At 6:42 p.m. [the garage.] She lit a candle on the dining table and went down to meet him. She smiled and licked her lips when they made eye contact.

George Hudgens was definitely the strongest, purest, and most handsome man Claire had ever known. He wasn't in the military anymore but he still did five hundred push-ups *every day,* usually half in the morning and the other half right before bed. He was a tall man and he was stout. His torso was like the trunk of a mighty oak. His chest was carved like a sculpture.

He stepped out of his Navigator wearing black slacks with a blue golf shirt tucked in neatly. In one hand he toted the briefcase Claire bought him just a few months before. In the other arm he cradled a huge vase stuffed with what had to be three dozen roses—some white, some pink. He looked up at Claire as she emerged from the back door and an eager smile lit his face.

George was 36 years old, like his wife. His skin was the color of a freshly baked croissant. He liked his head shaved completely bald, and Claire liked it like that too. George never allowed any facial stubble to mar his features. He had thick eyebrows and a stern countenance most of the time, but he looked seriously vexed as he eyeballed his woman this evening.

Claire stepped to him and put both arms around his neck. He was one of the few men she had to look up to. George's gaze went from her eyes to her cleavage and then back again.

"I would marry you all over again. Right now, if you wanted," he said.

Claire grinned and closed her eyes as they kissed. "Same here, soldier. Same here . . ."

HOW TO KILL YOUR YOUR HUSBAND

KEITH THOMAS WALKER

Genesis Press, Inc.

INDIGO LOVE STORIES

An imprint of Genesis Press, Inc.
Publishing Company

Genesis Press, Inc.
P.O. Box 101
Columbus, MS 39703

ISBN: 13 DIGIT : 978-1-58571-421-6
ISBN: 10 DIGIT : 1-58571-421-6
Manufactured in the United States of America

First Edition

Visit us at www.genesis-press.com
or call at 1-888-Indigo-1-4-0

DEDICATION

This book is for my mama and all the folks at the hospital who read my rough drafts, one chapter at a time. Thank you for driving me to meet my goals and fulfill your expectations.

ACKNOWLEDGMENTS

I would like to acknowledge Rachel Walker, Jackie Hafford, Janae Hampton, Jody Thomas, Anthony Douglas, Greg Johnson, Janean Livingston, Susan Vogel-Taylor and Mike Guinn. I would also like to give special thanks to Brandy, Shonya, Erika, Vicki, Alesia, Regina, Theda, Maricela, Letty, Lynda, Crystal, Amy, Charlene, Ben, Judd, Uncle Steve, Kierra, Vollie and Jason Owens. Thanks to everyone at the hospital who read my rough drafts and encouraged me to keep at it. And my most special thanks go to everyone who bought my book. I hope you have as much fun reading it as I did writing it.

Much love and God Bless!

CHAPTER ONE
A SPECIAL DAY

Claire hung up the phone with a loud sigh. She kneaded her forehead with the heels of her hands and eyed the clock mounted at the front of the office. It wasn't even noon yet, and already they were trying to take her there. They wouldn't like it if Claire went *there*—they complained to her supervisor the last time, as a matter of fact—but still they liked to push her buttons.

Hospitals had to be the most conniving corporations ever. There were so many charges and *charge types* and *room types*. The average medical billing professional might get befuddled and approve everything in her in-box. But after six years in the business, Claire knew how to spot bogus expenditures: Maybe Mr. Murphy did have *two* MRI's *and* a chest X-ray done on the same night, but Provincial Insurance wasn't paying for it—not if Claire Hudgens had anything to do with it.

She took out her ink pad and stamped the file on her desk with big red letters.

DENIED

That felt good, so she hit it again.

DENIED!

She was about to get jiggy with it, like the post office does when you send a registered letter, but a co-worker came and stood behind her computer.

"I swear, sometimes you act like that's *your* money." Rebecca was tall and thin, a couple years away from the big 4-0. She had long, blonde hair; it was beautiful, but she hid it away in a bun on most days. She usually wore wire-rimmed glasses, no makeup, and loose-fitting dresses to work. But Becky wasn't the *nerd-type* her appearance suggested.

"They can't give me an explanation for these charges," Claire informed her. "Who the hell gets two MRI's in one day—*and* a chest X-ray?"

Becky shrugged. "You never know what could be happening." Today she had on a simple blue dress; it was a one-piece with a sash around the waist and buttons down the middle. She was attractive, but there was so much more she could do to spice up her appearance. Claire thought she would change up her style a little after her divorce, but that was over a year ago, and Becky was still *Plain Jane.*

Claire frowned at her. "Girl, don't tell me you're over there approving mess like this."

Becky poked out her lips. "We can't *all* be employee of the month."

Claire grinned. "That only happened to me twice."

"Twice *this year*," Becky said and rolled her eyes.

"You going to lunch?" Claire asked, noticing the purse crooked under her friend's arm.

"*We're* going out to lunch," Becky said with a smile. "I'm taking you out for your anniversary."

"Aww. That's sweet. I wish George's memory was as good as yours."

"You always remembered my anniversaries," Becky said, and then a pained look took over her face. Claire was lost for words for a second, but Becky started to smile. "Gotcha."

Claire put a hand to her chest. "Girl, I thought we were going to have to break out the Kleenex again!"

Becky chuckled. "You ready?"

Claire looked around her desk. "I guess. Where we going?"

"Where do you want to go?" Becky smiled down at her pleasantly. She had cute dimples and nice teeth. Only the crow's feet in the corners of her eyes gave up her age.

"I don't know," Claire said.

"Where are you going with George?"

"I'm making him *lobster*," Claire said, "on a bed of wild rice with skewered jumbo shrimp on the side."

"*Ooh*. I like lobster."

"Sorry. I already sent out my invites," Claire teased. "You should have RSVP'd."

"Let's get Chinese," Becky said.

"That sounds great." Claire stood and retrieved her purse from the lowest drawer on her desk.

"You're not going to wear *that* to your dinner tonight, are you?" Becky asked.

Today Claire had on gray slacks with a white blouse. She was tall for a woman, teetering over five feet, ten inches. She was also slightly overweight. Like her friend, Claire's fashion sense settled into a mediocre groove after

3

sixteen years of marriage. She had long, beautiful legs, but rarely did her co-workers see them. Claire wore her shoulder-length hair down, but she never curled it, braided it, teased it, or colored it.

Claire was a beautiful woman, with brown skin like molasses. She had large eyes, a thin nose, and full lips. Her dark eyes were deep and alluring, but she didn't use mascara or fake lashes to draw attention to them. But then again, she was thirty-six years old with three kids and a great husband. Who was there to impress?

"I got some new outfits," she told her nosey friend. "I'll tell you about them at lunch."

The ladies left the office in good spirits. Becky was parked closest, so they climbed into her ex-husband's four-by-four rather than take Claire's Lexus. Inwardly, Claire hated riding in her friend's bigfoot Ford; the wheels were almost waist-tall, there seemed to be a lot of open space between the axles and the frame, and you had to stretch like a gymnast just to get in the damned thing.

But Becky's divorce was as bitter as they come. She got the house, the kids, and her husband's new toy—and damned if she wasn't going to enjoy all of it to the fullest. Becky didn't even have to back out of her parking spot anymore: She simply threw that bad boy in DRIVE and climbed over the parking block like she was at the motocross. Claire latched her seatbelt and said a quick prayer like she always did when Becky was behind the wheel.

They chose to dine at the Lotus restaurant because the self-serve buffet there worked best with their brief lunch hour. Midway through their meal, Claire pushed her crab Rangoon to the side and pulled a magazine clipping from her purse. She unfolded it and laid it out in front of her friend. Becky peered down her nose, and her eyes grew wide.

"Wow. Where is that from?"

"Victoria's Secret," Claire said. "I ordered it online. It just came in yesterday."

Becky sucked a broiled shrimp from its shell and chewed it eagerly. "Have you tried it on yet?"

"Yeah. Last night."

"And? . . ."

"And what?"

Becky looked from the curvaceous model on the ad to her average-sized friend across the table. "Does it still look like, like *that*?" she asked.

"What do you mean?" Claire said. "I'm just as fine as that lady."

Becky choked a little on her shrimp. She put a hand to her mouth and coughed, then took a few swallows of her tea. "Excuse me," she said, dabbing the corner of her eyes with a napkin.

"I might have a little cellulite on my thighs," Claire admitted.

"And your arms," Becky offered.

"What's wrong with my arms?"

"You know how old ladies get that flab under their triceps?" Becky asked. "When they wave at someone, that meat swings back and forth . . ."

"My arms do not look like that!"

"No—they don't," Becky said with a grin. "I'm just kidding. But you never know what could happen in twenty years, if you let it go."

Claire bent her arm and felt the skin under there. It still felt tight to her, mostly. "*Anything* can happen in twenty years," she muttered.

"And your stomach," Becky said.

"All right. I do need to do a few crunches."

"And your butt . . ."

Claire threw a hand up. "Hold up—George likes *every bit* of my ass. And what are you attacking me for? This is supposed to be a *celebratory* lunch!"

Becky chuckled. "I'm just fooling with you, Claire. You know you look good. I wish I had your legs."

"I wish I had your stomach," Claire said.

"I wish I was black so people would think my butt looks good," Becky said.

"Come to my next family reunion," Claire offered. "You'll have plenty of fans." She folded her picture and put it back in her purse. "I got a new dress to wear to dinner, too," she said.

"What does it look like?"

"It's red and strapless, tight around the waist, shows off my perky bosoms."

"Oh, I bet that looks nice."

"It does, girl. I modeled it for myself last night. I was standing in front of the mirror thinking: *Damn, that chick's hot!*"

Becky giggled. "So, what'd you get the colonel this year?"

Claire smiled. It was always hard to shop for her husband. What do you give a man who'd lived in more countries than he had fingers?

Since retiring from the Air Force, George has wanted for nothing that Claire was aware of. His salary at Boeing, coupled with his military pension, left their bank accounts quite full most of the time. George had every trinket imaginable from the golden iPod to multiple DVD screens in his Navigator, but Claire always found something special on gift-giving occasions.

"I had our wedding pictures restored," she said.

Becky's eyes lit up. "Oh, that's nice."

"*And,*" Claire said with a finger in the air, "I got our wedding video re-mastered."

"That's great!"

"Not just re-mastered," Claire went on. "I also went back and got everyone who was there to give a quick little blessing at the end. They say how proud they are that we made it sixteen years, and, you know, a bunch of corny stuff like that."

"You found *everybody?*"

"Well, there were some folks I *didn't want to find,*" Claire said. "Like my cousin Ray; he damned near ruined the original wedding with his drunk ass. I didn't put him in the new video. But I got our parents, our brothers and sisters. I got them all with the same backdrop, too, so it looks like they all came at the same time."

Becky's mouth was open. "How the hell did you do all of that?"

Claire shook her head. "It took months. It was hard, but it was fun, too. We don't talk to our families as much as we should. It was good to see everyone again and hear what they all had to say about me and George. You know some of them acted a fool! You put a camera in their face and they think they're on Oprah."

Becky laughed. "And you kept all of that a secret?"

"That was the hardest part," Claire confided. "All of these people started returning my calls—*at all hours of the night*—and I had to keep making excuses about who it was. You know I'm not the sneaky type, girl. I can't hardly keep a straight face if I'm lying to someone."

"He never got suspicious?"

"No. He trusts me. He didn't even ask who was calling most of the time."

"You have a great marriage," Becky said. She reached across the table and held her friend's hand. "I hope you guys get old and die together."

"We will," Claire said without hesitation. She never imagined it any other way.

The average pencil-pusher at Provincial Insurance worked a regular nine to five, but Claire never stayed later than two-thirty. She didn't have to work at all. It was actually George's preference that she didn't, but being a stay-at-home-mom got a little boring once the last kiddo started school.

When Claire got into medical billing, it was merely an interesting pastime at first, but her drive and diligence separated her from the rat pack right away. Each month she saved the company more money in her five hours than her co-workers did in eight. She could be manager, or at least supervisor by now, but that would mean working more hours. That would mean Nicole, Stacy, and George Jr. would have to ride the bus home from school.

And that was unacceptable.

Claire pulled to a stop in front of Wedgwood Elementary with ten minutes to spare. She got out and stood under the large awning that shaded the school's front doors. There were already a dozen parents milling around this area. A woman Claire recognized from the PTA meetings came over and made light conversation. After a few minutes, the bell rang.

Rather than let the kids explode from the building like a kicked ant pile, the students at Wedgewood Elementary had to follow their teachers out in neat, quiet lines. Once outside, they couldn't leave until their teacher saw a parent.

George's class was always among the last out of the building. Claire went to speak with his instructor as she always did, and her son rushed from the crowd and grabbed hold of her hand.

"*Mama!*"

"*Hey!* What's going on, man?"

"I planted a lima bean!" he announced, holding up a plastic cup filled with dirt. George was fair-skinned like his father, the color of a sugar cookie. He was a small boy, but he had a big head and large eyes. He wore khaki pants with a white golf shirt, and although all of the children were dressed similarly due to the dress code, Claire thought her boy was the most handsome fourth grader at the school.

"How was he today?" she asked his teacher, Mrs. Flores.

"He's great," the woman said immediately. "One of the few I *don't* have to worry about—*Justin, spit that out*! I'm sorry," she said and turned back to Claire. She put a hand on George's head. "He's great. Still don't have anything bad to say about him."

"Good," Claire said with a smile. "I'll see you tomorrow."

"Okay," the teacher said and wiped her brow. She turned away quickly. "Justin! *Get over here! No! Right here!*"

Claire walked away giggling. She never went to college, but education would have been her major if she had pursued a degree. Sometimes she regretted her decision, but scenes like that reminded her how sweet it was to sit behind a desk and deal with *adults* for a living.

"Can I get a new game?" George asked on the way back to the car.

"What kind of game?"

"For my Playstation."

"You got a new game for your birthday."

"I beat it already."

"You've got another birthday coming sooner or later."

KEITH THOMAS WALKER

"What? That's like, that's like *a year* from now!"

"You'll still want it then," Claire said with a grin.

"Huh?"

"Maybe this weekend," she said. "We can get you a *used* one from GameStop."

"I hope it doesn't have a lot of scratches."

Together, Claire and her husband brought in almost a hundred and fifty thousand a year. Not many children of such well-to-do parents would have to get used toys, but those video games were fifty dollars or more these days. It was hard, but Claire was determined to teach her children the value of a dollar.

"Can I sit in the front?" he asked.

"Yeah."

The boy rushed ahead of her, but Claire didn't have to chase him down. She parked with the passenger door next to the curb so he wouldn't have to go in the street. He was already seated and buckled in by the time Claire caught up.

"Did you make that card for your Daddy?" she asked when she started the car.

"*Oh yeah!*" George Jr. reached between his legs and ripped open his backpack. After a bit of rustling, he came up with a blue folder. He fumbled through it for half a minute and then produced a single sheet of paper with drawings on it. He handed it to his mother, and Claire immediately cherished it like it was an original Van Gogh.

Anniversary was misspelled, Daddy was as tall as a house, and one of Mommy's legs was relatively two feet

11

longer than the other, but Claire had never seen anything so precious.

"Aww. This is great. You did this all by yourself?"

"Yeah."

"It's very good work."

"I know. I'm going to be an artist when I grow up."

"I thought you were going to the Air Force like your daddy," Claire reminded him.

"I am," George Jr. confirmed. "I'm going to draw pictures from up in my jet."

Claire put her Lexus in drive and headed for Clarke Middle School. George Jr. chatted the whole way there. He was going to make quite a conversationalist one day—but Claire wasn't too concerned with the items on his lunch tray and the order he ate them in. She was a good listener, though; she nodded often and said *Hmmm* every time he stopped for a breath.

They couldn't park directly in front of Stacy's school because of the buses, so Claire met up with her middle child in the visitor's parking lot. Stacy got out at the same time as George, so she was always ready and waiting— usually on the steps of the gymnasium. Claire saw her there, and she saw that Stacy wasn't waiting alone. Once again there was a boy with her. He didn't attempt a hug or anything when Stacy got up to leave, but they looked like they wanted to.

Like her mom, Stacy was tall for a girl, but she had no problem showing off her long, yellow legs. She wore knee-length dresses and skirts whenever the weather permitted. She was only in the sixth grade, however, and the boys were not yet aware of the treasure they had among them. Well, most of them weren't.

"Why can't you ever pick me up *first*?" Stacy asked when she got to the car. Her hair was long like Claire's, and she wore it in two ponytails today. She had on a tight, pink T-shirt with the word HOTTIE printed across the chest. Her watch was pink, the ribbons in her hair were pink, and her lips were pink; naturally so. This was Mommy's bubblegum princess.

"You sure aren't having a hard time waiting," Claire said as Stacy climbed in the back. "Every time I pull up you're with some knot-head boy."

"No, I'm not. I'm usually with Crystal."

"Where's Crystal now?" Claire asked, backing out of her parking spot.

"She got detention."

"I'm not surprised."

"You don't even know what she did."

"All right. Tell me what she did."

"She went to the bathroom without asking the teacher."

"I'm not surprised."

"She did ask at first," Stacy said. "But he wouldn't let her go."

"That's against the law," Claire said. "You're not going to have me believing that."

"That's against the law," George Jr. said.

"Didn't nobody ask you," Stacy said.

"*Didn't nobody?*" Claire hit the brakes and eyed her daughter in the rear-view mirror. "Girl, it sounds like you need to go back in there. Didn't you have English class today?"

"*Nobody asked you,*" Stacy said to her little brother.

"That's better," Claire said. "And don't talk to your brother like that."

George Jr. sat up straighter and smiled. Stacy slouched and fastened her seatbelt.

⁓

Humboldt High School was right around the corner. Claire was glad for that because her oldest child had a sour disposition on most days. Nicole was fourteen years old. She was goofy at times, sometimes mature. Bold and beautiful some days, and insecure on the others; basically all things that came with that confounding age. She began to develop early—when she was just eleven—and Claire thought that had a lot to do with her daughter's social issues.

But Nikki was in high school now, and she didn't stick out like a sore thumb anymore. She was a freshman built like a senior, but that was a lot better than having that body in middle school.

The busses were already pulling away by the time they got to Humboldt. Claire parked in front of the main entrance, but she still didn't see her daughter milling around with the other restless souls. She sighed and checked her watch. It was already three-thirty. George Sr. wouldn't be home until after six, but she had a lot of getting ready to do on this special night.

"You want me to go find her?" Stacy asked, undoing her seatbelt.

"No, I don't," Claire said. "You keep your hot-tailed self right there."

"I'm not *hot-tailed*!" Stacy whined.

Claire frowned at her in the mirror. "You know how old I was before I let a boy wait with me after school?"

"I don't know," Stacy said. "But I know it was a *long time ago*. He was probably a *caveman*."

That cracked little George up.

"Oh, *ha ha*," Claire said.

"How old *were* you, Mama?" George asked.

Claire turned and smiled at him. "Thanks for asking, young man. I was a senior in high school," she told Stacy. "And that boy was your *daddy*."

"We were just sitting there," Stacy said. "We didn't hold hands or nothing."

"Or *anything*," Claire corrected.

"Anything."

"I don't like girls," George Jr. said.

"That's a good boy," Claire said.

"They don't like you, either," Stacy said.

"That's enough," Claire said. She checked her watch again. "Darn this girl . . ."

"There she go," Stacy said.

Claire looked up and was happy to see Nikki emerge from the building. "There she *is*," she told Stacy. "Or there she *goes*. You've got homework tonight."

"I already have homework."

"You have more now." Claire had plenty of reading and grammar worksheets at home. Sometimes the lessons she assigned her children were harder than the stuff they brought from school.

"*Man*," Stacy groaned.

"Ah-ha, you got homework!" George Jr. teased.

"Now you're getting some, too, for gloating," Claire told him.

"That's okay. I like homework," he said. And that was true. Claire couldn't do anything but smile at him.

Nicole Hudgens approached the vehicle on her mother's side with all the enthusiasm of a three-toed sloth. Of all her children, Claire saw more of herself in the oldest girl: Nikki was tall and dark-skinned with large eyes that were serious most of the time. She had her mother's legs and breasts, but she considered this figure a curse at this point of her life. Today she sported baggy jeans and a long-sleeved button-down that was equally over-sized. She wore her hair down, with a large bang hanging over her left eye.

"Another bad day?" Claire asked when Nikki opened the door.

"It was alright," the brooding beauty said.

"If you keep walking around looking like that people are going to think you're depressed," Claire warned.

"She needs a boyfriend," Stacy offered.

"*I/She do/does not need a boyfriend,*" Claire and Nikki said at the same time.

Claire met eyes with her oldest daughter in the rearview mirror and smiled at her.

Nikki smiled back, and then rolled her eyes—lest anyone think her and Mommy shared a *moment*.

CHAPTER TWO
CLAIRE'S GIFT

Claire didn't think she could pull it off, but she was a determined woman when she pulled into her two-car garage at 4:15 p.m. She went over the game plan in her head and then started barking orders.

"George, hurry and get up to your room. Change out of those school clothes and get started on your homework—"

"But what about my—"

"I'll bring a snack up there." She spun in her seat. "Nikki, you guys are eating early tonight."

"Can we eat pizza?"

"There's a tuna casserole in the fridge. I need you to put it in the oven for me—and some rolls. How much homework do you have?"

"A lot."

"What about you, Stacy?"

"I just have to read this dumb story."

"Okay, I need *you* to make a salad for me."

"You said you were giving her more homework," George Jr. reminded his mother.

Stacy kicked the back of his seat.

"That's right," Claire said. "All right. I'll make the salad myself. Did y'all get the cards?' she asked her daughters.

"Yes," they said at the same time.

"Well sign them," Claire instructed. "And write whatever you're going to put in there. Your father will be home at six-thirty. I want y'all fed and *smiling* and ready to get *out of our way* when he gets here." No one moved, so she clapped her hands. "Chop chop! Let's go! Let's go!"

Everyone exited the car and headed in separate directions once inside. Claire went upstairs and replaced her slacks and button-down with shorts and a T-shirt. When she got back to the kitchen, Nikki was putting the casserole in the oven like a good girl.

Claire grabbed a Lunchable from the refrigerator and headed back upstairs to George's room. On the way, she stopped in the office and found a worksheet that would help Stacy with her double negatives. She got a multiplication worksheet for George. She dropped these items off and barely stuck around long enough for a response.

"*Thanks, Mom!*"

"*Aww, man!*"

When she got back downstairs, Nikki was still in the kitchen.

"What are you doing?" Claire asked her.

Nikki took a large serving bowl from the cupboard. "I'm making a salad."

"I thought you had a lot of homework."

"It's not that much," Nikki said and looked away sheepishly.

Claire went to her and pulled her close for a sideways hug. "See, you *do* love me!"

Nikki grinned.

With *two* women in the kitchen, things didn't turn out so bad after all. Claire had her lobster tails thawing in the fridge already, and they looked perfect when she took them out. She put her large pot on the stovetop and grabbed a smaller saucepan for the wild rice. She skewered the lobster tails with wooden pins while waiting for the water to boil.

Behind her, Nikki sliced up tomatoes, mushrooms, and ham for their salad. Afterwards, she baked dinner rolls to go with the casserole.

At five o'clock the children's supper was ready. Claire thanked Nikki and then shooed her away so she could get started on her homework. Claire popped her lobsters in the colander and slid two potatoes in the oven before going upstairs to check on the terrible two. To her surprise, both Stacy and George Jr. were in their rooms working obediently. She praised them briefly then ran back downstairs to set the table.

By 5:45 the house smelled of *deliciousness*. Claire called the kids down for dinner, and she took a shower while they ate. When she got out, she slid into her *hot* red dress and did her hair as quickly as possible. She put on lipstick and a little blush for this special occasion and spritzed Fendi perfume on her neck, wrists and chest.

She checked herself in the mirror one last time at six-fifteen. The dress was perfect. It was strapless, and her bare neck and shoulders just begged for kisses. Her strapless bra pushed her breasts up, and they were full and inviting. Claire had more cleavage than a sixteenth-century aristocrat.

When she got back downstairs, the kids were already done eating and gone—except for Nikki. Not only had she cleared the table, but she had most of the dishes washed already. Claire walked up to her and put a hand on her forehead.

"What?" Nikki asked, backing away.

"Are you sick or something?" Claire asked good-naturedly.

"No."

"Why are you being so helpful?"

Nikki shrugged. "It's your anniversary," she said. "Aren't I supposed to do nice things for you today?"

"Who told you that?" Claire asked with a grin.

"You did," Nikki said. "You tell us that *every year.*"

"But I didn't have to tell you today," Claire said. "I'm proud of you. You're becoming quite a mature young lady."

Nikki turned away from the sink and looked at her mother's outfit. "*Wow.* You're busting out, Mama."

"*Busting out?*"

"Like, like, your, your breasts. They're like, like," she looked closer. "Are they gonna fall out?"

"Oh, yes," Claire confirmed. "But not till I want them to."

"*Ugh*!" Nikki said with a sour expression. "I don't want to think about you and Daddy—*Ah*! Now it's in my head!"

"Love is a beautiful thing," Claire said and wrapped her up for a longer hug this time. "One day you'll know exactly what I'm talking about."

⌒

At 6:42 p.m. Claire finally heard her man pull into the garage. She lit a candle on the dining table and went to down to meet him. She smiled and licked her lips when they made eye contact.

George Hudgens was definitely the strongest, purest, and most handsome man Claire had ever known. He wasn't in the military anymore, but he still did five hundred push-ups *every day*; usually half in the morning and the other half right before bed. He was a tall man, and he was stout. His torso was like the trunk of a mighty oak. His chest was carved like a sculpture.

He stepped out of his Navigator wearing black slacks with a blue golf shirt tucked in neatly. In one hand he toted the briefcase Claire bought him just a few months ago. In the other arm he cradled a huge vase stuffed with what had to be three dozen roses, some white, some pink. He looked up at Claire as she emerged from the back door and an eager smile lit his face as well.

George was thirty-six years old, like his wife. His skin was the color of a freshly baked croissant. He liked his head shaved completely bald, and Claire liked it like that too. George never allowed any facial stubble to mar his features. He had thick eyebrows and a stern countenance most of the time, but he looked seriously vexed as he eye-balled his woman this evening.

Claire stepped to him and put both arms around his neck. He was one of few men she had to look up to. George's gaze went from her eyes to her cleavage then back again.

"I would marry you all over again. Right now if you wanted," he said.

Claire grinned and closed her eyes as they kissed. "Same here, soldier. Same here . . ."

When they got inside, the kids were eager to spend as much time with their father as possible, but Claire already had a strict schedule in her head, and she aimed to stick to it. She let them read their cards and say how happy they were to have such great parents. She let them *ooh* and *ahh* at her flowers, and she even let them see the nice meal she prepared for their wonderful daddy, but after that they had to go.

When the kids went upstairs, the night took on the romantic aura Claire envisioned. The lobster was succulent, the rice was soft, and the flickering candlelight reminded her of their first anniversary dinner at the Italian Inn, exactly fifteen years ago. They weren't so well-off back then, and Claire's ten-dollar lasagna dinner was nowhere near as tasty as today's lobster, but she loved George just as much now as she did then. Even more so.

After their meal, Claire led her husband to the bed-room for phase two of the evening's festivities. George hadn't seen their wedding video in years. He watched the whole thing on the edge of his seat, totally in awe of the digital work Claire had done on it. When the new commentaries started to play towards the end, George held on to his woman and laughed and almost cried at times.

When it went off, Claire popped in a CD so they could listen to their wedding song. George took her hand and brought her to her feet. He put an arm around her waist and pulled her very close. He buried his face in her neck, and inhaled her scents, and they danced slowly.

They were still rocking quietly long after the CD player went mute.

At 9:30 Claire left the bedroom to make sure everyone was getting in bed as they should be. No one was getting in bed as they should be. Nikki was on the phone in the den, Stacy was on her computer, and George Jr. was down in the kitchen picking at the leftover lobster.

Claire sneaked up behind him and startled him purposefully. "*Whatchoo doing down here, boy?*"

He jumped, and then cracked a smile when he saw Mommy was happy. "How come we didn't get lobster?" he asked, his lips glistening.

"You're getting lobster tomorrow."

"Really?"

"No! Now go up there and brush your teeth." She gave him a soft swat on the heiney to get him going.

"*Hey!*"

She followed him up and was glad to see that everyone was bathed and in their pajamas at least. She shooed them to their respective rooms, but Claire wouldn't retire for the night until they were physically in the bed and under the sheets. She kissed her little goblins goodnight one at a time and thanked them for their good behavior today. She set the sleep timers on the girl's televisions so they could watch one more hour of High School Musical.

"You're still busting out of your dress," Nikki said when her mother turned off her lights.

"I thought you said you wanted another little brother," Claire teased.

"*Eww!*" Nikki shrieked. "Get out of here! I'm getting another mental picture!"

Claire left the room laughing.

Her good spirits didn't go away when she got back to the bedroom.

George was in his pajama bottoms only. He sat on the corner of the bed breathing deeply, and Claire knew he'd just finished his push-ups for the night.

Look at my man, she thought.

George's neck was massive. His traps were swollen like two small hills sitting atop his shoulders. His pectorals were huge and rippling, hard and smooth.

"Come here," he said. He stared at her like he was hypnotized.

Claire closed the door behind her and stepped to him. She stood between his legs and put her hands on those well-defined traps. George put his hands on her waist then slid them down to her hips. He looked up at her and grinned.

"This is a new dress?"

She nodded. "How do you always know?"

"I never forget anything," he said. He reached up and touched her breasts delicately, and then he slid his fingers down her stomach. Even after sixteen years, he still had the power to send a tingle down her spine.

"I love the dress," he said, "but how do you get it off?"

She turned so he could see the zipper running down the back. He reached up for it then stopped himself.

"Wait," he said. "Turn around."

She did. George took her hands and looked up at her like he was going to propose again.

"You know, baby, I've loved you since the first time I saw you."

"When was the first time you saw me?" Claire asked. She knew the story, but it was never a bad time to hear it again.

"I was in detention," he said with a smirk. "It was after school, and most of the students were already on their way home. Mr. Jensen opened the door 'cause it always got stuffy in his room, and about twelve seconds after he opened it *you* walked by."

"Twelve seconds?"

"I know it was twelve seconds because I was watching that damned clock," George said. "But I didn't care about that clock anymore when I saw you."

Claire put a hand on his cheek and grew a little misty-eyed.

"When he let us go," George went on, "I ran out there looking for you, but ten minutes had already passed. I couldn't find you anywhere. I must've run around that school three times."

Claire giggled.

"But I saw you again two weeks later."

"At assembly."

"I didn't let you get away that time."

"No," Claire said. "You didn't."

George reached behind his back and came up with a black jewelry box. It was too big to be a ring, but just the perfect size for a necklace. Claire took it with trembling fingers.

"I really loved that video," George said. "I can't believe you went through so much trouble for me. I want you to know I love you more than anything in this world. I know you've had your eye on that for quite a while. I'm giving it to you tonight because this day reminds me of how special you are, how you mean the world to me. You've given me everything I've ever wanted, so I want to do the same for you . . ."

With all the build-up, Claire almost couldn't get the box open in her excitement. But she managed. And although the item inside was beautiful, expensive and exquisite, Claire felt a brief pang of *let down* when she saw the necklace.

George got her a curving journey pendant with five diamonds set in white gold. The diamonds grew in size as they descended from the chain, but for the life of her, Claire couldn't remember ever requesting anything so extravagant.

But it was beautiful.

"It's wonderful," she said.

George stood and wrapped her in his arms. He kissed her deeply and pressed his body into to hers. Claire felt him growing against her.

"Turn around," he said. "Let me put that on for you."

Claire returned the pendant and turned her back on him. She raised her hair, and George secured the latch quickly. Claire stepped away when he was done so she could admire the necklace in the mirror over their dresser. George followed. He stood behind her and unzipped her dress while she leaned in for a closer look.

"*Oh, my God, George.* This is incredible!"

"Nothing's more beautiful than you," he said.

She turned to face him. He slid the dress down her frame, and Claire stepped out of it gingerly. She didn't feel self-conscious at all with his eyes on her. She even felt comfortable with her belly. She peeled off her undergarments slowly, and George's eyes grew larger by the second.

"Wow," he said when she was down to everything but his gift. He put his hands on her sides then held her hips and caressed her butt. Claire backed him towards the bed with a hand on his throbbing member.

"Why don't you take your pants off?" she suggested.

He jumped out of the britches like they were poisonous and sat down on the mattress. Claire climbed on top of him like a leopard. She put her hands on his neck and looked him in the eyes as she eased down and took him into her. George grabbed her hips again and she moaned, already close to climax.

"I've been thinking about this for *too long*," she whispered. "I'm already ready . . ."

He cupped her left breast and suckled the nipple delightfully.

"Go ahead," he said. "I'll make sure you get another one."

And he did.

❧

Claire woke up at 3:43 a.m. That was odd because she had wine with dinner. Alcohol coupled with the pipe work George laid down last night should have had her knocked out until the alarm went off. But Claire wasn't tired at all. She didn't even feel like she'd been asleep.

She sat up carefully and looked over at her husband. George lay on his stomach, snoring lightly. Claire slid her legs over slowly and *crept* out of the bed, though she had no idea why she needed to be sneaky.

But then again, she did know why. She just didn't want to accept it right then because thinking about it made her nauseous.

Claire never put much stock in the idea of *women's intuition*, but she couldn't deny the other-worldly vibes she felt. George's words played over and over in her head until they didn't make sense anymore. And yet they did make sense.

I never forget anything.
I know you've had your eye on that for quite a while.
I never forget anything.
you've had your eye on that
never forget

If she was married to any other man, Claire would have thought nothing of this *faux pas*. What husband doesn't give his wife the wrong gift every once in a while? But George was no ordinary man. He really did have a memory like an elephant. And if he said she had her eye on it for quite a while, then she *did* have her eye on it for quite a while.

The only question was; who was *she*?

Claire tied her robe closed and slipped out of the room with pin-needles pricking the bottom of her feet. Her underarms were moist. Her mouth was dry, and her heart jack-hammered in her chest. In sixteen years she never felt like this. Maybe she was wrong for feeling this now.

Or maybe she was right.

Claire really didn't want to know. But she kept moving.

She navigated the hallways like a ghost and found herself in George's office almost unintentionally. She was afraid to turn on the lights, so she fumbled through her husband's belongings like a cat burglar, flipping papers, scrutinizing little post-its.

She didn't know what she was looking for, but she knew it would be in his office, and she knew it wouldn't be hard to find. Claire never invaded her husband's privacy, so he wouldn't keep his secrets in a safe.

She found George's briefcase on the floor next to the coat rack. She took it to the desk and opened it slowly. The small clicks sounded like firecrackers to Claire. She stopped and listened to the darkness several times. She held her breath as she opened it.

Then she closed it again.

This was ridiculous. Was she going to throw away all these years of trust over one misunderstanding? There were a million explanations for what she was thinking.

But Claire was no fool.

I know you've had your eye on that for quite a while.

She never once told him she wanted a diamond necklace.

I never forget anything.

She opened the briefcase again and found what she was looking for in the first pocket she searched. Claire pulled out the Hallmark card and read it slowly in the darkness. It was nothing, really. It was innocent. It definitely wasn't something she could shove in his face as hard evidence.

But it was enough; enough to make her start crying on what was supposed to be a very special day.

It was a *Thinking of You* card. Written in blue ink were the words:

Good luck with your meeting today.
I believe in you.
You make me proud.
Kim

Claire's face folded in on itself, but she gritted her teeth and forced herself to remain strong. This card didn't prove anything. Kim could be anyone. If Kim was Asian, he could actually be a *man*.

And the handwriting wasn't necessarily *feminine*. Calligraphy was originally a male-dominated field. Surely there were men out there who still wrote this beautifully . . .

I know you've had your eye on that for quite a while.
I believe in you.
I never forget anything.
You make me proud.
I know you've had your eye on that for quite a while.
Kim.

Claire breathed fire from her nostrils. She decided right then and there that if her suspicions were true, she was going to murder her husband. No ifs, ands, or buts about it. If George was cheating on her, she was going to kill his sorry ass.

CHAPTER THREE
THE CARD

Claire sat at her desk the next morning still lost in a flood of emotions. Everything seemed to be happening around her without much thought or action on her end. She knew she got the kids ready for school. She knew she made breakfast for them, and she kissed George Sr. on the way out of the house, but it all had the hazy sensation of *déjà-vu*.

Claire approved the first ten files in her box without much scrutiny, not really wanting to argue with anyone. Becky came and stood behind her computer when it was time for their mid-morning break. Without a word passed between them, Rebecca knew something went wrong with Claire's special day.

"Hey," Becky said with a guarded smile.

"Hey," Claire mumbled.

Today Becky wore a flowing sundress with a pink background and colorful floral prints. Claire wore black slacks with a gray sweatshirt. She had her hair pulled back in a ponytail for convenience, but the move left her whole face exposed on what was not one of her prettier days.

She didn't have on makeup. This was the norm, but Claire's trademarked cheeriness—which usually added a glow to her countenance—was missing. She looked tired and stressed, angry and haggard.

"*Sooo*, how'd it go last night?" Becky queried.

Claire shrugged. "It was fine," she said without looking up.

"Did, um, did George have to work late?" Becky asked.

"No. He got home around six-thirty."

"So he didn't like your video? You burned the lobster? He wouldn't give you any? Come on, girl, tell me what happened. You've been over here looking pissed all morning."

Claire looked up at her friend, and she didn't look pissed at all anymore. Her eyes were glossy, and Becky saw that she was close to tears.

"*Claire*, what's wrong, honey?"

Claire shook her head. "I don't know. Maybe nothing."

"It doesn't look like nothing. You want to go to the break room?"

"No," Claire said, thinking about all the gossips in there.

"Let's go outside," Becky suggested.

Claire sighed and stood slowly on stiff legs. "All right."

⌒

The spring morning was warm and beautiful. The daily temperatures in Overbrook Meadows, Texas, would skyrocket to a hundred-plus in a few months, but in April it rarely got over eighty degrees. A soothing breeze tickled the branches of rejuvenating dogwood trees, sending pink petals drifting through the air like snowflakes.

Becky led her friend around the building where concrete benches were set up for a smoking section. Smoking was no longer allowed on the Provincial campus, so the area was pleasantly vacant. Claire took a seat and stared out at the traffic blazing by on Hulen Avenue. Becky sat next to her and waited anxiously.

Claire looked her friend in the eyes and chuckled nervously. "I hope I'm going crazy," she said.

Becky reached into her lap and held Claire's trembling hand. "You're scaring me," she said.

Claire took a deep breath and the tears started to fall again. "I can't believe I'm thinking this," she said. "I don't even want to say it—not about George." She let go of her friend's hand and retrieved the *Thinking of You* card from her purse. She handed it over without saying anything.

Becky took it hesitantly and didn't open it right away. She kept her eyes on Claire's. "What's this?"

Claire shook her head. "Just read it."

Becky did, but she didn't have the look of horror Claire expected when she was done. "Where did you get this?" she asked.

"Out of George's briefcase."

Becky was confused. "So what is it? Is this what you're upset about?"

"Last night," Claire said, "George gave me a diamond necklace for our anniversary. It's a journey pendant. It's beautiful, and expensive."

Becky nodded and listened intently.

"He told me . . ." Claire took another breath, but couldn't stop her voice from hitching. "He told me I meant everything to him, and, and he wanted me to have everything I wanted."

"That's beautiful," Becky said.

Claire held a hand up. "He said he knew I had my eye on that necklace for a long time, but I *didn't*." She shook her head. "I never *once* said anything about wanting that necklace, or any other necklace."

Becky's look of confusion changed to concern. She gazed down at the card in her hands again. "So . . ."

"So I knew he had me confused with someone else," Claire said. "George has a great memory, but he slipped up this time. I think some other bitch has been nagging him about that necklace, but he got it for me accidentally."

Becky's mouth fell open.

"I found that card in his briefcase last night," Claire said. "What kind of message does that sound like to you?"

Becky was still too shocked to speak.

"It could be one of the managers," Claire mused, "but, but she said 'I believe in you. You make me pr-proud.'" Her features started to crumple again, and Claire put both hands up to hide her sorrow. "That's something *I* would say to him," she moaned through her fingers. "That sounds like someone who *loves* him!"

"Aww, honey." Becky put an arm around her shoulder and comforted her as best she could. "You, you can't believe that."

"Why not?" Claire bawled. Becky's husband left her two years ago after similar infidelities. Claire didn't understand how her friend could be so naïve after going through the same thing so recently.

"You've been with George since you were in high school," Becky said. "You guys love each other more than any couple I know. I mean, you *really* love each other, you're not just putting on a show for the kids."

Claire nodded and sniffled loudly.

"George would *never* cheat on you," Becky said. "If he was, you'd know something by now. I think this is just a misunderstanding."

Claire took her hands from her face and wiped her eyes, glad she didn't have any messy mascara to contend with. "He works late almost every night," she said. "He goes on business trips all the time. A lot of times he's gone for a whole week."

"Why are you talking like that?" Becky asked.

"I was thinking about it," Claire said, "this morning, when I couldn't go back to sleep. I was just lying there thinking about all the times he was gone, all the times he came in after I was asleep. Everything started to make sense."

Becky smiled encouragingly. "Claire, George is successful at work. You tell me all the time how good he's doing. He's working hard for *you guys*. Everything he does is a sacrifice for the family."

Claire knew her friend's words were true, and she was eager to accept them, but still . . . "What about that card?" she asked. "What about the necklace?"

"Are you sure you didn't maybe say it on a whim?" Becky offered. "Maybe you were walking downtown and you said you liked it, not thinking much about it. Or maybe you saw it on TV one day. Maybe he thought it meant more to you than it really did. That's not such a bad thing, Claire. It just means he's attentive."

Claire took a deep breath and took a napkin from her purse. She blew her nose and wiped away the last of her tears with the back of her hand. "You really think so?"

Becky grinned. "I *know* so," she said. "I've been around you guys. I know how much he loves you. It's real. You know it is."

Claire smiled too, but it was mostly forced. "What about that card?" she asked, staring down at her friend's hands.

"I think it's one of his co-workers," she said. "Or maybe his secretary. They're doing a lot of good things in those big companies nowadays. They treat their employees like *real people* with feelings. I don't think that card is from his *lover*, Claire. I mean, come on. Do you really think George would cheat on you?"

Claire giggled nervously and shook her head. "No," she said. And she meant it.

"Come on," Becky said. "We were supposed to be back five minutes ago. Mr. Roubidou is going to make us eat lunch at our desks."

Claire chuckled. "I think I forgot my lunch today," she said. "My head's been so cloudy." She stood and her muscles cried out, protesting the night with no rest. "Oh," she said, rubbing her spine. "I'm tired, girl."

"I'll bet you are," Becky said. She stood and gave the card back. "I brought some leftover meatloaf, but I can take you to Golden Corral if you don't have anything."

"No," Claire said. "I'll take *you* to Golden Corral. You're a good friend, Rebecca. I was losing it."

"It's okay. Even perfect people go crazy sometimes," she said with a smile. "And don't call me *Rebecca.*"

Becky thought her full name made her *feel* all thirty-nine of her years. This woman was as quirky as they come, but she was also rational and sensible, all things Claire needed on a day like this.

They went back in and Claire found fault in the very next file she looked at. She took that as a sign that her shattered emotions were on the mend. At lunch they dined pleasantly and talked about the earlier incident only briefly. It took the tone of a *silly moment in time*, like the time Becky wore a dark blue pump and a black pump to work.

But by the time Claire got off, the journey pendant was at the forefront of her mind again. She picked up George Jr. and Stacy like any other day. But on the way to Nikki's school, she started to grill them, not really knowing what she was doing at first.

"How was school?"

George was in the back this time. Stacy sat up front, staring out of the passenger window like a tourist. All of the middle school kids lucky enough to *walk* home were a mystery to her. She thought they probably had jobs and wood-chopping chores and everything.

Stacy wore denim capris this afternoon with another pink T-shirt. This one had *100% NATURAL* sprawled across the chest. Her modest raisins barely dented the fabric.

"How was school?" Claire asked again.

Stacy looked over at her and shrugged. "It was okay, I guess."

"What about you, boy?"

"It was great!" George Jr. bounced in the backseat like they had cotton candy right before the last bell. "My lima bean is growing!" he announced. He held up his plastic cup, and Claire nodded.

"That's nice. Did you guys have fun with your daddy last night?"

"Yes!" George Jr. said. Stacy shrugged.

"What's your deal?" Claire asked her. "You too cool to have fun with your daddy now?"

The little girl smiled. "I'm not too cool."

"What do you like to do with your dad?" Claire asked. "Where's the best place he takes you guys?"

"I like the tracks," George Jr. said immediately.

The Lone Star Park was one place that was just for George and the kids. Possible animal cruelty aside, Claire simply didn't see what was so enjoyable about sitting in the sun all day waiting for thoroughbreds with odd names to streak by. The fact that her father was a dysfunctional gambler probably had a lot to do with Claire's opinion. And then there was the possible animal cruelty . . .

"I like the racetrack, too," Stacy said.

"What do you like about it?" Claire asked.

"I like the horses' names," George said. "And people stand up and yell at them."

"I like watching Dad," Stacy said. "When he wins, he gets so happy. He buys us whatever we want."

"Sometimes he takes some of his friends with him, doesn't he?" Claire fished.

"Mr. Hodges comes with us sometimes," George Jr. confirmed.

"Just him?" Claire asked.

"He brings his wife sometimes," George Jr. said. "*She* doesn't hate horses."

"I don't hate horses," Claire said.

"She just doesn't like them," Stacy said.

"I never said I don't like horses," Claire said.

"Horses are cool," George Jr. said.

"When Mr. Hodges brings his wife," Claire went on, "does she ever bring any of *her* friends with them?"

No one said anything right away, and Claire felt a quick stab of pain behind her sternum. *I was right! I knew it.*

"What do you mean?" George Jr. asked.

Claire sighed. "Mrs. Hodges," she said. "I haven't seen her in a while. I thought she used to have a couple of friends she hung around with all the time, friends that were *girls.*"

"I never seen any of her friends," Stacy said.

"*I've* never seen," Claire corrected.

"She only comes with Mr. Hodges," George Jr. said. "She doesn't have any friends."

Claire let out a pent-up breath, suddenly embarrassed about what she was doing. But *in for an ounce, in for a pound*, she figured. "What about any *other place* Daddy takes you?" she asked. "Does he ever have friends there that Mommy doesn't know?"

Another awkward silence ensued. Claire thought she was going to get a revelation, but no such luck.

"You know all of Daddy's friends," Stacy said. "Mr. Hodges, Murray . . ."

"Mr. Billy!" George Jr. shouted.

"Mr. Tucker," Stacy said. "Humphrey, Mr. Dalton, Pat . . ."

"Sherman," George Jr. offered.

"What was that last one?" Claire asked her daughter.

"Patrick," Stacy said. "You know him."

Claire nodded. She did know him.

She dropped the conversation before they pulled to a stop in front of Humboldt High. Nikki was a little older and wiser; she'd want to know why mother was so concerned with such things.

When they got home, Claire was able to get things off her mind for a while as she got into her normal routine of servitude to the children. George Jr. liked to eat a snack while doing his homework, so Claire popped a corny dog in the microwave before she went up to change clothes.

She let him eat it in his room afterwards because George Jr., unlike his sisters, knew how to munch neatly and clean up his crumbs afterwards. Nikki and Stacy had ants in their rooms two summers in a row. Claire wouldn't even let them eat a peppermint outside of the kitchen.

After she got everyone started on their homework, Claire went back downstairs to prepare what she hoped was a meal for *five*, but George Sr. called while she was dicing onions. Claire cradled the cordless on her shoulder and washed the pungent juices from her hands.

"Hello?"

"Hey, baby. It looks like I'm not going to make it for dinner tonight."

This wasn't an unusual announcement at all. Boeing built aircraft twenty-four hours a day, and George was a lead engineer. Plus he was young and still on the uphill slope of his career. Claire got this call at least twice a week. It used to give her a sense of security, knowing her husband was doing so well. But today things felt *different*.

"I thought they brought in a few new guys," she said.

"And they ain't worth a shit," George countered. "Don't know their assholes from a fuselage. *Goddamn Aggies*. One of them even helped put up that bonfire in '99. Now he's in there trying to tell *my* guys what to do. I'm not leaving till he's gone."

"Do you want me to keep a plate for you?" Claire asked.

"No. I'll pick up something in the cafeteria. Don't wait up."

"Okay," Claire said. "I'll see you later." She hung up the phone with a keen understanding that there wasn't much she could say in situations like this. George was a great provider. He bought her a two-thousand-dollar pendant for their anniversary just yesterday. What kind of wife would Claire be if she nagged every night he had a little overtime?

She called her friend Melanie when she hung up with her husband.

"Hello?"

"Hey, girl. Whatchoo doing?"

"Looking for something to put in the oven."

"I'm making chicken cacciatore," Claire said. "You interested?"

"George is working late again?"

"Yeah. He told me not to wait up."

"That sounds good," Melanie said. "But I haven't fixed anything for Rodney and Trevon. They're not gonna want these leftovers."

"I think George is cheating on me," Claire said.

"I'll be right there."

CHAPTER FOUR
SMELLING LIKE A ROSE

Melanie Sturgis knocked on Claire's door fifteen minutes later carrying a rolling pin, a Tupperware bowl, and a box of Kleenex. Claire had a lot of good friends in high school, but Melanie was the only one she still kept in touch with after all this time. Melanie was short and top heavy. She had long hair she wore in tight curls and beady eyes always on a fault-finding mission.

Melanie was married with one child, and she was the bread-winner of her family due to her husband's recent stint of unemployment. After ten lackluster years in the automotive industry, Rodney finally decided to go to technical school so he could get the job he wanted. Melanie worked a regular nine-to-five at a genetics lab, so it was Rodney's job to pick up their son from school and make a dinner for the family on most nights.

Claire let her friend in and laughed at the accessories she brought with her.

"I guess you want to take some food home with you . . ."

"Yeah," Melanie said. "If that's all right with you." She walked through the living room, wielding the rolling pin like a lead pipe. "Did he come home yet?"

Melanie wore denim overall shorts with white sneakers. She was a big girl, knot-kneed with pudgy arms and full cheeks. If Claire ever *did* need to have someone beat up, this was the first person she'd call, but she didn't think she gave that impression over the phone.

"No," Claire said. "And if he *was* here, I'm pretty sure I wouldn't want you to attack him."

Melanie turned and frowned at her. "Why not?"

Claire closed the door behind her. "What do you mean, *why not?*"

"Oh, 'cause of the kids," Melanie said. She nodded. "That's good thinking, Claire. How you holding up? You look like shit. You been crying? Here, girl, I brought some tissues."

"I look like *what?* I haven't cried since this morning." Claire leaned over her glass coffee table and tried to assess her features in the reflection. "I look bad?"

"Uh, naw," Melanie said. "You look good."

"You just said—"

"Don't worry about it, Claire. We ain't got time for that. What time is he gonna be here? Do you want to get some bleach going in the tub for his clothes, or do you want to burn all his stuff? I would go with the bleach, just cause everybody wanna call the police these days. But if you really want to get his attention, nothing works better than fire. I got a five-gallon can in the trunk. I filled it up on the way over here."

Claire chuckled. "Melanie, I don't even know for sure if he's doing anything. All I said—"

"It's all right, girl. Go with your heart. You can always apologize later. Just say, '*My bad*,' like Left Eye did."

"I'm not bleaching those good clothes I bought him," Claire said. "I don't even know if I'm right. And even if I *am*, I'm pretty sure I don't want to start a fire. I'd rather kill his ass than deal with the property damage."

Melanie shook her head. "I don't know if I can help with a *murder*, Claire. I can give you technical support, but nothing hands-on."

Claire laughed. "What—?"

"You wouldn't help me kill Rodney if I asked," Melanie said. "Tell the truth. You know you wouldn't."

"Back it up," Claire said. "I just want to *talk* to somebody right now. That's why I called you over. I don't have any evidence that he cheated, and I'm pretty sure I'm making something out of nothing. *Damn, girl.* You're jumping to conclusions worse than me."

"All right," Melanie said. She sighed and took a seat on the couch. "Tell me what's going on."

Before Claire could say anything, George Jr. slid down the banister and hopped into the living room like Peter Rabbit.

"Hey, Aunt Melanie!" he shouted. "Hey, Mama! Is dinner ready yet?"

"Yeah," Claire said. "Go get your sisters. And stop sliding down that banister! You're not going to be happy till you bust your head."

"Okay," George said, but he turned and eyed Melanie before heading up. "What's *that* thing?"

"That's a rolling pin, baby," she said, "for making bread and cookies."

George looked confused, but he ran upstairs anyway.

"Can we talk after dinner?" Claire asked.

"Sure," Melanie said.

"You know we're going to have to make something with that thing now," Claire informed.

"For real?"

"For real."

After dinner the girls went upstairs, but George Jr. stuck around to find out what a rolling pin does. Claire mixed flour, baking soda, eggs, sugar and a little vanilla extract in a bowl. She kneaded the dough on the counter and let Melanie flatten it out with her *husband-beater*. They made a quick batch of sugar cookies and shooed little George away when they put them in the oven.

Claire sat at the table and rubbed her temples when he was gone. Melanie washed her hands and sat across from her.

"All right, girl. Tell me what's going on. If you don't need help starting a fire, I can't stay out too long."

Claire grinned at her. "All I really want is for you to tell me I'm crazy."

"We already know you're *crazy*," Melanie teased. "Just tell me what you're being crazy about this time."

"Last night was our anniversary," Claire said.

"For real? Happy anniversary, sugar. I got you something, but I forgot it at home."

Claire frowned. "What is it?"

"Huh?"

"Go ahead and commit to it," Claire said. "Just make sure it's something you can get *really* quick, 'cause I'm coming to collect after work tomorrow."

"It's a, it's a flower pot," Melanie said. "You like azaleas, don't you?"

"Is that the same pot of azaleas you have in your living room?"

"No, *it's not*," Melanie said with a little *umph* in her voice. "I have *four* azalea plants. I was going to give you the one from the den."

Claire shook her head. "Anyway, I had everything set up perfectly for last night. I made him lobster for dinner, I got our wedding video re-mastered, and—"

"That's what you had all of them people calling you about, right?"

"Yeah," Claire said. "I got the last video added just two weeks ago."

"That was a lot of work," Melanie said. "I wouldn't never do nothing like that for Rodney."

Claire was tempted to get her friend one of Stacy's grammar worksheets. "I bought a new dress," she said. "It's red, and *tight*. I wore it last night, and I looked *good*."

"What did George get you?"

"That's where the trouble started," Claire said. "He got me a necklace. It's a pendant, but it's curved. It has five diamonds on it."

"Big spender," Melanie noted.

"Yeah," Claire said, "but he messed up when he gave it to me. He told me he knew how *badly I wanted it*, and he was going to make sure *all* of my dreams came true."

"That's sweet."

"Yeah, except I never told him I wanted that necklace," Claire said. "I never told him I wanted any kind of necklace."

"He slipped up," Melanie agreed.

"Becky thinks I asked for it and forgot about it."

"Who's Becky—that lady you work with?"

"Yeah."

"*Did* you ask for it?"

"No," Claire said, "and he made it sound like I've been really sweating him for a while."

Melanie nodded. "Like someone's been saying, '*Please, George. Please buy that for me.*'"

Claire felt the same way, but it still hurt to hear her friend say it.

Melanie saw the change in her demeanor. "Ooh, I'm sorry, girl. I get so caught up in the *hate*, I forget how it feels to find out stuff like that."

"It's all right," Claire said. "But, yeah, that's pretty much what I figure she's been telling him."

"Did you confront him?"

"No. I woke up early this morning and started snooping."

"*You* snooped?"

"Not that much. I just looked around the office a little. I found a card in his briefcase. I'll be back." She went upstairs to retrieve the Hallmark. Melanie was checking on the cookies when she got back.

"These smell good, Claire. I never knew you could use a rolling pin for *good.*"

Claire chuckled and returned to her seat. She slid the card across the table when Melanie sat down. She waited anxiously for what seemed like a long time while her friend read.

When Melanie finally looked up at her, her beady eyes were even *beadier.*

"That's his *bitch,*" she said with no uncertainties.

Claire knew it would hurt to get confirmation, and it did. Her friend's words hit like a wrecking ball to the gut. "How do you know?"

"Well, first of all, do you know somebody named *Kim?*" Melanie asked.

Claire shook her head.

"So this can't be his *mama,* or an *aunt* or *sister* or nothing like that, right?"

"It's no one I know," Claire said, speaking softly. "But Becky thinks it might be one of his co-workers at Boeing, like a friendly motivation sort of thing."

"She's too trusting," Melanie said. "She'll find something good to say about a mass murderer."

Claire grinned because that was actually true. Becky thought John Wayne Gacy was eccentric, like her, and mostly misunderstood.

"What else did you find?" Melanie asked.

"That's it," Claire said. "It was dark, and I didn't want to turn on the lights."

"You didn't find anything else today?"

Claire shook her head. "I didn't go back in there."

"Why not?"

That was a good question, and Claire didn't have a good answer. The office was off-limits to the kids, but it wasn't George's room any more than it was Claire's. The fact that George had more stuff in there was coincidental.

Claire went in that cluttered room almost every day to get worksheets and other office supplies, but she couldn't force herself to go in there today. Twice she tried, but was unable to cross the threshold; something in her heart kept pulling her away.

"I don't know," she said. "I'm not used to snooping. What if one of the kids catches me?"

"This is *your house*," Melanie reminded her. "Send their nosey asses to bed. You can go right now."

"What if George comes home early?"

"Do you want me to look out for you?"

"Look out—what, are you serious?"

"Yeah. Come on," Melanie said and stood. "You go in the office, and I'll wait in the hallway. If I see George, I'll go, like, *hootyhoooo!*"

"*Hootyhoooo*? Girl, what the hell?"

"I can't whistle," Melanie confided.

"Can't you knock on the wall?" Claire suggested. "Or stomp your feet? Where'd you get *hootyhoooo* from?"

"I can knock on the wall," Melanie said. "That would work better anyway."

"You think?" Claire teased.

"All right, come on," Melanie said.

"What about the oven?" Claire asked.

Melanie checked the stove and grinned. She put on one of Claire's cooking mitts and removed the baking sheet. A sweet aroma filled the kitchen. They only made six cookies, but they were big and golden brown. She put the pan on the counter and tossed the glove on the table. "Come on."

"I can't search the office," Claire said.

"Why not?"

"It's not right. I just don't feel good about it. Not with the kids here."

"What he's doing to you ain't right."

"I might be wrong," Claire said. "I don't want to go through all of this, the deception, lies and suspicions. I don't want to think about George like that and then find out I'm wrong."

"Sounds like you don't want to know if you're *right*," Melanie said. "You're going to be okay with that, him having another woman? Don't get me wrong, Claire. Some women *can* live like that. Just as long as they man don't bring home no diseases, and they don't never *see* his mistress."

"I'm not like that."

"If you are, it's cool," Melanie said, continuing to bait her. "Long as he keeps giving you expensive gifts and stuff . . ."

"No," Claire said. "I'm not like that, Melanie. If George is cheating on me, I'm going to kill him—I swear to God."

"So that's why you don't want to know?" Melanie guessed. "You don't want it to ever come to that? Ignorance is bliss, girl."

Claire shook her head. "Stop talking to me like that. I'm not sharing George with another woman. And I'm not *ignorant*. I already know he bought my necklace for some other bitch, and I know someone named Kim cares a lot about him, probably loves him."

"But you don't want to get to the bottom of it?" Melanie asked.

Claire shot daggers with her eyes, and then her features softened. "I thought I did," she said. "But the more I think about it, I kind of don't . . ."

"It's hard," Melanie said.

"You don't know."

"Yes, I do," Melanie snapped. "I knew you *before* you met George. I helped you get dressed for the prom. *I* was the maid of honor at your wedding. I know how long y'all been together. I know how much you sacrificed for him; you gave up your whole career. You could have went to college, Claire, but he made you his *housewife,* moved you all around the world with him so you could stay home and raise *his* kids.

"Now he's all successful, and you work part-time at an insurance company. I know you're worried about what kind of life you'll have if you lose him. But more than that, you're worried about how much it's gonna hurt if you're right. I know exactly what you're going through, Claire. Don't ever think I don't understand."

Claire sighed and a lone tear fell from her eye. She dabbed it with a trembling knuckle and stared at her friend, for the first time really. Melanie was loud, obnoxious and violent; pretty much all things you'd expect from a *hood chick*. But she was also smart and beautiful, caring, and understanding—the kind of person Claire would need to lean on if her suspicions turned out to be valid.

"I don't want to do it while the kids are here. I might freak out if I find something, and I don't want them to see me like that."

"Do you want to do a stake-out?" Melanie suggested. "We could go up to his job next time he says he's working late."

"You're crazy."

"If you really want to get to the bottom of it, I can help you," Melanie offered. "Rodney doesn't do nothing all day. He can stay home and watch Trevon sometimes. We can go tomorrow if you want."

"Go do a stake-out?"

"If you want."

"Tomorrow *is* his poker night," Claire mused.

"Prolly ain't no damned poker night," Melanie guessed. "Do you ever smell him when he gets in?"

Claire shook her head. "I'm usually asleep."

"Next time he comes in all late and shit, put your face up to his neck and take a good whiff," Melanie suggested.

"All right," Claire said.

"So we're doing the stake-out tomorrow?" Melanie asked.

Claire shook her head. "I don't think so. We'll see."

Melanie was about to start arguing again, but the smell of confections lured one of the rug rats down the stairs. George Jr. crept like an Indian on the warpath, and the women pretended not to see him until the last moment.

"*Argh!*" he screamed, jumping from around the corner with a plastic Conan sword in hand.

"*Ahh!*" the girls screamed in unison.

"I got you!" George said.

"Yeah, baby. You got me," Claire said.

"You got me, too, little man," Melanie agreed. "You're a big *sneak*, just like your daddy."

Claire was in dreamland when George Sr. made it in that night, but she awakened when she heard him flush the toilet in their restroom. She feigned sleep until he crawled into bed with her, and then she rolled over and pressed her body close to his. George lay on his side with his back to her, and Claire spooned him pleasantly.

"You still awake?" he asked.

"I just woke up when I heard you," she said. "What time is it?"

"It's almost one," he said. "It was a bad night."

Claire scooted up on the mattress so she could kiss the back of his neck. While there, she stuck her nose under his ear and took a long, healthy sniff as advised.

After a sixteen-hour shift at work, George somehow came home smelling like a rose. Well, technically he smelled like Irish Spring soap, the Moisture Blast scent to be specific, but *smelling like a rose* was how Claire planned to describe it tomorrow.

"You already took a shower?" she asked. She planned to get up and check the tub if he said *yes*, but George wasn't going to get busted so easily.

"No. I'll take on in the morning," he said.

Claire rolled back over the other way with the weight of a dump truck on her chest. She didn't think it was possible to remain completely silent while crying, but that night she found there's a lot you can do if you give it your all. George wasn't even bothered by the continuous hitching of her sorrow-laden shoulders.

CHAPTER FIVE
AGITATION

"So, if you're not too busy sometime maybe I can call you."

Claire cocked an eye at the man standing in front of her desk. It was Cordell, an employee of the United States Postal Service. Cordell was about forty years old. He was light-skinned with short, curly hair. Claire thought he was of mixed cultures, most likely black and Hispanic. Cordell didn't have any facial stubble, and his postal uniform was generally clean and free of wrinkles. Claire always thought he was handsome, but that was the last thing on her mind this morning.

"Huh?" she said, snapping out of a fog she didn't know she was in.

"I said maybe I could call you sometimes, you know, if you've got time . . ."

Cordell had his mail basket propped on his hip. He wore short sleeves today, and Claire saw that his forearms were well toned—and hairy. He had his shirt open midway down his chest, and she could see a tuft of hair poking out there, too.

"I'm sorry," Claire said. "I must've been daydreaming for a second. What are we talking about?"

Cordell grinned. "We're talking about *physical attraction*," he said. "I was telling you about how I come in here every day and see your pretty self sitting there. And every day I come up with an excuse not to talk to you. But today I decided to say *the hell with it*, ya know?"

"The hell with it?"

"You're a beautiful sister," he said. "You're tall. You've got long legs, an *awesome* body, pretty face. I know you got that ring on your finger, but I also know most women aren't happy with the man they're with. I'm hoping you'll at least consider my offer."

"Your offer?"

"Damn, baby. You really weren't listening to me?"

"I'm sorry," Claire said. "I've got a lot on my mind. I saw you come up to my desk, and I knew you were talking about *something*, I just—okay, I wasn't paying attention."

The mailman laughed politely. "Okay," he said. "Fair enough. What I was saying was—"

"Wait," Claire said. "Are you hitting on me?"

He smiled. "Something like that."

"And did you say you *know* I'm married?"

He nodded. "I see your ring."

"So why are you still trying to talk to me?" Claire wanted to know.

"Just 'cause you're married doesn't mean you're happy," he countered.

Claire sneered at him. "That's messed up," she said. "I see you walk in here every day. I don't know you, but I figured you're a hard-working guy. You're handsome, and you've got a pretty good job. I thought you were a good dude."

"I am a good dude."

"No, you're not. You're running around here hitting on *married women*. How many marriages have you ruined? You're *disgusting*. Don't you know what it means to stand in front of God and all your family and say *Till death do us part*? Isn't that sacred to you?"

Cordell's smile fell. He tried to back away, but his retreat was thwarted by his own mail cart. He stumbled into the buggy and dropped the envelopes in his hand. Claire stood and berated him further while he picked them up.

"You're probably married yourself, aren't you? You probably got a wife at home, and you make her cry every night while you go out and do whatever the hell you want to do. Do you think women are objects you can treat however you please?"

"I'm, I'm sorry, ma'am . . ."

"Your mother is a *woman*! Your sister, aunt—your grandmother is a woman *just like me*. Do you want people treating them like that? Don't you care anything about their feelings?"

Cordell scooped up the last of his envelopes. He threw them on his cart and rolled quickly in the opposite direction. "You have a nice day, ma'am."

Claire stared after him with a hand on her hip until Becky stepped in her line of sight.

"Claire?"

Claire stared at her friend, but it took a few seconds for her features to soften.

"Huh?"

"Are you doing all right?"

"Yeah, why?"

"You just cursed out our mailman," Becky informed her.

"I didn't curse."

"Everybody's looking at you," Becky reported.

Claire scanned the room, and her co-workers quickly looked down at their keyboards. Some of their desktops were empty, but they stared at the wood anyway.

Claire sighed. "What time is it?"

"Time for our break," Becky said.

The clock mounted at the front of the office indicated it was still a few minutes before ten, but no one gave Claire and Becky a hard time when they exited the building.

❧

It was cloudy that morning, and that fit Claire's mood perfectly. Today she wore black slacks with a long-sleeved, black button-down. She had her hair down, but there was nothing flashy about her. Her slacks were a little tight, however. Maybe that's what attracted the perverted postman.

Claire stomped around the side of the building and made her way to Provincial's abandoned smoking section with Becky quick on her heels. Becky took a seat on the concrete bench, but Claire preferred to stand. She leaned with her back against the building and her hands in her pockets. A steady breeze ruffled the hair on her forehead.

"You're still upset?" Becky asked.

"No shit, Sherlock," Claire said. Becky was queen when it came to stating the obvious, but that wasn't nice. Claire immediately felt bad about snapping at her. "I'm sorry."

"Is it George?" Becky asked.

Claire nodded. "I think you're wrong about him not cheating on me."

Becky's mouth fell open, and it looked like she would be the one crying this time.

"Claire, why would you say that?"

"I told you about the necklace and the card, right?"

"Yeah, but I thought we said—"

"No, *you* said it didn't mean anything. I went along with you because that's what I wanted to hear, but I can't keep lying to myself. George is working late all the time. He goes on *business trips* at least twice a month, and sometimes he's gone for over a week."

"He's always been like that," Becky said.

"I know. And I'm starting to wonder how long he's been cheating on me, how many times, how many, *God*, how many women?"

"Why don't you just ask him about the card?" Becky suggested.

" 'Cause he's a liar," Claire snapped. "All men are liars. George came home at one o'clock this morning smelling like a rose."

"He brought you flowers?"

Claire was mad, but she couldn't help but laugh at that. "No, Becky. He didn't bring me flowers. He didn't smell like roses *literally*. Damn, I thought that was a good analogy."

Becky knitted her eyebrows in confusion.

"He smelled *clean*, girl," Claire clarified. "He left the house at seven-thirty and didn't come home till one in the morning. And he smelled *clean*—like he was fresh out of the shower. I got real close to him so I could make sure."

"Maybe he took a shower at work," Becky said. "Don't they have a gym there?"

"Yes, they have a gym."

"You know he likes to work out."

"Why are you defending him?"

"I'm not defending him, Claire. I just don't want you to jump to conclusions and make a mistake you'll regret. If he's not doing anything and you run up and throw all of these accusations at him, he's not going to like that. It may hurt him. He might resent the fact that he's working so hard, and all you're worried about is him being with someone else."

"You're right," Claire said. "That's why I'm not accusing him of anything right now. Even when I smelled the soap on him this morning, I didn't say anything. Unless I know for sure, I'm keeping my mouth shut."

"That's good," Becky said.

"But I am going to find out for sure," Claire said decisively. "I'm not going to live like this. It's too hectic. I'm stressed out."

"That's why you cursed out our mailman?" Becky asked with a giggle.

"Girl, he was hitting on me. He saw the ring on my finger, acknowledged that he knew I was married, and still hit on me. What's this world coming to?"

"Get out of the Dark Ages," Becky advised her. "Everybody cheats nowadays. Just 'cause you're married doesn't mean another man can't call you. It just means he can't call *at certain times.*"

"Is that the way people really act?"

"I'm no statistician," Becky said, "but I'll bet at least half of all married people have cheated on their spouse at least once. A quarter of them probably do it on a regular basis."

Claire shook her head. "I don't believe that."

"It happened to me," Becky said. "Trent cheated on me with *four* different women, and they all knew he was married."

A year ago Becky couldn't talk about her ex husband without crying. It was good to see how much progress she had made. Claire wondered if she would one day have to get over George like that.

"I may have been fooled," Claire said, "but it's over now. My blinders are off. I pray that everything will be okay, but if George is cheating on me, I'm going to *catch him* and *expose* him. He had a pretty good life going there. He could come and go as he pleased. But until I find out what's going on, I'm going to be on his ass like white on rice."

"What are you going to do?"

"I'm saying I'm not taking anything he says for granted anymore. My friend thinks I should follow him tonight, and I think I'm gonna do it."

Becky shook her head. "Claire, you're going off the deep end."

"Am I? Or am I taking control of my own life? I've been doing what George wanted for a long time, Becky, since high school. I gave him freedom to take care of whatever he had to do, and if he used that freedom against me . . ." She shook her head. "I, I can't even think about what's going to happen."

"So you're really going to follow him?"

"Wouldn't you?" Claire asked. "If you had a chance to catch Trent sleeping around, wouldn't you want to do it?"

Becky nodded. "By the time I found out, he already had another apartment and half of his stuff moved."

"George isn't moving *shit* out of my house," Claire said. "I'm going to know before he *thinks* I know."

"Who's your friend?" Becky asked. "Who's going to help you follow him?"

"You remember Melanie, the one who came to my Christmas party last year?"

"The one you said you knew since high school?"

"Yeah. The stakeout is her idea."

Becky smiled. "Can I go, too?"

Claire chuckled. "You want to help me follow George around?"

"Yeah. I wish I had friends to help me when I went through this. I still hope you're wrong. But if you're right, I want to be there for you. That's the worst feeling in the world."

"I told you I was going to kill him if he's cheating, right?"

"You're not going to kill George," Becky said with a snicker, but when she looked up Claire wasn't smiling at all.

❧

When they got back inside, Claire called Melanie at her job to tell her it was on.

"Biotech Industries . . ."

"Hey, girl. This is Claire."

"What's up, honey? What you doing?"

"I'm at work," Claire said, "about to go to lunch."

"We should hook up for lunch sometimes," Melanie said.

"That would be cool," Claire said. "Except you work in *Grand Prairie*."

"We could meet in the middle."

"If I drove to Arlington, I'd have to turn right around as soon as I got there," Claire said.

"We could—"

"Melanie, I didn't call to chit-chat."

"Oh, well. What's up, then?"

"*It's on*," Claire said.

"What's on?"

"The stakeout."

"For real?"

"Yeah," Claire said. "It's on. Becky wants to go, too."

"*Cool!* You must have put on your big-girl drawers this morning. What changed your mind?"

"When George came home late last night," Claire said, "he smelled like a *fresh shower*."

"I told you."

"Don't say that. We still might be wrong."

"Maybe," Melanie said. "If we are, no harm done. But if we're not, we're going to *get his ass*. I want to run up on him with a camera like they do on Cheaters."

Claire laughed, but none of this was funny, not really. What they were joking about may very well be the end of life as she knew it.

"We gonna get his ass," Melanie said again.

"Don't forget," Claire said, "we want to find him doing *nothing* wrong. If he's cheating, that's like, the worst-case scenario."

"Ooh, I'm sorry, girl. I told you, I get so wrapped up in the *hate*—"

"It's okay," Claire said. "I'm pretty sure we'll all be wrapped up in hate by the end of it."

∽

Claire went out so infrequently that she decided to break the news to the kids before they got home. On Friday nights (when George had poker night with the guys) Claire usually rented a movie everyone wanted to see and gathered the kids in the living room for family time. She would make popcorn, or popcorn balls, or whatever else they wanted, and they would genuinely enjoy each other's company.

After the movie, Claire was known to declare a few hours of Electronics Free time. The goal was to get the kids to play a board game with her, but if they wanted to read a book, that was fine, too, so long as they stayed in the living room.

But instead of making her announcement, Claire sat outside of Humboldt High School looking over the note Stacy's teacher sent home with her. Stacy fidgeted in the backseat, very near panic. By the time she was done reading, Claire wanted to reach back there and grab her by the hair.

"Why the hell would you *cheat* on a science test?" Claire's face was set in a deep scowl. She turned in her seat so she could watch her daughter's eyes.

Stacy couldn't respond right away. She scooted back as far as she could, but unless she was going to get in the trunk, there was no escape.

"*You answer me!*"

George Jr. cowered wide-eyed in the front seat. He flinched when his mother screamed, as if she struck him.

"*I, I, I, I didn't-*" Stacy's bottom lip quivered like she was freezing.

"You didn't *what*? Don't tell me you didn't do it, girl. I'll slap the black off you!"

Stacy didn't have much melanin to begin with, but Claire's mom always told her that, and it sort of trickled down subconsciously.

"It was *Crystal,*" Stacy blurted. "*She* made that for me."

Stacy was referring to the cheat-sheet her teacher sent home with the letter. Claire already knew it wasn't written in her daughter's handwriting, but she wanted to hear Stacy say it herself.

"Why would Crystal make *you* a cheat-sheet?"

"I don't know . . ."

"Why'd you use it?"

"I didn't, not really."

"You calling your teacher a liar?"

"I had it on my desk," Stacy admitted. "But I wasn't looking at it!"

Claire thought these explanations were getting more and more ignorant. "Why'd you have it on your desk, then, Stacy?"

"Crystal gave it to me. She made one for herself and another one for me—but I wasn't looking at it. *I swear.*"

Claire studied her daughter's face, and she suddenly understood everything perfectly. "So why didn't you tell Crystal you didn't need it? Even better, why didn't you tell Crystal she shouldn't cheat, either? Are you that much of a *follower*? You would rather pretend to cheat than tell her you could pass the test without her help?"

"She said it was hard," Stacy explained. "She said she failed the other one."

"What's that got to do with *you*?"

"I, I, I—"

"You're a *follower*," Claire said, realization slowly dawning. "So now instead of making an A on this test like you were going to, you got a zero so you could be *cool*. Was it worth it? You smoke cigarettes in the bathroom, too?"

"No."

"You skip classes sometimes so you can get high? You smoking *weed*, girl?"

"No, Mama."

"Why not?" Claire barked. "You want to do what everybody else does."

"No, I don't," Stacy said. She was crying now.

Claire didn't even know her oldest daughter was out yet, but when she looked up Nikki walked around the front of the Lexus and got in behind her mother. She looked around from Stacy's to George's to Claire's face.

"Why everybody mad?"

"Why *is* everyone mad?" Claire corrected. She sighed loudly and backed out of her parking spot, glad to be headed home.

"What's wrong with you?" Nikki asked her sister when they got on the freeway.

Claire watched the girls in the rearview, but Stacy didn't want to share.

"She got caught cheating at school," Claire said. "She made a *zero* on her test, and now she's mad cause she can't use the phone for two weeks."

"*Two weeks?*" Stacy looked like she got shot.

"The computer, either," Claire said.

"But I use the computer for my homework," Stacy whined.

"If you want to do some research, you can use *my* computer," Claire offered, "in *my* room while I'm sitting there watching your sneaky self."

"I thought you liked science . . ." Nikki said to her sister.

"Oh," Claire interrupted. "That's the best part: *Miss Attitude* didn't even need to cheat. She just did it so her friend would think she's cool."

Nikki giggled.

"Don't laugh at me!" Stacy spat.

"Don't yell at your sister!" Claire shouted. "If you weren't such a *follower*, this never would have happened!"

"I'm not a follower!"

"Prove it!" her mom snapped back.

George Jr. giggled. "We should watch a movie about not being a follower tonight," he suggested.

Stacy kicked the back of his seat. "Shut up!"

"You keep your feet on the floor!" Claire warned. She knew her anger was being misdirected, but it was hard to be civil right now. She sighed. "I can't watch a movie with you guys tonight," she told George Jr. "Mommy has something to do."

"What?" he asked.

"You gonna do your insurance stuff?" Nikki guessed.

"No."

"You gonna work on your crosswords?" George Jr. asked.

"No."

"You gonna clean the bathrooms?" Nikki pondered.

"*No*," Claire said, a little chagrined that her life was so boring and predictable.

"What *are* you doing tonight, Mommy?" little George asked.

And here it was: For the first time in recent memory, Claire had to lie to her children. She gritted her teeth and wondered how George Sr. was able to spout mistruths so easily.

"Me and Becky are going to the movies," she said.

Little George swallowed it easily enough, but Nikki said, "Really?"

"Yes. What's wrong with that?"

"You *never* go out, Mom."

"I know. But I'm not in jail; I can if I want to."

"Who's going to take care of us?" George Jr. asked.

Claire grinned at him. "Your sister's fourteen years old," she said. "And Becky's daughter is coming over, too, to help out."

"Courtney?" Nikki asked.

"Yeah."

"Ooh, I like Courtney," George Jr. said.

"That's good," Claire said, and she meant it. It was hard enough leaving her children with a babysitter. She didn't think she could do it if they were opposed.

CHAPTER SIX
THE STAKEOUT

Claire got the kids started on their homework, and then she showered and changed for her night out with the girls. She had no idea what to wear to a *stake-out*, but she figured the less flashy the better. She put on blue jeans with a white T-shirt and white sneakers. She pulled her hair back in a pony tail and went back downstairs to start dinner.

Melanie called while she was rinsing carrots.

"Hello?"

"Hey, Claire. It's me. I'm just now getting off."

"I'm getting the kids' dinner ready," Claire said.

"It's still on?" Melanie asked. "You haven't changed your mind, have you?"

"No," Claire said. "I'm still going. I already showered and got dressed. George will be here at six, and he leaves at *six-thirty*. We need to get in position before then."

"I'm gonna go home and change, and I'll be ready," Melanie promised.

"You don't have to cook dinner?" Claire asked.

"No. I already told Rodney I was going out with you. How you feeling?"

"Like shit. My stomach's upset. Stacy got caught cheating on a test today. I had to yell at her on the way home. I'm already stressed."

"You need to beat her ass," Melanie advised.

"Maybe," Claire said, but they both knew she wasn't going to do it. In fourteen years of parenting, she hardly ever had to get physically violent with her offspring to get them to mind.

"You still want me to go after him first?" Melanie asked.

"Yeah," Claire said. "When he gets here, I'll tell him I'm going to the movies with Becky. I'll wait for him to leave, and you can get behind him as soon as he backs out of our driveway. When you call and say you're on his tail, me and Becky will leave and catch up to you."

"Damn, Claire, you sure you never did this before? You sound like you know what you're doing."

"George told me a lot of war stories," Claire said. "I guess some of those military tactics stuck with me."

"*For real!*" Melanie agreed. "You're on some old, Desert Storm type of shit. Some *counter-surveillance* type of shit."

Claire didn't bother telling her friend she was using that term inappropriately.

⌒~

Becky called at 5:45 while Claire was setting the table.
"Hello?"
"Hey. It's me."

"You just get home?"

"Yeah." She sounded out of breath. "I'm changing clothes now. What time did you say we were leaving?"

"George will be here in about fifteen minutes," Claire said. "He's leaving at six-thirty, and I only want to give him five minutes, just in case he forgets something and doubles back."

"Okay. Me and Courtney can be there at six-fifteen."

"What about Craig? You don't have to cook for him?"

Becky had one boy and one girl, ages seventeen and sixteen, respectively. Claire figured they could probably feed themselves, but she had no idea how things went down over there.

"He's not even here," Becky said with a chuckle. "He spends the night with his girlfriend a lot."

"Girl, you're letting Craig get down *like that*?"

"Like what?"

"Like openly sleeping with his girlfriend?"

"You don't want them to hide it from you," Becky warned. "It's better this way. I keep telling you, these are different times."

George came home, as expected, at 5:59 p.m. He came in from the garage wearing khaki Dockers with a long-sleeved, blue button-down. He was comfortable, but his shirts always looked too small for him because he was such a big man. His pecs stood out in this outfit as much as they would in a T-shirt.

George toted his special briefcase in one hand and his car keys in the other. He stepped into the dining room with a swagger like John Wayne. He had a big smile on his face. He stopped at the table and looked proudly upon the family God gave him.

"Y'all sure are some good-looking people," he said.

"Daddy!" George Jr. started to get up, but his father stepped forward and palmed the top of his head.

"Naw, sit there and eat your food. Don't leave the table until you're finished."

Today Claire had a succulent meal of chicken and dumplings prepared. The rolls were still warm. Nikki's salad was fresh and colorful. Claire sat at the head of the table with George Jr. on her right and two ebony princesses on her left. Everyone was clean and neat. Everything was perfect, just as Claire wanted it to be. She stared up at her husband, wondering if he saw what she saw. Didn't he know life was wonderful just the way it was?

"Hey, baby," he said to Claire. "How y'all girls doing?" he asked his daughters.

"Fine," they said in unison.

"That looks good," he said to Claire and licked his lips. "I wish I had time to eat with y'all."

"You going to play cards tonight?" she asked.

"Friday night is my time to *shine*," he confirmed.

"I can fix you a plate," she said. "Can't you be late? They'll be there all night."

George grinned. "Maybe, but I want some of that *early* money."

Claire nodded. "I'm going out tonight, too," she said, "to the movies with Becky."

George looked puzzled for a second, and then he smiled. "That's great, baby. What are you gonna see?"

It suddenly struck Claire that she hadn't come up with a lie for that. Her eyes widened, and she blinked quickly. "Um, I, I don't know. What's playing?"

The kids giggled.

George's eyes narrowed. Claire's face felt very warm. But then George smiled again.

"Baby, *I* don't know what's playing. You the one who said you're going to the movies. This must be some mess Becky talked you into."

Claire nodded; happy for the escape. "Yeah."

"All right, *darling*. Well, have fun." He turned and headed for the stairs. "Is somebody watching the kids?" he called over his shoulder.

"I'm old enough to watch the kids!" Nikki shouted.

"And *I'm* not a kid," Stacy said.

"Me, neither," George Jr. tacked on.

"Becky's bringing Courtney," Claire said.

"I like Courtney," George Jr. said.

৩——

At six-fifteen Melanie called Claire on her cell phone. "Hello?"

"Is it still on?"

"Yeah, *unfortunately.*"

"He hasn't left yet, has he?"

"He's getting ready now."

"All right. I'm sitting over here in my car waiting."

"Where are you?" Claire asked.

"Down the street. Don't worry. I'll see *him*, but he won't see *me*."

‿つ

At 6:19 Becky showed up wearing the most ridiculous getup Claire could have imagined. She had on black jeans, a black sweater, a black bandana on her head, and black combat boots. Claire stepped out onto her porch quickly and closed the door behind her.

"Becky, what are you doing?"

Her friend held her arms out. "What do you mean?"

"Why are you dressed like that?" Claire hissed.

"We're doing a *stake-out*," Becky whispered. "I thought we were supposed to, you know, dress like the night."

Claire cracked a smile and couldn't help but laugh. "Okay, so why are you wearing *combat boots*?"

"These are the only black shoes I have," Becky explained. "Except for heels, and I didn't want to look *crazy*."

"All right," Claire said. "But take that handkerchief off at least."

Becky did, and Claire muffled her chuckles with a hand over her mouth as she led them inside.

George Jr. was in the living room waiting. He really did like Becky's daughter, but not for the reasons Claire would have preferred. Courtney was of average height and medium build. She was blonde and blue-eyed, and pretty—but it was her busts that made her special. Courtney was one of few high school sophomores toting around perky 32C's, and she was already starting to harness their power. Almost every time Claire saw her, Courtney had on something with a V-neckline.

Today she wore blue jeans with a red tube top. George Jr. jumped from the couch and ran to greet her.

"Hi, Courtney!"

"*Georgie Porgie.*"

She bent to hug him, and George grinned like a Jack-o-lantern with his face smushing her bosoms. Claire rolled her eyes at him. If she didn't know any better, she'd think he *knew* what a lucky guy he was.

George Sr. came downstairs at 6:29 wearing dark-colored slacks with a short-sleeved, gray golf shirt. His loafers were black and polished to perfection. He brought the smell of Michael Jordan cologne down with him. He gave Claire a kiss goodbye, as he always did, and he didn't look like he was about to do anything even remotely evil.

At 6:35 Melanie called and said the dreaded deed had begun; she was three vehicles behind George on McCart Avenue. They were headed north, towards the freeway.

Claire and Becky left a few minutes later. They took Becky's monster truck, although that thing was just as conspicuous as Claire's Lexus. Claire called Melanie back as soon as she buckled her safety belt.

"Hey. Where are you now?"

"We're on 20," Melanie said, "headed towards 35. Where is he supposed to be playing poker anyway?"

"On the east side," Claire replied. "Near Bridge Street."

"Well, we're headed in that direction," Melanie said. "Where are you? Did y'all leave yet?"

"Yeah, but we just got on McCart. I don't know if we can catch up with you."

"Don't worry," Melanie said. "I got him in my sights, and he ain't going *nowhere.*"

"Thanks, Melanie. I really appreciate it."

"It's cool. How you holding up?"

"I still feel like shit," Claire admitted. "If I'm wrong, I'm never going to forgive myself."

"Doesn't look like you're wrong," Melanie said.

"What do you mean?"

"He's got his blinker on. He's about to get off on Hemphill."

"*Hemphill?* What's over there?"

"I don't know," Melanie said. "That's *your* husband."

Claire waited in silence and she racked her brain for answers, but none were forthcoming. Melanie filled in another piece of the puzzle half a minute later.

"Okay, there's a Chevrolet dealership on the corner up here. He's turning in there."

Claire knitted her eyebrows. "A *car dealership*?" She thought and prayed and hoped beyond hope but couldn't make any sense of it. Their oldest child was two years from even taking driver's ed, and neither Claire nor George drove a Chevy.

"Are you going in there with him?" she asked Melanie. Her voice was shaky and her hands were as well.

"Yeah. I'm turning in now, but I had to give him some slack. There's not a lot of traffic in here. Where are y'all?"

"We just got on the freeway," Claire said. "I don't think we're going to make it in time."

"That's all right," Melanie replied. "As a matter of fact, you probably shouldn't get too close in your car."

"We're in Becky's truck."

"*Damn.* That's even worse. Take the exit before Hemphill and wait at that Stop 'N Go. I think that's Crowley."

"Yeah, it is," Claire confirmed. "We're coming up on it now. Exit here," she instructed Becky.

"He's stopping," Melanie said. "*Yep.* He just pulled in front of a building. He's not parking, though. He's sitting in the fire lane."

"What building?" Claire asked. "What's he doing?"

"I don't know," Melanie said, "but I need to find somewhere to park or I'm going to—*oh* . . ."

"*Oh*? What's *oh*? What the hell does that mean?" Claire was frazzled, nearly frantic. Becky looked over at her and put a hand to her mouth.

"He's picking someone up," Melanie said softly, and there was a long pause.

Claire's eyes blurred over before she could get the question out: "Who, who is it, Melanie?"

Melanie sighed loudly into the phone. "It's a *female*, Claire, about your age. She's wearing a business suit. She's smiling, getting in on the passenger side."

Claire felt like a punctured balloon; she exhaled hot breath and really didn't want to take another one in. She felt light-headed. Streams of gray and black flowed in her peripheral vision. Her sick heart struggled for one pitiful beat, and then another, and Claire realized she wasn't going to die. And that was a shame. Moisture leaked from her eyes and nose like acid rain.

Becky pulled into the Stop 'N Go on Crowley Avenue and reached in her purse for a tissue. She had plenty. There were more in the glove compartment and another box under the driver's seat, just in case.

The rest of the evening didn't make a lot of sense to Claire. She felt like she was intoxicated, watching someone else's life crumble before her tear-filled eyes.

George and his unidentified passenger exited the dealership with Melanie still on their tail. Claire wasn't much good with the phone anymore, so Melanie started giving her directions to Becky. They got back on the freeway headed east, and George didn't exit again until they were near the Six Flags Mall.

He pulled into the parking lot of a Saltgrass Steak House and Melanie did the same. She got there in time to see him get out with his date, but by the time Becky made it, the adulterers were already in the safe confines of the restaurant.

Melanie got out of her car and came to sit in the truck with Becky and Claire, but they were without a leader by then. Claire was more distraught than they had ever seen her. No amount of consoling or promises of revenge could dry her eyes.

For a while Claire could barely speak. Her sorrow brought Becky to tears as well, but Melanie's heart became more cold and calloused by the minute. She wanted to vent her anger on George's vehicle. She wanted to go into the restaurant and attack George's tramp as well, but Claire wouldn't condone it.

Claire didn't have any alternatives in mind, but she knew she didn't want to confront *anyone* with snot running from her nose. The most obscure reference saved her from a hasty decision she might later regret: Her no-good husband once told her, "*If you're not sure what to do, then sit your fool ass down and don't do anything. Never run in half-cocked, and* never *breach a perimeter unless you have a game plan.*"

"Take me home," she told Becky between sniffles.

Melanie thought that was asinine. "*Why*, Claire? We're *right here*! She's in there *right now*! Don't you want to wait so you can see what she looks like? Don't you want to confront your husband? I know you're not going to let that *bitch* get away with this."

"I'm not," Claire sobbed, "but I'm not right. I'm no good right now."

"But—"

"It's all right," Claire assured her friend. "I'm going to take care of it. I promise. I appreciate what you did for me, but this is as far as I can go. Take me home," she told Becky again.

Melanie looked defeated, but then her eyes narrowed. Fire burned behind her pupils. "I'm not leaving," she said abruptly. "You're not mad right now, but I'm gonna be mad for you. I'ma wait for them to get out, then I'm gonna follow them some more and find out where that bitch lives."

"Don't say anything to them," Claire pleaded.

Melanie sneered at her. "Why are you taking up for them? I can't believe you're gonna let them do you like this. We got they ass *right now!*"

"I'm *going to get them!*" Claire growled, and everyone within earshot knew she meant it. "This is *my* deal," she said, "and *I'm* going to handle it *myself.* They're not going to get away, Melanie. I swear to God they're not."

Melanie stared into her eyes for a second, and then she nodded. "All right, Claire. We'll do it your way."

Melanie got back in her husband's car and continued her stake out, and Becky left the restaurant without incident. Halfway home, Claire forced herself to stop crying.

She refused to show this *weakness* in front of the kids—no matter how bad she felt.

And Claire knew she would have to wear a mask for George, too. He would come home from his bullshit poker night around one, and Claire wouldn't let on that she knew he was a low-down, dirty, two-timing, adulterer asshole.

She went over a few scenarios in her head as she stared out at the crowded freeway. She knew she wasn't strong enough to hold a pillow over George's face, but she figured she could drop a radio in the tub while he bathed. Stuff like that happened all the time, and she wouldn't even have to explain why her fingerprints were on the murder weapon.

CHAPTER SEVEN
DADDY TOLD ME

Claire found it virtually impossible to feign sleep when George climbed into bed at 1:30 that morning.

It was even harder to keep her composure five and a half hours later at breakfast.

George usually worked six days a week, but occasionally he stayed home and enjoyed a lazy Saturday morning with his family. Any other time Claire would have been thrilled with his company and the sense of family *togetherness*, but she hated everything about her husband today.

Claire labored at the stove, tending to a hot skillet crackling with bacon. The grease from the shrinking meat bubbled and popped, and for the life of her Claire couldn't think of *one good reason* why she shouldn't dump the contents of the pan on Mr. Hudgens's head. In a pleasant daydream, she imagined what the burns would look like on his bald dome, pink and blistering, maroon and painful.

George sat at the table behind her with his newspaper and the cup of coffee she made for him. Much to Claire's chagrin, there were no crushed pills in his coffee and no anthrax on his newspaper.

George wore sand-colored canvas shorts with a blue tank top. He sipped pleasantly and smiled at his wife every-so-often when they made eye contact. He was done with his morning push-ups, and all of the muscles involved were perky and swollen, especially in his neck and arms.

George looked like he was ready for a body-building competition. Seeing him like that usually ignited within Claire a sense of *urgency.* She would want to stop whatever she was doing so she could rub him down as if applying sun screen.

But she felt nothing like that now.

Instead Claire imagined walking up behind him with the skillet in hand. She thought maybe she could trip over her own feet and stumble towards him. That wasn't *totally* inconceivable, was it? Surely people spilled pans of scalding grease every now and then.

And if she fell particularly *clumsily*, she could swing her arm out and bang him behind the ear with the hard metal as well. He probably wouldn't die, but the suffering would be memorable. It would be *exquisite,* even. It might not alleviate the pain she felt, but it would be a start.

Of course there were the kids to consider. They were already awake and soon they'd come downstairs, lured by the smell of Mama's cooking. They would wonder if their father was home, and when they saw him, they would be excited about the opportunity to smile at him and eat with him and tell him about their week at school. Claire loved her children immensely, and she knew they deserved to have those precious moments.

They did not deserve to run down in a panic, lured by Daddy's horrific screams as bacon grease melted his skin like water on cotton candy. No, that was the stuff repressed childhood memories are made of.

So Claire poured the bubbling grease in an old jelly jar instead. "Did you have fun with the boys last night?" she asked over her shoulder.

"Yeah, baby. It was nice."

Claire stared at the clock on the back of the oven rather than turn to face him. "Do y'all still play at Murray's?" she asked.

"Yeah. Sometimes we play at Sherman's house."

Murray was a longtime friend from the Air Force. George met Sherman when he went to college on the G.I. Bill.

Claire scooped the bacon out with a metal spatula and went to the fridge to get milk for the children's oatmeal. On the way back to the stove, she glanced over at George, who was still deep in his black-and-white world of current affairs. Maybe the United States was going to repair volatile relations with Iran, but that wasn't the *current affair* Claire was interested in.

She sighed heavily and thought about the mystery woman her husband was with yesterday. Claire never saw George's date for the evening personally, but she did see his Navigator at the restaurant. Plus Melanie gave her a pretty good description later on, after Claire got the kids in bed for the night. According to Melanie, George's slut was tall, like his wife, and she had long hair like Claire as well. There weren't many similarities after that.

Melanie said she was light-skinned and thinner than Claire. Melanie said she dressed *professionally*, and wore make-up. Melanie thought she was very attractive. She didn't go as far as saying George's tramp was prettier than Claire, but she didn't say she wasn't, either.

They would have had more information, but Melanie didn't follow George again when he left the restaurant like she said she would. George and his date were still dining an hour and a half after Becky took Claire home, and Melanie found the stakeout to be a little tedious without her girlfriends around.

"What time did you get home?" Claire asked, her back to George again.

"About one-thirty."

That was the truth, but Claire suspected it was the only one she'd get.

"How'd you do?" she queried.

"Great."

Lie.

"What does '*Great*' mean? Did you turn a profit?"

"I came out about even."

Lie.

"Do you eat a sensible dinner there," Claire asked. "or do you eat hot wings all night?"

George chuckled. "Hot wings, mostly. And chips, and beer . . ."

Damn, you lying bastard.

Claire gritted her teeth and stared up at the ceiling. How could he sit right there and not have any guilt at all? She wished she had the strength to overpower him. She'd knock him to the floor and get on top and ask, *What the hell were you thinking?* as she bashed his head into the floor.

Why are you lying to me?

Bam! Bam!

How the hell could you do this to me? How could you do this to us?

The only saving grace Claire could cling to was the fact that he didn't know she knew yet. That had to put her in a situation of advantage, even though it didn't feel like at the present moment.

"Why don't y'all ever have your poker games *here*?" she asked. "I could make fajitas or burgers when you get hungry."

"Most of the guys smoke cigars," George said. "I don't want that in here with the kids. You know that."

That was probably true, but given how there was no freaking poker night, Claire still counted that one as a *lie*. She added milk and cinnamon to the oatmeal, and then she heard footsteps behind her. Before she could turn, she felt George's hands on her waist. He stepped close to her and pressed his chest against her back. He wrapped her up in a hug and kissed the side of her neck.

"Do you miss me much when I play cards?"

His touch was *evil* yet *comforting*. Claire didn't know how that was possible. She wanted him to hold her, *needed* it, in fact, but it still wasn't right. She knew it would never be right.

"I miss you all the time," she said. She stared at the oven dial again, and her eyes glossed over with tears. How screwed up was this? How can you hate someone yet love them so much at the same time?

Claire wondered if she would stay with him if he came clean and promised to give up his secret lover. If someone asked her that a month ago, she would have responded with a resounding, *Hell no!*, but now she wasn't so sure.

"It's going to get better," he promised. "Next year I won't have to work on the weekends at all."

What does that mean? Claire wondered. *You get more time with me or more time with your bitch?*

"Oh," she said.

"We can go to the lake house when the kids get out for summer," George offered. "Spend a whole week there if you want."

"That would be nice," Claire said. "But what about all the hours you work *during the week*? When is that going to slow down?"

"Not as long as we've got war-hungry politicians in office," he said jokingly, or seriously—Claire couldn't tell. "But this is *good*, baby. Trust me. It may not seem like it now, but it will in the long run."

In the long run for who, me or that bitch you're seeing?

Claire's eyes narrowed and she wondered just how long her husband's affair had been going on. Maybe he cared enough about his other woman to leave her something in his will. That was reason enough to kill him while he was still young and unsuspecting.

"What are you doing today?" she asked.

"I'm going riding with the guys," he said. "We're going down to Houston."

Next to hard work (and adultery), George's souped-up Harley was his other favorite pastime. Unless his new broad was a biker chick, Claire figured he was probably telling the truth about today's agenda.

"Are you going to be home for dinner?" she asked. Houston was a good four hours away. Depending on what they did there, it was possible.

"We'll see," George said. He slapped her on the bottom and then headed back to the table. "We'll see."

❧

Becky called an hour later while Claire and George Jr. were clearing the table.

"Claire?"

"It's me. What's up?"

"What are you doing?" Becky asked.

"We just finished breakfast. I'm about to wash dishes."

"Um, what about *George*?"

"What about him?"

"Is he, he's all right? *Is he all right?*"

Claire looked down at the top of George Jr.'s big head and sighed. "He's fine," she said. "*So far . . .*"

"I was thinking about you *all night*. Claire, I'm *so sorry*. You're a great person. I can't believe this is happening to you."

"It's still pretty hard for me to believe, too," Claire admitted.

"You're not really going to do something to George, are you?"

Claire looked down at her son again. George Jr. brought the last few glasses from the table and set them on the counter. He grinned at his mother, and she smiled back at him, and then she shooed him up the stairs.

"He deserves it," Claire said, "but the kids don't."

Becky sighed. "I'm glad you said that. You know, *you* don't deserve that either. You don't want to end up in jail, right?"

Claire didn't think prison could be any worse than the hell she was currently simmering in.

"I let myself get fat," she said abruptly.

"Stop right there," Becky said. "You're *the perfect woman,* Claire. I know you want to blame yourself and try to figure out what's wrong with *you*, but it's not *you*. It's *George!* He's an *asshole*, and he doesn't realize what he's got.

"When Brent cheated on me, I started thinking I was ugly, and *dorky*, and not hot anymore. My self-esteem was shot. I was thirty-seven years old, thinking my whole life was over. Who's gonna want an old divorced lady with two kids?"

"I've got *three* kids."

"You don't want to fall into that kind of depression," Becky warned. "Plus you really do look good, Claire. The mailman was hitting on you just yesterday."

Claire chuckled. "Maybe I shouldn't have been so hard on him," she mused.

"That's the spirit! Get right back on that horse."

"I was kidding."

"Oh."

"Hey, let me call you back later."

"You didn't still want to go to the Omni, did you?" Becky asked. "I can understand if you don't."

Claire forgot all about those plans. "Was that today?"

"It's okay," Becky said. "I know you've got a lot of other things on your mind."

"No," Claire said. "We might as well go. George isn't going to be here, and that damned office has been calling me. I'm going to tear that room up if I stay here all day."

"Maybe you *should* look in there," Becky suggested. "Your suspicions aren't going to go away. Whether you find anything else or not, at least you'll have closure."

"Not today," Claire said. "I'm starting to think ignorance really is bliss."

⌒

The Overbrook Museum of Science and History was one of the best places in the city for learning and adventure. The most stand-out feature was the Omni Theatre. Enjoying a movie there was really not comparable to any other cinema.

The Omni was a large auditorium topped with a huge dome. The chairs were all tilted up towards the ceiling, and the feature presentation played all around you. The sense of being *lost* in their films was so prevalent, you actually had to wear safety belts to keep you from leaning and possibly falling forward.

There were plenty of other things at the museum that were both fun and interesting, but Claire's children had already been there a few times on field trips. Just the thought of the place reminded them of school.

"I thought I was grounded," Stacy whined from the back seat. "Why do I have to go?"

"If I thought you were going to enjoy yourself, I would have left you at home," Claire said. "But since you hate it so much, it still counts as punishment."

"I do hate it," Stacy confirmed. "It's boring."

"You think *everything's* boring," Claire chided.

"I think it's boring, too," Nikki said.

The girls sat next to each other with their lips poking out. They both wore T-shirts and jeans this afternoon, but Stacy's outfits were always more stylish. Her pants were tight, and they flared out into bell-bottoms. Stacy wore brown sandals, and her toenails glistened with a fresh coat of pink and glitter. Her T-shirt was short and small with the word *DIVA* splashed across her chest.

Nikki's pants were loose fitting, and her solid blue T-shirt was an extra large on her medium frame. Nikki didn't even have her fingers painted, let alone her toenails.

George Jr. sat up front, cheesing pleasantly. He was always ready and willing to embark on any project an authority figure presented. At school, he took *Teacher's Pet* to an all-new high.

"I like the Wild, Wild West town," he said. "And the reptile exhibit."

"You like *everything*," Stacy said.

"He's a nerd," Nikki explained.

"I'm not a nerd!"

Claire smiled at her little boy and put a hand on his head. "It's all right," she said. "They used to call Bill Gates a nerd, too."

"Who's Bill Gates?" George Jr. wanted to know.

"Another *nerd*," Stacy informed.

"A *rich* nerd," Claire clarified. "People with big brains make *big money* when they grow up."

"I want to be a rich nerd," George Jr. decided.

"You're not going to have a girlfriend," Stacy teased.

Before Claire could chastise her, George Jr. had his own comeback.

"I don't want a girlfriend," he said. "They just want your money."

Claire's eyes widened and she was briefly filled with pride for her youngest child. "How did you know *that*?" she asked.

"Daddy told me," he said, and his mother's delight was immediately replaced with angst.

CHAPTER EIGHT
A FATE WORSE THAN DEATH

Claire called her friend when she pulled into the parking lot, and Becky met them at the main entrance. Becky's uncle worked as a fine arts curator, and he always gave her free tickets whenever a new exhibit was in town. Becky's children had gotten a little too old and independent for the outing, so she usually offered the tickets to Claire and her family.

The girls rushed from the car as soon as Claire turned the motor off, but George Jr. waited to cross the street with Mommy. Becky waited for them on the other side, standing next to a giant tortoise sculpture made of iron. She had her daughter Courtney in tow, and George almost yanked his mother's arm off trying to get to her.

"*Hey, Courtney!*"

"*Georgie Porgie!*" she shouted back.

"Boy, she ain't going anywhere," Stacy mumbled.

"She isn't," Claire corrected.

Becky wore blue jeans with a white camisole this afternoon. She had on a new pair of spectacles Claire hadn't seen before. The lenses were large, and the thick, plastic frame was reminiscent of 80s sunglasses.

"Hey," Claire said as she stepped up on the curb.

"Hi!" Becky reached for her and they exchanged a brief hug.

"How are you guys?" she asked the kids.

"Fine," the girls said with all the enthusiasm of a wilting flower.

"They're *great*," Claire said. "Very happy to be here and thankful for the tickets."

The Omni's presentation of *Deep Sea* was a lot better than everyone expected. Even without 3-D glasses, Claire didn't think they could get more *immersed* without scuba gear. The lights and sounds were exceptional, and the experience of being under water with the cameraman was so complete, Becky found herself holding her breath a few times.

And it was great to see the girls watching with wide-eyed fascination. It was even better to see them flinch when a few menacing-looking predators swam close to the screen.

Afterwards, Becky took them on a general tour of the museum. Claire liked the Cro-Magnon room because they had a display set up with small figurines depicting what early brain surgery might have looked like. The models were small, and they couldn't sculpt too much expression on their little faces, but you could almost feel the pain of the poor sap being held down while a witch doctor sliced at his scalp with a sharp rock.

After lunch, Claire let her girls roam freely with Courtney while she and Becky took George Jr. to KID-

SPACE, one of the few areas in the museum were little ones could touch anything they wanted.

Claire took a much-needed rest on one of the benches provided for parents while George Jr. went to the soap rings and tried to make a bubble big enough to put his head in. Becky came and sat next to her friend.

"Having fun?"

"*Oodles*," Claire said sarcastically.

Becky put a hand on her shoulder. "Come on. It's not *that* bad, is it?"

"The museum's fine," Claire said. "It's my head that's messing with me."

Becky nodded. "I know how you feel."

Claire leaned back and closed her eyes. "Everything I see reminds me of him," she said. "Every married couple makes me want to cry, especially if they're our age. I've been with him since *high school*. I've been with him for half of my life, Becky. Everything I've ever done as an adult has been with him."

"I know," Becky said. "It's hard."

"I know I'm not supposed to," Claire said, "but I keep thinking, *maybe if I stayed smaller*. I put on thirty pounds since we graduated. Maybe if I dressed sexier . . ."

"I told you not to do that."

"I know. But I don't think I can stop. If he still wanted me as much as he used to—"

"Claire, you are a beautiful woman. You're tall, you've got long, sexy legs. You've got big boobs and a nice butt."

"I'm not beautiful," Claire said. "Look at me." She fingered her shirt with disgust. "Look at my clothes. I don't blame him for not wanting me."

"Claire, don't say things like that. You know it's not true. Remember how you felt with your red dress on? You're still just as desirable. Trust me, you're hot. Maybe a makeover will help you feel better."

"Yeah, right."

"I'm serious."

Claire rolled her eyes.

"You know," Becky said, "if you and George break up, you're going to find another man who will love you more. There are plenty of guys out there—"

"Oh, please don't start with that."

"It's true."

"Becky, I'm *nowhere near* thinking about another man. Let me kill the one I have first, and then we'll talk."

"That's another thing." Becky brushed the hair from her face. "I don't like hearing you talk like that. I'm starting to think you're serious."

Claire gave her a look to let her know she was.

"See? That's what I'm talking about. Honey, you need to see that this isn't the end of the world. You still have three beautiful children who need you, and you still have a whole life to live. I would like to think you're just upset, but if you really are thinking about . . ." She looked around and whispered, "*Murder*—"

"Let's not talk about it right now," Claire suggested.

Becky saw that her eyes were tearing up again. "Just tell me you're not serious."

"Serious?" Claire sniffled. "How should I respond to the worst betrayal I've ever known? I gave George everything I have. I never once looked at another man that way. What if he plans on leaving me to be with *her*?"

"Then you'll make him pay," Becky said. Her eyes narrowed and her eyebrows knotted together. "I didn't have *any* evidence like you do," she said, "and I still got the house *and* Brent's truck. There are ways to kill a man without laying a finger on him, Claire. I can give you the number to my divorce lawyer."

Claire wiped away a tear and stared into her friend's eyes. *Divorce lawyer* was a dirty word she thought she'd never utter, but it did sound better than *guilty of murder* and *penitentiary*.

"Can you get out later on?" Becky asked. "We should go have drinks."

Claire chuckled woefully. She couldn't imagine George's reaction if she told him she was going out again. This would be twice in one week. *Screw him*, she decided.

"That sounds great."

"Good," Becky said with a bright smile.

"I'm getting drunk though," Claire announced. "So you can't."

"Fine. I'll be your designated driver."

"Can I invite Melanie? She's been asking me to go out for a while."

"Sure." Becky's eyes glistened like an infant's. "The more the merrier."

⌒

George still wasn't home when Claire cleared the table and washed the dinner dishes, but she didn't let that spoil her night out. She didn't really need a babysitter.

Nikki was brooding and obnoxious most of the time, but she *was* fourteen years old. Stacy minded her, and George was obedient to any authority figure.

Claire went upstairs and showered, and then she put on a pair of black slacks with a gray blouse. She searched for her pearl earrings in the bathroom, and the reflection staring back at her made Claire do a double-take. She stopped everything and stared at the woman in the mirror for a long time.

Becky was right, she was still attractive, but she wasn't doing a lot to show it off.

Claire shook her head slowly and almost cried right then. It was hard to accept, but the truth was glaring: She'd become drab and plain and *average*. Claire looked over her color-scheme for the night and realized she wore stuff like this every day; grays and blacks and browns and whites. She couldn't remember the last time she colored or curled her hair. And her eyes—they were still big and beautiful, but she used eyeliners back in high school, didn't she? Claire couldn't remember anymore.

"No wonder," she said aloud, but that wasn't right. That was the self-hate Becky warned her about. It was easy to blame herself, but Claire refused to go down that road again. Maybe she did lose a little flair over the years, but that didn't give George the right to break the vows he made before God. He should have manned up and asked for a divorce if he lost interest.

She undressed and looked in the closet for something different to put on. She pulled out a few pairs of jeans that used to hug her hips in sexy and *exciting* ways, but that ended up making her feel worse. No way had her waist ever been that small. After an unsuccessful attempt to squeeze her ass into the last pair, Claire felt her emotions getting the better of her again. Her cell phone rang, and she was grateful for the distraction.

"Hello?"

"Hey, girl! What's the damned deal?"

"I'm not doing so good," Claire admitted.

"What's wrong?" Melanie asked. "George won't let you go?"

"*Please*," Claire said. "I'm way past letting *him* tell me what to do. He's not even here."

"So what's the problem, sister?"

"My jeans don't fit anymore," Claire said. "I've been through three pair—"

"Why are you wearing *jeans*?" Melanie asked. "If I was as tall as you, I bet you wouldn't never catch me in no jeans. 'Specially not in 80-degree weather."

Claire thought about that for a second. "Why am I wearing jeans?" she asked.

" 'Cause you've been married too long. Don't you have any skirts in your closet?"

"A skirt?"

"Something that stops *above* your knees."

"I don't need to wear anything like that," Claire said. "I'm not trying to meet anyone, and I don't want—"

"You think dressing sexy is all about trying to hook up?" Melanie asked. "Claire, I think that's what got you in the rut you're in. You and George got together when you were young and skinny. You got older, and you stopped caring about what you looked like. You took it for granted 'cause you already had a man. I'll bet you've got a whole closet full of tight skirts you forgot about."

"What good do they do me now?" Claire asked with a hitch in her throat. "He's already looking somewhere else."

"It's not always about pleasing your man," Melanie lectured. "Sometimes you have to think about pleasing *yourself.* You'd be surprised what a freakum dress will do for you spirits."

"A *freakum* dress?"

"Don't act like you don't got one," Melanie said. "Everybody got a freakum dress."

Claire checked the closet again when she got off the phone and was surprised to find she *did* have a freakum dress in there. She had three of them, in fact. She selected a black Chanel for her night out with the girls. She squeezed into it in the bathroom, and right away she knew this is what Melanie was talking about: The dress was too tight, too short, and the shoulder straps were non-existent; giving plenty of freedom to her luscious breasts.

Any doubts about her sexiness were dismissed when George came home a few minutes later. Claire was still in the bathroom, applying eyeliner for the first time in Lord knew when. George walked up behind her, and Claire watched his expression in the mirror. His eyes lit up, and his smile was both devilish and genuine. He put his hands on her hips and tried to kiss the back of her neck.

"Damn, baby. You look—"

But Claire turned and stepped around him, leaving him standing in the bathroom alone.

"I'm glad you're here," she called over her shoulder. "I'm going out with the girls tonight."

He caught up with her at the bed and watched anxiously while Claire transferred the necessities from her Coach bag to a smaller evening purse. George had on his biker outfit. The tight jeans, combat boots and leather vest made him look like a sexy Hell's Angel, but Claire barely gave him a second look. George took the black bandana off his head and tossed it on the bed.

"You're doing what?"

"I'm going out," Claire said without looking up. She pulled items from her hobo bag and looked around impatiently. "Where's my compact?" she asked herself.

"You, you look *good*," George said.

"Thanks."

"When I saw you, I thought, I thought you were looking *all good* for me. Thought maybe you were feeling a little amorous . . ."

Claire looked up at him, and he cocked his head and grinned.

"Nope," she said. "I wasn't thinking about you at all."

George's smile fell, but he brought it back quickly. "You're really dressing like that to go out?"

Claire turned and stood straight so he could admire the full measure of her beauty. The dress fit her like a glove; accentuating her Coke-bottle figure. The fabric stopped midway down her thighs, leaving three feet worth of smooth, creamy legs. Her push-up bra was doing a very good job, and her hair was smooth and flowing.

"Are you, are you wearing makeup?" George asked.

Claire turned and grabbed the last few items she needed in her little purse.

"What's wrong with makeup?" she asked. "You like girls with makeup, don't you?"

She enjoyed watching him struggle to respond.

"Um, I, uh, yeah, I guess I do."

"I know you do," Claire said and winked at him. On the outside she smiled, but on the inside she sneered and despised everything about him.

It felt good to be witty, on the other side of the joke for a change. She stepped forward and gave him a very brief kiss so she wouldn't smear her lipstick.

"I gotta go, honey. Becky will—"

DING DONG!

George looked around curiously like he didn't recognize his own doorbell.

"Oops," Claire said with a big grin. "*That's my ride,*" she sang.

She turned and left the room without another word. George followed her to the head of the stairs but didn't go down.

"Claire, what are you doing? How long are you going to be out? What about the kids?"

"I'm going to the Coco Lounge, the bar closes at two, and the kids have already eaten and bathed. Just read them a bedtime story and they'll be all right." She didn't stop or turn to see his expression, but she wished she would have. George *never* got caught off-guard. This was so awesome, she should have taken pictures.

∼⌒

The Coco Lounge was a popular nightspot on the west side of town. On Friday and Saturday evenings, the manager brought in a live band and usually pulled in pretty decent crowds of middle class nine-to-fivers. They had a huge bar, a decent dance floor, and enough room to seat three hundred.

Becky and Claire walked through the doors at 9:45 p.m., and they spotted Melanie right away. She sat at the bar with her back to them, but there were only four black people in the whole building, so it wasn't too hard to find the short, chubby one. Claire sneaked up behind her friend and patted her shoulder.

"So, your husband let you out again?"

Melanie spun on her stool, and her beady eyes grew as big as cantaloupes.

"*Oh, snap*! Look at you, Claire! You got it going on in that dress!"

A few patrons turned to see, and Claire's face reddened. Melanie wore black slacks with a blue top. Becky had a one-piece schoolteacher dress that was both long and unflattering. No one else within eyeshot looked as good as Claire.

"How long you been here?" she asked.

"Twenty minutes," Melanie said. "I bought you two shots, but I already drunk them. *Dang, Claire.* You really look good in that dress."

"I know, right?" Becky chipped in.

"I *feel* good, too," Claire said. "You were right. You should have seen the look on George's face when I left."

"He was jealous, wasn't he?" Melanie asked with a grin.

"He didn't ask me to stay home, but I knew he wanted me to. He followed me to the stairs talking about, *Where are you going? What am I gonna do? What about the kids?*"

They all laughed.

"You ready to get drunk?" Melanie asked. "I'm buying your first shot. You're getting a *double*."

"*I* wanna buy her a double," Becky whined.

"*Girls, girls,*" Claire said. She put one arm around Becky's shoulder and threw the other over Melanie. "You can both buy me doubles."

"That's a *quadruple!*" Becky noted.

Melanie shook her head and Claire laughed.

By one a.m. things were still flowing smoothly with the sweet, mellow buzz of inebriation. The girls sat at a table with a dozen empty glasses and bottles scattered before them. Becky was *tipsy* and more talkative than Claire ever knew her to be. Melanie was drunk; but she was that special kind of drunk, the one that makes you think you can still operate a motor vehicle. Claire was fully *wasted* and loving every minute of it.

"See . . ." Melanie leaned over the table with a finger in Claire's face. "See, you, you can't keep thinking you're sparter than the police. *Nobody* takes a bath with a radio these days. They know better."

"Yeah, they do," Becky agreed.

"Wait," Claire said giggling. "Did you just say '*sparter*?'"

"Huh?"

Claire leaned on the table chuckling. "You said '*sparter*!' You can't even talk right."

"No, I didn't."

"Yes, you did," Becky said. "You said, '*sparter than the police.*' "

Claire laughed even harder because Becky was trying to match Melanie's accent. Police came out *poe-leece.*

"*Whatever*," Melanie said and took another swig of her Miller Lite. "All I know is you can't hardly get away with stuff like that these days."

"Yes you, you can," Claire said with a finger in the air. "I've been thinking, and I think I got it . . ."

They all waited, but Claire didn't say anything.

"You got *what*?" Melanie asked.

"Huh?"

"See? You need to take her home," Melanie told Becky. "She's had it."

"No, no, no," Claire said. "I got it. I remember now." She sat up straight in her chair but couldn't get her eyes to focus. "What if he gets *mugged* and they *shoot him*? . . ." She looked around and nodded. "Yeah. Y'all can't say anything bad about *that* one."

"You don't have a gun," Becky said.

"And you can't hire somebody to do it, because they'll snitch," Melanie informed her.

"And you can't do it yourself, because you could *never* shoot George," Becky predicted.

"Yes I can," Claire said.

"Maybe if you're drunk, but then you won't be able to aim."

"And somebody will probably hear the shots," Melanie said. "With your luck, you'll get pulled over right after you do it."

"Oh, oh," Clair had an answer for that one. "I'll leave the gun *at the scene*." She said it as if no one had ever done anything so daring.

"They can test your skin to see if you fired at shome-body," Melanie said.

Claire laughed, but didn't point that one out. "Poison?" she asked no one in particular.

"Way too much evidence," Melanie said.

"He's *thirty-six years old*," Becky said. "They'll do a *really good* autopsy."

"Probably," Claire said. "Ooh, I could strangle him! And then, and then y'all help me move the body. We'll tie him up with ropes and blankets and weigh him down with bricks, and we'll send him to the bottom of the Trinity River." She nodded. That was it.

But Melanie shook her head. "You're too little to strangle George, first off."

"And *I'm* not helping carry a dead guy," Becky said.

"Me neither," Melanie said.

"And even if you get him in the river, the police aren't going to leave you alone," Becky said. "Until they find a body, you're going to be the number-one suspect."

"And you can't get any insurance money until *after* they find the body," Melanie said.

Claire put her head down. "Y'all just don't want me to kill my husband," she moaned.

Melanie laughed.

"What about what we talked about earlier?" Becky asked. "Remember? You can kill him *without* killing him . . ."

"The slow way," Claire said without much enthusiasm.

"What are y'all talking about?" Melanie asked.

"I was telling her about my divorce lawyer," Becky said. "You know I got my ex's truck, and I got the house and the kids, too."

Melanie grinned broadly. "Yeah, Claire. That doesn't sound like a bad idea. You already got proof he's cheating. You could get him for the house, the kids—"

"His Navigator," Becky piped in.

"The lake house," Claire said. "And his Harley. *And* the boats." She lifted her head slowly and her eyes widened too. "You know . . . George has a lot of shit; accounts everywhere, stocks and bonds, a couple time shares . . ."

"That could all be *yours*," Becky said with a conniving smile.

"Y'all got boats?" Melanie asked.

Claire frowned as she really considered that avenue for the first time. "You know what?" she said. "I think it would be better to just divorce his ass. I always thought of court as some long, drawn-out thing. But it might be the best way to go."

"Especially if you get him first," Becky said.

Melanie nodded.

"That's all good, except for one thing," Claire said.

"What?" they both asked.

"I don't even know if he's cheating on me."

Melanie smacked her lips. "Girl, don't start going *backwards*. I'd like to think George is a good man, too, but we saw what we saw."

"What did we see?" Claire asked.

"We saw him pick his bitch up from work and take her to dinner," Melanie reminded her.

"We saw him pick a *woman* up and take her to a *restaurant*," Claire clarified. "We don't know who that woman is or what their relationship is."

Melanie shook her head. "Claire, I know you don't want it to be over, but you need to quit being such—"

"No, she's right," Becky said. She was deep in thought. "What if that was a business meeting? What if it was a client? What if that was the first time they met each other?"

"If *if* was a *fifth* we'd all be drunk," Claire said.

"Well, why would he lie?" Melanie asked. "He told Claire he was playing poker."

"What if that was someone Claire knew?" Becky pondered. "What if that was his cousin and they were meeting secretly to plan something special for Claire?"

Melanie chuckled. "You living in *Never-never-land.*"

"No," Claire said. "I mean, she *is*, but we don't know for sure what was going on. I don't think I have enough evidence to talk to a lawyer."

"I think you should call him anyway, and he'll tell you what you need," Becky suggested.

"All right," Melanie said, and her smile came back. "So that means we got to do another stakeout?"

Claire sighed. "I guess we do . . ."

Becky clapped her hands. "*Goody!*—Wait. This isn't going to be another *sad* stakeout like last time. That was *depressing*. I thought it was going to be fun."

"I promise I won't cry," Claire said with an unsteady hand in the air. "I give you my word. Now, help me up."

Becky did, but Claire wasn't very steady on her feet.

"Where are you going?" Melanie asked. "I *know* you're not getting more to drink."

"No," Claire said. "I gotta throw up."

She took off with a hand over her mouth. It didn't feel like she was going to make it, but nothing came up until she was safely hovering over the toilet. With some of the liquor gone, Claire's head cleared a few degrees. She thought about the new plans they made and felt like she was on the right track.

Contrary to what she told her friends, Claire definitely felt George was cheating on her, but that didn't matter tonight. Tonight she felt good, and according to the mirror in the ladies room, she still looked good, too.

As if for confirmation, a nice-looking Jewish fellow hit on her when she left the restroom.

"Oh, no. No thanks," Claire told him. "I'm married. He's dead to me, but he's still mine. For now . . ."

CHAPTER NINE
MAKE A MOVE

Two weeks passed without incident.

Claire didn't think she could live with someone she utterly despised for that long, but it was just an issue of mind over matter. When they lived in Alaska some ten years ago, George had a big, ugly St. Bernard named Chuck. Claire hated that dog, but George wasn't around much, and Chuck became her responsibility. She walked him, played fetch, and even let him slobber on her a few times. Claire decided if she could pooper-scoop those monster turds day after day for two years, then certainly she could tolerate a nastier dog named *George* for another month or so.

The girls made plans to follow his sorry ass a few more times, but George was stuck at the office the past two Fridays. Claire considered that good news, figuring he wasn't able to commit adultery if he really was at work, but Melanie wouldn't let her fall into that pathetic groove of acceptance.

What if he's going straight to her house after work? she would ask. *What if he's having lunch with her every day? Just 'cause he's not doing it on his poker night doesn't mean he's not doing it.*

Claire took all of that in and remained vigilant. Deep inside she wished the affair would just blow over, but things didn't seem to be headed in that direction. She watched her husband like a hawk for fourteen days, and George's pattern of infidelity became clear. He came in late from work smelling like Irish Springs soap on three separate occasions. Once he brought home the scent of a strange perfume.

On a pleasant Wednesday afternoon, three weeks after the original stakeout, Claire took Becky to lunch at a newly opened French bistro. The *quiche aux poireaux* was divine, and the *salade aux lardoons* was interesting. Midway through the meal, their waiter even offered them two complimentary glasses of wine. Claire was pleasantly surprised, but she told him they had to go back to work after the meal. Becky voiced her disapproval when he left the table.

"Man, you're such a stickler."

Claire cocked an eye. "A *stickler?*"

"You know, *stickler for the rules.*"

Claire frowned at her friend and shook her head. "Becky, you can't call someone a *stickler* without saying *stickler for the rules.* Stickler makes no sense by itself."

"My son calls me a stickler," Becky said.

"That's sweet," Claire said. "But in your case it's a term of endearment."

Today Becky wore a black skirt with a turquoise blouse. Claire still wasn't at the point of wearing skirts to work, but she did have on a yellow blouse with her navy blue slacks. She had on eyeliner and a little lipstick as well.

"No way are you going to still feel that wine by the time we get back to work," Becky said.

Claire checked her watch. "We have to leave in fifteen minutes. And it only takes ten minutes to get back to the office. You'll be sitting at your desk at thirteen-hundred, still buzzed."

Becky laughed at her.

"What?"

"You said '*thirteen-hundred*,'" Becky pointed out.

Claire thought about it and frowned. "Damn that man," she said. "You know, he walks around the house doing that all the time: '*Come on, girls. Get a move on. It's oh-six-forty-five, and we're leaving at oh-seven hundred!*'"

Becky giggled at her George impersonation. "You're good at that."

Claire rolled her eyes. "Try listening to it for sixteen years."

Becky nodded and her smile faded a few degrees. She put her elbows on the table and laced her fingers together as if praying. She rested her chin on her knuckles and stared into her friend's eyes.

"What?" Claire asked.

"How's it going with George?" Becky asked. "What did he smell like last night?"

"Like regular man funk," Claire said. "He came straight home from work."

"I don't see how you can do it," her friend said. "If Brent ever came home smelling like a *fresh shower*, I would have had it out with him right then."

"Patience is a virtue," Claire said and looked away uneasily.

"You don't want to kill him anymore?" Becky asked.

"We decided not to do that, remember?"

"Yeah, but we didn't decide to do *nothing*," Becky said. "We haven't done any more stakeouts or anything."

"He didn't play poker the last two weeks," Claire said. "I told you that."

"Yeah, Claire. You did . . ."

"What's that supposed to mean?"

Becky shrugged. "I don't know. It just seems like you're okay with the way things are, like you're glad he didn't play poker because you didn't want to follow him anyway."

"I *don't* want to follow him," Claire said. "I told you so."

"So if he doesn't play poker anymore, you're done with it?" Becky asked. "You're going to forget everything you already know? Pretend he's not taking showers before he gets home?"

Claire put her fork down, and her stomach rolled with discomfort. "What am I supposed to do?"

"Have you searched the office again?"

Claire shook her head.

"That doesn't seem odd to you?" Becky asked.

"What are you saying?"

Becky shrugged again. "I don't know, Claire. It just seems like you're trying to back away from everything. You're hoping it will just go away."

Claire hated her friend for being so damned perceptive. Her nose filled with moisture and a tear fell from her left eye. She wiped it casually and sniffled quietly. "I don't want to cry every time we go out to lunch, Becky."

Becky reached across the table and held her hand. "Honey, I don't want you to cry. I just don't want you to get complacent, like you're going to accept his mistress."

"I'm not accepting her."

"You're not going to kill him anymore, which is good, but you're not searching the office, you're not following him around, and you're not calling a divorce lawyer, either."

"*Oh, God.*" Claire put her hands to her face. "You think that's what I'm doing, accepting it?"

Their waiter approached the table with their bill, and Becky shooed him away quietly. She reached for the tissues in her purse, but she didn't need them. Claire put her hands down and she wasn't crying anymore. She looked tired, and worn out.

"Here," Becky said. She removed a business card from her wallet and slid it across the table. Claire took it and grinned at the name printed in bold lettering.

"*Trevor Smiley?*"

"Don't let the name throw you off," Becky said. "He's good, and handsome, too."

"Becky, I don't care what he looks like."

"I'm just saying," Becky said, still digging in her purse. She took out her cellphone, pushed a few buttons, and then handed it to Claire. But Claire wouldn't take it.

"What's that?"

"I'm calling him for you."

Claire's heart leapt up in her throat. "What? I don't— *what are you doing?*"

"Take it," Becky said.

"No!"

Becky tossed the phone into Claire's lap and threw up her hands. Claire had to scramble for the cellular because it was going to hit the floor. Someone answered as soon as she got hold of it.

"*Burns and Smiley.*"

Claire looked at the phone, and then she stared at Becky with her mouth ajar. Becky smiled and leaned back in her seat.

"*Burns and Smiley?*"

Claire put the phone to her ear hesitantly.

"Huh, hello?"

"Hi!" a chirpy female responded. "You've reached the law offices of Nathan Burns and Trevor Smiley."

Claire took a deep breath. Her mouth was very dry. "Um, yeah . . ." She wiped at the beads of sweat forming on her forehead. "I, uh, I think I need a lawyer."

"*Okay,*" the receptionist hummed. "Mr. Burns and Mr. Smiley are both *divorce lawyers*. Do you need a *divorce lawyer?*"

The woman was talking down to her, and that brought Claire to her senses. If she was at work, someone would have gotten told off. She rolled her eyes at Becky and took a deep breath.

"Yes," she breathed.

"Okay," the receptionist said. "Would you like to make an appointment to consult with a lawyer?"

"How much are the consultation fees?"

Becky was shaking her head.

"There are no consultation fees," the secretary said.

"Well then, yes. I suppose so," Claire said. "I would like to make an appointment to see a lawyer," she stated more firmly.

"Would you like to see Mr. Burns or Mr. Smiley—or does it matter?"

"Hold on," Claire said. She put a hand over the phone. "They want to know which one I want to see," she told Becky.

"*Trevor*!" Becky said quickly. "He's the cute one."

"I don't care if he's cute," Claire snapped.

"He's the one I used," Becky said. "He's *really* good."

Claire frowned at her as she said to the receptionist, "I would like to see Mr. Smiley."

"Okay," the woman said. "Hmm, you know what? Mr. Smiley had a cancellation this afternoon. Would you like to come in at two?"

Claire put a hand over the phone again. Her heart banged in her chest.

"They want me to go today!" she hissed.

"When?"

"At two."

"Well go!" Becky said. "What's the problem?"

"I'll still be at work," Claire whispered.

"You can take the rest of the day off," Becky said knowingly. "You've got like, *perfect attendance*."

That was true.

"I can come at two," Claire told the lady on the phone. "But I have to pick up my kids at thrwr, three-thirty." She moved her tongue around, but still couldn't get any saliva. "This isn't going to take more than an hour, is it?"

Becky started shaking her head again.

"No," the receptionist confirmed. "An hour would be the longest for a first consultation."

"Okay," Claire said. "So, I guess I'll be there at two."

"Do you need directions?"

"No," Claire said, still shooting daggers across the table. "I was referred by a friend. I'm sure she can tell me where you are."

"Who referred you?" the secretary asked.

"Becky Adair."

"*Ooh*, could you tell her Pat said hi? I miss Becky. She's great."

"Yeah," Claire said sarcastically. "She's a real *peach*."

Claire didn't have any problems at all getting off a little early that afternoon. She requested personal time so infrequently, her manager automatically assumed the worst. After she assured him everyone was all right and she would be in bright and early the next day, he let her clock out at 1:30. Claire got into her Lexus and headed downtown.

She pulled into the underground garage at the Mallick Towers twenty minutes later and then sat there for an additional five minutes debating whether she should even get out of her car. It wasn't that she wanted to accept what George was doing; it was that she knew she really couldn't prove anything. The only thing they knew for sure was that her husband took a strange woman to dinner.

And he gave you the wrong gift for your anniversary.
And you found that card.
And he bathes before he comes home sometimes.
And he smelled like perfume that one time . . .
Claire still didn't think that was enough.
If you're not sure what to do, then sit your fool ass down and don't do anything.

That was George talking in her head, and that was the one thought that got her moving. Claire was done listening to the likes of him, in real life and in her mind.

CHAPTER TEN
THE DIVORCE LAWYER

Claire stomped out of her Lexus bold and confident, but she was afraid and unsure again by the time she got off the elevator on the tenth floor. She approached suite 112 with weak legs that threatened to buckle any moment.

Go get back in your car before you ruin your marriage.

That was great advice. Claire was about to take it, but the suite she was approaching had glass doors and there was a secretary posted right up front. The woman looked up, and she and Claire made eye contact. They stared at each other for an awkward moment, and then the receptionist waved hello. Claire was obliged to wave back. The woman mouthed something that looked like, *You can come in.*

Claire coughed nervously. She stuck her head inside and asked, "Is this the Burns and Smiley law office?"

"Yes," the secretary said. She was a redhead, about twenty-two years old. She had a serious acne problem, and she wore metal braces. She wasn't absolutely *hideous*, but she was nowhere near as attractive as she sounded over the phone. She wore a gray pants suit with a white blouse and black pumps.

"How may I help you?' she asked.

Claire stepped into the foyer and slowly made her way to the woman's desk. "My name is Claire *Hudgens*. I have an appointment with Mr. Smiley."

"Oh, hi!" Her face brightened. "You're Becky's friend, right?"

Claire nodded.

"I'm Pat. I spoke with you earlier."

"Yeah," Claire said. "I was caught off guard when we talked. I, I really didn't plan on calling a lawyer today. Becky dialed the number and sort of *threw* the phone at me."

"Good for her," Pat said. "How's she doing?"

"She's great," Claire said. "I thought I was never going to see her smile again after that mess with Brent, but she's back to her happy-go-lucky self now."

"That's good," Pat said. "I love Becky. She didn't deserve that."

"None of us do," Claire said.

"You're right." Pat looked Claire in the eyes and held the gaze for a beat. "No one *ever* deserves to be cheated on."

At that moment, Claire knew she would get along well with this woman.

Pat picked up her telephone and pressed a few digits. "Your two o'clock has arrived," she announced into the receiver. A second later she said, "Yes, sir," and hung up. "He's ready for you," she told Claire. "It's that first office on your left."

She pointed, and Claire followed her directions, wondering what sort of man might work behind that door.

All Becky harped on was how cute he was. She said he did a good job, too, but she bragged on his attractiveness more than she did his résumé. Claire hoped that was coincidental.

It wasn't.

As soon as she walked into the office, Claire knew Mr. Smiley's physical attributes would stay on her mind long after she left the Mallick Towers. Becky said her lawyer was *cute*, but Claire would never disrespect him with such a weak description. This man was more of a *chocolate Adonis*. He was tall, dark, and handsome. He was a lot of other things Claire wouldn't allow her mind to entertain, but Mr. Smiley was definitely not *cute*. Puppies are cute. Trevor was more like a black stallion.

He stepped around his desk and held a hand out for her to shake. "Good afternoon, Mrs. Hudgens."

Claire took it weakly, like a Southern belle. She almost curtsied and said, *How do you do?* "Hi."

Mr. Smiley wore black slacks with a white button-down. He was a little over six feet tall with large hands and a bright smile. He had smooth, dark skin the color of a Hershey bar, and he was clean cut; with thin eyebrows and no facial stubble.

His hair was short, the same length all around. He had deep waves that reminded Claire of the ocean at night. He had a strong jaw line, a thin nose, and full lips. His eyes were deep ebony. Claire stared into them, and then looked away nervously.

"I'm, I'm sorry," she said. "I'm a little uncomfortable about being here."

"It's okay," he said. "Have a seat and tell me what's going on."

He gestured to the chair in front of his desk. Claire sat in it slowly and cradled her Coach bag in her lap. Mr. Smiley went back around to his side of the desk and plopped down in a leather executive chair. He leaned forward with his hands together and stared into her eyes again.

Claire was suddenly anxious to see what the *other* lawyer in this firm looked like. This would probably be a lot easier with an ugly guy.

"Uh," she said and sighed. "I really don't know if I need to be here."

"You're here for a reason."

"It was, it was my friend, Becky," Claire said. "Becky Adair. She was one of your clients."

He smiled. "Yes, I remember Becky. How is she?"

"She's better," Claire said. "She says you did a really good job on her case."

"She suggested you call me?"

"Yeah," Claire said. "But I don't want to sound like a fool."

"Women's intuition is strong," Trevor said. "I believe in it *one hundred percent.* Just tell me what's on your mind."

"All right," Claire said. "I'm married. I've been married to my husband for sixteen years. I met him in high school, and he asked me to marry him when he went into the Air Force."

Mr. Smiley nodded.

"I uh . . ." Claire wiped her forehead. "Is it hot in here?"

The lawyer chuckled. "No, ma'am."

She looked around for the thermostat.

"Has something gone wrong in your marriage?" he prompted.

"I think so," Claire said. "I mean, I'm pretty sure my husband is cheating on me."

Trevor leaned back in his chair. "Why do you think that?"

"All right," Claire said. "I'm just going to lay it out and you can tell me I'm crazy."

"You're not crazy," he said.

She smiled. "Well, thank you. But that would mean a lot more if you heard what I have to say first."

"Okay," he said. "I just thought it would be a lot easier for you to talk to me if you knew I don't think you're crazy."

"All right," Claire said. "Thanks. Okay, it all started about a month ago, on our anniversary."

The lawyer gave her a look.

"Yeah, I know," Claire said. "George—that's my husband—he gave me a gift that, that just *wasn't right*. It was a necklace, and it was *beautiful*, but I don't think it was for me. When he gave it to me, he said, '*I know how long you've wanted this*,' and I never told him I wanted a necklace at all."

The lawyer nodded.

"That's crazy, right?" Claire asked.

"Why do you doubt yourself?"

"I don't know. I thought some people might think that was silly."

"But it's not silly to you, is it?"

She shook her head. "No. It's not."

"Then it's not silly to me," he said, and Claire almost melted right then. "If you say you didn't ask for a necklace, I believe you."

"All right." Claire took a deep breath. "So I looked in his briefcase later that night, and I found a card." She started to dig in her purse as she spoke. "It's just a Hallmark, and it doesn't say anything, you know, *bad*, but it made me wonder . . ." She produced the card and handed it over the desk.

"This is it?"

"Yes," Claire said. "I was going to put it back, but I didn't want to go in his briefcase *twice*. I can't throw it away. I tried, but . . .." She got quiet while he read. When he looked up at her again, Claire looked away. "It's nothing, right?"

"I think a woman in love with him wrote this," the lawyer said.

Claire met his eyes again. "Really?"

"I know there's more," he said. "Tell me."

Claire had no idea where he got so much insight, but it was really easy to talk to this man. "After I got suspicious, I started smelling him when he got home from work—my friend told me to do that."

The lawyer cracked a big smile.

"I don't normally smell my husband," she said.

He nodded, chuckling.

"George works at Boeing. He's an engineer. He works a lot, usually six days a week. I never thought anything of it until he gave me that necklace. Anyway, I started to smell him when he got in bed late at night, and sometimes George comes home smelling like he *just* bathed— like within the last thirty minutes. And a few days ago I smelled perfume. My girlfriends and I followed him one night when he was supposed to be playing poker."

Trevor leaned forward with one eyebrow cocked.

"We saw him pick up a female and take her to a restaurant," Claire said. "We didn't see them kissing or anything, and we don't know what type of relationship they have, but . . ."

"But you know, don't you?" Mr. Smiley asked.

Claire sighed. Her eyes started to water, so she looked up at the ceiling to keep the tears in. "The dinner by itself, maybe means nothing," she said. "But all of it together—especially the showers—makes me think bad about him."

"Do you and George have children?" Trevor asked.

"Yes. Three."

"Do you own your house?"

Claire nodded.

Trevor nodded too and rubbed his smooth chin. "Let me ask you something," he said. "If you had proof that your husband is cheating, what would you want to do?"

"Kill his ass," Claire said quickly. She made eye contact again and her nostrils flared.

The lawyer grinned. "I'm not a hit man. Tell me what you want *me* to do for you."

"I want to destroy him," Claire said. "I want the house, the kids, the lake house, the cars—whatever he has. I want child support and alimony. I want to split the savings right down the middle. I want the kids' college funds in *my* name. I want to take away everything he cares about. I want to leave him so destitute no other bitch would ever want him—not even the one he has now."

Trevor's eyes widened. "Wow."

Claire shrugged. "You asked."

He smiled. "You're right. I did." He leaned forward in his seat again. "You know, if he's having the affair it sounds like he is, I can get you just about everything you're asking for. I can't promise he'll be *destitute* afterwards, but I can guarantee his lifestyle will take a serious nosedive. If he's an engineer, he'll probably recover, but it will take a decade to get his finances back in order. His life will never be as good as it was with you."

Claire nodded. "You're reading my mind."

"Two things," Trevor said. "First off, if you were to hire me as your lawyer, a divorce of this magnitude would not be inexpensive. Once we win, we can get your husband to reimburse your legal fees, but that's not until after we win."

"How much do I have to pay you?" Claire asked.

"I would need a three-thousand-dollar retainer."

Claire nodded. She could get that out of their savings account, but George would notice it gone. If he didn't notice until after he got served with court papers, then it wouldn't matter.

"What else?" she asked.

"Well, we would need to get definitive proof of his infidelities," he said. "What you have is a good start, but it's not enough to take to court. He could say a co-worker wrote that card. He could say he showers before he gets home because he wants to be fresh for you. Does he work out?"

Claire nodded.

"See, that's even better. And as far as the dinner he had, that could be an old friend from high school. Maybe he met up with her casually. Maybe he didn't tell you because he knows you wouldn't believe him."

"I would have believed him," Claire said.

"That's your word against his," Mr. Smiley countered.

Claire shook her head and put a hand over her mouth. "I knew it," she said. "I shouldn't be here."

"No, Mrs. Hudgens. That's not what I'm saying. I'm fully convinced your husband's cheating on you."

Claire met his eyes, and they were warm and honest.

"And that's a shame," he went on. "You're a beautiful black woman. A *strong* woman. You know how many wives have sat across from me and went to pieces over stuff like this? You deserve to be *loved*, and honored, and *respected*. I don't know anything about George personally, but he's a fool for not putting you first. Excuse me for saying that, but I don't bite my tongue."

His words made Claire feel warm and important, but also a little uneasy. She looked at his hands, and grew even more uncomfortable when she saw there was no ring on his finger.

He watched her, and his eyes narrowed. "Did I offend you?"

Claire took a nervous breath and blinked quickly. "I, uh, I . . ."

"Is it because I said you're *beautiful,* or because I said you deserve love, honor and respect?"

Claire was unable to meet his eyes. "Um, both . . . All of it . . ."

He smiled. It was a big, hearty smile. "Mrs. Hudgens, I am a professional. Those are just my observations."

You think I'm beautiful?

"Wha." Claire wiped at her forehead again. "Is it hot in here?"

He laughed. "All right, Mrs. Hudgens. Let's talk business. Here's what I think you should do. First, find out for sure if he's cheating on you. We need something black and white we can show a judge. We need to catch him with his other woman. If we could get pictures, that would be great. That card you have may turn out to be valuable. If we can prove his mistress wrote it, that would be excellent. Have you looked around your home for any other evidence?"

Claire shook her head.

"Okay. Well you probably should do that. What I would suggest is that you hire a detective to spy on your husband. I can get one for you—"

"No," Claire said with a smile. "I already have access to a small detective agency."

Trevor smiled back at her. "Well, that would work, too. When you get your evidence and you're sure you want to divorce George—"

"I want to *destroy* George."

"I would love to help you destroy George," Trevor said.

"Good," Claire said. "I think you'd do just fine . . ."

&2

As tumultuous as her day already was, there's always the propensity for more drama. When she got home, George called and said he wouldn't be working late that night. He didn't have any extramarital event planned either, so the Hudgens enjoyed one of those rare family dinners with every member present. And even though she was still very much disgusted with her husband, Claire found herself crossing her fingers and ignoring the evidence again as they ate.

The kids truly loved this man. Watching their inter-actions with George made Claire feel like rusted daggers were being plunged into her chest. She felt like *she* had all the secrets now. The visit with the lawyer rested on her shoulders like a huge boulder, and Claire felt like she was the one trying to rip the fabric of their family. Anything that happened was ultimately her fault, because all she had to do was shut up, keep her nose down, and go along with the program.

Yeah, George might come home late, but that was just putting more money in their bank accounts. Yeah, he bought her the wrong necklace, but it was still a very nice and expensive gift. Who would complain about that? And yeah, he might be banging another broad a couple times a week, but at least he had the decency to *bathe* before he came home to his wife. He didn't flaunt his affair, and if Claire was really so upset about it, all she had to do was stop sniffing on him when he came in. If she kept her nosey ass to herself, things could be as they used to be.

In the good old days.

Claire might have gone along with that line of thinking, but a good friend pulled her from that stagnant pool of acceptance once again. Becky called while she and Nikki were cleaning up after dinner.

"Hello?"

"Hey, Claire! Whatchoo doing?"

"Washing dishes."

"How'd it go with the lawyer?"

"Fine."

"What'd he say?"

"I'm washing dishes *with Nikki*," Claire said.

"Oh."

"Who is that?" Nikki asked.

"It's Becky."

"What is she talking about?" Nikki wanted to know.

Claire frowned at her. "*Noneya.*"

"Well, just tell me if he wants to take your case," Becky said.

"He does, but I don't know," Claire said.

"What do you mean you don't know?"

"I just, I don't know."

"Is George home?"

"Yeah."

"Just because he's home today doesn't mean he's going to change, Claire."

"I know."

"You deserve better," Becky said. "I know George is handsome, and he's got this *great career*, but that doesn't mean you have to take whatever he gives."

"I know. You're right. Hey, I'll talk to you about it tomorrow."

"Okay. Wait—you didn't tell me what you think of *Trevor*."

"What do you mean?"

"He's cute, right?"

Claire chuckled. "He's way more than that and you know it."

"You know he's single, right?"

"I noticed," Claire said. "What about it?"

"He told me he was looking for Miss Right when he was working on my case," she said. "Maybe he still is . . ."

"That's totally not my concern."

"*Aww, come on . . .*"

"I gotta go," Claire said, "upstairs, with my husband *George*." She hung up thinking Becky was crazy for those insinuations. Mr. Trevor Smiley was successful and good-looking, but surely he wasn't desperate enough to hit on his heartbroken clients, was he? He told Claire she was beautiful, but she took that more as a self-esteem booster. He knew she was about to cry, and he wanted to comfort her. That was all.

But Claire was still thinking about her would-be lawyer when she got into bed that evening. She thought about his words of encouragement and the good advice he gave, but she also found herself thinking about his dark eyes and his chiseled physique. Unfortunately George was in bed with her, and he was interested in *someone else's* physique; tonight it just so happened to be Claire's.

Fresh from his stint of push ups, George sat next to his wife and pulled the sheets from her body. Claire had on a pair of panties and a white tank top. This was typical sleepwear for her, but she felt uncomfortable and exposed on this night. She reached up and snatched the covers from his hand, and then she rolled away from him.

Undaunted, George got under the sheets and positioned himself close to her body. He wore only a pair of boxer briefs, and the feel of his chest on her back made Claire excited even though she didn't want to be.

When she felt his erection on her backside, she scooted away from it. George followed. Claire scooted again, but soon she ran out of bed. George still had plenty penis.

"I have a headache," she said without looking back.

"I can help, baby." He put his hands on the back of her neck and started to rub sensually. "Tell me where you're tense," he whispered.

"It's not going to work," Claire said. "I don't feel like it tonight."

"Sure you do," George said. He continued to rub the back of her neck with one hand, and he reached around with the other to fondle her breasts. Again Claire tried to resist, but he had one of her nipples erect within seconds.

"Stop," she warned. She sent an elbow to his rib cage, but among so many other things, George was a third-degree black belt. He evaded the blow easily, and the hand on her chest slid down between her legs with the quickness of a striking cobra. Before Claire could even gasp, he had his fingers in her panties, figuring things out for himself.

"Naw, I think you *are* ready," he said.

Claire couldn't argue with that because she was as moist as a damp sponge. "Come on, baby," he urged.

He stroked her mound tenderly and worked a finger between the lips. Claire inhaled sharply and found herself at the devil's crossroads. Her body was going to respond regardless because they hadn't been intimate since the night of their anniversary. Her brain knew it was wrong to succumb to his advances, but that organ wasn't offering much of an exit plan. As a matter of fact, her brain worked to facilitate the evil.

Remember what the lawyer said: You don't have any evidence of adultery. What reason will you give for denying his advances?

Claire knew she was listening to the little devil on her shoulder rather than the angel, but her life was so disorganized right now it didn't matter what decision she made.

She stopped fighting with him, and George removed her panties tenderly. He crawled on top of her, and Claire reluctantly spread her legs for him. When he entered,

137

Claire closed her eyes and tried to force the mental turmoil from her head. George filled her fully and pleasantly, but she still couldn't clear her mind—not totally.

Claire thought about the fresh smell of *clean* he brought in with him after late nights at work. She thought about the faint scent of perfume she encountered just a few days ago. She wondered if he knew how much she loved him and how much joy and pleasure he brought to her life. Claire wondered if he made his other woman as happy. Did he touch her like he touched his wife? Was he gentle with her? Did he kiss her neck like he did with his *first* love? Did she want to close her eyes and scream when they became one?

Claire opened her eyes and stared into her husband's hazel orbs. She stared at him with pain and longing. George returned her gaze, but he didn't notice that his wife's eyes were blurred with tears.

When she climaxed it was both bitter and sweet.
But mostly sweet.

CHAPTER ELEVEN
MELANIE'S WAY

Claire rose from her seat the next morning and scanned the office curiously. Her eyes widened when she saw the blue uniform. She left her desk and crossed the room quickly. Their postal carrier didn't have time to run or pull any of the evasive maneuvers he'd been using as of late. Claire walked up behind him and put a hand on his cart. He turned and jumped a little when he saw her standing there.

"Uh, um, hey. Hey. How are you doing, today, ma'am?" Cordell was seriously spooked. Claire took a mild satisfaction from that.

"I'm fine," she said. She stood with one hand on his buggy and the other on her hip. Today she wore a white blouse with a navy blue *skirt*; it was long, revealing only her ankles when she sat down, but it was still a skirt—the first one she'd ever worn there.

She had her hair pulled back in a ponytail, and her features weren't forlorn or haggard this time. Claire looked bright and well-rested. Her lips were full and pink. Her eyes were big and brown.

"Um, how, what can I do for you?" Cordell asked.

"I've noticed you don't bring my letters to my desk anymore," Claire said.

The mailman had on short sleeves and short pants today. He was a hairy fellow; his arms and legs were covered with a dense fur. He was still attractive, though.

"I, I talked to Mis-Mr. Roubidou," he stammered. "He said I can leave it up front from now on."

Out of the corner of her eye, Claire noticed Becky and a few other co-workers watching her. "You *can* leave it up here," she said. "But I want to let you know that there are no hard feelings between us. You can bring my mail to my desk if you want to. I'd actually prefer it that way."

His eyes narrowed a little like he expected a trap. "I, I thought you had a problem with me."

"I was having a bad day," Claire replied airily. "I didn't mean to yell at you like I did, but you kind of caught me off-guard. It wasn't a good time for what you were saying."

He smiled, his confidence returning by degrees. "Really?"

"I didn't think you were going to stop bringing my mail," Claire said with a grin. "I don't bite."

"Oh?" He leaned on the other end of his basket and gave her a cheesy smile. "Well, um, I can start bringing your mail to your desk again if you want me to."

"Thanks," Claire said. "I would appreciate that." She turned to leave, but her apology left an expected opening.

"Hey," the mailman said. "You said I approached you with the wrong words on the *wrong day*. Does that mean I should ask you out on a *different* day?"

Claire chuckled. "I guess so, Cordell."

"So—"

"But not today," she said. She turned again and headed for her desk. Halfway there she stopped to see if he was still watching her. He was. She gave him a flirty grin, and he waved.

Becky came and stood behind her computer a few seconds later.

"What's going on?"

Claire looked up and smiled cheerily. "Hey. What's up?"

"Are you okay?" Becky asked. "You feeling all right today?"

Claire shrugged. "Yeah. I guess so. Why?"

"I see you made up with our mail guy."

Claire chuckled. "Are you sitting over there watching my every move?"

"After what happened between you guys last time, I think a lot of people are watching."

"People love drama," Claire said. "I just told him I wasn't mad at him and he can start giving me my mail personally again. I feel weird with him leaving my stuff up there, like I'm a leper or something. Everybody thinks he and I have issues."

"That's great," Becky said. "Glad you got that squared away. But what about all that other stuff?"

"What other stuff?" Claire asked innocently.

"Why'd you turn back and smile at him when you were on your way back to your desk?"

"Oh, my God. Are you watching me like *that*?"

"You were all out in the open. I just happened to look up."

141

Claire rolled her eyes. "You know, I realized something yesterday, Becky."

"What?"

"Let's talk at lunch."

"*Uh-uhn*!" Becky grabbed her arm and dragged her to the break room. "I think we need some coffee *now*."

❧

It was a full hour before their first break, so the lounge was pleasantly empty. Becky directed Claire to a seat at the lone table. She ran around the other side and sat across from her. She leaned forward in her chair with both elbows on the table and a dopey grin on her face. Claire frowned at her.

"You need a life."

"I've got a life," Becky said. "Yours just happens to be more interesting at this exact moment."

Claire shook her head. "All right. I came to a decision yesterday."

"When you talked to Trevor?"

"*No*," Claire said. She looked away uncomfortably. "When George and I were, *together . . .*"

Her friend's eyes widened. "*You didn't.*"

"He was in the mood. What was I supposed to do?"

"Make him sleep on the couch."

"For what reason?" Claire asked. "I'm not ready to confront him."

"You could have told him you had a headache."

"I did," Claire said. "He rubbed my neck. It was nice." She closed her eyes, lost in the memory.

Becky looked pretty pissed. "You could've—"

"We made love, Becky. But that's not what I want to talk about. Can I finish the story?"

Becky lowered her eyes, pouting a little. "I was just going to say you could have told him it was your *womanly* time."

"Thanks, buddy. We'll send that memo back in time when it might have been useful."

"I'm just trying to be helpful."

"*All right*," Claire said, laughing.

Becky smiled, too. "*Fine*. Tell me what happened."

"Okay," Clair said. "George and I were *having relations* last night, and I couldn't get his girlfriend out of my head. I kept thinking about, you know, him and her, together."

Becky frowned.

"I know," Claire said. "How do you think I felt? Not only was I picturing it, but something *even worse* struck me."

"What?"

"I was really tripping. I told myself, *it's bad enough you're sharing him. Don't you think you need some protection?*"

Becky's eyes grew wide. "*No.*"

"*Yes*," Claire said. "The only protection I've ever used with George was the pill, but I was thinking we needed some *condoms*."

"George doesn't have any diseases," Becky said.

"I know he doesn't," Claire said. "But the thought was in my head. You know, it *is* possible. I have no idea what kind of nasty whore he's with."

Becky shook her head.

"Hear me out," Claire said. "That's not even what my revelation was."

"Well, what was it?"

Claire sighed. "I don't know why that was the catalyst, but it was, Becky. You were right; I am trying to ignore it. I *was*, but I'm not anymore. I don't know much right now, but I know I can't sleep with George anymore—not until we get to the bottom of this."

Becky nodded. "It's about time."

"When I was weak, you were there for me," Claire said. "I love you for that. I always will."

"*Aww*," Becky said. She took off her glasses and wiped at her eyes. "You're going to make me cry."

Claire reached across the table and squeezed her hand. "So here's what we're going to do," she said. "First off, we're going up beef up our efforts. George has poker night tomorrow. Are you still down?"

"Hell, yes!"

"If he doesn't come home, then we'll go to his job and wait for him to leave the plant. And if he doesn't do anything, then I'm trying again the next day."

"Good for you," Becky said.

"And I'm searching our office *today*," Claire declared. "If I find anything else with that Kim bitch's name on it, that's his ass."

"This is great," Becky said, her eyes twinkling. "I'm actually getting jittery over here."

"I'm going to get him so good," Claire promised.

"Claire, I'm so proud of you. It feels like the old *you* is back. Is that why you were flirting with our mailman?"

"I was not flirting with him."

"I saw you look back and smile."

"Becky, I would *never* go out with our mailman."

"Why not?"

"Because he's *hairy*, for one. Plus he tried to hit on me, knowing I was married."

"So what was all of that about?"

Claire smiled. "When we were in high school, I used to have George wrapped around my little finger."

"You wanted to see if you've still got it?"

"That was just a little experiment," Claire said with a sly smile.

"Were you practicing for *Trevor*?"

Claire giggled. "I knew you were going to ask that, and *no, I was not*. What is it with you and that lawyer?"

"Claire, he's good looking, *and single*. You're good looking and about to be single. You guys would look good together."

"He told me I was beautiful."

Becky's mouth dropped. "I knew it!"

"He just said that because I was depressed," Claire guessed. "He said I was beautiful and I deserved to be loved, honored, and respected."

"Oh, man."

"There's no *oh man*, Becky."

"He never said *I* was beautiful."

"Well . . ."

"He didn't say I deserved to be loved, honored, or respected, either."

"I'm sure he meant to."

"I'm sure he likes 'em tall and dark . . ."

"I'm, not going there with you, Becky. I'll probably hire him to work my case, but that'll be it."

"But what if—"

"*That'll be it,*" Claire said. She stood to leave, and Becky did, too. "Now come on before you get us in trouble. You know we're not on break. I'm going to get fired messing around with you."

Becky rolled her eyes. "They are not going to fire you, Claire. Mr. Roubidou thinks you're the best."

"Do you really think that lawyer thinks I'm beautiful?" Claire asked.

"I knew it!"

❧

When she got home, Claire got the kids started on their homework, but she kept coming up with excuses not to search the office. First she decided it was better to get dinner started first. After that, it seemed like a good time to take a shower. When she got out, it was time the set the table for supper. She didn't search the office while the kids ate because they were known to discard their asparagus if there wasn't an adult at the table with a keen eye on them.

George called during the meal to say he wouldn't be in until after ten. Claire took that as a stroke of fortune; she still had four hours to do her dirty work. But when they were done eating, *someone* had to clear the table and wash the dishes. That someone could have been Stacy or

Nikki, but Claire was in the mood for housework for some reason.

When she finished in the kitchen, Claire felt obliged to check on the children's homework and get George Jr.'s bath started.

She called Melanie at eight o'clock when she was all out of things to do but still didn't want to go into that damned office.

"Hello?"

"Hey, what are you up to?"

"Nothing. Watching Tila Tequila. Girl, this bitch is *nasty*. What you doing? Why do you sound so down?"

"I'm having trouble with this thing I have to do."

"What?"

"The office."

"Claire, you still haven't searched that damned office?"

"Uh-uhn."

"Why not?"

"I can give you several reasons. I've been coming up with them for a while."

"Man, you crazy."

"What if I find something bad and I start freaking out? The kids will see me. They'll tell George—"

"Do you know how many bitches *love* to look through their man's shit?"

"They've probably had a little more practice than me," Claire said. "I only did it once in sixteen years, and it didn't turn out too good for me that time."

"Are you really scared?" Melanie asked.

"I am," Claire said. "I really am."

"All right, girl. I'll come over and we'll do it together. But if you make me miss my Tila Tequila, and you still don't want to look, I'm going up there *by myself*!"

"I thought you said she was nasty."

"She is, but who doesn't think about that sometimes? I'd get in the bed with her fine ass at least once. Wouldn't you?"

Claire knew her friend wasn't playing around as soon as she opened the front door. Melanie stood there wearing a baby blue pajama suit with fuzzy footies. She had her hands on her hips and her head cocked to the side. A few tight curls hung over her beady eyes. In one fist she gripped a hammer. She held a small a crowbar in the other hand. Claire didn't know whether to laugh or slam the door and lock it.

"What, *wha*?"

"You ready?" Melanie asked.

Claire held her arms out, blinking quickly. "What are, what are the tools for, Melanie?"

"If we need them, you'll know," she said.

Claire wavered in indecision, contemplating all that could go wrong with this. George was the most on-time person she knew. If he said he wouldn't be home until after ten, then he wouldn't be home until after ten. But with Claire's luck, today he might surprise his wife by showing up early. If he caught them in the midst of their search, Claire was pretty sure Melanie wouldn't attack him with the claw end of the hammer, but *pretty sure* seemed a little inadequate.

"We're not going to need tools," Claire said. "Leave them in your car."

"*You* called *me* over," Melanie reminded. "If you wanted to do it your way, then you should have done it by now." She stepped through the doorway, pushing Claire to the side a little. Claire said a quick prayer before she closed and locked it behind her.

"Y'all already ate?" Melanie asked, headed for the kitchen.

"Yeah, but I can make you plate if you want." Claire followed her with butterflies in her stomach.

"What'd y'all eat?"

"Vegetable lasagna." Claire went to the fridge, but Melanie headed for the stairs.

"What are you doing?"

"I thought you wanted something to eat."

"Claire, quit trying to get out of this. I wanted to take a plate home with me. I don't want it now."

"Oh."

George Jr. stomped down the stairs like a three-legged horse. "Aunt Melanie!"

"Hey, boy!" She positioned her tools in one hand so she could throw an arm around him. "What you still doing up?"

"It's only eight-thirty," he said. "I can stay up for another hour!"

"Cool. Do you think you can stay up for another hour *in your room*? Me and your mama have a little job we need to take care of."

"What's *that*?" he asked, pointing at the hammer.

"That's a hammer."

"I know what a hammer is. What's that other thing?"

"That's a crowbar," Melanie said.

"What's it for?"

"*Ooh*, there's a lot you can do with crowbars," Melanie said.

"Like what?"

Claire held her breath in the background.

"You can screw things on," Melanie said, "and screw them off. You can hold it like a sword; you can poke things and hit things. If a monster comes out from under your bed, you can beat him with it. What *can't* you do with a crowbar? That's the real question."

The little boy stared in wonder. "Mama. I want a crowbar!"

"You have to wait till you're eighteen," Melanie said. "Now go on up to your room before I poke *you* with it!" She tickled his ribs, and the little boy clomped back up the stairs laughing. "Come on," she told Claire. "We've only got an hour and a half."

"That should be enough," Claire said.

But she had no idea.

CHAPTER TWELVE
THE SUNFLOWER GIRL

The Hudgens' office was not a very large room, but *large* is such a relative term. If your goal was to play a game of badminton in there, you probably wouldn't think it was very spacious at all. But if you wanted to find one sheet of paper or something small among all of the files, shelves, desk drawers and boxes, then the office was a very large place indeed.

Claire had no idea where to begin the search or even what they were looking for, so she didn't put any limitations on her friend. On the east side of the room, they had bookshelves covering the whole wall from corner to corner. At the bottom of these shelves was a row of identical drawers for additional storage. Melanie started on that wall, and Claire headed for the desk in the middle of the room.

Their mission was simple: Everything needed to be looked at, and anything with Kim's name on it was like the Holy Grail. The girls got started solemnly and didn't speak much for a while.

After about thirty minutes of searching the desk, Claire figured this probably wasn't where she would find the incriminating evidence she sought. George sat there often, but only when he had to work on drawings for work. All Claire could find in those drawers were small engineering tools: pens, pencils, protractors and rulers.

Similarly, Melanie wasn't having much luck on the other side of the room. There were no hidden papers among the many manuals and textbooks George kept over the years. And Claire's Stephen King collection was just that. There were no secret compartments behind her Dean Koontz novels, either.

Melanie did find a lot of interesting things in the row of drawers, but nothing that confirmed the existence of George's secret lady. She interrupted Claire every few minutes with something new in her hands.

"What's this?"

"Those are worksheets I made for the kids."

"What's this?"

"Those are old report cards, transcripts."

"What's all this?"

"Uh, *oh*, that's a couple of books I wrote back in the day."

"*You* wrote books?"

"I played with it for a couple of years."

"What are they about?"

"One's about a pimp and his main girl. The other's about a sultry love affair."

Melanie's eyes widened. "Nigga, I didn't know you wrote books."

"I don't. I just wrote those two. I wrote them when little George started school, before I got into medical billing."

"Damn, Claire. You should've told somebody. How do you know enough about pimps to write a whole book?"

"What's there to know?" Claire asked. "I know what they do for a living, and all of the characteristics I gave him came out of my head. It wasn't that hard."

"Did you ever try to publish them?"

"No. It was just a hobby."

Melanie took a seat and starting flipping through the pages.

Claire brushed the hair from her face and closed the last drawer on the desk.

"I can make you a copy if you want to read it *later . . .*" she suggested.

"Oh. Oh, yea." Melanie returned the papers to the drawer and moved on to the next one.

"What are y'all doing?"

Claire looked up and saw Stacy lounging the doorway.

"I'm looking for some papers I stored away," she said quickly. "Melanie's helping."

"Can I help?"

"*No!*" Claire said, almost too forcefully. "I mean, no, sweetie. You've got to get ready for bed. What time is it anyway?'"

"9:15."

"Oh." Claire stood quickly. "I gotta go check on George Jr.," she told Melanie.

"Gone," Melanie said without looking up.

When Claire got back, Melanie was on the other side of the room examining a model plane George Sr. put together.

"Did you find anything?"

Melanie shook her head. "What about that?" She pointed to a file cabinet Claire kept her important papers in.

"I'm about to check that," Claire said. "We only have about forty minutes, though. I don't want to be in here when George gets home."

"What's in there?" Melanie pointed to a small closet this time.

"Should just be clothes," Claire said. She went to the file cabinet and pulled out the first drawer. There were only more worksheets in there.

"What's this?" Melanie asked. She backed out of the closet with a well-worn briefcase in hand.

"That's George's," Claire said. She stared at it oddly. "He hasn't used that one in a couple of years."

Melanie crossed the room and set it on the desk. She fiddled with the lock unsuccessfully. "What's the combination?"

"I don't know," Claire said. "I don't think I ever knew the numbers for that one."

"*Umm, hmm,*" Melanie hummed. She went back to the bookshelves and found her crowbar.

"Girl what are you doing?"

"I'm gonna open it."

"Can't you use something else? You're going to break the lock."

"You said he doesn't use it anymore."

"Yeah, but what if he sees it?"

"Throw it away," Melanie said. "I'll take it with me if you want."

Before Claire could voice another objection, Melanie slid the tip of the tire iron between the leather and wrenched it open like a huge clam. It took no more than four seconds.

Claire watched from the file cabinet, unable to move. She felt cold and prickly. Her heart sunk low in her chest.

"Come over here," Melanie said. "You know I don't know what I'm looking for."

Claire stepped hesitantly. "You shouldn't have done that."

"Well, it's over now," her friend said. "Umm, hmm. And here's another card."

Claire thought she was kidding, but Melanie held up another Hallmark. She opened it, and then smiled and snapped her fingers.

"*Got him, baby.* We got another one."

She handed it over, and Claire read, in a daze. Like the first one, this card wasn't given on a holiday or for any other specific occasion. Someone gave it to her husband *just because . . .*

> *I had a great time at the party.*
> *You make me feel so special.*
> *I was just thinking about you,*
> *and I thought I'd let you know*
> *how much I love you.*
> *Kim*

Claire's mouth went dry. Her stomach flipped, and the contents came rushing up her esophagus. She managed to swallow it back down, but the gastric acids burned the back of her throat. She put a hand to her mouth and blinked hard, trying to see through the tears.

"Wha, where did you find this?"

"Right behind that flap," Melanie said. She put an arm around her friend's waist. "You okay?"

Claire's whole body shook; the card trembled in her hands. "It's, it's—"

"It's that *same bitch*," Melanie confirmed. She turned back to the briefcase and started pawing through the other pockets. Claire was frozen in both time and place.

"Come on, girl," Melanie urged. "You still got that whole file cabinet to search. We're running out of time."

Claire dropped the card on the desk and staggered back to her work area. She leaned on the drawer and drew in deep, hot breaths. Her shoulders hitched with each sullen heartbeat.

Two years ago?

"Mama, how long are y'all going to be in here?"

Claire didn't turn to face the door, but she knew it was Nikki standing in the hallway. Melanie rushed to the girl when her mother didn't respond.

"Nikki, ain't you supposed to be in bed?"

"No. It's only nine-thirty."

"Well you need to go back to your room *anyway*. Me and your mom are doing some *grown-folk* stuff."

"*I'm* grown."

"Girl, you'd better get in that room before I go get a switch."

Claire hadn't spanked Nikki since the fifth grade, and Aunt Melanie never laid a hand on her, but those fun facts matter so little when you're being threatened. Nikki hastily turned tail. Melanie moved quickly to her friend when she was gone.

"You gonna be okay?"

Claire shook her head. Her hair hung over her face, and a fat tear wobbled on the tip of her nose. "They, they had a relationship, fuh, for two, *two years*." Claire's words were low, resonating with the foul grief only death or heartbreak can bring. "She *loves him*. He probably *loves her tuh-too*."

Melanie grabbed her shoulders and turned her so they could see eye to eye.

"That's right, Claire. George has a girlfriend. And yeah, she loves him. You already knew that."

"*No! No I didn't*," Claire blubbered.

"Well you do now," Melanie said. "And what it's gonna come down to is this right here: Are you gonna ball up on the floor and start crying, or are you going to get his ass back? All of that pain needs to be switched to *hate*, or you're always gonna be his foot stool."

"I'm not his foot stool."

"Well, what do you call it? He doesn't respect you. He's got another woman *right under your nose*. He lies to you *every day*. He's doing *both of y'all*. Back in high school, you wanted to kick Shonda's ass when she started following George around after football practice. Do you remember that?"

Claire nodded, her face a mess because of the recently acquired mascara.

"Is that bad bitch still in there?" Melanie asked, poking at her chest.

Claire wiped her tears and nodded.

"Huh?"

"*Yes*," she breathed.

"Then what are you gonna do, let him play you like a fool?"

"No," Claire said. She sniffled loudly and looked her friend in the eyes.

"Then what are you gonna do?"

"I'm going to make him pay." Claire's eyes narrowed and her nostrils flared. Her look of despair was replaced with a deep scowl.

Melanie nodded. "That's good. You still a bad bitch."

Claire threw her arms around her. "Thank you."

"Ain't nothing, girl. We in this *together*."

Claire went to wash her face while Melanie turned the briefcase inside out. There was nothing more. They didn't make any discoveries in the file cabinet, either. Counting the first card she found, George left only two incriminating items in the whole office. It wasn't a lot, but it was enough to dispel any hopes Claire had of a happy ending. From that moment on it was war, and Claire was on the offensive. George wouldn't even know he was being attacked until she was ready to yell *Checkmate!*

Melanie left at 9:52, and Claire climbed into bed a little while later. She was still awake when George sneaked under the sheets at 12:45, but she pretended to be in the midst of a pleasant dream. She rolled over drowsily to spoon with him, and damn if the sonofabitch wasn't as fresh as a clean load of laundry.

Claire opened her eyes and stared at the back of his head for a long time that night.

Live it up, sweetheart.

Live it up.

The next day things got a little hairy when George called and said he was getting off at five o'clock rather than six.

"Are you still playing poker tonight?" Claire asked him.

"Yeah, baby. But I'm leaving earlier than usual."

"How come?"

"We're playing at Sherman's tonight. I'm going to help him set up before the other guys get there."

"What time are you leaving?"

"Around six, why?"

"I'm going to the movies with Becky today."

"*Again?* You've been going out a lot lately. What's up with that?"

"I don't know. I get bored sometimes," Claire said. "I feel like I don't have any excitement in my life. Why don't you take me with you to the poker game?"

George laughed. "Yeah, right. Have fun at your movie."

Claire called her friends at work when she got off the phone with him.

"Biotech Industries."

"Hey, Melanie?"

"Yeah, Claire. What's up?"

"George just called. He said he's getting off at five today."

"*Five?*"

"Yeah. He's leaving here at six. Can you still make it?"

"I leave at five-thirty," Melanie said. "I'd have to dip out a little early . . ."

"You don't have to pick up Trevon?"

"Rodney ain't doing nothing. He can pick him up."

"I really appreciate it."

"It's cool. But if I ever think Rodney's cheating on me, you'd better be the *first one* offering to help me follow his ass around."

"You got it," Claire promised. She hung up and called Becky.

"Provincial Insurance."

"*Becky?*"

"Hey, Claire. You ready for the big night?"

"*No.* George just threw a monkey wrench; he's getting off at five today instead of six."

"*Five?*"

"I just found out. Can you still come?"

"I leave at five, Claire."

"I know."

"I have to pick Courtney up from school. I can't make it to your house until six."

"That's fine," Claire said. "That's what time George is leaving. Melanie's going to be waiting on him just like last time."

"Okay," Becky said. "I'll be there. You can count on me."

"I know I can," Claire said. "Thank you."

The plan was laid perfectly, and George was none the wiser.

Claire already had the kids at the dining table when he got home at five-thirty. He went upstairs to change, and she didn't follow him. She enjoyed her chicken primavera like a good wife and listened to the children recap their peculiar days.

At 5:45 Melanie called and said she was in position.

At 5:50 George came downstairs wearing gray slacks and a long-sleeved black button-down. He asked his wife if she'd seen his Stacy Adams loafers. Claire directed him to the spot in the closet where she took all of the shoes he left out. George gave her a kiss on the forehead and headed back upstairs with a big smile on his face.

At 5:58 Becky and Courtney arrived just in time to see George leave at 6:02.

Melanie called at 6:07 to inform them she was on his tail.

Claire and Becky left a few minutes later.

George's second stakeout proceeded much like the first one, but there were two notable exceptions: First, he didn't stop at the car dealership to pick up the mystery woman. Second, he didn't head towards the south side of town where Sherman lived. He got on I-35 headed north, and he was still on that freeway thirty minutes later.

No one knew where he was going, but there was an advantage to all of this time on the road: Becky booked it ten miles over the speed limit for a while, and she was able to catch up to Melanie. They pulled within eyesight once, but Melanie urged them to hang back a little.

"If you can see *me*," she said, "then George can see *you*, 'cause I'm right on his tail. Get that big-ass truck outta here."

Becky lowered her speed and put a couple of exits between them.

George stayed on 35 past the Meacham exit, and then he got on Highway 820 headed east. He booked it all the way to 121, and Claire had to throw up her hands. She knew of absolutely no destination in that direction. They were headed for the airport, and Claire decided to call the stakeout off if that's where he was going. There was no way they could follow him in the terminal without being spotted.

But George didn't stop there. He zipped by all of the airport exits, and continued his drive all the way to the fair city of *Irving*. Melanie called to voice her disapproval as soon as they entered the city limits.

"Claire, where the hell is your husband going?"

"Melanie, *I don't know*. He's still on the freeway?"

"Hell, yea! Girl, I've been following his ass for more than *forty-five minutes*. I'm gonna have to get some gas soon. I didn't know he was going this far."

"If you need to stop, then we can stop," Claire said. "We'll try again tomorrow."

"I'm still over the E, but—hold on, Claire. I think he's getting off."

"He is?"

"Uhh, *yeah*. He's about to get off on Story Road. You got lucky."

"No," Claire said gloomily. "I don't think I'm lucky at all . . ."

They followed George from the freeway, through the business district, and into a residential neighborhood Claire had never seen before. Just when Melanie started complaining about her gas again, George pulled into the parking lot of a private school called St. Martin's Academy. Melanie parked a block away, but she crept past the entrance when George got out of the car. The school's parking lot was bustling with parents arriving for *God-knew-what*, and George entered the building alone. It was exactly seven p.m.

Becky parked around the corner a few minutes later, and Melanie got out of her car to meet them.

"What the hell is your husband doing *here*?" she asked when Claire rolled down her window.

"I don't know," she said. "I don't know anything about this city. I don't know anyone who lives over here, and I damned sure don't know anyone who goes to *that* school."

"Well, George does," Becky said, stating the obvious.

Claire's face was like granite; they couldn't tell how this news was affecting her.

"Well, let's find out who," she said.

Claire wanted to go in right away, but her friends thought someone should look the place over first. George might be waiting right inside the lobby for all they knew. After a quick discussion, they decided to let Becky go inside by herself. Fresh off work, she was dressed as professionally as all the other guests. Plus she was the most *innocent-looking* of the three. She headed off on foot, and Claire and Melanie waited a mind-numbing fifteen minutes for the news she would bring back.

Claire knew it was going to be bad, and she wasn't disappointed. She held her breath when Becky returned to her truck, a little paler than before.

"Uh, you guys better see this for yourself."

The trio crossed the street and walked around the side of the building with little regard for the negative attention they garnished. They walked through the front doors of the school boldly and were greeted by two fourth-graders handing out programs for tonight's presentation. Claire took one, and the sweat from her hand left a large stain on it by the time they made it to the auditorium.

Becky led them in, and they found three seats near the back. A dozen small students were on stage singing *Texas Our Texas*. It didn't take a lot of looking around to locate George's bald dome and broad shoulders in the crowd. He sat on the third row; next to the woman who most likely held the seat for him.

"*That's her*," Melanie whispered. "From last time . . ."

Claire leaned forward in her chair and tried to memorize every detail, but mostly all she saw was long hair that was auburn tinted and slightly curled. George turned a few times to whisper in his lady friend's ear, and Becky took a couple of pictures of his perfect profile.

Sitting there watching her husband enjoy time with another woman was hard enough. Trying to figure out why George was there in the first place was even more stressful, but luckily they had to wait only ten minutes to figure that part out. The first group of youngsters finished their song, and a first-grade teacher with pudgy cankles took the stage after they departed. She started to brag about the many extracurricular activities the students at St. Martin's were involved in. She harped on about the Girl Scouts in particular, because she was once a member of that fine organization herself.

"So, without further adieu," she screamed, "let's bring out our girls from Troop Number 84!"

Everyone cheered as a group of fifteen children marched onto the stage in full Girl Scout regalia. In addition to their uniforms, some of the girls also wore cardboard cutouts that resembled the sun, the moon, and an assortment of simple flowers. They arranged themselves on the stage and began to sing a song Claire recognized from Nikki's stint with Camp Fire so many years ago.

"*If all of the raindrops were lemon drops and gumdrops, oh what a rain it would be. I'd stand outside with my mouth open wide. Ah, ah, ah ah, ah, ah ah, ah, ah ah!*"

When they got to the last part, all of the girls looked to the sky with their mouths open, as if to catch imaginary candy falling from the clouds.

"What's this shit about?" Melanie asked.

"Look," Becky said.

They did, and they all saw the same thing: George wasn't sitting anymore. He was standing with a camcorder, following the actions of one of the little girls.

"Who's he recording?" Becky asked, but that question pretty much answered itself. St. Martin's Academy didn't have very many students of color, and only one of the girls on stage was black. She was as cute as a button, light-skinned like George Jr., wearing a card-board cutout that looked like a sunflower.

Claire was out of her seat before she knew her legs were moving.

"If all of the snowflakes were chocolate chips and cupcakes, oh what a snow it would be!"

She stomped down the middle aisle with her fists balled and her teeth clenched. She had no definite plan in mind, but yanking George's girlfriend's hair out seemed like a good start. Claire got within ten feet of her husband then someone grabbed her in a bear-hug from behind; lifting her feet almost off the ground. They turned her and let her go when she was facing the opposite direction.

A good number of parents stared in awe, but Claire didn't give a damn about them. She turned back towards George, but Melanie blocked her path sufficiently.

"Go," she said. "Get out of here, Claire."

It seemed odd to move in one direction when her heart and soul tugged her in the other, but Claire heeded her friend's advice. She allowed Melanie to push her down the aisle, and soon they were in the foyer again. She could still hear the children singing behind her.

"If all of the flash floods were lemonade and Kool-Aid . . ."

Melanie grabbed her shoulders and stared into her eyes. "Are you gonna cry?" she asked.

Claire shook her head. "*Hell, no.*"

"You gonna blow our cover?"

Claire shook her head again.

"Then what are you gonna do?" Melanie asked.

"*I'm gonna get his ass,*" Claire hissed.

Melanie squinted at her. "You sure?"

Claire chuckled nervously. "Oh, yeah. *I'm so freaking sure.*"

CHAPTER THIRTEEN

GEORGE'S SECRET OTHER FAMILY

Claire stood at the kitchen sink the next morning slicing a banana for George Jr. and George Sr.'s cornflakes. Today she wore a white sundress with pink floral prints. When she pulled it from the closet a couple hours ago, Claire had to rack her brain to remember the last time she wore the dress. But it still fit, and it was pretty, and sexy. The billowy fabric stopped right at her knees, exposing brown legs that were smooth, long, and freshly shaven. Today Claire would wear sandals to work for the first time since—*ever*.

She turned with the knife and cutting-board in hand and looked upon her beautiful family. The girls were neat and clean, bright-eyed and bushy tailed. They both sat on one side of the table eating oatmeal with toast rather than cereal like the men.

Actually, Nikki wasn't eating too much. She had a notebook on the table and was rushing through a vocabulary assignment she had *all last night* to complete. She chose to watch movies and shoot the breeze with Courtney instead, and now she was in danger of receiving an early morning butt-whooping if she didn't finish within the next sixteen minutes.

That whooping was going to come from her mother, even if it was wrong.

Claire made her way to the table with the detached airiness of a phantom. When she got there, she served her son first. That was a notable taboo, but Claire was simply girding her mind for the inevitable: George Sr.'s days were numbered, and little George would be the new man of the house. Claire even gave him the majority of the banana slices.

"*Wow!* Thanks, Mom!"

Her husband looked on with obvious envy. "Damn, baby," he chuckled. "You gonna save any for me?"

Today George Sr. wore a navy blue Polo with khaki Dockers. Claire picked out that shirt at Christmas, and she bought him those slacks two months ago. Come to think of it, she purchased his socks, shoes, and even the drawers he had on. George was a good-looking man, but a lot of his fashion sense came from his wife. Claire wondered if his floozy knew that.

She whipped the knife quickly in a small arc that peaked right under George's Adam's apple. A beam of light glinted on the smooth blade. She hadn't sharpened the utensil in years; Claire expected it to scrape his skin and maybe leave a long, red welt once it healed.

Instead she opened him up like a cantaloupe. The hole was only two inches in diameter, but apparently every artery in his body ran through that small space. Blood sprayed the dining table as if from a shower nozzle. Stacy threw up her hands to block most of it, but Nikki just watched in astonishment, and she got splattered worse than Carrie did in Stephen King's tale.

George Jr. didn't have the sense to turn away either, but most of the gore landed on his chest and in his bowl of cornflakes. He stared at his mother in awe, and then looked down at his food oddly. He looked back up at his mom with a huge scowl pulling his chipmunk cheeks.

George Sr. gawked at his wife with more of a horrified expression. His eyes bugged like boiled eggs. He grasped at his neck with one hand and clawed at Claire's with the other. She backed away and he tried to follow. He stumbled out of his chair like a drunkard and fell to the floor, sucking air like a fish out of water.

"Why'd you do that?" he asked.

"Hmm?" Claire looked down and realized she dumped his bananas from too great a height. They fell into his bowl with a large splash; sending a couple teaspoons of milk flying at his shirt. The stain wasn't that big of a deal, but it was surely not a good way to start the day. George stood and brushed his stomach with a cloth napkin.

"Why'd you do that?" he asked again.

"Huh?" Claire asked, returning from a most pleasant daydream.

"Did you do this on purpose?" George asked.

Claire frowned at him. "Of course not, honey." She looked at the knife in her hands and was almost surprised there was no blood on it. "It's not the end of the world," she said. "Trust me; it could have been *a lot* worse."

∽

For lunch that afternoon, Becky took her to the Don Pablo's down the street from their office. She choked a little on her shrimp fajita when Claire told her about her *vision* this morning. Becky put a napkin to her mouth and patted her chest lightly.

"Ooh, excuse me."

"Don't laugh," Claire said. "For a minute, I thought I really did cut him. And you know the worst part about it?" She leaned forward and took a conspiratorial tone. "It felt *good*, Becky, the thought of him *bleeding*, staggering towards me on his knees." Claire shook her head and sighed pleasantly. "It still feels like something I'm supposed to do."

"Oh, no. We already went down that road," Becky warned. "Trains go forward, not backward."

Claire frowned. "I'm not sure that really relates here, but I was just fantasizing. It's okay to still think about it, right? Long as nobody gets hurt?"

"I guess," Becky said. "What time did he get home last night?"

"Around one, *freshly showered.*" Claire's smile went away. She looked in Becky's direction, but stared past her, into nothingness.

"It's okay," Becky said.

Claire met her eyes. "Really? How so?"

" 'Cause your stakeout was a success." Becky grabbed her purse from the seat next to her and dug through it in her lap. She came up with a handful of photographs wrapped in a plastic sandwich bag.

"You got those developed already?"

"Mmm-hmm." She handed them over the table, and Claire fiddled with the wrapping.

"Wal-mart's getting a little cheap, aren't they?"

"*No*," Becky said with a bright smile. "I developed those at home."

Claire cocked an eye. "You've got a darkroom?"

"No, silly. I have a digital camera and a computer. You can buy photograph paper anywhere."

"I guess I'm behind on the times," Claire admitted. "You're going to have to . . ." She trailed off and gaped at the first of six photographs. It was a good shot of George and his mistress, not blurry at all. Becky zoomed in for a close-up, but both subjects had their back to the camera and neither offered a profile. Still, it was shocking to have it in her hands. A judge may not view the photo as definitive proof, but that bald dome was unmistakable to Claire.

Raw emotions knocked at her soul like a restless tide, but she closed them off quickly. She squeezed her eyes shut, and when she opened them, they remained dry. She was getting into a habit of crying at lunch every day, but no more of that. She hated how George made her feel so weak and powerless.

"The next one's better," Becky said.

Claire flipped to it and sighed raggedly. In the second photograph, George made the mistake of facing his girlfriend fully. His profile was unequivocal.

"This is a good one," she said numbly.

"Keep looking . . ." Becky said.

The next picture was as useless as the first, but the one after that was definitely a keeper. Claire leaned forward to get more light, and she stared at this one the longest. She didn't think George's floozy made herself available for any good shots, but Becky snapped one when George was standing with the camcorder. His girlfriend looked up at him, and the scene was now preserved for eternity.

"You got her," Claire breathed, unconsciously sizing up her competition. George's girlfriend *was* thinner than his wife; you could see it in just her face and neck. Her skin was the color of a walnut shell. Her hair was long and layered. It was full and rich. She had a thin, almost European nose. She wore a little blush on her cheeks, and autumn-red-colored lipstick. Her eyes were large and curious. Claire tried for a long time, but couldn't come up with anything bad to say about her.

"*Bitch*," she mumbled, but that seemed immensely inadequate.

The next photo was another good profile of George.

The last two pictures were from a sick nightmare: Like Claire, Becky assumed George was there to support the one black Girl Scout on stage. She took a full body shot of the child and another that was a close-up of her face. Claire studied the girl's features for a long time before speaking.

"George has his own kids at home," she said. "I can't believe he'd risk it all so he could support *hers*."

Becky made a face but didn't say anything.

"What?"

Becky shrugged. The girls had come up with lots of opinions about George and his woman and the girl on stage, but so far no one wanted to state the unthinkable. Becky surely didn't want to be the one.

"You, you don't think that's *George's* little girl.." Claire prompted.

Becky pursed her lips.

"It's not," Claire said. "This girl, she's, she's in the *first grade*. That would make her at least seven years old, right?"

Becky nodded. "She looks about seven."

"That means he would have had to get that lady pregnant eight years ago," Claire deduced.

Becky shrugged.

"So this *couldn't* be George's child," Claire said. "We were still in New York then. We've only been in Texas for seven years."

"All right," Becky said.

"What do you mean, '*All right*'?"

"All right, if you say it's not . . ."

"Don't patronize me, girl. Just say what you think."

"Well, I think she looks a lot like him." Becky looked away nervously. "She looks a lot like George Jr., too."

Claire's nostrils flared. She looked at the picture again and accepted it for what it was. She couldn't deny the resemblances between this *abomination* and her husband. The Girl Scout was physically similar to her son as well. Claire could even see bits of Stacy . . .

"So what are you saying, George has been cheating on me for *eight years*?"

"I'm not saying that."

"Then why are you making all of those faces?"

"I'm not making faces."

"Well, why'd you take the *damned pictures*?" Claire spat. She stacked them roughly and stuffed them back in their wrapping.

Becky observed her friend's pit bull countenance but didn't back down. "So it's okay if he's cheating on you, so long as that's not his daughter?"

"That's *not* his daughter!"

"What's the difference, Claire? He's having an affair either way, right?"

" 'Cause *I'm not a fool*," Claire hissed. "Do you know how stupid I'd have to be to let that go on for *eight years*?"

"Claire, you're not a fool."

"Easy for you to say. At least Brent didn't have a secret other family. God, this is sick."

A woman at the table next to them dropped her fork. Claire looked over and saw that she and her friend were eavesdropping openly.

"Like your marriage is all *perfect*," she growled at them.

The strangers looked away quickly.

"Is that what it is?" Becky asked. "You think his infidelities are somehow a reflection of *you*?"

"I've heard about stuff like this," Claire said. "I don't want to be *that woman*, the one who loved her man and never second-guessed him, who thought her life was *just wonderful*, but it turned out he had a whole 'nother life right behind my back—a *whole goddamned family*."

"Don't start," Becky said. "You're not supposed to have to look through his stuff. Do you think it was your *job* to figure this out?"

Claire sighed. "I don't know."

"You're victimizing yourself," Becky informed her friend. "You're like the battered woman who tells herself, '*Oh, if I wouldn't have burnt his eggs, he wouldn't have hit me.*'"

Claire shook her head.

"No," Becky said, "that's what you're doing. You can't blame yourself for *anything* George did. He's a liar and a cheat. When he said he was working late, you believed him because *that's what you're supposed to do*. He's your husband, and your husband isn't supposed to lie. Even if George has been with her for ten years, Claire, it's not your fault."

Claire rubbed her eyes and took a long breath. She smiled at her friend and removed the pictures from the plastic again. "When'd you get your therapy license?" she kidded.

"Everything I just said to you, Trevor said to me," Becky said.

"The lawyer?"

"Mmm-hmm."

"What is he, a counselor, too?"

Becky shrugged. "No. He's just really understanding."

Claire examined the close-up of the sunflower girl again. "This *is* George's baby, isn't it?"

Becky shook her head. "Either way, it's not your fault."

"This is his baby," Claire said definitely. "I don't know much, but I know my husband's child when I see it."

When they got back to the office, Claire devoted her whole brain to her job. That helped get her mind off things for a little while, but Melanie called thirty minutes before it was time to clock out.

"*Girl*, I thought you were going to be in *jail* today! If I find out Robert has some kids by some *other bitch* I'm messing him up."

"She might not be his." Claire knew she was in denial but didn't know what else to say.

"Both of them is his!" Melanie informed. "Don't get it twisted."

Claire's heart fell into her stomach. "*Both*?"

"Didn't you get my message?"

"What message?"

"On your cellphone?"

"My battery's dead," Claire said. "I meant to charg— what do you, what do you mean '*both of them*'?"

"I told you I was going to follow his ass after they left the school."

"You said that last time. I didn't think you did it."

"I wasn't at first," Melanie agreed. "I was running out of gas, but when I saw them leaving, they were headed back towards the freeway. I figured since they going the same way I'm going, I might as well roll with them, you know? Claire, they went right around the corner; that's where she lives! I got that ho's address and everything!"

"What do you mean '*them*', Melanie?"

177

"Oh, yeah, when they left the school, it was George, his *bitch*, that Girl Scout chick, and another little boy. The two kids look like *twins*. Can you believe that nigga got *two* kids?"

"Melanie, tell me you're playing."

"You know I wouldn't play about that."

"You followed them to her house?"

"*Yeah*. I can take you over there. It's a one story, but it's nice. She stays right around from the school, so you know it's in that *good* neighborhood."

"There were *two* kids?"

"A boy *and* a girl, same height, and looked like the same age. Both of them is high-yellow—just like George."

"I'm gonna be sick," Claire said, and she really was. Her stomach flipped, and her mouth filled with saliva. She pulled the waste basket from under the desk but managed to keep it down, for now.

"I feel like I coulda been a private eye," Melanie went on. "Your husband's been getting away with this shit for *too long*. He wasn't even looking over his shoulder or nothing. Girl, do you know how paid you're gonna be when the judge finds out he got a whole 'nother family?"

Money was the last thing on Claire's mind. "How, how could he do that?"

"He's been lying about *everything*," Melanie explained. "His ass probably don't even got a job for all you know."

That was ludicrous, but Claire found herself considering it. George called her from his company cellphone whenever he was at work, and Claire returned his calls to the same number. *Surely George has a job* was just as bankable as *Surely George isn't cheating*, and *Surely George doesn't have another freaking family*.

"What time is the stakeout today?" Melanie asked.

"What do you mean?"

"We ain't doing a stakeout?"

"George doesn't play poker tonight," Claire said. Her head spun. She leaned on the desk for support. "I think he's coming home right after work."

"I'm talking about staking out *his bitch's house*," Melanie said.

"This is, this is just a lot. I need to think about things . . ."

"*What?* Claire, don't go getting soft on me again. The only thing you need to think about is *what's that bitch's full name?* You need to be thinking about getting some mail out of her box."

Oh, my God. Claire realized she had created a monster. "We don't have to do that today."

"What's wrong with today?"

"I just found out my husband has *two illicit children*," Claire whispered.

Melanie sighed loudly. "Claire, I'm not going to let you back away from all of this like you did last time."

"I'm not—"

"I got that ho's address, and I already told Robert I was going out. I got a full tank of gas, and I'm going to Irving *tonight*. I'm hyped up, girl. I can't stop now."

"You'll go all the way over there without me?"

"It's for the *greater good*," Melanie said. "I ain't never did this much for nobody, but it kinda feels nice, like when white people find money and turn it in—not even thinking about a reward or nothing. What's that called?"

"Benevolence," Claire mumbled.

"Huh?"

"I gotta go."

"So are you going with me tonight or what?"

"I don't know," Claire said. She stared at the papers on her desk until they became a white blur. "I'll call you later."

Claire hung up and took out her pictures again. She studied them all in more detail, giving the most scrutiny to the two shots of George's bastard child this time.

She decided divorcing him was definitely not as good as killing him. She didn't understand how she could have ever seen it any other way.

CHAPTER FOURTEEN
FREEZER BAGS

Claire had her emotions under control by the time she picked up the kids, but camouflaging her *mood* was a bit more difficult. George Jr. was the first to notice something was awry. He sat up front with his short legs dangling over the seat. He had his backpack on his lap and his most recent spelling test in hand.

"No one else got a *hundred*," he chirped. "Teacher says I'm going to set the curve when I get to middle school. What's a *curve*, Mama?"

"It's what nerds do to make everyone hate them," Stacy explained. She sat in the back wearing a white T-shirt with the word *PRECIOUS* pasted across the chest. Nikki slouched next to her wearing baggy jeans.

"They don't hate me!" George Jr. exclaimed.

"They will when you get to middle school," Stacy predicted.

"Mama, will they hate me when I get to middle school?"

"No, honey," Claire said without looking over.

"See. I told you!"

"Mama hasn't been in school in *twenty years*," Stacy guessed. "She don't know what goes on."

"*Ooh*!" George Jr. patted his mother's leg. "Mama!"

"What, dear?"

"She said, '*don't know*.'"

"That's nice, honey."

"Shut up and mind your business," Stacy warned.

"*Mama*!" He smacked her more persistently. "She was supposed to say '*doesn't* know.'"

"Hmm?"

"Stacy said she *don't know*, and she was supposed to say she *doesn't know*."

"Okay, baby," Claire said.

"But Mama—"

"She said it's fine, so leave her alone!"

"Mama, did you see my test?" George Jr. whined.

"Yes, sweetie."

"You didn't even look at it."

"Hmmm?"

Little George studied her countenance for a few seconds, and then he turned and eyeballed his sisters. "Something's wrong with Mama," he announced.

Stacy sat up in her seat. "What's wrong?"

"Nothing's wrong with me," Claire said, her eyes still on the road.

"Did you have a bad day at work?" Nikki asked.

That seemed like a good excuse. "Yeah. I guess I did."

"Are you tired, Mama?" Stacy asked. "You look tired."

"Do you want me to help make dinner tonight?" Nikki offered.

"Sure," Claire said. "I'd appreciate that."

"I can make macaroni," Nikki said.

George Jr.'s face lit up. "Me, too!"

"Thanks," Claire told him. She stopped at a light and turned to face him fully. "You're a very special young man."

He grinned like a Jack-O-Lantern.

Claire looked in the rearview and made eye contact with her girls. "I appreciate you guys, too. You're all perfect, *precious* children. You didn't do anything wrong."

Stacy was glad for the endorsement, but Nikki was a little confused.

"Dang, Mama. All I did was offer to make macaroni."

⌒⌐

Claire got dinner started, and she took a shower while the girls boiled noodles. When she got out of the tub, George Sr. was home. He came into the bathroom and ogled her wolfishly while she dried off.

"You should have waited on me," he said. "I would have got in there with you."

"Like I know when you're going to be home."

"I'm just kidding, baby." He sat on the toilet and ran a hand up her inner thigh. Claire stepped away from him and snatched her robe from behind the door. She turned her back and slid into it quickly. When she faced him again, George gave her a peculiar look.

"What's up, baby? You doing all right?"

She rolled her eyes and went over to the sink. "I'm just fine, *dear.*"

She checked her features in the vanity and started to brush her hair. George got up and stood behind her. He tried to grab on to her, but Claire increased her brush strokes to an almost dangerous speed. She aimed to knock him on the forehead, but George bobbed out of the way like a prizefighter.

"Damn, baby! You almost hit me."

"You see me trying to do my hair."

"You coulda gave me a black eye."

"Give me three feet and you'll be fine," Claire advised him coolly.

George grinned. He moved in for another hug, but Claire timed her downstroke just right this time. She jerked back, *hard,* and the brush exploded from her head as if from a cannon. George backed away and brought a hand up simultaneously. The wooden brush banged hard on his pinky finger, and he yelped loudly like a frightened puppy.

"*Ouch! Dammit, Claire!*" He shook his hand briskly and rubbed on the sore digit. "What the hell is wrong with you?"

"I told you to give me some room," she said without looking back.

"Yeah, but you didn't have to hit me!"

"I didn't hit you. You stuck your hand up there on your own."

"*I stuck my hand up to protect my head!*"

"Well, your head shouldn't have been there, then."

George scowled at her reflection. "You *crazy.* I didn't do nothing to you."

That was almost laughable. Claire wanted to show him the pictures so badly her fingers trembled.

"You got problems," he said and disappeared through the bedroom.

"And you're a *disgusting asshole*," Claire muttered when he was gone. She couldn't wait to say that to his face.

Dinner was great, but the tension at the table was so thick it could have been a side dish. Claire sat across from her husband, and they frowned at each other for most of the meal. The kids didn't know what was wrong, but they knew when to keep quiet. An awkward silence ensued; only the clinking of forks scraping plates disturbed the hush. When the phone rang, George Jr. jumped as if struck. Claire went to the kitchen to answer it.

"Hello?"

"Claire, your phone's still dead," Melanie said.

"Oh. I'm sorry. It's on the charger, but it's not on. I wasn't thinking about it."

"How are you *not* thinking about it? I told you we were going over that bitch's house today."

"Yeah, Melanie, I don't think I can make it."

"Why not?"

"It's just not a good time. I'm not feeling well."

"That's good," Melanie said. "You can use that *hate*."

"Melanie—"

"Do you want to know what George's kids are doing right now?"

"What?"

"I mean, I'm looking at both of them little bastards *right now*. Don't tell me you're not curious."

"You went over there?"

"Claire, I already told you I was going."

"I know, but, by yourself?"

"Listen, girl, I got your back—even when you don't want me to have it. We in this together, right?"

Claire put a hand to her mouth. "Yeah. Thank you, Melanie."

"They've been in the yard for an hour. I got some pictures of them, they mama, too. I'm about to leave if you're not coming."

"Can you give me directions?"

"That's my girl," Melanie said. "You get your ass over here."

As surprised as George was that his wife would strike him with a hairbrush, that was nothing compared to his shock when Claire told him she was leaving—in the middle of dinner.

She went upstairs without a word and grabbed her cellphone. She passed through the dining room on the way out of the front door. "I'll be back."

"You'll what? Where are you going?" George left his seat and caught up with her in the living room. The kids looked on with clear foreboding.

"I said I'll be back."

"Back from where, Claire? Where are you going? We're eating dinner. You can't just *leave*."

She tilted her head. "Why not?"

George softened. He put his hands on her shoulders. "Listen, baby. I don't know what's going on, but we need to talk about it. If there's something you want, if there's something you *need*, just tell me. If I did something— what is it?"

Claire stared into his brown eyes and smiled. She put a hand on the side of his face and pulled him close for a kiss. His lips were as warm and full as they always were, but they were just dead meat as far as Claire was concerned.

"You're fine, baby," she said. "You didn't do anything at all."

"So where are you going?"

"I'm going to Melanie's house. Trevon needs help with his algebra."

"In the middle of dinner?"

"Are you going to miss me?"

He smiled.

"Stop acting like a baby," she said. "I'll be back in time to put the kids in bed."

"And then you can put *me* to bed?" He grinned perversely, and Claire saw the young Girl Scout superimposed over his features.

"Yeah, baby," she said. "Anything you want."

He slapped her on the butt on her way out, and Claire gritted her teeth and endured it. She never thought it possible, but even his touch sickened her.

And that was a rotten feeling; an awful, stinking feeling.

∂

The ride on the freeway felt like it was taking longer than yesterday. Claire found herself bouncing a knee and biting her nails. She called Melanie when she got on I-35.

"*My nigga*! You made it out?"

"Yeah. You still there?"

"I was getting ready to leave. I didn't know if you were going to call back or not. It's getting dark."

"Did they go inside yet?"

"Yeah."

"Damn."

"I took some pictures," Melanie said again, "of them *and* they mama."

"I really appreciate that."

"I told you, I got your back."

"You and Becky seem to have my back more than I do. I don't know how to thank you."

"Just as long as you break George's ass down to the *barest essentials* I'll be happy. Mostly I'm doing it 'cause I love you, but I also *can't stand* to see a man do a woman like that, especially a good woman like you. I want to go to court and see him crying like a baby. I want your lawyer to hold up one of those pictures, and I'm going to be like, '*Yeah! I took that one, nigga!*' "

Claire laughed. "So you're going home?"

"Not if you're coming. They're about to eat dinner. I can see her setting the table."

"You can see *inside their house*?"

"She's got her blinds open," Melanie said. "By the time you get here, it'll be dark enough for us to go in their front yard, but I've got binoculars, too."

Claire chuckled. "Oh, my God, Melanie. You're a fool."

"You need to hurry up."

"I'm coming," Claire said. "I'm doing eighty."

"Do ninety."

❦

Claire called her friend back when she exited on Story Road, and Melanie directed her the rest of the way. The mistress's neighborhood was as nice as Melanie described. Most of the houses were brick with circular driveways and St. Augustine lawns. The sun had almost set, but there was still a beautiful auburn tint in the horizon.

A few neighbors were out walking their dogs. Claire had to slow for a gang of skateboarders when she turned onto Stevens Court. She pulled to a stop behind her friend's Impala and crept from her Lexus like a Navy SEAL. She climbed in on the passenger side and looked around anxiously. Melanie frowned at her.

"Girl, what you doing?"

"This is crazy," Claire said. "I've got goose bumps."

"*And* you're sitting on my Snickers," Melanie informed her.

Claire raised up and pulled the squashed candy bar from under her. "*Eww!* Why didn't you tell me?"

"I just did."

Claire looked around for somewhere to put it, but *everywhere* looked like a trash. There were potato chip bags on the floorboard, empty soda cans on the backseat, and a huge turkey leg on the center console. It was skinned all the way to the bone.

"You got a little hungry?" Claire teased.

Melanie smiled pleasantly. "Girl, you know you can't do no stakeout without *food*."

Claire chuckled softly. She loved this woman; every pudgy pound of her.

"Just throw that anywhere," Melanie said.

Claire looked around uneasily before depositing it on the dashboard. She scanned the nearby houses anxiously. "Which one is it?"

Melanie affixed an evil eye on the house right across from them and nodded in that direction. "There that bitch go."

Claire leaned forward and peeked around her friend's heaving bosoms. "Oh, my God! You've been sitting *right here?*"

"Naw. I moved down here once the kids went inside."

"But still . . ."

"You know what I learned?" Melanie asked. "People don't live their lives looking over their shoulder and stuff. No one looks at every car on their street when they go outside. It ain't like the movies; mostly people just go on about their business."

Claire still didn't feel comfortable, but it was almost dark, and the house they were posted in front of had a

FOR SALE sign in the yard. At least no complaints would come from that direction.

"Here," Melanie said. She handed over a pair of binoculars, and Claire scrutinized them curiously. Nikki had a pair when they lived in Alaska, but that was a long, long time ago.

"Just point and look," Melanie directed her. "Roll that knob on top to focus."

Claire followed those basic instructions, and soon everything was crystal clear. George's mistress had a huge picture window at the front of the house, and the blinds were indeed pulled back. Claire saw a dining table set with both a main course and side dishes. There was a vase in the center filled with fresh flowers. There was a familiar woman sitting at the head of the table with her two children on either side of her.

Claire was mostly interested in the second child, but she zoomed in on the interloper instead. This woman was of the devil. She was the destroyer of all things good, but Claire still couldn't find anything physically wrong with her, and that was very frustrating.

George's other woman was dressed casually now in jeans and a T-shirt, and her hair was pulled back rather than flowing voluminously like a model's. But even without all the flair, she was very beautiful. She had smooth skin, an easy smile, and nice teeth. She was about Claire's height and at least thirty pounds leaner. Her breasts were perkier than Claire's. She didn't look any older than twenty-eight.

"You know them his kids," Melanie said.

Claire moved her sights to the offspring, glad for the distraction. The girl offered no new information; Claire studied Becky's pictures so thoroughly she could draw a portrait of George's illicit daughter. But seeing the boy was like getting the wrong anniversary gift all over again. He was definitely the girl's twin. Much worse, Claire felt like she was watching a younger version of her own son.

Melanie mistook her shock for disagreement. "You don't think those are George's kids?"

"I didn't say that."

"So you know they are, don't you?"

Claire watched the woman twirl spaghetti on her fork and consume it daintily. She chewed with her mouth closed and didn't have her elbows on the table. The kids didn't, either. They looked well behaved and well groomed. Claire looked away from the binoculars and met her friend's suspicious eyes.

"They look like George," she said.

"They *are* his," Melanie insisted. "Do you need to get closer for a better look?"

"No. I can see fine from here."

"So what's the problem?"

Claire looked away uneasily.

"What is it, Claire?'

"I already know what you're going to say."

"Say to what?"

Claire sighed and met her eyes again. "I still think we need more definite proof."

Melanie opened her mouth, but Claire stopped her.

"We saw George with her at the restaurant and at the school—but we never saw them hug or kiss. We never saw them go to a motel."

"Claire, you know—"

"*I know what I know!*" she cried. "But none of what I know is one hundred percent positive. We can't tell a judge, '*Well, they sure do look like his kids.*' "

Melanie nodded. "You got a point. Come on. Let's get some proof." She opened the door and started out of the car. Claire grabbed her arm.

"What are you doing?"

"It's some trash cans on the side of the house," Melanie said. "Let's go dig through 'em."

"*Eww!*"

Melanie leaned and reached to the back seat. She came back with a box of latex gloves and a few freezer bags. She dumped the supplies in Claire's lap and gave her a long, hard look.

"What's your excuse now?"

"Where'd you get these?"

"From my job."

"What, what are you—"

"We're going to get some *proof*," Melanie explained. "I'll take it to work and run the DNA."

Claire was flabbergasted. Melanie did work at a genetics lab, but she was a secretary.

"I'm not doing it *myself*," she said, reading Claire's expression. "I'll ask Nathan to do it for me."

"Who's *Nathan?*" Claire asked, still taken aback.

Melanie smiled. "He work in the lab. You remember when I used to work nights, back before I had Trevon?"

Claire nodded.

"Well," Melanie beamed, "I was going through some stuff with Anthony back then, and Nathan was always there at work. He was cool. We talked a lot." She cleared her throat. "And um, things got a little confusing for a minute there, when I got pregnant . . ."

Claire's jaw dropped.

"We got it figured out," Melanie said quickly. "Trevon is definitely Anthony's baby."

"*Melanie!*"

"Don't look at me like that. I went to church and prayed about it. Me and Anthony got past *our* paternal issues. You need to deal with yours."

Claire gave her a crazy look, but she put the gloves on. Melanie did, too.

Claire felt odd to find herself sneaking around the side of a strange woman's house—at seven thirty p.m., on a work night, when her kids were at home with homework that needed to be checked and baths that needed to be run—but it was no more odd than seeing George at a private school function with a camcorder in hand.

Melanie led her to the back door where there were two trash bins next to the steps. The blue one contained recyclables. The brown one had regular garbage. In this day of identity theft and credit scams, Claire didn't expect to find any unshredded letters in there, but people only destroy paperwork with confidential information on it. There was nothing confidential about the fact that Kimberly Pate graduated from Texas Lutheran University, so the discarded alumni newsletter was sitting right on top.

Melanie handed it to her, and Claire stared at it in silence. The *Kim* from the Hallmark cards finally had a full name. She had an address, and a face, and Claire even knew what her perfume smelled like. Claire knew what kind of soap the mistress bought for her household.

At that moment Claire understood that everything they suspected was true, but Melanie wasn't taking any more chances. From the brown trash bin, they bagged a pint-sized milk carton, a few Styrofoam cups, and a handful of small rubber bands with little hairs still tangled in them. Melanie would have preferred a toothbrush or hairbrush, but Claire desired nothing further; she had a face for the dreaded *Kim*, and, for now, that was all the torment she needed.

CHAPTER FIFTEEN
IT'S A GO

George had plans to take the kids to the track the next morning, and Claire was happy to be excluded from the venture. She sat on the corner of Stacy's bed with a hot curling iron crimped in her daughter's hair. Stacy wore a denim skirt with leather sandals. Her white T-shirt had the word *SPUNKY* doodled across the chest in yellow lettering. Claire wore a green terry bathrobe with fuzzy slippers. She also wore the look of a woman not long for this world. Nikki eyed her mom curiously from Stacy's computer desk.

"Are you going back to sleep?" she asked.

Claire looked over at her lackadaisically. "No. Why?"

"You look tired," Nikki observed, "like you're gonna pass out."

Stacy looked up with a start. "*Don't burn my hair!*" She held up a hand mirror and scrutinized her mother in the reflection.

"I'm not going to burn your hair," Claire assured her.

"Did you and Daddy argue last night?" Nikki wanted to know.

"What makes you say that?" Claire asked without looking away from Stacy's head.

"Y'all was mad at dinner," Stacy said.

"*Were* mad," Claire corrected. "And what did we do to give you that impression?"

"Y'all weren't talking," Nikki said. "You're usually happy when Dad eats dinner with us, but you weren't yesterday. Y'all just looked at each other crazy the whole time."

"And then you left," Stacy reminded her mother.

"In the middle of dinner," Nikki noted. "Where'd you go?"

Claire gave her a look then. "I'm pretty sure, no . . . Yeah! I remember now: *I* was in labor for seven hours giving birth to *you*—not the other way around."

Nikki rolled her eyes. "I know that."

"Stop trying to act like you're the mama, then," Stacy said. "Right, Mama?"

Claire grinned weakly.

"So, where *did* you go, Mama?" Stacy asked.

Claire thumped the back of her ear. "Hypocrite."

"*Ouch*! I'm not a hypocrite!"

"You don't even know what hypocrite means," Nikki ventured.

Stacy opened her mouth to say something and then shut it angrily.

"A hypocrite is someone who tells people not to do something, but then they turn around and do it themselves," Claire explained. "Like when America built all of those nuclear bombs and then got mad at any other country that tried to build nukes. And I went to Melanie's house last night, *nosey*."

"Was Trevon there?" Stacy asked with a slick grin.

"He doesn't like *you*," Nikki informed.

"Shut up."

"Was Aunt Melanie in trouble?" Nikki asked her mother. "Is that why you were mad?"

"Everything's fine," Claire assured her. "Why are you so concerned?"

Nikki shrugged. "I don't know. I don't like to see you and Daddy like that."

Claire stared into her daughter's soft eyes, and she felt a little guilty for last night's antics. Melanie had her focused so much on the *hate* that Claire forgot there were three innocent souls in the middle of all this. She knew that no matter what the outcome, the kids would still love and respect their father. The girls wanted to marry a man just like him, and George Jr. wanted to grow up and be his dad. Claire wondered how they would respond to her once she divorced their hero.

"I think you should go with us," Stacy suggested, "so you and Daddy can make up."

"What would I look like at a horse race?" Claire asked. "You know I don't like to see that. It's almost as bad as calf-roping."

"Daddy says they like it," Stacy argued. "He says they love to run."

"Of course thoroughbreds like to run," Claire admitted. "But they don't like those broken bones. They don't like to get old and unwanted."

"I never saw one break a bone," Nikki said.

"Look up Eight Belles," Claire suggested.

"Who?"

"Daddy says they get to relax and make babies when they're old," Stacy informed.

Daddy said he would forsake all others and keep hisself only unto me, Claire wanted to tell them.

"He doesn't know everything," she said instead, and the girls looked at her like she blasphemed.

Claire rolled her eyes at them. She frowned at an odd sound until she realized it was George Jr. stomping down the hallway. If she didn't know any better, she'd swear that boy was part camel. The little squirt paused in his sister's doorway and surveyed the scene cautiously.

For his day out with Dad, George Jr. wore peanut butter-colored canvas shorts with a white golf shirt and white sneakers. He took a hesitant step in his mom's direction, and Stacy responded like R. Kelly was crashing her slumber party.

"*Get out of here!*"

George Jr. made his usual retreat, but Claire was seriously taken aback. She knew the girls gave their brother a hard time, but she didn't know it had come to this.

"*Don't talk to him like that*," she snapped. "George, get in here."

Even under his mother's direction, George Jr. was tentative about encroaching on his sister's territory. Stacy scowled at him when he made it to the center of the room. Claire put down the curling iron and turned her daughter so she could see her face.

"Why are you talking to your brother like that?"

"He got—I mean he has his own room," Stacy said with a frown. "He doesn't need to come in here."

"What's wrong with him being in here?" Claire asked. "What's wrong with him visiting with you? You, too," she said to Nikki. "What's wrong with treating him like he's someone you love? Your family is the most important thing you have," she told the girls. "Never forget that."

"Your mama's right."

All eyes moved to the newcomer in the doorway. George Sr. wore a white golf shirt like his son. Recently awakened by morning pushups, his muscles stretched the fabric on his chest and shoulders. He wore baggy denim shorts with leather sandals and no socks. A dark blue baseball cap shaded his eyes.

"Never put *anyone* before your family," he said.

Rather than feel appreciation for his words, Claire felt angered and betrayed all over again. How dare he?

Here's one right here, she wanted to tell Stacy. *Your daddy's a perfect example of that hypocrite we were talking about.*

⌒⌒

Becky called later while Claire was scrubbing the tiles in the bathroom. She propped her cellphone on her shoulder and brushed a few wild hairs from her face.

"Hello?"

"Hey, Claire. What's going on?"

"Nothing much."

"Did George go to the races today?"

"Yeah. He took the kids. I've got the house all to myself."

"Do you want me to come by? We could make s'mores."

Claire chuckled. "You come up with the strangest ideas. But no, I think I'll pass. I've got a lot of cleaning to do—*Oh, my God*. You'll never guess what happened last night."

"Did George want to *do it*?"

"*Eww*. No."

"Did you tell him about the pictures?"

"No. Why would I do that?"

"Did you—"

"Wait—what are you doing?" Claire asked.

"I'm trying to guess what happened."

"Becky, when people say, '*You'll never guess*,' that doesn't mean they want you to start guessing. That means you're not going to guess, so they're about to tell you . . ."

"Really? I've been doing it the other way."

"That doesn't surprise me."

"Okay. Hurry and tell me what happened."

"Melanie called me at work yesterday and said she wanted to do another stakeout."

"*Goody*! I want to go."

"That was yesterday," Claire said. "We already went."

"Why didn't you tell me?"

"I wasn't going to go myself. It was a spur of the moment thing."

"Where'd y'all go?"

"Did you know Melanie stayed at that private school after we left?" Claire asked.

"No. I thought she was right behind us."

"So did I. But she waited for the program to end, and then she followed George and his girlfriend to her house," Claire informed her friend. "Last night Melanie called and asked if I wanted to go spy on her. I didn't at first, but she was already there so I went."

"You know where that lady lives?"

"I know more than that," Claire said. "First off, her name is *Kimberly Pate*, and she went to Texas Lutheran."

"*Wow!*" Becky exclaimed. "How'd you find that out?"

"We went through her trash," Claire said with no shame.

"You *what?*"

"I know. A lot of this stuff I wouldn't normally do. But it's like, no holds barred at this point. Anything goes, you know?"

"You and Melanie always do the *good* stuff."

"Wait till I tell you why we looked through her trash," Claire said. "You know that Girl Scout you took pictures of?"

"Yeah . . ."

"Well, she has a twin brother."

"*No.*"

"Yes."

"Oh, my."

"That's what I said!"

"George has two children?"

"Well, technically he has *five*, but yeah, he has two with that other lady."

"Claire, that's *terrible*. Are you all right?"

"I wasn't at first, but Melanie was there. She helped out a lot."

"So what else did you get out of the trash?"

"First we were looking for that lady's full name," Claire said. "After we got that, Melanie picked out a few things she thought the kids' DNA might be on."

"Oh, man . . ."

"You know Melanie works at that genetics place?"

"Yeah, but I thought—"

"She's a secretary, I know. But she knows a guy who works in the lab—that's a *totally* different story. The bottom line is she says she can check for DNA on the stuff we took and find out for sure if the twins really are George's. I already know they are, but we're going to get paperwork we can show a judge."

"This is *surreal*."

"You don't have to tell me. I feel like I'm in the Twilight Zone."

"George is a *monster*."

"Yeah. It's starting to look like it. Do you know the worst part?"

"There's *more*?"

"I can't stand the way he walks around here like everything is okay. Do you know what he told our kids this morning?"

"What?"

"He said, '*Never put anyone before your family.*' Can you believe that crap?"

"He's a piece of work," Becky mused.

"He's a piece of *something*," Claire agreed.

"I feel so bad for you."

"Don't," Claire said. "I feel better than I did last week. I know what's going on now, and I know what I have to do."

"So it's over?" Becky asked. "You're ready to go ahead with the divorce?"

"I think so," Claire said. "I've got his mistress' name. I've got her address, and I'm getting DNA evidence from her garbage analyzed."

"Analyzed," Becky said with a giggle.

"It's tripped out, right?"

"When are you going to call the lawyer back?"

Claire sighed. "I don't know. Sometime next week, I guess."

"Why next week? Don't you want to get it over with?"

"It's Saturday," Claire reminded her. "I can't call him today."

"Yes, you can. His office is open every Saturday."

"Oh, well, I still think I should wait till Monday."

"All right," Becky said, then, "hold on. I've got another call."

Claire didn't hear her phone clicking, but she didn't say anything. She listened to dead air for a few seconds, and her friend finally came back to the line. Oddly, Claire heard another phone ringing in addition to her friend's soft breaths.

"Becky, are you still there?"

"Yeah."

"What's that ringing?" Claire asked. "Did you call someone on three-way?"

Before Becky could respond, the third party picked up.

"Burns and Smiley."

Oh, no you didn't, Claire thought. She remained quiet, hoping Becky would say something, but her friend's lips were sealed. The silence was more than uncomfortable. Claire almost hung up.

"You've reached Burns and Smiley," the receptionist announced again.

Claire sighed. "So you're not going to say anything?"

"Excuse me?" the secretary asked.

"All right. *Hi*. My name is Claire Hudgens. I believe I spoke with you a few weeks ago. I'm Becky Adair's friend. She's actually on the line right now if you want to say hi."

"Um, Becky?" the secretary asked.

"Hi, Pat," Becky chirped. "How are you doing?"

"I'm fine. How are *you* doing? Is everything going okay?"

"Yes, thank you."

"How are the kids?"

"They're great. I'm calling to get an appointment for my friend, Claire. She met with Trevor once before."

"Oh, I remember," Pat said. "You're the one who was standing out in the hallway, afraid to come in the office?"

"I wasn't afraid," Claire said. "I was weighing my options."

"So you'd like to set up another appointment with Mr. Smiley?" Pat asked.

"Yes," Claire said. "I think Becky would like that very much."

The secretary laughed. "Alright. When would you like to come in?"

"As soon as possible," Becky said. "Her husband's *way worse* than Brent."

"I can get you in Wednesday," Pat said, "unless you want to come *today*. Mr. Smiley has an appointment at three, but until then he's just doing paperwork."

"She wants to come today," Becky said.

"You don't know what I have to do today," Claire said.

"What do you have to do?" Becky asked.

Claire couldn't think of anything, but still . . .

"So you'd like to schedule it for Wednesday?" Pat asked.

"No," Claire said. "I can come today."

"*Yay!*" Becky said.

"Would you like to come in at noon?" Pat asked.

Claire checked her watch. It was only ten-thirty. "I suppose so."

"All right," the receptionist said. "I'll let Mr. Smiley know you're coming. We look forward to seeing you."

"Thanks," Claire said.

"I'll talk to you later," Becky told Pat.

"Okay. You guys take it easy."

"You can be so persistent," Claire said when Becky hung up the other line.

"You'll thank me for it."

"I know. I can do that right now, actually. Thanks for being such a good buddy."

"Are you going to wear a skirt?" Becky asked.

"Why would I wear a skirt?"

"*I don't know,*" Becky hummed and abruptly disconnected the line.

Claire stared at the phone for a few seconds after she hung up.

CHAPTER SIXTEEN
WORKING LUNCH

As illogical as it was, Becky's advice was still on Claire's mind when she got out of the shower twenty minutes later. She had plenty of sensible pantsuits in her closet, but she pulled out a black skirt with white tropical prints instead. The garment was loose-fitting on her when she ordered it online some four years ago, but it fit like a glove today. Claire squeezed into it and liked the way the fabric stretched on her skin. She topped it off with a sleeveless white blouse and modeled the outfit in her bathroom mirror.

Claire knew she was attractive, but George had her feeling inadequate as of late. Claire thought about Ms. Kimberly Pate as she stared at her reflection. The mistress was definitely slimmer, but Claire thought her own full-figured curves were more appealing. She used to think George felt the same way.

Claire's breasts were definitely fuller than *Miss Thang's*, and her stomach wasn't all that pudgy. It didn't look bad at all in this outfit. Claire had a nice, slim waist that blossomed into ample, child-bearing hips. Plus she had legs for days. She turned and even liked the way her butt looked in the outfit.

I'll bet Trevor likes women with curves.

That thought didn't seem right at all, but Claire didn't question herself or change clothes before leaving the house.

The Mallick Towers were a lot less crowded on the weekends. Claire found a parking spot on ground level, right next to the elevators. She made it to the tenth floor in a matter of minutes and didn't have any of the anxiety she felt the first time she traipsed down that hallway.

Her nerves started to get the better of her when she got to suite 112, but she clenched her teeth and walked through the glass doors with no outward signs of the inner turmoil she felt. The receptionist looked up at her like she was a long-lost friend.

"*Mrs. Hudgens*! How are you today?"

Pat had her hair down, and the curly red locks took a lot of attention away from her acne issues. She wore a gray skirt with a white blouse this afternoon. She didn't look at all overwhelmed with her Saturday morning workload. She lounged lackadaisically with her elbow on the desk and her chin propped in the crook of her palm. She closed down a game of computer solitaire when Claire approached.

"You and Becky are *so crazy*," she said. "I wish all of our clients were like you guys."

"Becky's a nut," Claire agreed. "But I would have had a few mental breakdowns by now if it wasn't for her."

"I'm glad you've got someone," Pat said sincerely. "It sure is easier if you've got a friend you can lean on. I went through this myself five years ago."

Claire narrowed an eye. This girl didn't look old enough to have been married *and* divorced already.

"It was an odd situation," Pat said, reading her expression. "I was a freshman in college, young and naïve, and he was a student in South Africa. We met over the internet, and I flew over there twice to meet him. He seemed like a nice guy . . ."

"You *married* him?"

"At the time I didn't know he just wanted to get his U.S. citizenship," Pat explained. "I didn't know he was a womanizer, a liar, and a cheat, either," she mused.

"I'm sorry to hear that," Claire said.

"Oh, it's okay," Pat assured her. "We live and learn. There's no way you can truly know someone you met on the computer."

"You can grow old together and still not truly *know* someone," Claire informed her. "I've been married sixteen years, and look at me."

Pat opened her mouth to respond, but one of the office doors to their left swung open. Mr. Trevor Smiley stepped out, and all eyes moved in his direction. Today he wore khaki slacks with a long-sleeved, maroon button-down. His shoes were snake-skins, brown and cognac-colored. He stepped to the receptionist's desk with a stack of file folders in hand. When he saw Claire, he smiled with recognition.

"Mrs. Hudgens. How are you?"

"Not good," Claire admitted.

"I'm sorry to hear that," Mr. Smiley said. He stared into her eyes, and Claire met his gaze. His orbs were dark and comforting; Claire's were large and vulnerable. "Could you make a few calls for me?" he asked his secretary without looking away from his client. Pat took the folders from his hand and Mr. Smiley half-turned back towards his office. He held a hand out and gestured for Claire. "Right this way . . ."

She stepped past him and caught the scent of Joop cologne. She liked that fragrance. Smelling good is so important for a man. She wished more fellows understood that.

She walked into his office, and Mr. Smiley closed the door behind them. He went around to his side of the desk, but he didn't take his seat until she did. Claire couldn't explain why, but that gesture made her feel warm and safe, like she was in the company of a real man for a change. She crossed her legs and watched him nervously. He leaned back in his chair and rubbed his chin slowly.

Trevor had large, smooth hands; obviously strangers to the abuse of manual labor. His skin was dark like brandy, rich like an African prince. His hair was perfectly cropped, and the waves were still mesmerizing. Being with a bald man for so long, Claire forgot how attractive a full head of hair was.

"I was hoping I wouldn't see you again," he said.

Claire was glad to hear those words. It may have been part of his technique, but this lawyer was good at disarming. He made her feel like the three-thousand-dollar retainer wasn't his driving concern at all.

"I still wish I wasn't here," she said.

"Have you done more research?" he asked. "You definitely want to go ahead with the divorce?"

DIVORCE was still a big, ugly word, but the more Claire thought about *Kim*, the fewer negative connotations it had. "It's a go," she said. "My husband is definitely cheating on me."

The counselor nodded. He leaned forward on the desk with his hands together as if in prayer. "The last time I saw you, you showed me a card you found. Presumably that card came from his lover. And you said you saw him take a woman you don't know into a restaurant."

"Right." Claire forced a smile. "You've got a good memory."

"I remember your case," he agreed. "You're not an easy woman to forget."

Claire felt comforted by his words. She felt exhilarated, as a matter of fact, but this man made a living turning phrases. She didn't want to read too much into it.

"You said you were going to get more proof of George's infidelities," the lawyer went on.

"You remember his name, too?" Claire asked.

"You don't come across too many people as foolish as George," Mr. Smiley said. "It's kind of hard to forget."

Claire frowned then. "Wait, I need to get something off my chest. Some of the things you say, I mean, I don't want to take it the wrong way—"

He laughed. It was a rich, hearty chortle. "I know what you're thinking."

Claire waited.

"A lot of the women I represent are in the midst of the most severe emotional trauma they will ever encounter," he explained. "They hire me to make things right. They want me to exact revenge sometimes. They want me to punish their husbands. But mainly, it's been my experience that they basically want to feel better. By the time things get to a divorce, most women have been run through the mud. Their self-esteem is shot."

"So you say stuff like that to help their egos?" Claire guessed.

"I don't *lie* to them," Mr. Smiley said. "The wives who sit across from me don't know they're beautiful. They don't know they're worthy of greater things. They pay me to hurt their husbands, but most of the work I do doesn't show up on the bill."

"Becky told me about that," Claire said, a little put off. "I'll bet you get a lot of referrals."

"Don't think I'm using those tactics with you," Trevor said.

"You have said a lot of nice things," Claire reflected.

The lawyer shrugged. "I have flaws," he admitted. "I'm one-hundred-percent ready to take your case and do a great job with it, but, on the other hand, I'm a single man, and you're a beautiful, soon-to-be-divorced woman. I'm willing to hand your file over to my partner if this makes you uncomfortable."

Claire blushed. "No," she said. "I don't think that's necessary."

"I have *never* had a relationship with a client," the lawyer stated.

"I didn't say that."

"But I want you to know this doesn't happen to me often."

Claire was afraid to ask what *this* was.

The lawyer leaned back and smiled at her again. "Are you okay?"

Claire nodded, though she did feel quite warm.

"Would you like to continue with me?" he asked.

Continue with me might be laced with many innuendos. Either way, Claire responded, "Yes."

"Great." Mr. Smiley opened the file on his desk. "What do you want to tell me?"

Claire had no idea. She quickly scanned her memory bank. "Oh, *my husband.* I've been working hard on this, and I think I have the proof you need." She reached into her hobo bag and retrieved the new evidence. She laid a few items on Trevor's desk one at a time. He picked them up and scrutinized each one thoroughly.

"This is the card I read?"

"No," Claire said. "Here's the card you read." She held up the first Hallmark. "That's the second one I found."

He read it and looked up at her. "The first one is signed *Kim* too, isn't it?"

Claire nodded.

"This is great," he said. "Good stuff." He picked up the Texas Lutheran newsletter next. He regarded it oddly until he saw the address box on the front. His eyes grew large then. "Is this . . ." He reached for the card again and compared them.

"Kimberly is Kim," Claire confirmed. "I know where she lives."

He watched her eyes and grinned. "Wow. You're making my job easy . . ."

"I've got pictures of her, too," Claire said.

Mr. Smiley dropped the items in his hands and scooped up Becky's photographs like they were money. "Is your husband in any of these?"

Claire leaned over his desk and pointed. "He's that bald-headed guy right there. That woman next to him is Kim."

"Where's this?" he asked.

"Those pictures were taken at a placed called St. Martin's Academy," Claire informed him.

"What is that, some kind of—"

"It's a school."

The lawyer was perplexed, but Claire let the pictures do the talking. He looked up at her again when he got to the Girl Scout.

"Who's this?"

"That's the girl George went to the school to support," Claire said.

The lawyer flipped through the pictures again. "This is *Kim's* daughter?"

"Her daughter, George's daughter, my step-daughter . . ."

He frowned. "He has a child by this woman?"

"He has two children by that woman," Claire clarified. "That girl has a twin brother. I don't have his pictures developed yet."

"You, you found out all of this since the last time I talked to you?"

"I'm still waiting on DNA results, but yeah, I'm positive George is the father of that lady's twins."

Mr. Smiley sat the photos on his desk and stared at her curiously. "Back it up," he said. "You're saying your husband is not only cheating with this woman, but they have two illegitimate children together?"

"George has a secret family," Claire said calmly, shocked she could get the words out without crying. "My husband spends a lot of time away from the house, sometimes a whole week at a time. He says he's on business trips, but I don't think he's *ever* been on a business trip. I think he goes over to *her house* and lives there. He spends more time with me, but it's almost fifty-fifty. The twins are in the second grade, so this has been going on for a long time."

The lawyer shook his head. "This is outrageous."

Claire chuckled nervously. "You mean you don't get clients with this situation every day?"

"I've heard about it," he said. "But no one's ever come to *my* office with this, this *situation*. Does she know about you?"

Claire shook her head. "I don't know. But we moved down to Texas seven years ago. Those twins are in the second grade, so I think George brought her down from New York."

If Mr. Smiley was shocked by this, he didn't show it. He turned to a clean page in his ledger and found a good ink pen. "All right. Start from the beginning, and tell me everything you know."

Claire sighed. She sat up in her seat and let the whole tale spill, from the wrong anniversary gift to the stake-outs. When she was done talking, a full hour had passed, and the lawyer had three full pages filled with his chicken scratch. He sat back heavily and shook his head in disappointment.

"Well, Mrs. Hudgens, this is definitely one of the worst cases of adultery I've ever seen."

Claire figured as much. "Do you think I have enough evidence?" she asked. "I have more pictures being developed."

"I think you're on the right track," Trevor said. "If we can prove those twins are his, this case is going to be open and shut. You've done most of the hard part already."

"They're his," Claire said.

"If they're not, we can still—"

"*They're his*," Claire said more firmly, and he didn't question her again.

"All right," he said. "And your friend, Melanie, will be able to get official paperwork with the DNA results?"

"Everything will be in order," Claire promised.

Mr. Smiley beamed at her. "You've done a great job, Mrs. Hudgens. I have to say, I'm surprised."

"Why?"

"Most people think if you give a lawyer a lot of money, *he's* supposed to do all of this stuff."

"Well, you are, aren't you?" Claire teased.

"Yes, but it works a lot better when the wife is as motivated as I am. Plus if I billed you for all of that surveillance and DNA work, it would have been pretty hefty. You did good to take care of it yourself."

Claire smiled back at him. She was proud of herself. It was a tender, gratifying feeling.

Mr. Smiley checked his watch. It was after one. "Would you like to go over some of the finances and properties you'd like to recover? I was going to step out for lunch before I meet with another client at three."

"We can do it next week," Claire said. She gathered her things to leave.

"We can do it today," he offered, "if you'd like to have lunch with me."

Claire was ravenous, but that seemed *highly* inappropriate. The lawyer noticed her unease.

"I'll take my briefcase," he said with a smile. "And you can pay for your own meal."

"That still seems kind of weird," Claire admitted.

"All right, I'll pay for your lunch." He smiled brightly, and it was infectious.

Claire giggled. "That's not what I meant."

"I know."

"Mr. Smiley, I—"

"Call me Trevor."

"Trevor, I . . ." *I'm what?* Claire wondered. *I'm married?* That was a farce. *I'm in love with my husband?* That didn't seem to be the case anymore, either. *I'm faithful?* That was true, but why should she be? *I'm scared?* That was the most valid argument, but she was getting braver every day. And she was going to need a boatload of courage to follow through with a divorce of this magnitude.

"I would like that," she decided.

"Great!" He stood, and she did, too. On the way out of the office he placed a hand on the small of her back. It was only for a moment, but Claire felt a sensation in her heart and mind, and at that moment she knew she was in big, big trouble.

He led her down to the garage, and they left the tower in separate vehicles. Trevor wanted her to ride in his Town Car, but Claire told him she had an errand to run after their *meeting*. She followed him to a Red Lobster restaurant with a full understanding of the evil she was getting involved in, yet she felt powerless to stop it. It was as if her Lexus was tethered to the bumper of his Lincoln; even if she let go of the wheel, they were going to end up at the same place.

And to make matters worse, Trevor didn't open his briefcase at all during lunch. He nibbled his butter biscuits with those soft, juicy lips and eyed Claire like she was the main course. She told him about her and George's mutual properties and laid out her plans for total annihilation, and Trevor listened, but he seemed a bit preoccupied.

Halfway through her Seaside Shrimp Trio, Claire shook her head and laughed at him.

"What?" His eyes twinkled like an infant's.

"Don't you think this is a little *cliché*?" she observed.

"What do you mean?"

"Getting involved with the divorce lawyer?"

He grinned. "We're not *getting involved . . .*"

"You haven't touched your briefcase," she pointed out.

"I didn't want to spill food in it," he countered.

Claire rolled her eyes at him.

"I want to get to know you," he admitted. "I think you're beautiful, Claire. I think you're smart and resilient . . . *strong*. I've never met a woman like you."

"And I'm vulnerable," she pointed out. "You meet women all the time who're at the end of their marriages. Surely you've felt the same way about some of them . . ."

"I told you, I've never been involved with a client. You can ask my secretary."

Claire giggled. "I'm not asking Pat."

"Then you'll have to take my word for it," he said.

"It's a little hard for me to take any man's word for *anything* right now."

"I understand." He reached across the table and held her hand. His touch was comforting, but Claire responded as if shocked. She felt his energy shoot down her arm, into her chest and throughout her limbs. She even felt it in her toes.

"Let's just enjoy our lunch," he said. "I want you to be happy. I have no other agenda this afternoon."

Claire liked that. She relaxed and the time with him took on a calm and pleasant quality she hadn't felt in years, not since before she and George were married. Trevor told her about his college days and his decision to go to law school. He told her about his hobbies, his likes and dislikes. He told her how pretty she was more than a few times, and by the end of the meal Claire didn't remember how badly George had hurt her.

Trevor walked her to her car at two-thirty, and they lingered there awkwardly for a couple minutes. Claire wouldn't have kissed him if he tried, but she was curious as to whether he'd make the attempt.

He didn't, and they left the restaurant with *some* lawyer-client professionalism still intact.

CHAPTER SEVENTEEN
REGARDING TREVOR

The following Monday George embarked on one of his notorious *business trips*. Supposedly he was going to Anaheim, California, for six days. The Boeing plant there was in a transitional phase, and a lot of engineers from the Overbrook facility were going over to help with training and other technical support.

But Claire was a fool no longer. She knew he wasn't leaving the state—wasn't travelling more than forty-five miles as a matter of fact—so she played with his head a little while he got dressed that evening.

"Baby, do you want me to take you to the airport?"

He stuck his head out of the closet, buttoning the collar of his shirt. "Huh?"

"I said, '*Do you want me to take you to the airport*?'" Claire sat on the corner of the bed, packing his suitcase like she always did. She knew she was folding underwear for him to wear at his other wife's house, but she'd been doing it for sixteen years. He might get curious if she stopped now.

"Naw," George said and stepped back into the closet. "You know I like to leave my car there."

"Aren't you ever worried about it?"

His head poked out again. "Huh?"

"Are you ever worried about your car at the airport?"

He frowned. "Why would I be?"

Claire shrugged. "I don't know. It just seems like you'd feel safer with it here at home. I know how much you love that thing."

He ducked back inside. "Nothing's gonna happen to my Navigator. And the airport's way more secure than this house, if you want to know the truth."

"What about that robbery a few years ago?" Claire asked. "They took fifty million dollars worth of diamonds from that *highly secured* airport."

"That was a fluke," George retorted. "And they're even more secure now because of that."

Claire conceded, but that was okay. Her goal was not to win the argument; she just wanted to see how good a liar he was. "Are you going to go to the beach while you're there?" she asked next.

"Naw, baby. All work, no time to play."

"Oh. I wanted some beach sand," Claire said.

George stepped out of the closet again, tucking in his shirt this time.

"You want *what?*"

"Some sand from the beach," Claire said.

"You want me to grab some sand? What for?"

"I don't want you to scoop it up with your hand, silly. You know those souvenir things they make; it's like a plastic cup. They color the sand and pour it in layers. Actually, you don't have to get it from the beach. They have those everywhere in California."

"So you want me to bring you a souvenir?"

"Some sand."

"I can get you something," he said, "but I don't know if it will be sand."

"As long as it comes from California," she said.

Claire knew he could pull it off. He had six full days, and a couple of his old Air Force buddies lived in the golden state. If he could cover up an affair for eight years, surely he could get someone to FedEx him a cup of dirt. Claire didn't really care how he got it, so long as he got it. This was her war, and she could spark as many minor battles as she wanted along the way.

George left the house at seven that evening. Melanie called at ten after to say she was on his tail. He got on I-35 headed north, but Big George didn't take 121 towards the airport. He went east instead, headed for Irving, as everyone knew he would. Melanie stayed on his ass when he exited on Story Road. She followed him all the way to Kimberly Pate's house and took a few pictures of his car in her driveway.

A lot of the evidence they were collecting would become superfluous once the DNA results came in, but Melanie was like a woman possessed. They couldn't have reined her in if they wanted to. Plus Claire didn't want George to have an explanation for *anything*. She planned to bury him with a mountain of indisputable facts. She wanted to leave him awed, dazed, and confused. She wanted to laugh at him when he dropped to his knees and begged for mercy.

⌒

The next day, the girls decided to have a margarita night. The original plan was to meet at the Coco Lounge again, but Claire didn't want her kids to have two parents out gallivanting at the same time. Becky said she'd come over and help Claire make flautas, and Melanie was all for any activity that involved a tasty treat at the end.

Claire bought corn tortillas on the way home from work, and she had a whole chicken boiled by the time Becky showed up. Melanie had to go home after work and fix her family a meal, so she didn't get there until sunset. By then Becky, Nikki and Stacy were shredding chicken like authentic *cocineras*. Claire kicked the children out of the kitchen at eight and had the first batch of frozen margaritas ready by eight-fifteen.

By ten-thirty the kids were in bed, and the whole house smelled like a traditional Mexican eatery. The women lounged in the den with full bellies and altered levels of awareness. Martin Lawrence's *You So Crazy* DVD played in the background, but Melanie's recently developed pictures held center stage. They passed them around like vacation photos.

"Wow. She *is* pretty," Becky said, a drink in one hand, and a snapshot of Kim in the other.

Claire and Melanie shot mean looks at her simultaneously.

"I mean, she's *ugly*," Becky said. "You're definitely better-looking, Claire."

Claire reached over and snatched the picture from her hands. Ms. Kimberly Pate stood at the head of her dinner table, handing a saucer to her bastard son. Melanie leaned around Claire's arm to get a look.

"She ain't pretty."

"I know. I just said that," Becky informed her.

"You said—"

"Don't worry about it," Claire interrupted. "Whether she's attractive or not has nothing to do with what we've got going on."

"She's not, though," Becky said.

"Yes, she is," Claire said. "Y'all know she's pretty. *I* know she's pretty, and George knows she's pretty. That's why he's over there."

Melanie patted her friend's knee. "Are you okay?" she asked solemnly.

Claire frowned at her. "What? Do you think I'm going to cry over it?"

"She's done crying," Becky said.

"Yeah, but he's over there *right now*," Melanie reminded her.

"Thanks," Claire said sarcastically. "I keep forgetting."

"I'm just saying," Melanie went on, "You know *exactly* where your husband's at. You know who he's with. You know what she looks like. You've been to her house. That don't make it harder to live with?"

"It doesn't hurt anymore," Claire said honestly.

"Claire's got someone else on her mind," Becky explained.

Both Claire and Melanie's mouths fell open at the same time.

"*Bitch*!" Melanie hissed.

"I *do not* have someone else on my mind," Claire warned Becky.

"Who is it?" Melanie wanted to know.

"It's no one," Claire said.

"It's *Trevor*," Becky crooned.

"No, it's not," Claire said. "Becky, don't start telling that lie."

Melanie slapped Claire hard on the arm. Her eyes were wide and glossy. "Who's Trevor? Why didn't you tell me?"

"Ouch!" Claire said. "Girl, stop hitting me!"

"Why didn't you tell me?"

"Because there's nothing to tell," Claire said. "Becky thinks there's something going on with me and my lawyer. But I told her it's *nothing*." Claire gave her friend the eye. "I don't know why she won't just *drop it*."

"Tell her what he said," Becky urged Claire with an intoxicated grin.

"Becky, *stop*!" Claire gasped.

"What he say?" Melanie asked.

"There is nothing going on with me and my lawyer," Claire promised.

"What he say?" Melanie asked again.

Claire sighed. She frowned at Becky, then turned to face her other friend.

"Melanie, don't go over the deep end with this. I didn't tell you because it's nothing."

"It's *something*," Becky countered.

"It's *nothing*," Claire said.

"What he say?" Melanie bounced impatiently in her seat.

"He said she was beautiful!" Becky shouted over Claire's shoulder.

Melanie's mouth fell open again.

Claire turned and tried to glare at Becky, but she couldn't stop from smiling herself.

"Would you let me tell it? You make it sound all *sordid*."

Melanie grabbed her shoulder and whipped her back around. Claire felt like a ping-pong ball.

"Who are y'all talking about?"

"My lawyer," Claire said. "His name is Trevor Smiley."

Melanie frowned. "That's a stupid name. What is he, short? Does he wear glasses?"

Claire couldn't help but laugh at that. She shook her head while wiping her eyes.

"He's not short," Becky said. "He's tall, dark, and *ooh-wee* handsome!"

"He is," Claire admitted. "Mr. Smiley is a very good-looking man."

"And he likes you?" Melanie asked.

"He just said I was beautiful," Claire said.

"And he took her to lunch," Becky squeaked.

Claire couldn't believe it. "Is there anything you don't blab about?"

Melanie grabbed her shoulder again. "He took you to lunch?"

"It was a *business meeting*," Claire clarified.

"Yeah, right," Becky chirped. "That's why he didn't open his briefcase?"

Claire closed her eyes and shook her head. When she opened them, Melanie was still right there, waiting for an explanation.

"Okay," she admitted. "My lawyer kinda said he likes me."

It was funny watching Melanie's beady eyes grow.

"I *didn't reciprocate*," Claire said quickly. "He was saying a lot of nice things, and when I asked him why, he said he was attracted to me. He asked me if I wanted another lawyer, and I said no. Then I had a *business lunch* with him, so Becky thinks we've got something going on."

"They do."

"We *don't*," Claire said. "Now stop instigating."

Melanie couldn't speak for a few moments. When she could, she didn't want to talk to Claire.

"He fine?" she asked Becky.

"Oh yeah," Becky said. "He's sweet, and smart, and funny . . ."

"But is he *fine?*" Melanie asked.

"He's built like George," Becky said. "He's got a big chest, big arms, a big butt."

"*Ooh*," Melanie squealed. "I like a big butt!"

"It's not that big," Claire said.

"It's nice," Becky said. "He's all-around good-looking. If you saw him in the store or something, you'd definitely stop and do a double-take."

"Nnn, nnn. *Shame, shame, shame*, Claire," Melanie teased.

"Nothing's going on," Claire said again.

"Then why'd you go to lunch with him?" Melanie asked.

"It was supposed to be business," Claire said.

"Why you didn't leave when it wasn't?"

"I didn't want to be rude."

"Why you didn't tell him you wanted another lawyer when he said he liked you?"

"Because Becky said he was the best?" Claire offered, but no one bought it.

"You telling me you don't like him *at all?*" Melanie asked.

Claire didn't even have to say anything. They read her look, and that was enough to get the girls going again. Claire sat back and marveled at their yip-yapping. She knew that no matter what she said, they were going to believe whatever they wanted to believe anyway. Plus they were so close to the truth, there was really no sense in trying to argue them down.

Before her friends left for the evening, Claire went up to Nikki's bathroom and snatched one of her old tooth-brushes from the holder. She gave it to Melanie so she could get her friend at work to compare the DNA to the unknown samples from Ms. Kimberly Pate's garbage. The rubber bands they pilfered didn't have enough roots attached to the hairs to retrieve a sample, but the milk carton and Styrofoam cups still looked hopeful. Melanie said they would know for sure if the twins were George's within a week or so.

CHAPTER EIGHTEEN
CALIFORNIA SAND

The next day, Claire left work a few minutes early so she could drop off her retainer to Mr. Trevor Smiley. He wouldn't file any paperwork until the bloodwork came back from Melanie, but there were a lot of preliminary things he wanted to get started on.

Claire wrote the check from her personal account, but she had to take fifteen hundred dollars from their joint savings to cover it. George wasn't too involved with the bill-paying side of their marriage, but he did check their balances every so often.

Claire knew it was a gamble, but fifteen hundred was a pretty small percentage of the bulk they had in there. Plus George had a birthday coming up in a couple of months. If worse came to worst, Claire could say she was planning something very special for him. Technically, that wasn't even a lie.

Before she left his office, Mr. Smiley reached to shake her hand. Claire offered it, and he stared longingly into her eyes when he shook. Claire knew his advances were serious, but she didn't have him figured out yet. She'd been out of the dating game for a long time; almost two decades. She had no idea what men really wanted anymore. She was pretty sure she didn't want to find out. But then again . . .

"What do you want from me, Trevor? *Seriously* . . ." she asked him.

The lawyer leaned back against his desk and smiled warmly. He wore a suit today. The coat and slacks were a soft maroon. His shirt was tan. He was smooth, poised, and confident.

"That's not a fair question."

"Why not?"

He shook his head. "Because if I say *I just want to be friends*, you'll know I'm lying. And if I say anything *but* that, then I'm out of line. You're a married woman, Claire. You're not even separated yet. And as soon as your check clears, you're officially my client. I'm not in a position to want anything at all from you."

"So why do you persist?"

"Why does a moth chase a flame that might devour him?" he asked. "I can't explain my actions anymore than he can. All I can say is this: When you walked out of my office after that first meeting, I *knew* you were a good woman. I knew you were beautiful, strong, kind, and intelligent. I didn't think it was possible for a man to cheat on you. I thought you would discover you were wrong, and I'd never hear from you again."

Claire listened intently and she watched his eyes. She didn't believe he was lying.

"When you came back," Trevor went on, "I was torn. I knew how much it hurt you to find out your suspicions were true, but I also believed you deserved a better man who would never cause you pain like that. I felt that right away. I told you, George is stark raving mad to disrespect you in this manner."

"But what do you want?"

"I want to make you happy," the lawyer said. "I know it's wrong. I know I shouldn't. I'm going to win this case for you, and if that's the only happiness I can ever give you, I'll accept that. But you're no old maid, Mrs. Hudgens. It may not feel like it right now, but you *will* date and probably marry again. That may not be any time soon, but when you're ready, I'd sure like to take you out sometime." He threw up his hands. "That's it. That's my story; the whole truth."

Claire liked his answer, but this guy was starting to sound too good. "I think you're a player," she said.

He chuckled softly. "A *player*? No, ma'am. I grew up in a household with seven sisters and no brothers. Plus my dad left when I was two, so I was the only boy in our home. I respect women to the utmost. I've never hit a woman or cheated on one. I've broken a few hearts in my time, but I was the recipient of the heartbreaks more often than not. Girls used to tell me I was *sensitive*. They thought I was the nice-guy type—which wasn't so good, considering I grew up in the ghetto."

Claire smiled. "Well, if you're such an all-around good guy, why are you not married yourself?"

"I was," Trevor said, and his smile went away completely. "My wife died of breast cancer four years ago."

Claire felt bad for being so nosey. "I'm sorry."

"You had no way of knowing," he said. "I've dated a few women since then, but none who struck me as *marriage* material. The game's changed a lot since I was young. A lot of women don't like to cook nowadays. They don't like to take care of kids. They act like I cursed them out when I ask them to do my laundry."

Claire laughed.

"The game's going to be a lot different for you, too," Trevor warned. "There aren't too many straight-laced, hard-working black men out there."

Aye, there's the rub.

"So you think I should hook up with you so I don't waste my time searching."

He grinned. "I knew you were smart."

"I'm married, too."

"I'm working on that."

"Well, let's take care of that first," Claire said. She knew she was giving him hope, but what was wrong with that? George had a whole family on the side. Maybe she should have an ace in the hole as well.

"Do you ever look at my card?" he asked. "There's a cell phone number on there. That's my personal line. I have it with me all the time."

"I'll keep that in mind," Claire said.

She left his office with a tight squeeze in her stomach, and it didn't go away until she got to her car. She sat behind the steering wheel breathing slowly, trying to calm her heartbeats. She knew it was wrong to carry on with her lawyer in that manner, but it was thrilling, and it was *different*. Nothing George could do right now would put a smile on her face, but when Trevor said she was beautiful, Claire felt like she might float out of the room. And she believed he meant it, too.

She wouldn't call his personal number, but a fine man like Mr. Smiley could compliment her as often as he wanted. If that violated some lawyer/client protocol, then so be it. She sure as hell wasn't going to be the one to report it.

⌒

With the retainer paid, Claire knew the façade of her happy marriage would collapse in a matter of weeks rather than months. She felt it was time to have a long talk with the only parties still left in the dark, but discussing DIVORCE with the kids was a worst case scenario. How do you tell them their life is going to be altered in ways that might still affect them twenty years from now? How do you explain that their father is not the fair and honest man they looked up to?

Originally, Claire wanted to wait until the papers were filed. George would move out, and she could sit her babies down and explain why Daddy was never coming back home. But Becky thought that might be too much of a shock, especially if they didn't think Mom and Dad had problems previously. Claire definitely wasn't ready to tell them today, but she thought she'd test the waters a little bit.

She started with George Jr. since he was the first one to be picked up. She pulled in front of Wedgwood

Elementary and got out so she could stand under the large awning that shaded the front door. The bell rang a few minutes later, and the students started marching out in orderly lines, headed by their teachers. George Jr. rushed from the pack as soon as he saw his mother.

"Hey, Mama!" He threw his arms around her waist, and Claire patted his back.

"Did you tell your teacher you're leaving?" she asked.

"I saw him," a flustered Mrs. Flores called over her shoulder. She turned quickly to yell at another student. "*Justin!* Justin, get over here! Sit down! *I mean it!*"

Claire walked away hand-in-hand with her little one. "You don't hang around with Justin, do you?" she asked.

"No, I don't like Justin. He never shuts up, and he *never* makes good grades. He can make milk squirt out of his nose, though."

"Well that's special," Claire quipped.

"I know," George Jr. said. "He's got a girlfriend and *everything*."

When they got to the car, Claire found she didn't have to work too hard to get little George's opinion of his dad. She didn't even have to initiate the conversation, as a matter of fact.

"Is Daddy coming home today?"

"He just left a couple days ago," Claire said. "Do you miss him already?"

"Yeah."

"Why?"

"Huh?"

"Why do you miss your Dad?"

He shrugged. "I don't know. Because I love him?"

"Are you asking me or telling me?"

"I'm telling you," he said. "Don't you miss Daddy?"

"We're not talking about me. Tell me, what do you like to do with your Dad?"

"I like when he's not at work and he can take us to the race track, and sometimes he takes us fishing. He taught me how to swim, and we swimmed in the lake before."

"You *swam* in the lake," Claire corrected.

"Oh yeah, swammed."

Claire giggled. "What about when he's gone all the time?" she asked.

"I miss him."

"What if he left one day and didn't come back to live with us anymore?" she asked with a straight face.

George Jr. had to think about that. "Why not?"

Claire shrugged. "I don't know. Maybe he wanted to live somewhere else . . ."

Now he was confused. "Why would he do that?"

"I don't know," Claire said. "I'm just asking how you think you would feel about it if that happened."

"If he didn't come home?"

"Mmm, hmm."

"Could I go live with Daddy, too?" he asked.

Oh, God, Claire thought. She'd forgotten that was even an option. "No, you'd still be with me."

"Why couldn't we all stay with you?" he asked. "I don't like it when Daddy doesn't come home." He folded his arms and pouted.

"Daddy *is* coming home," Claire said, realizing what a total mess this was. "I was just asking a hypothetical question."

"What's *hypothetical?*"

"It's when you ask a question that can't really happen. Like if I asked you, 'Would you like it if you had cauliflowers for ears?' "

She tugged his earlobe and he giggled.

"There's no way you could have cauliflowers for ears," Claire said. "That's why it's called a *hypothetical question.*"

She was glad to get the smile back on his face, but George Jr. never came across a bit of new knowledge without sharing. As soon as Stacy got into the car, he showed off his new word.

"I got a hypo-medical question." He turned and grinned at her. "What would you do if Daddy didn't come home?"

Claire's mouth dropped open, and she stared at him with wide eyes. But the damage was done. Stacy's face fell also. She glared at her mom in the rearview mirror.

"Daddy's not coming home?"

"Daddy's coming home," Claire assured her daughter.

"Did he get in a plane crash?" Stacy asked.

"No."

"Train wreck?"

"*No.*"

"Hurricane Katrina?"

"No! Girl, where are you coming up with this stuff?"

"That's how they did my friend when her brother died. Instead of coming right out with it, they asked how she would feel if he didn't come home anymore."

"Well, that was wrong," Claire said, "but there's nothing wrong with your father. I talked to him earlier today. And Hurricane Katrina was a one-time thing. You can't get the same hurricane twice."

Stacy kicked the back of George's seat. "Why you playing?"

"I'm not playing. Mama asked *me* that."

Stacy's angst went back to her mom. "Mama, why'd you ask us that?"

"I didn't ask *you* anything," Claire pointed out. "I asked George Jr. And I didn't tell you to ask your sister," she scolded her son.

"But are you asking because it really is happening?" Stacy asked.

"No," Claire said.

"So there's nothing wrong with Dad?"

"Nothing."

"He's not dead?"

"I *promise* you, he's not dead. He's just fine, and he'll be back in less than a week. So can we just drop it?"

They did, until Nikki got in the car.

"I got a *hypo-medical* question," George Jr. announced as soon as she sat down.

"What did I tell you?" Claire snapped.

"Oh yea."

"What?" Nikki asked.

"Nothing," Claire said.

"Mama asked George what he would do if Daddy didn't come home," Stacy blurted.

Claire couldn't believe her ears.

"Daddy's not coming home?" Nikki asked.

Rather than exit the parking lot, Claire pulled up the emergency brake. She turned in her seat so she could look at all three of her crumb-snatchers at the same time.

"Your father will be home in *four days*," she told Nikki. "He's not dead," she told Stacy. "And I was just making conversation," she told George Jr. "If I would've known it was going to turn into this, I wouldn't have said anything. So we're going to drop it, okay?"

Everyone nodded.

"I'll let you guys call him as soon as we get home."

"I wanna talk first," George Jr. shouted, and that seemed to settle things.

Unfortunately, none of Claire's children rode the short bus to school. Nikki crept into her mother's room a little after eleven that night. Claire was lying down, but she wasn't asleep yet. She was actually daydreaming, thinking about her two-timing husband. She wondered if he was making love to Ms. Pate at that exact moment, or if they were simply in bed together snuggling and spooning.

Nikki sat on the corner of her mother's mattress wearing the long Scooby Doo shirt she slept in. Claire sat up and studied her forlorn features.

"What's going on?"

"Nothing."

"Why aren't you in bed?"

"I wasn't sleepy." Nikki always looked somewhat depressed, but she appeared to be on the verge of tears now.

"Come here." Claire patted the spot next to her. Nikki got up and sat closer. Claire put an arm around her and touched her cheek with the back of her hand. "Are you feeling okay?"

"I'm not sick," Nikki said.

"So what's going on?"

"Are you still mad at Dad?" she asked, and Claire knew she should have kept her mouth shut earlier.

"Is that what's bothering you? You still thinking about what your brother said?"

"Why'd you ask him that?"

Claire hated to be dishonest with her children. She didn't think she could even pull off a lie of this magnitude. "Is Stacy still tripping about that, too?" she asked.

"No."

"Then why are you?"

"Stacy's still a kid," Nikki informed. "She doesn't understand things."

"Oh, and you do?"

"I'm *fourteen*."

"Really?"

Nikki frowned at her.

"Listen," Claire said, "I know you think you're a big girl, but you're not so old. You've still got a lot of growing up to do. Take your time and enjoy it."

"I will," Nikki promised, "*after* you tell me what's going on with Daddy."

"Your father's fine," Claire said.

"Are y'all getting a divorce?"

Claire almost choked on her own tongue. "Uh, ahem—where did you get *that* idea?"

"If there's nothing wrong with him, why else wouldn't he come home?" Nikki asked.

"He *is* coming home," Claire said. "I told you that. You talked to him just today."

"Tell the truth, Mama. I know you and Dad have been mad at each other. And then you asked George how he would feel if Daddy didn't come home."

Claire wondered if she had a child psychology book in the office somewhere. If so, she should have read it before free-styling with such a delicate subject. "Married people don't get divorces just because they're mad at each other sometimes," Claire said. "Your dad's fine, and he's coming home, and I wish I never said anything. It was just a hypothetical question that got blown all out of proportion."

"*Hypo-medical,*" Nikki teased.

"Right, hypo-medical," Claire said with a smile. She pulled her daughter close and held her tightly. "It's time for you to go to bed. You feel better?"

Nikki nodded, and it broke Claire's heart to comfort her child with a fib. This wasn't Santa Claus or the Tooth Fairy. This was a real live grown-up lie that was going to bite her in the ass within a month. She wondered if her daughter would hold it against her when the bottom finally fell out from under them.

"I love you, pumpkin," she said and kissed her temple softly.

"I love you, too, Mama," Nikki said and squeezed a little tighter.

⌒〇⌒

The next four days without George were nothing special to the kids, but Melanie's prediction took hold and became an actuality for Claire. It was nearly impossible to get her adulterous husband off her mind. Claire wondered if Ms. Kimberly Pate cooked big breakfasts for George. She wondered if Kim liked to jump on him after his morning push ups like his real wife used to.

During the sunlight hours Claire was able to occupy her mind with trivial things, like work, cooking and child-rearing. But at night she tossed in her sheets like a ship lost in a storm. Claire knew exactly what George's mistress looked like, and that travesty helped her imagine awful, horrible things. When she closed her eyes at night, Claire not only saw them making love, but she saw candle wax, rose petals and satin sheets.

Before George gave her the wrong anniversary gift, he could make Claire smile with just a goofy look or a simple gesture of kindness. It broke her heart to know that he was making another woman smile with his silly antics. George used to play with Claire's toes when they were spent and exhausted but still caught up in the raptures of love, and she wondered if he bonded with Ms. Pate in this way.

Imagining the sex was torment enough, but it was the little things that set Claire's soul on fire.

She didn't think it was possible to literally *hate* her husband, but by the time George returned from *California*, Claire wanted nothing to do with him. He came in at dinnertime wearing tan shorts with a white shirt and a brown Cuban fedora. He had his suitcase in one hand and a large paper bag in the other. The kids left their seats and rushed to him like he was returning from war.

"Daddy!"

He picked up his son with one arm and threw the other one around his daughters. He smiled brightly and passed out kisses like candy. "Heh, hey! You guys miss me?"

"*Yes!*" they screamed in unison. "What'd you bring us?"

"Whoa! I thought y'all missed *me!*" he said with a big grin. "Well, come on over here and let's see what we got." He moved to the dining room with three monkeys hanging on his arms. "Hey, baby," he said to Claire. "I got something for you, too."

He put the bag on the table and the kids crowded around like it was Christmastime. "These are for my *middle child*," he said, producing a pair of leather sandals with large soles and long straps. Stacy grabbed the shoes and pirouetted like a ballerina.

"Thanks, Dad!"

George Jr. got a remote-controlled Hummer, and Nikki got a new journal, complete with pens, bookmarks, and a small locking mechanism. Claire made a mental note that none of those gifts necessarily came from California, but George didn't pull off a decade-long affair by being foolish. The next item he retrieved from his big bag of treats was a plastic bottle filled with sand, just as Claire had requested. The sand was layered and colored blue, yellow, purple and pink.

"Here, baby. I don't know what you want this for, but I'd do anything for you."

Claire took it and forced a smile as best she could.

"I got something else for you," he said, still digging in the bag. He produced a jewelry box this time, and it suddenly struck Claire that George *always* brought her a nice gift when he came back from his long business trips. He opened the box for her, but the glimmer from the gold bracelet was all but lost in a fire that raged behind Claire's pupils.

This asshole's trying to buy me off, she realized. Just like the husband who brought flowers after giving his wife a black eye, George was trying to lessen the guilt he felt for living with his second family for the past week. Claire felt like an idiot for letting him do this to her for so long. How many times had she run to mirror with a new trinket while Kimberly Pate's perfume lingered on his lapel?

"Thank you," she said.

"What's wrong? Don't you like it?"

"I do. It's fine."

"Well, I'm glad I'm home," George said with a hearty grin. "Shouldn't have to go back for a week or two."

"That's fine," Claire said numbly, knowing that if everything went the way she wanted it, the next time he went to Irving it would be a permanent move.

CHAPTER NINETEEN
A NIGHT AT MILLE FLEURS

George returned from his bogus California trip on a Tuesday. After spending six full days with his mistress, Claire thought he might want to give his *real* family a little quality time, but no such luck. He worked late the following Wednesday and Thursday. When he called from the job on Friday and said he was playing poker with the guys that night, Claire nearly lost it. She didn't care about his attention personally, but their kids certainly deserved better. No way should those bastard twins get top-billing.

"What do you mean you're *playing poker*?"

"Today is Friday, baby. I always play poker on Friday."

Claire was in the process of making eggplant parmesan for supper. She had to put her steak knife down because it was shaking in her hands, and the large vegetable was starting to look like George's face.

"No, you don't," she grunted. "You didn't play last week."

He chuckled. "That's 'cause I was out of town."

"So you don't *have* to go," Claire said. "It's not going to kill you to bring your ass home."

"What?"

Claire had to catch herself because none of her reasoning could be revealed at this time. She had no cause for anger as far as he knew.

"You got back in town Tuesday," she said. "And you haven't eaten dinner with your children since."

"I haven't played with the guys in a while," George countered. "Maybe I haven't eaten with the kids this week, but I do see them *every day.*"

"They can pull out a photo album if all they wanted was to *see* you."

"What is it with you?" George asked. "You've got to be the most wishy-washy woman I know."

"What are you talking about?"

"Claire, I don't know what your deal is, but you haven't been very happy to be around me lately. When I got back Tuesday, you looked like you wanted to put me right back on the plane."

Plane, my ass.

"What's that got to do with the kids?" she asked, and the words rang in her ears with a backwards déjà vu quality. Rather than feel like she'd asked that question before, it felt like a phrase she was destined to repeat many times in the future.

"Why don't you tell me what's wrong with you," George offered. "Let's start there."

Claire couldn't imagine being more aggravated. So many things were on the tip of her tongue; so many devastating, tragic, and life-altering sentences were just *begging* to be screamed, but she couldn't voice a one of them.

"Nothing's wrong."

"*Mmm-hmm.* You've been saying that for quite awhile. I guess nothing was wrong last night, either."

"What about last night?"

"I massaged your back," George reminded her. "I tried to get your pants off. You don't remember any of that?"

Claire did remember, and it caused her a bit of revulsion to think about it now.

"Do you want to tell me what the deal is?" he asked.

"There's nothing wrong with *me*," Claire said.

"Good," George said. "Then I'm playing poker tonight. If you decide maybe you want to tell me what's going on, let me know."

He hung up and Claire slammed the receiver on the counter so hard she hurt her hand. She stood over the sink fuming, rubbing her sore digits. There were a lot of people she could call for support at a time like this, but neither Melanie nor Becky had what Claire needed right then. Instead, she went upstairs and fetched a business card from her purse.

George got home from work at six-thirty. He headed straight for the bedroom to change for his poker night. By then the kids were already fed and Claire was on her way out. She wore a white cocktail dress that flashed a lot of skin about the chest and back. The gown stopped right at her knees, and her stockingless legs were smooth and alluring. She had her hair down in lose curls. She wore mascara and peach-colored lipstick. Her fragrance was soft, and she exuded confidence.

The look on George's face when he saw her almost made up for his whole affair.

"*Claire*? Buh-baby, you're looking real good."

"Thanks." She stood before their bathroom mirror putting on the journey pendant he gave her for their anniversary. This was the first time she ever wore the thing. She couldn't think of a more fitting occasion.

"You, you didn't call back," he said. "I'm going to play poker tonight. You know that, right?"

She rolled her eyes at his reflection. "I know you're not going to be here. I heard you just fine."

"So what's with, where . . ."

"I'm going out, too," Claire said.

"With who?"

"*Becky*," she said with no hesitation. It was uncommon for Claire to lie about her whereabouts, but she didn't feel guilty at all.

George stepped into the bathroom with her. Claire turned and tried to slip by him. He grabbed her arm when she passed, and Claire jerked it away roughly.

"Let go of me."

They stood, staring at each other for a moment, and then she stepped past him again. She scooped her purse from the bed without stopping, but George sprinted ahead and cut her off at the stairs.

"Baby, stop. Tell me what's going on."

Claire couldn't believe he had the nerve. This was like the fox asking the hen, '*What did I ever do to you?*'

"You're going to play poker," she said. "What do you care what I do?"

George never faced such opposition in his marriage, and it showed. He looked stressed and flustered. His wife was *easy* to manage. He didn't know what to make of this woman.

"Is that what this is about? I can stay home, Claire. If you want to be with me, I won't go."

Kim won't like that. The words were on the tip of her tongue, but she swallowed them down. "It's too late," she said instead. "Becky's meeting me, and she already left her house."

"Who's gonna watch the kids?"

"Nikki's fourteen," Claire said. "We have to stop treating them like babies. She's old enough to look after them."

George reached out and grabbed her wrist again. "I said I'll stay home," he said more sternly.

Claire was about to tell him what he could do to himself, but their oldest daughter stepped into the hallway. Nikki was already suspicious enough. Claire smiled and embraced her man.

"I'm sorry," she said close to his ear. "I already made Becky get dressed, so I have to go."

George smiled, too. He wrapped his arms around her and palmed her butt unabashedly. "You're not doing this 'cause you're mad at me?"

"I'm not mad at you, baby. I love you." She poked his stomach playfully. "Now stop that. Nikki's standing right behind you."

He let go of her and turned to grin at the curious girl. "Hey, hey! I hear you're going to be holding down the fort tonight."

"I'm almost fifteen," Nikki announced with a bright smile.

"*Fifteen?*" George sounded truly surprised. "Girl you're old enough to get your *own* babysitting jobs. Wouldn't that be nice, honey, if she could start bringing some money in every once in a while?"

"That'd be great," Claire said, but she was halfway down the stairs by then, and she didn't stop. "I'll see you later," she called over her shoulder.

Mille Fleurs was the hottest French restaurant in the city. There was a lot on the menu Claire was unsure about, so she ordered *magret de canard roti*, which turned out to be a delicious roasted duck breast over raspberry vinegar sauce. Trevor had *pave de boeuf Rossini*, which was a sautéed beef filet with *foie gras* (goose liver) and truffles with *Madeira* sauce. Claire thought he was making a big mistake when he made the order, but he let her taste some of it when their plates arrived, and she had to admit it was scrumptious.

For his date this evening, Mr. Smiley wore a black suit with a red shirt and a black tie. His tie clip was gold, with one diamond in the center. His cufflinks were gold as well. They glistened every time he brought a forkful to his mouth. His eyes were bright and glistening. His smile was fresh and confident. His briefcase was nowhere to be seen.

Claire took a dainty sip of her wine and dabbed her lips with a cloth napkin. She looked up at her date and smiled, and her heart fluttered slightly. Trevor seemed to be watching her every move. He took a sip of his liquor and cheesed pleasantly.

"I like your lips," she told him.

He cocked an eyebrow. "Excuse me?"

She smirked at him. "You heard me."

He smiled. "I did, but if I'm not mistaken, that's the first compliment you've ever paid me."

"It is," Claire agreed.

"Well, I feel grateful."

"You should."

He chuckled. "So, to what do I owe this honor?"

"George, of course," Claire said. "Every day I despise him a little more."

"Then let's not talk about him," Trevor said. "Tell me something else you like about me."

Claire giggled. "You never struck me as the insecure type."

"I'm not asking because I want you to feed my ego," he replied. "I just want to know if you really like me, or if you're running to me because you have something terrible at home."

"I like you," she said. "I wouldn't be here if I didn't."

He leaned forward with his elbows on the table. "Okay, then tell me what you like about me."

Claire stared dreamily into his eyes. "Well, you know you're a handsome man."

"Oh, please go on . . ."

She giggled. "I like your eyes," she said. "I like your skin tone. I like the waves in your hair. I think about touching them all the time."

"See. I definitely didn't know that. Would you like to touch them now?"

"Not in a restaurant," she said flirtatiously.

"Maybe I could let you do that later," he said suggestively.

Claire knew she should shoot him down, but she didn't. "Maybe."

"Is there anything else you like about me?" he asked.

"Are you sure you don't have low self-esteem?"

"Do you like it when I compliment you?" he asked.

Claire nodded and blushed a little.

"Should I feel any different because I'm a man?" he asked.

"No. I guess not."

"Then stop giving me a hard time," he said good-naturedly.

"Okay," Claire said. "You're smart and professional. I like that about you. I like the way you dress. I like your smile. You're smooth and self-assured."

"I work out at Bally's, too," he kidded.

"I was getting to that," Claire said, but the thought of his physique embarrassed her even more. "Trevor, you know you're fine. You don't need me to tell you you've got it going on."

"You're the one who's got it going on," he said. "Shall *I* elaborate?"

"You'd better."

He smiled. "Well first off, you're pretty in the face, a natural beauty. And you're definitely the sexiest woman to ever step foot in my office. That first time you came in with your legs showing . . ." He looked up to the high heavens. "I almost lost it right then. And I'm not even a leg man."

"What kind of man are you?" Claire asked. That was bold for her, but Trevor was good at disarming. He made her feel like anything goes.

"What do you mean?"

She frowned. "Don't go getting all tight-lipped now."

He looked around nervously, and then pulled at the collar of his shirt. He looked around again, and his glance paused on her breasts for a second. Claire laughed at him.

"All right, you don't have to say."

"Either way," he said, "you've got it. No matter what kind of man I am. That's why I don't understand your husband's motives."

"I thought we weren't going to talk about him," Claire reminded.

"I think you're a strong woman," Trevor said. "You remind me a lot of my mom. She raised all of us by herself. She worked, but she made sure she was there for us most of the time. She had to get government assistance to cover the bills, but she was still proud. She made sure all of us did well in school. Of her eight children, six of us graduated college. The other two dropped out, but at least they went."

"That's incredible," Claire said.

"I know. My mom died three years ago. Just one year after Michelle."

Claire knew it must have been hard to lose two loved ones so close to each other, and it showed. Trevor was immediately downcast. Claire felt her own heart sinking.

"Was Michelle your wife?"

He nodded. "She was a teacher. She worked at Sam Houston in Arlington. You should have seen her funeral. There were so many kids. I think almost the whole school was there. She was a good woman. One in a million."

Trevor looked up at his date and smiled weakly. "Look at me carrying on. I know you don't want to hear about that."

"It's okay," Claire said, feeling a little misty-eyed herself. "I don't mind."

He shook his head and grinned sheepishly. "It's stuff like *that* that gives me the misconception of me being sensitive."

"All men can't be cavemen," Claire said with a smile. "Who would open the doors for pretty ladies?"

They talked about his family a little more, and Claire was obliged to tell him about her little ones. Trevor was a good listener. Some of that may have come with his profession, but he wasn't the type to say whatever he thought a woman wanted to hear. He was honest and frank. His interest in Claire was genuine.

255

They drank more wine and eventually returned to the inevitable topic of *George*, but Trevor didn't consistently down her husband. They talked about her case more than anything, and Claire felt very comfortable with him by the end of the evening.

∽

She didn't think she was comfortable enough to go home with him, but that's where she found herself at exactly 10:42 p.m. She knew what time it was because Trevor had a bronze clock mounted over his fireplace. Claire looked up at it and thought to herself, *You know, I should probably be at home—or at the very least I should call to make sure Nikki's got her brother in bed.*

But Nikki had her mom's cell number, and Claire's phone hadn't rung all night. Plus Trevor had his tongue in her mouth, and it was kind of hard to think about anything past that.

They sat on the leather sofa in his living room. It was money green, a color Claire generally disdained when it came to furniture, but Trevor's layout was nice. His shag carpet had shades of green and brown, and his plants served to further coordinate things. Two large ivies hung from the bar, and a ficus tree posted in one corner reached for the ceiling fan with strong, thin branches and shiny leaves.

He had a huge plasma television on the wall opposite the couch, but it wasn't on right now. The only light in the house illuminated from the kitchen where Trevor went to take their doggy bag from Mille Fleurs.

The only sounds were Claire's ragged heartbeats and the barely audible music emanating from a stereo somewhere to their left. Trevor set up the tunes with a remote, but he kept the volume low because they were going to *talk*.

They conversed for a full eight minutes before he reached and brushed the hair from her eyes. His hand lingered on her cheek for a second, and then it moved to the back of her neck. He urged her forward ever so gently, and Claire easily succumbed to his will.

When their mouths touched for the first time, it felt like a jolt from a defibrillator. Trevor's lips were warm and soft, and a bit moist. He placed a hand on her side, tentatively at first, but Claire was receptive and his confidence grew.

Now he had her left breast fully in hand. He wasn't squeezing or groping, but his hand was there, and it was intentional. In the background the infamous Pied Piper of R&B crooned, and R Kelly was somehow on the same, exact page. It was odd. Claire closed her eyes again, and darted her tongue, and listened to the music while feeling this man in so many ways.

It seems like you're ready.
I could've sworn you were ready.

And maybe it was that song, more than anything, which caused her to back away from the pleasure, at least for a moment, and look at things logically.

Was she ready?

She could answer that with a resounding, *Hell yes*! This man was strong and hard, yet sympathetic and compassionate. He treated her like a lady and made her feel like a woman; a beautiful woman, a confident woman, a sexy woman.

Claire didn't think she could ever reach this level of emotion and sensuality with anyone but George, but here they were. And this wasn't some fluke encounter. This was divine. This man was sent to heal her, to soothe her, to make her *feel good*. And for all of those reasons and more Claire was willing and eager to accept him.

But at the same time, she knew she couldn't.

And it wasn't because she was such a *good person*. She had flaws just like everyone else. It wasn't because she was married and feared adultery, either.

Claire knew she couldn't go any further with Trevor because this was too much like something *George* would do. She would be a hypocrite and a cheater, just as low-down as him. She felt she totally deserved this *guilt-free* affair, but on a deeper level she knew that no such thing was possible.

She backed away and put a hand on his chest. "I can't."

The hand was not needed, because Trevor backed away as well.

"I know."

His chest rose and fell, and his lips glistened with her lipstick. Claire wasn't sure she heard him right.

"What?"

"I said '*I know*'. I know you can't do this."

With so many emotions raging within her, Claire didn't think she had room to register confusion, but she did. Trevor watched her expression and chuckled softly.

"What are you laughing at?"

"You," he said. "Why do you look so perplexed?"

"You *knew* I would stop you?"

He nodded. "I was pretty sure."

"So why'd you let it go on?"

He smiled. "Me?"

"Yeah, you," Claire said, feeling a little embarrassed.

"I might have been wrong," he said. "*I* wasn't going to stop you, but if you stopped yourself, I was okay with it."

She frowned. "You're not mad?"

"Why should I be mad?" Trevor asked. "I just got to, like, *second base* with the woman of my dreams. I don't regret that at all."

Claire smiled too. "Why do you say stuff like that?"

"Like what?"

"*Woman of my dreams . . .*"

"Everybody's got to have dreams," he said. "If you don't have a dream, then your life's meaningless."

"But why me?"

It was Trevor's turn to frown then. "I don't get it. You're the best, Claire. Don't you know that? Has no one told you that lately?"

She shook her head and searched her memory bank. "I can't remember the last time someone told me that."

"Well let me make it clear," he said. "You are an outstanding woman. You're the best at what you do. You're the best I could have hoped to find. George is a fool, and I'm darned lucky, and I'm not upset at all about anything that happened tonight."

"Thank you," she said softly.

"What about you?" he asked.

"What about me?"

"Do you regret anything?"

Claire had to think about that one, too. "I guess I regret being such a *prude*," she said. "I think it would have been nice."

"Oh, yeah. I would have totally rocked your world."

She laughed.

"Is that all you regret?" he asked.

She nodded. "Yeah. I think so."

He kissed her again, slowly and tenderly. They talked for a few minutes more, but at eleven p.m. Claire thought she should get home. Trevor was respectful of her decision. He walked her to the door and gave her a long, healing hug under his porch light.

CHAPTER TWENTY
DNA RESULTS

Claire's legs were still trembling when she got behind the wheel. By the time she made it home, it was her fingers that were shaking. She crept into her house like a burglar, knowing she wasn't going to pull this off without repercussions. Surely one of her kids would still be up, and they would see her, and they would know *intuitively* that Mama did something bad. They would smell Trevor's man scents on her, and they would see the whole sordid episode in her eyes.

But when Claire got up to the second floor, no one stirred. She went into her bedroom and changed into a robe quickly, and then she checked on her precious bundles one by one. All were asleep, nothing was awry, and at 12:30 Claire was finally calm enough to lie down and try to catch a few Z's herself.

But her guilt made slumber elusive. She stared at the ceiling for a long time, wondering why she didn't nip this in the bud in the beginning. She could have told Trevor she wanted another lawyer when he first came on to her. She wasn't a weak woman, and it wasn't like her to succumb to temptation.

Claire was on the verge of condemning her lawyer and all of their twisted encounters altogether, but good old George came home at 1:30 and put everything back into perspective. He snuck into bed as daintily as a mouse. Claire waited thirty minutes before she rolled over to sniff the back of his neck.

The bastard was fresh and clean again, and all of her guilt was transformed into a sudden fury. Her initial thought was that she should have cheated, but after a few minutes of soul searching Claire decided things were better the way they were. When they got to court, she wanted it to be a clear case of good versus *pure evil*.

George was making that job easier every day.

The rest of the weekend proceeded without much friction. George had no plans Saturday morning, so he slept late and ate breakfast with the family when he got up. The kids were very happy to have his company, but Claire was past the point of needing him. She saw the worst in him and expected the worst from him. If he grew horns and sprouted a forked tongue, she wouldn't be on bit surprised.

She still took care of him, but everything she did was out of habit. She picked up his discarded socks because that's what was supposed to happen. She fed him and washed the dishes afterwards because that, too, was expected of her. She even let him put his arm around her when the family gathered in the den for movie night.

On Sunday George left to ride his Harley, so Claire took the kids to Six Flags for the day. She thought about Trevor often when she was away from her husband, but she didn't call him. Even when the kids were stuck in ridiculous lines and she knew she had twenty minutes to herself, she didn't call him. Her feelings were already deeply involved, but they still had a task ahead, and she knew she had to stay focused on it. She didn't even allow herself to contemplate what life with Trevor might be like after George was out of the picture.

On Sunday night, things got a little hairy when George came home feeling amorous, but Claire took a page from the Book of Becky and told him it wasn't a good time of the month. He was known to insist anyway or request *other* things as a substitute, but George accepted her lie this time and slept with his back to her.

Claire knew things were going to come to a head quickly, because his suspicions were on the rise. Pretty soon he was going to accuse *her* of having an affair.

On Monday Claire was glad to get to work and be away from her husband, but George could still ruin her day from miles away. Melanie called right after lunch with a highly predictable bombshell.

"Provincial Insurance."

"Claire?"

"Melanie? What's going on?"

"My friend just got finished with your tests."

Claire put a hand to her mouth as a sudden chill enveloped her. She already knew what her friend would say, but this was still the biggest news of her life. If those weren't George's twins, she would feel lower than a tick on a horned toad.

"Do you want to know what he found out?" Melanie asked.

"Girl I'm fixing to have a heart attack over here. *Hurry up and tell me.*" The phone was slick in her hands. The whole room tilted and swam around her slowly.

"We didn't get anything off the rubber bands. I told you that, right?"

Claire nodded as if her friend could see her.

"We got a sample off the milk carton and one of them Styrofoam cups," Melanie went on. "They turned out to be from the same person, but that was cool. Nathan checked that sample against what we got from Nikki's toothbrush, and it was a match. Yo daughter is *definitely* related to somebody in that house."

The air left Claire with a big whoosh, and it threatened not to come back. She literally had to force herself to make the next inhalation. When she looked up again Becky was standing at her desk looking very concerned.

"You hear me, Claire?" Melanie asked.

"Yeah, I hear you."

"So that's it," Melanie said. "I can bring you a copy of the paperwork. It's a done deal."

It sounded pretty definite, but something still bothered Claire. "Wait," she said. "George is over there all the time. He could have used that little milk carton."

"That's not what Nathan says," Melanie informed. "He says it's *brother-sister* related, not *father-daughter* related. Trust me, they can tell."

"Can you bring the papers today?" Claire asked numbly.

"Yeah. We kicking it at your house tonight?"

"We can. I'm out of tequila, though."

"I'll bring some of that bumpy face," Melanie offered.

"Okay," Claire said, not at all sure what she was talking about. They got off the phone, and Claire looked up at her doting coworker. "The DNA was a match," she said weakly.

Becky stepped around the desk and stood next to her. She put a hand on Claire's shoulder and rubbed gently. "Are you okay?"

"Melanie's coming over tonight," Claire said. "I think we're getting drunk."

"Can I come?"

Claire looked up at her and grinned. "You know it's no fun getting drunk without you."

Claire made it through the rest of her shift like a half-powered robot, but she couldn't understand why the DNA results bothered her so much. It was like when a terminally ill relative finally goes to be with Jesus: You know it's coming. You wait for the bad news every day, in fact. But when they eventually pass on, you're still going to cry if it was someone you loved.

When Claire picked up the kids from school, they recognized immediately that Mama was not in a good mood, and they did their best to stay out of her hair for the rest of the day. Stacy picked up her room without a million and one requests, and George Jr. sought Nikki when he got stumped on his multiplications rather than disturb Mom.

George called while Claire was slicing onions for an enchilada dinner.

"Hello?"

"Hey, baby. I gotta work la—"

"It's fine."

"Huh?"

"Go ahead and work late," Claire said. "That's fine."

"Are you okay?"

"I'm great. Melanie and Becky are coming over tonight anyway."

"Oh, well, okay," George said. "We're getting backed up over here. I think I'll be in around t—"

Claire hung up before he could get the rest of his lie out. The bastard had been lying about his whereabouts for the last freaking *decade*; what was the point in listening to him anymore? Even if George told her it was raining outside, Claire would check for herself before she grabbed an umbrella.

Melanie arrived at Claire's house at six-thirty and Becky got there at seven. The kids weren't in bed yet, but they were still in their Act Good 'Cause Mama's Mad mode. They greeted their play-aunts quietly, and then hustled back upstairs to their computers and video games.

Claire served her friends leftover enchiladas when it was time to put her offspring to bed. She went upstairs and set the sleep timer on George Jr.'s TV for ten. The girls got an extra hour, but under no circumstances were they allowed downstairs for the rest of the evening.

"Are you going to get drunk?" Nikki asked when Claire turned her light off.

"Ladies don't get *drunk*," Claire informed her daughter. "They may get *tipsy*."

"Whatever it takes to make you happy," Nikki said. "You're mad *all* the time."

Claire was eager to get downstairs and see Melanie's papers for the first time, but she couldn't let that misconception slide. She went and sat on her daughter's bed.

"Drinking doesn't make you happy," she said. "When you get bigger, don't ever think you can find happiness at the bottom of a bottle. You'll turn into a depressed alcoholic."

"I can't wait till I'm—"

"You'd better not say it."

"What? I was gonna say I can't wait until I'm as smart as you."

"Oh, you're such a butt-kisser," Claire said, but Nikki made her more and more proud every day. She kissed her on the forehead and left the room with a smile on her face.

When she got back downstairs, Becky was in the den alone.

"Where's Melanie?"

"She went to get those papers and something called *bumpy face.* I don't know what that is."

"I don't, either," Claire said with a chuckle. She sat next to her friend and sighed heavily. "Oh, Becky. This is going to be really bad, isn't it?"

Becky nodded and patted her knee. "Probably so."

"What did I do wrong?" Claire asked her. "That's the only thing I don't understand. Why would he do this?"

"Maybe it was an accident," Becky said. "Maybe he got drunk at a party one time and didn't know what he was doing."

"He knew what he was doing for the last *ten years,*" Claire said.

"Maybe when she told him she was pregnant, he decided to do the right thing," Becky offered. "A lot of guys would walk away, but maybe he wanted to be there for his children, even if they were illegitimate."

"Why are you taking up for George?"

"I don't know. I thought you wanted me to."

"No, Becky. We hate him and he's an asshole, remember?"

"Oh, well I think he did it 'cause he's an asshole," Becky said. "If he wanted to do the right thing, then he should have told you and let you decide if you wanted to accept his mistake or not."

"That's my girl," Claire said.

They heard a sound at the front door. Melanie rounded the corner a few seconds later with a folder in one hand and a huge jug of clear alcohol in the other.

"What's that?" Claire asked.

"These are your papers," Melanie said. She approached them a little winded from her trip outside.

"I mean what's that bottle?" Claire asked.

"That's gin," Melanie said. She handed it over, and Claire almost let it fall to the floor. She bobbled and caught it just in time.

"*Girl, whatchoo doing?*"

"I wasn't prepared for the weight." Claire said. "Why do you call it bumpy face?"

Melanie smiled. "Feel the thang, girl."

Claire shook her head, but as she caressed the glass she understood. The Seagram's people designed their gin bottle with a lot of small knots on the outside that might feel like someone's *bumpy face*—if this person had a terrible, terrible skin condition.

"I'll go get some orange juice," Claire said, but Becky shot to her feet.

"I'll get it."

"Well, let me see those papers." Claire sat the bottle down and took the folder from her friend. She flipped through the pages aimlessly, not making sense of all the technical information. "Where does it say there's a match?" she finally asked.

Melanie took the folder from her and went straight to the last page. "Right there. You see that number *ninety-nine point nine, nine, eight, nine, nine, nine, nine?*"

"Yeah."

"That means them twins is George's."

Claire stared at the computer-generated data for a long time. Science was awesome. It was funny how man's greatest achievement was now used to crucify men day after day. "So this is what I need to give my lawyer?"

"That's it," Melanie said. "You got his ass."

Claire knew she did, and it was the very thing she wanted, but still it didn't feel like a victory.

***

The girls stayed up for another three hours drinking gin and juice and talking bad about Claire's husband. When George got home at one they were still in the midst of the revelry. He stepped into the den and all noise stopped as if shut off by a switch. Six mean eyes settled on him with undisguised hate.

"Huh-hey, y'all," he said. "How you ladies doing?"

No one answered.

George stood uneasily, shifting his weight from one leg to the other. "I'm, um, I guess I'll go upstairs . . ." he told his wife.

Claire frowned, and the ladies continued to stare him down.

"Um, okay. Well, I guess I'll see you later." He paused a few moments longer but still didn't get a response. He backed out cautiously as if expecting someone to throw something at him.

The girls burst into laughter when he was gone.

Her friends stayed only thirty minutes more, and when they left, they did so without ever hearing about Claire's special night with her lawyer. She was dying to tell them, but she knew that conversation would get very loud and rowdy. They would want to know all the particulars. It was bad enough they were talking about the divorce while the children were home, but Claire couldn't live with herself if the kids accidentally found out she'd been carrying on with another man.

Plus, her time with Trevor was special. The longer she kept it to herself, the more special it felt.

CHAPTER TWENTY-ONE
ONE LAST THING

With her final bit of evidence secured, Claire felt no need to delay the inevitable. George was clearly an adulterer. He was a proven liar, and he was *definitely* not the man she married. If he wanted to be with another woman, that was fine. He could marry Kimberly Pate (if they weren't already married) and live happily ever after for all Claire cared. The only thing left was to make him pay what he owed.

George owed Nikki, Stacy, and George Jr. an upper-middle-class upbringing, and Claire would be damned if they wouldn't have it. He owed them a college education, and they would have that, too. Keeping the house and car were a given, but if Claire had it her way, George would give up a lot more. She wanted the lake house and the time shares. She wanted the stocks and bonds. She wanted *all* of their savings, but would settle for merely half.

The odd thing was, even if Claire got all of those things, she still didn't think she'd be happy, because what she wanted most of all was an explanation. Before things got ugly in the courts, she wanted to sit her husband down and get an honest answer.

Why would you do this to us, George?
How could you do it?
Why, George, why?

Trevor said he could almost guarantee her every-thing else, but no judge in the country could force George to explain himself. Claire thought that was a travesty of justice.

She sat in her lawyer's office on a balmy Saturday afternoon. Strewn across Mr. Smiley's desk were photo-graphs, receipts, account statements, mortgage paper-work and titles. In his hands was the folder Melanie gave Claire five days ago. Trevor studied the genetics informa-tion with more sense of understanding than Claire had when she looked over the documents.

He wore a dark green button-down with black slacks and a black tie. He was serious today, all business so far. He made it to the last page, and then flipped back to the middle and looked up at his client.

Claire wore blue jeans with a blue T-shirt. She thought about wearing something a little more upbeat, but she didn't feel sexy at all today, not even in this gen-tleman's company.

"Where'd the first sample come from?" he asked. "The one they got off the toothbrush?"

"That was from my oldest girl. Her name's Nicole."

Trevor nodded. "So she definitely has a relative in that house. I guess she's got two . . ."

Claire wondered how Nikki would react if she found out she had another little sister, and heaven help us, another little brother. Claire didn't think she should tell her, but she had to, didn't she? She was sure to find out anyway.

Trevor closed the folder and sat it atop his desk with the other things. He had quite an impressive pile of evidence. He looked past it all and stared into his client's eyes. Claire had her hair in a ponytail. She wore no lipstick or eyeliner this afternoon.

"Are you doing okay?" he asked.

She nodded. She knew this was coming. Trevor always played lawyer first, then counselor.

"As well as to be expected, I guess."

"Don't worry about expectations," he said. "Tell me how you feel."

Claire considered her response. She hadn't cried since she first found out about the affair, but the closer they got to filing papers, the less confident she felt. Just yesterday she found herself misty-eyed while setting the table for dinner.

"I've been going back and forth," she admitted. "Sometimes I think, *It's okay. You don't need him. If he would do this to you, you're better off without him.* But other times, I feel like he's all I have. He's all I've ever known. I get scared to step out in this world by myself."

"You don't have to do it alone. You know that."

"I know," Claire said. "I know you want to help, but even that scares me. I worry about what it would be like to be in a relationship with another man, to learn all about someone new." She chuckled. "You know, there are just so many things. With George, I *know* he's going to leave a face towel in the sink after he shaves. I know he's going to soak the floor when he tries to wash dishes. I know what he likes to do, what makes him mad. I know which relatives he likes to visit over the holidays . . ."

"You can learn all of that about someone new. It might even be fun."

"I know it's possible," Claire said, "but lately I've felt like, like it's something I don't want to do." She looked away, unable to meet his eyes. "I can't even *imagine* introducing my children to another man . . ."

Trevor nodded. He didn't seem upset. "That's disheartening," he said. "You're too young and beautiful to be an old maid."

Claire met his eyes again. "Of course *you're* going to say that."

He smiled. "Claire, you're not the only one who's ever felt this way. People have written whole textbooks about women in your situation. Even me, I felt just like you do when Michelle died."

That got her attention.

"Except I probably had it worse because my wife never cheated on me," he said. "She never did anything wrong. She was the perfect woman, and then she was gone. I didn't even think about dating again for a year. And when I did, I knew none of them would measure up. I went on a few dates expecting substandard women, and that's what I got. After a while, I quit looking altogether. It's too hard to be in the rat race. I did that when I was a young man. I knew I wasn't going to find another Michelle, so why bother?"

Claire was right with him. If she could somehow have a *faithful* George, she'd be the happiest woman in the city.

"But I was only thirty-two," Trevor went on. "I decided okay, I'm probably not going to find another woman like my wife, but that didn't mean I shouldn't find another woman *period*. Michelle would want me to be happy. So I got back out there and put my heart on the line again. It hasn't worked out for me yet, but I thought I was getting close . . ."

Claire didn't know how to respond.

"When are you going to file the papers?" she asked.

Trevor's face went slack for a half-second, but he pulled himself together quickly.

"I can do it anytime you want. When do you want George to get served?"

"I don't know. Sometime this week, but he's hardly home."

"I could get a constable to go to his job," Trevor offered.

Claire shook her head. "No. I want to be there. When he gets those papers, I want him to turn around and look at me. I want to tell him what I know, and then I want him to explain himself, and then I want him to leave."

"Are you sure?" Trevor asked. "You don't think he might respond violently?"

"George would never hit me," Claire said. "If he did, I guess I could get that lake house for sure," she kidded.

"I don't care about that lake house," Trevor said. "If you think—"

"George isn't going to hit me," Claire said. "I'm positive."

"All right. So when do you want the subpoena to come?"

"How about next Saturday? A week from today."

"Okay," Trevor said. "We'll do it Saturday morning."

"Around what time? I want to get the kids out of the house."

"Either nine to twelve or twelve to three."

"Nine to twelve would be good," Claire said. She did a few mental calculations in her head. "Yeah. That would be perfect."

"If you change your mind, call me before Thursday."

"I'm not changing my mind. You can pay with cash if you want. It's a done deal."

"All right. I'll get it typed up." Trevor leaned forward in his seat and stared at her for a second. "I guess I shouldn't ask why I haven't heard from you since, since we went out . . ."

"I wanted to call," Claire said. "I actually dialed your number twice. But George came home early the first time, and my son walked into the room the other time. I got real nervous and hung up, and I started feeling *really* guilty." She frowned. "I didn't like that feeling. I don't see how George can do that every day. I mean, I guess you get used to it after a while, but it's just not in me to be deceitful."

"That's good," Trevor said earnestly. "But if he fights this, you know it could go on for months . . ."

Claire knew what he was getting at, and she knew he wouldn't like her response.

"I'm thinking maybe that would be okay," she said. "It'll probably take that long to clear my head."

"When he moves out, you'll be legally separated," Trevor said. "I don't want to wait three months to see you again."

Claire looked down at her hands.

If Trevor was upset, he didn't show it. He pushed his chair away from the desk and pulled open the top drawer. He reached in and came out with a small, hard-cover book with a cartoon drawing on the front. He handed it over the desk and Claire took it curiously.

The drawing was a big block of Swiss cheese, which made sense because the book was titled *Who Moved my Cheese*. Claire flipped through it and saw a few more illustrations. This didn't look like a serious text at all.

"It's very helpful," Trevor said, studying her expression.

"What's it about?"

"It's about change," he said. "Living with change. Adapting to change. Expecting change as a part of everyday life."

"I would have expected a thicker manual," Claire said honestly. Nothing she could get through in a few hours was likely to change her life significantly.

"Sometimes the most complicated subjects have the simplest explanations."

Claire nodded. "Thanks." She stood to shake his hand. Trevor stood also, and it was a regular lawyer/client handshake this time, no funny stuff.

"Make sure you read that," he said.

"I will," Claire promised. "I guess I'll talk to you later."

"You can call me Saturday," he said, "to let me know how things went, if you want."

Claire smiled and said she might, but she was pretty sure she wouldn't.

୶

She thought she'd feel better to have all of that out of her hands and officially *in the system*, but Claire was as depressed as ever when she got back on the freeway. She was upset because her marriage was virtually over, but she also felt bad about the way she treated Trevor.

She knew he was a good man, but she wasn't ready for *any* man right now. She never should have gone to his house. She felt like she led him on, and that was a terrible feeling because that wasn't the type of person she was.

୶

George took the kids to the track earlier, so Claire didn't have any particular place to be for another few hours. She felt like there was *something* she should do but didn't know what it was. She got on I 35, not really sure where she was going, but after forty minutes on the road things started to look familiar.

Claire realized she wasn't driving aimlessly after all. Somehow she made it all the way to Highway 121. While she considered how odd this was, powers beyond her control made her exit on Story Road. Claire navigated the beautiful Irving neighborhood from memory and turned onto Stevens Court five minutes later.

She pulled to a stop across the street from Kimberly Pate's house. She knew she shouldn't be there, but she put her car in park and turned off the engine anyway. She decided that if she had to be there, she *definitely* wouldn't get out of the car, but moments later Claire stood, confused, in the middle of the street.

Ms. Kimberly Pate was in her front yard, no more than ten feet away. She was on her knees near the curb, pulling stubborn weeds up by hand. George's mistress wore denim capris with a short-sleeved T-shirt this afternoon. She had a red handkerchief wrapped around her head to keep the hair out of her eyes.

The sun and hard work had her skin a shade darker than Claire remembered. Kim had a crimson tint now, like the Native Americans. Beads of sweat stood on her forehead, and her chest was stained with a dark bib as well. Claire walked right up to her, still with no particular game plan in mind. Kim looked up and regarded this stranger oddly.

"Hi," she said.

"Hi," Claire said.

They stared at each other uncomfortably.

Kim tilted her head, and then looked around at Claire's car. "Did you come to look at the Swanson's house?" she prompted. "I have the keys. I could let you inside."

Claire looked back and saw that the FOR SALE sign was still in the yard across the street. "Yeah," she said. "I came to look at the house."

Kimberly Pate stood and stared her visitor in the eyes. She pulled off one of her gardening gloves and stuck a hand out to Claire.

"My name's Kim."

Claire shook it gingerly. "I'm Claire."

"*Claire.* I like that name. Do you have a family?"

"I'm married," Claire said. "With three children."

"Great," Kim said. She leaned in conspiratorially. "It would be good to get a little more *color* around here, if you know what I mean . . ."

Claire meant to smile and nod, but she had no idea what her face was doing. It apparently wasn't doing what she wanted, because Kim looked upset all of a sudden.

"Oh, my God," she said. "If your husband's white, I didn't mean to offend you. I don't care what color my neighbors are. I was just—"

Claire did crack a smile then. "No. My husband's black."

Kim put a hand to her chest. "*Whew.* Girl, you scared me. I would've had my foot in my mouth for *real.*" She turned and headed for her house. She stopped when Claire didn't follow. "Um, I've got the key in here somewhere. You can come in and get out of the sun while I look for it."

Claire didn't know why she was at this location, and she didn't know what to expect while there, but she knew she *absolutely* wasn't going into that lady's house. Or was she? Her legs started moving, and that made up her mind for her.

"Have you lived here long?" she asked.

"About seven years," Kim confirmed without looking back. "I came down from New York."

New York.

The words hit Claire like a contraction and her knees buckled for a second.

"I miss my old neighborhood," Kim went on. "But I guess it's better over here. It's definitely safer, but everything's too slow for me. It's too hot, too." She turned and smiled. "You like it in Texas?"

"It is hot here," Claire agreed.

"You from somewhere else, too?" Kim walked around to the back door, and her visitor followed.

"I've lived a lot of places," Claire said. "I lived in New York too; right before I came to Texas, like you . . ."

"*Really?*" Kim stopped again and regarded her kindly. "What part?"

"We lived in Yonkers."

"*Really?*" Kim's eyes lit up. She really was pretty, and fit. Claire could see why George was attracted to her. "Where at?"

"On Hudson."

Kim put a hand on her hip and shook her head. "What a *small world*. I lived on Prospect."

The two streets ran parallel to each other, just one block apart. The Hudgens family lived in New York for only four years. Claire was young and naïve in those days, saddled with three small children. George cheating on her was the very *last* thing on her mind then, but that was probably when his affair started. They lived so close to Kim, he could have met her anywhere; the corner store, the marina, Washington Park.

"Wouldn't that be cool if we came all the way from the same Yonkers neighborhood, then ended up living right across the street from each other in *Texas*?" Kim asked.

"Yeah," Claire said. "That would be funny."

"This is *crazy*," Kim mused, still caught up in the weirdness of the encounter. "What a coincidence."

That's not the only thing we have in common, Claire wanted to say.

Kim turned and disappeared inside her back door. "Come on."

Claire took a deep breath and let it out slowly before following. She didn't know if she would make friends or end up attacking this woman. Either scenario still seemed possible. She prepared herself for the worst and entered the interloper's house with her teeth clenched.

Kimberly Pate had a nice kitchen. It was large, with enough hip room for three to four cooks. It was also bright and clean. The burners on the stove all had identical covers featuring a napping Garfield cartoon. A wooden sign over the sink asked visitors to *Bless This Mess*, but everything was neat and tidy—except the refrigerator. It was crammed with a huge assortment of magnets, everything from letters of the alphabet to dancing cows. There were a couple school papers affixed to the fridge by way of these magnets.

Claire immediately wanted to make her way over to those papers so she could get more information on George's children, but she didn't have to: The twins were seated at the table to her right eating corny dogs. Claire jumped a little when she turned and saw them there.

"Those are the twins," Kim said, "George and Gina. They scare me sometimes, too," she said good-naturedly.

"George?" Claire's head swam. *Please don't let me fall out on this woman's floor.*

"He's named after his father," Kim explained. "I know *George* is a little old-school, but he likes it. Don't you, *Georgie Porgie*?"

The little boy smiled, and Claire's stomach churned. A little vomit reached the back of her throat.

How the hell did he let her do that? His first born *son is the junior! He can't just throw that name around like that! It's got to be illegal!*

"Are you okay?" Kim asked.

"I'm all right," Claire said. "Just tired, all of a sudden. I've been looking at houses all day." She had no idea where that lie came from, but she liked it. It was timely and believable.

"You look pale," Kim said. "Here, come sit down." She went to the table and pulled out the chair next to the *wannabe* George Jr. She dragged her guest over to it, and Claire was obliged to sit down. The boy grinned at her and licked ketchup off of his corny dog. The girl licked mustard from hers. They were even more adorable up close, and Stevie Wonder could tell you they were George's babies.

"Do you want something to drink?" Kim asked.

Claire shook her head.

"All right, I'll go get that key," she said. "You guys wait in here with Mrs. . . ." She was talking to the twins, but the pause was for Claire to fill in the blank.

"Hudgens."

"*Hudgens*?" Kim looked ready to blow a fuse.

Claire realized her mistake immediately. "Hutchens," she said. "I said *Hutchens*."

Kim put a hand to her chest. "Girl, I thought you said *Hudgens*. That's my boyfriend's last name. That's the twins' last name, too."

Claire was glad she was sitting down.

"If you would have said *Hudgens*," Kim went on, "I was gonna freak out right here. That would be like, way too many coincidences!"

"No," Claire smiled weakly. "I'm Claire Hut-*chens*."

"I'm Hudgens," Gina said.

"Me, too," the fake George Jr. announced.

Kim giggled. "And I'll be right back."

She turned and disappeared through the doorway, and Claire was left with way more than she bargained for. The twins talked her ear off as soon as Mommy was out of the room.

"Who are you?" George asked boldly, ketchup glistening on the tip of his nose.

"Uh, my name is Claire. I came to look at the house across the street."

"Are you going to buy that house?" Gina asked suspiciously. They were both missing their bunny-rabbit teeth, but she looked goofier without hers.

"I might," Claire said.

"That house cost a lot of money," George Jr. said.

"A lot of money," he sister agreed.

Claire grinned. "How do you know that?"

"Mommy said so," they said almost in unison.

"Do you have a dog?" the boy asked.

"I like puppies," the girl said.

"I don't have any pets," Claire said.

"We have a dog," George Jr. said. "His name is Boogie."

"He got too big," his sister informed Claire.

"He used to be little," her brother explained.

"Do you have a little girl?" Gina asked.

"I do," Claire said. "I have two daughters."

"I don't have any friends over here," Gina said.

"Do you have any little *boys*?" George Jr. asked.

"I do have a son," Claire said. "And I'm pretty sure you'd like him."

"Does he like rabbits?" George Jr. asked. "I'm going to get a rabbit."

"*It's going to be mine's, too,*" his sister whined.

"*I'm* naming him," George Jr. announced.

"It's going to be a *girl* rabbit!"

Kim came back before things could get any more heated. "You guys stop arguing in front of her. She's going to think you don't have no home-training."

"Our rabbit's gonna be a girl rabbit, right, Mama?" Gina pleaded.

"Child, I don't know. I found the key," she said to Claire with a big smile.

"Okay." Claire stood with a smile on her face as well.

"Sorry about leaving you in here with *Thing 1* and *Thing 2*."

"They're fine," Claire said honestly. "I actually enjoyed their company."

They both cheesed.

"Hurry and get through eating," Kim told them, "so we can finish up in the yard."

"You've got them picking weeds, too?" Claire asked.

"Girl, yes," Kim said. "I can't wait till they're old enough to do it by themselves so I can stay in the house!"

Kim took Claire across the street and gave her a great tour of a beautiful house she was never going to buy. Claire steered the conversation back to Kim's boyfriend when they got to the guest bedroom.

"Are you still with the twin's father?"

"Yeah," Kim said. "I've been with George for almost nine years now. I met him in New York, and we moved down here when he got transferred on his job."

"What kind of work does he do?"

"He's retired from the Air Force," Kim said. "He's an engineer now. He works for Boeing." She was proud the same way Claire was proud when she talked about George. That was wrong on so many levels.

"He lives with you?"

Kim frowned. "If you want to call it that. He's not here most of the time because of his job. They send him all around the country. I'd say he only sleeps here half the year. But he makes good money, though, and our bills are never late. He says he's going to slow down on his hours pretty soon."

Good luck with that one, Claire thought. "How come you haven't married?" she asked.

Kim shook her head. "George ain't the marrying type. I've been trying to get him to jump the broom since before we had the twins. I gave them his last name and everything—you know, thinking it was going to help when we finally did it—but he's not going to get married." She said it with the certainty of a woman who was all nagged out. "I know what I got with George, though, and I don't stress him about it anymore. We're happy, and he ain't going nowhere."

Claire forced a smile. Kim didn't know it, but she was about to get her man full-time within the next week or so. Hell, George might even step up and marry her once his real excuse was out in the open.

Just then Claire understood why she sought Kim out today. She wanted to see how bad George's life was going to be when he moved out. Now she wished she'd just gone home, because his Plan B wasn't too shabby at all. They had a nice house, Kim was beautiful, and his twins were adorable. Claire wanted to die right then. She had to turn away so the mistress wouldn't see her tears.

"That's great," she said. "That's just, great . . ."

CHAPTER TWENTY-TWO

GETTING EVEN WITH GEORGE

After the open house, Kim took Claire back across the street and they had tea and cookies. Kim was a gracious host, and by the time Claire got back to her car, she didn't hate the woman at all anymore. They were truly in the same boat.

Claire wanted to tell her who she really was a few times, hoping they could band together and leave George with *nowhere* to run, but Kim was going to have to make her own decisions. For all Claire knew, she would be happy to have George to herself after the divorce. Claire began to wonder for the first time if it was possible to destroy a man who seemed to be prepared for the inevitable.

She left the Irving neighborhood with more answers, but she still had a boatload of questions. George was the only one left who could give her the answers she needed.

One more week, she told herself. *Let that pig get a little fatter before you gut him . . .*

On Monday Claire told her friends about the night at Mille Fleurs and the subsequent break-up with Mr. Trevor Smiley. Becky said she understood, but she thought Claire was making a mistake. Melanie thought Claire was crazy for not jumping the lawyer's bones. Claire thought they were both right, yet they were both wrong.

On Wednesday night things came to a head again when Claire wouldn't yield to the tender passions of her husband for an unheard of *ninth* time. George jumped fully out of bed and stood with his hands on his hips, his erection pitching quite a fine tent in his boxers.

"So what the hell's the problem tonight?" His scowl was hard and rigid like a sculpture. Claire rolled her back to him, pulling the sheets over her body. In some marriages, that move might have led to her getting snatched out of bed by her hair, but, like she told Trevor, George would never lay a hand on her.

"I've got a headache," she said. She wanted to tell him they'd talk about it this weekend, but her husband would never let her sleep if she said that. Simply acknowledging there was something to talk about was cause for an all-nighter.

George tried to rationalize. "Baby, you're going to have to tell me what's wrong with you *sooner or later*. I'm your husband, and I need attention. Things aren't going to be good around here if you keep stalling me out. The adult thing would be to get it off your chest. I'm not waiting around on you forever."

That was an unmistakable and undisguised threat of retaliation (take it how you wanna), but Claire didn't swallow the bait like she was supposed to. She didn't respond at all, as a matter of fact, and that was even stronger medicine. George began to breathe roughly behind her, and Claire sensed he was fuming, with heat waves and smoke wafting from his smooth dome.

"Okay, forget it then," he said. "I'm not even going to ask you about it no more. And you don't need to worry about what the hell I'm doing either."

Another threat of retaliations? Wow, Claire mused. She really had his goat this time.

She went to sleep with a smile on her face that night.

On Friday George came home from work and changed quickly for his infamous *poker night with the guys.* Claire didn't leave the dinner table and follow him up, and she didn't have any tails on him when he left the house.

When she got into bed later, she did start to wonder if Ms. Pate would tell him about her odd visitor. But when George got home at two, he didn't say anything, even though Claire was still awake.

"Did you have a nice time?" she asked as he slipped into his pajamas.

"You ready to give me some?" he asked.

"Nope."

"Then don't worry about it."

Claire was curious about whether he was clean and fresh that night, but she didn't roll over to sniff him when he got into bed. She couldn't bear the *closeness* of the encounter anymore. It didn't matter anyway, because the sun was going to rise in just a little while. Everything would come to a head when a constable knocked on their door between the hours of nine and twelve.

Claire closed her eyes at 2:14 a.m.

She opened them again at 4:33. She wasn't sure what woke her but she felt remotely alarmed about *something*. She didn't feel like she slept enough for this feeling to come from a dream. She sat up and scanned the bedroom slowly. When her gaze fell upon her husband, a sudden chill rolled down her spine.

George lay on his side with his legs pulled up almost in a fetal position. The house was dark and eerily quiet. George didn't snore loudly, but he usually made *some* noise when he slept. Claire held her own breath and listened for his, but her husband remained mute. She knew George wasn't *dead*, but the thought filled her heart with a brief exhilaration.

What if he is? That would be, this could be . . .

Her eyes adjusted to the darkness, and Claire saw his broad shoulder rise and fall slowly. She could hear his soft breaths then, too. Rather than feel relieved that she wasn't in bed with a corpse, Claire stared at the back of her husband's head and a deep sneer marred her beautiful features. She wasn't aware of it, but she looked evil, almost demonic with the shadows shading all but her eyes and teeth.

She slipped out of bed slowly, pausing every few seconds to see if he would awaken. It occurred to her that he might very well be awake *right now*, waiting like a lion in the brush to see what she would do. If that were so, things were about to get pretty ugly. Claire left the bedroom on the balls of her feet, and she ducked into the office two doors down.

The room immediately filled her with the foul pangs of pain and betrayal, but that was okay. She could think of no better place to end this drama. This was the place where George's lies first began to unravel. And this was the place Claire would find an end to her suffering.

There were three firearms in the Hudgens' household. George had a Remington 12-gauge in the bedroom closet, and there was a Glock .45 in the nightstand next to the bed. The last gun, a chrome .380 automatic, had been in the office closet for the last three years. George bought the pistol to keep his wife company on those many nights he was away on *business trips*. Claire went to the shooting range a few times to familiarize herself with the weapon, but they never had a burglary while George was home or away.

The semi-automatic got stored away but never forgotten. Claire found the lock box on the top shelf in the closet. The key was a few feet away in George's desk.

Claire worked like a thief in the night. Twenty seconds later she was armed with anguish, malice, and now a loaded gun.

She crept back to the bedroom more boldly than she left it. George still lay with his back to her. Claire gritted her teeth and pointed the pistol at the back of his neck. Goosebumps stood out on her arms. Her trigger finger twitched.

She knew she'd lost it, but her heart was filled with so much hate. If she didn't kill her husband, he was going to get off, just like Robert Blake and OJ. George had enough money to hire an excellent lawyer. Even if worse came to worst and he had to pay child support for all five children, Trevor said the most the Attorney General could take was fifty percent of his income. George made eighty thousand a year—plus he had a whole family to fall back on.

A divorce wasn't going to destroy this man. George was resilient, and he was smart. Killing him was the only way to make it better. Claire pulled the top back on the .380 slowly, but it still let out a loud *CHA-CHICK* when cocked.

Claire froze again, expecting him to roll over. She held her breath and waited, but nothing happened. George's breaths were deep and steady. The rise and fall of his shoulder hadn't changed at all. Claire exhaled slowly. She took a few steps closer and leaned over the bed. She got the barrel within five feet of his head, and then she heard a sound behind her.

She turned slowly, like a child with his hand in the cookie jar, wondering what the hell she could say to explain *this*. If George Jr. was standing there half-asleep, she could tell him Mommy and Daddy were playing a grownup game. But Nikki wouldn't believe such rubbish. She already knew Mom and Dad were not having the best of times.

Claire cursed herself for being a fool, but when she looked around there was no one in the doorway. She strained her ears but didn't hear any retreating footsteps either. She wore a look of confusion when she looked back at George. The confusion gave way to horror because George was looking right at her. Claire was so shocked she gasped and almost dropped the gun.

But, those weren't his eyes at all. That was still the *back* of his head she was looking at. Claire rubbed her eyes, cursing them for playing tricks on her. She wondered if the noise she heard behind her had even been real.

I'm going crazy, she realized, and that understanding explained a lot of what was going on right now. She had a gun to her husband's head in the middle of the night while her children slept just a dozen yards away. This was the most ignorant thing she'd ever been party to.

He's taken so much. Are you going to let him take your sanity too?

Claire lowered her weapon and backed out of the room. She took the .380 to the office and locked it in the gun box just as she had found it. She didn't go back into the bedroom out of fear of whatever else she might do. It was hard to believe she hated someone that much, but she honestly wanted that man to die. With every ounce of her being, she wanted him dead.

She went downstairs and called Becky, and they talked until the sun rose at 6:42.

Claire got the children up without too much fuss at 8:00. She told them they were spending the afternoon with Aunt Becky, and they were too sleepy to give her a hard time about it. Claire usually made big lumberjack breakfasts on the weekends, but she prepared a meal of cereal and juice for the kids today. She wanted George to stay in bed as long as possible—preferably until the constable came—and she didn't want the delectable aroma of sausage and eggs to wake him up.

Becky left with the children at 9:00 a.m. sharp. Claire took a seat on the living room sofa and waited quietly. She listened to the muffled ticks from their grandfather clock and prepared herself for the biggest confrontation she'd ever known. She wondered if she should show George her evidence right away or spring it on him after he tried to weasel his way out of it. She wondered if it wasn't too late to call Kim Pate and invite her over for the show.

When someone knocked on the front door Claire jumped like she'd seen a mouse. It was odd to her that someone would *knock*, considering they had a perfectly good doorbell right next to the knob. This had to be a visitor who didn't ring doorbells. She looked at the clock and saw that it was 9:32.

Claire crossed the room on stiff legs, still in her bathrobe. When she got there, she craned her ear in the direction of the staircase and listened for the bedroom door to open. She didn't hear anything. She leaned forward and squinted through the peephole. The view was distorted, but she saw enough to know there was a policeman standing on the opposite side.

In the eight years they lived in this house, this was the first time an officer ever had cause to pay them a visit. That was an odd thing to think about, but it was the first thought on Claire's mind.

I wonder who died, she kidded, but the joke did little to shake her jitters. She turned and listened for the stairway again. Everything was still silent in that direction. She took a breath and cleared her throat softly. She twisted the knob and cracked the door a bit.

"Hello?"

The constable was tall and stocky with blond hair and brown eyes. He had a fold of papers in his hand.

"Hi," he said. "Is there a George Hudgens at this residence?"

Claire opened the door a little more. She was about to tell him the adulterer was upstairs asleep, but at that moment she realized she wasn't ready to serve George his papers yet. There was still one more thing that needed to be done.

"He lives here," Claire said, "but he's not home right now. He just left to go to the store. Could you come back in thirty minutes?"

The cop frowned and looked at his watch. "He'll be back at ten?"

"Ten o'clock would be perfect," Claire said.

He checked his watch again. "I'll still be in the neighborhood. I could come back at ten, if you're sure he's going to be here."

"I'm *positive*," Claire said. "And I really appreciate it."

"Okay, ma'am. I'll be back."

He turned to leave, and Claire shuddered as she closed the door on him. She couldn't believe she just lied to a lawman, but her new plan was going to be much worse than that. She redid the deadbolt and stormed off towards the dining room, rolling her sleeves up as she went. If she wasn't going to kill her husband, at least she could destroy one more of George's dreams before he moved in with his mistress.

Claire entered the garage via the kitchen and pulled the chain at the foot of the stairs to turn the lights on. There were three vehicles in the large room: her Lexus, George's Navigator, and the crown jewel, his souped-up chopper.

George first purchased the bike nine years ago, when they were still in New York. Since then he shipped the Harley off to four different shops to get customized handlebars, wheels and pipes. It was truly a thing of beauty now, but it took many years of patience, money, and hard work to get it there.

Claire didn't believe she could totally wreck the motorcycle in just thirty minutes, but she was certainly willing to give it a try. George was a good mechanic, and he had tools of all sorts hanging from on walls of the garage. Claire scanned them until she saw the weapon she preferred. She hefted the heavy sledge hammer with two hands. She didn't think she'd have the strength to wield it, but once she got it over her head, gravity was happy to bring it down on the target all by itself.

As planned, George was awakened by the racket. He stepped into the garage twenty minutes after the constable left wearing only a pair of boxers. His look of weariness was immediately replaced with a look of sheer horror when he saw his wife wild and sweating in the center of the room.

Between Claire's legs lay the remnants of his Harley. It was not propped on the kickstand as it should be, and it was not in one piece like it should be, either. Every light and reflector was smashed. The seat was shredded and its innards were strewn here and there. The tires were flat as well.

The entire bike had huge dents covering every square inch. Most of the bruises were fist-sized and at least an inch deep. The Harley's beautifully crafted motor looked more like a radiator now. The chrome pipes were smooshed, almost flattened. The fender was cracked and detached. Nearly every spoke on the wheels was bent out of shape.

Claire had the sledgehammer poised over her head for another blow when she looked up and saw her husband. They stared at each other without words for half a second, and then he started for her. Claire brought the hammer down one more time before he could stop her.

The metal head slammed into the chassis with the sickening sound of dreams, sacrifice, and hard-earned money rushing down the drain.

George reacted as if he'd taken the blow himself. He doubled over and fell to his knees. He crawled, then staggered, to the remains of his bike like a mummy. His eyes were wide and his jaw was slack like he took a shot of heroin. His big chest rose and fell. A weak moan escaped his lips.

Claire dropped the hammer and took one step back. Her eyes were low and her teeth were bared. Sweat drenched her face and neck. She crossed her arms and stared at her husband defiantly. They stood no more than ten feet apart. The twisted machinery between them was much like the remnants of their marriage.

George looked at her, and Claire thought he might cry. She was ready to explain herself, but just then they heard a noise from upstairs.

KNOCK

KNOCK

KNOCK

Claire smiled. There was no way this could go any better. But George either didn't hear or didn't care about their visitor. His eyes never left his wife's. He held his hands out to his sides and attempted to ask the most obvious question.

"What did, why, what . . ."

"There's someone at the door," Claire said coldly.

"Wha . . . Wha? . . ."

"The *door*, George. There's someone at the front door. I think you need to answer it."

He looked over his shoulder, and then back down at his bike. A slight twitch formed on the right side of his face, but he was still too shocked to look angry. He regarded his wife again and actually balled his fists. Claire couldn't believe her eyes.

"Why did you do this?"

"Go answer the door, George. When you get back, we can talk about *everything*."

He looked over his shoulder quickly, as if expecting a trap.

KNOCK

KNOCK

KNOCK

"You're going to pay for this," he declared. Most of his senses were back now. "I don't know what the hell's wrong with you, and I don't know how you're going to get the money, but best believe you're going to pay for this."

"Yeah, fine," Claire said. Her heart hammered in her chest. "Now will you go answer the door, please?"

She didn't think he would do it, but George was never one to let his temper get the best of him. He gave his wife one more hard glare before turning towards the steps. Halfway up, he looked back and pointed a finger.

"You stay your ass *right there*."

"I'm not going anywhere," Claire promised. He disappeared, and she leaned against the Navigator and waited. And she waited some more. After five minutes she started to go up and see what was taking him, but George appeared in the doorway just as she headed up the stairs. Claire backed away and took her original position on the other side of the wreckage.

George still wore only his boxers. He had a stack of papers in his hand, and for now, this material had his full attention. Claire put her hands on her hips and held the pose like a model. George looked up at her after scrutinizing each page thoroughly. He didn't look angry or upset or even surprised.

"What the hell is this?"

"You just read it," Claire said. "Do you need me to read it to you again?"

"You, you taking me to court?" he asked. "You wanna get a divorce?"

"I definitely have just cause."

"What the fu—what *just cause*?" He was starting to get upset again, and that's just where Claire wanted him. She knew she could shut him down with just two words:

"Kimberly Pate."

The blood drained from his face, and the look of doom he wore now was better than when he first saw the Harley.

"Oh, you recognize that name, huh?" she teased.

George didn't respond. His mouth fell open, and he blinked rapidly. His Adam's apple bobbed as if he was drinking.

"What's wrong?" Claire asked. "Cat got your tongue? Okay, well, I guess I'll do the talking then. First, let me start by saying you're a *disgusting pig*, George. I've wanted to say that to your face for quite a while now. You want to know why I won't sleep with you anymore? Want to know why I'm *stalling you out?* It's because you're *filthy* and you're *nasty*. You're low-down, you're *dirty*, and you're *rotten*."

George was still at a loss for words, and that was just fine with Claire.

"I've been following you," she said. "I followed you to the Chevy dealership when you picked up your other woman. I followed you to the steakhouse when you took her out. I followed you to that school, George. At first I couldn't believe any of this. I certainly couldn't believe you actually had *children* with this woman, but I know all about it now. I know about the twins. I know you let her name that boy *George Jr.* How the hell could you do that?" Her eyes glossed over, but Claire wouldn't let a tear fall.

"I talked to her!" she spat. "I was in her house, George. I sat at that table right next to those twins! I've got pictures! I've got DNA tests!"

Her nose started to run. She wiped it with the back of her hand.

"I loved you," she said. "I gave you *all I had*. I followed you anywhere you wanted me to go. I would have done *anything* for you, George. But you betrayed me. You betrayed our children. Do you have any idea how bad you've hurt me? Do you know how you've hurt your family?"

The tears started to fall, and Claire hated herself for it. She wanted to be strong. She wanted to be the one in control for a change. She wiped her face angrily and glared at her husband, who was still wide-eyed and open-mouthed.

"*Well, answer me!*" she screamed. "*Tell me why you did it!*"

George continued to stare, but his eyes ran in and out of focus. The papers fell from his hand and scattered around his bare feet. He reached up and touched the left side of his chest. Claire would remember that move for many years to come. He didn't grab it or squeeze it; he merely *touched* his chest, as if there was a button there that would fix what was going wrong inside.

George's eyes rolled back in his head, and his knees buckled. Claire thought he was playing, but when he fell backwards, he didn't throw an arm back to brace his fall. He didn't stick out his butt to catch most of the impact.

George fell straight and flat like a two by four; his back and legs hit the ground at the same time. His bald head connected with the concrete floor with an audible *SMACK*, but he didn't reach for the pain like normal people do when they injure themselves. Both of his arms lay limply at his sides. His eyes were closed, and that's how they would remain.

Oh, I know you're not going to die without answering me!

Claire rushed to his side and commenced CPR.

CHAPTER TWENTY-THREE

THE AFTERMATH

Claire never knew her husband had a Type A personality, but everything made sense once they sat her down and talked to her. In retrospect, she knew George was impatient, highly competitive, aggressive and excessively time-conscious. Like others with the personality trait, George was a workaholic and he was always unhappy with the smallest setbacks or delays. At Boeing he drove himself with quotas and deadlines, and with the affair he took multitasking to an all-time high.

People with Type A personalities often made things worse by drinking too much and smoking. And while George managed to avoid these pitfalls, he put his body in a state of high stress on a daily basis. The stress kept him in a constant fight of flight mode, and over the years his body released tons of adrenaline and epinephrine. These hormones sped up his heart rate, which soon constricted his arteries and eventually lead to heart disease.

George was diagnosed with CAD (coronary artery disease) over two years ago. Always a manly man, he did not tell his wife about his treatments, medications, or ongoing chest pains. Claire guessed his main reason for secrecy was because he knew she would try to help him.

Had she known he was sick, Claire would've gone out of her way to reduce the stress in her husband's life, and she would have certainly paid more attention to his comings and goings.

It was a near-fatal catch twenty-two: George couldn't confide in his life partner because in doing so he would have to divulge all, at which point he was likely to lose his life partner.

Claire had plenty of time to make these suppositions because her husband didn't regain consciousness for three hours after the ambulance wheeled him into the emergency room. Claire talked to George's ER doctor as well as his primary care physician, who provided the information on his cardiac history.

Claire was pissed he would keep something like that from her just as she was still pissed about the affair, but all of her anger took the backseat while she was at the hospital.

She was at her husband's bedside when his eyes fluttered open, and the sight filled her heart with unexpected cheer. Claire let out the biggest sigh of relief ever as she looked down on her poor, poor George. It was a peculiar situation, considering how badly she wanted him dead the night before.

It didn't seem possible for one heart attack to change a person so drastically, but George was but a shell of the man who stood over his mangled bike four hours ago. He lay on his back with an oxygen tube running from his nose and a mess of EKG leads stretching from beneath his gown. Next to his bed a monitor glowed brightly with jagged lines that skated across the screen from right to left. Claire didn't know what any of those readings meant, but as long as those lines weren't flat, she knew they were still in business.

George was on the third floor of Jackson Memorial's heart tower. This was a blessing because the first floor had cardiac ICU patients, and the second floor was for the unfortunates who had to have heart surgery. George was merely on a telemetry floor, which meant he wasn't expected to go live with Jesus any time soon.

Claire stood when he woke up. She hovered over the bed with fat tears in her eyes. She smiled hopefully, but it wasn't a pretty scene. George's cheeks were sunken and his eye sockets were dark. Pharmaceuticals dripped from an IV bag over his head. A catheter snaked from between his legs down to a collection bag hanging on the side of the bed.

George blinked quickly. He looked around the whole room before his eyes settled on Claire. There was no anger, foreboding or fear in those eyes. It was as if nothing he saw surprised him.

"I . . ." He cleared his throat, but his voice was still raspy. "I had a heart attack?"

Claire sighed, happy his loss of consciousness didn't leave him a vegetable.

"Yeah, you did," she said. "How come you didn't tell me about your chest pains?"

George breathed in slowly and took in his surroundings again. His eyes were low and he appeared inebriated. It was a strange sight because Claire never saw her husband high or drunk. George always had his wits about him.

A nurse walked into the room looking down at a plastic binder that contained his chart. She looked up and smiled brightly when she saw that her patient was awake.

"Hey. How are you doing?" She was a large woman with dark chocolate skin and big, beautiful lips. She wore an all blue scrub suit that could barely contain her breasts and hips.

George watched her but did not respond.

The nurse approached the bed and proceeded to take his vitals. "You doing okay?" she asked again and wrapped a blood pressure cuff around his arm. "Do you know what happened?" She put on a stethoscope and propped his arm on her hip.

George nodded weakly. "I had a heart attack."

"Good," the nurse said, counting his heartbeats. "Not good that you had a heart attack, but good you can speak. That's always a positive. According to your EEG you don't have any brain damage, but I need to ask you a few questions if that's okay with you."

"Okay," George said with a nod.

"Can you tell me your name?" the nurse asked.

He frowned and said, "George Hudgens."

"All right. Do you know what day it is?"

"It's Saturday," George said. "I don't know the date."

"He never keeps up with the date," Claire offered.

"That's fine," the nurse said. "Do you know what year it is?"

"2010," George said with another frown.

"Great," the nurse said. "And do you have any idea what time it is?"

George tilted his head so he could see the clock mounted on the wall behind her.

"It's one-thirty."

The nurse turned and eyed the clock herself. She looked back to George with a sly grin. "Oh, you're sneaky. You're also doing very well. Your heart attack was bad, but it wasn't the worst. I'll be right back. I'm going to call the doctor and let him know you're awake."

She left the room, and George's attention quickly went back to his wife. They watched each other for a while, neither wanting to speak about what happened earlier. George finally bit the bullet.

"I, I dreamed you smashed my bike."

Claire forced a smile. "That wasn't a dream, George."

He nodded. "I know. I was, I was hoping you'd let all of that go, because I'm laid up . . ."

Claire reached down and held his hand. "I want to. I'm sorry, George, but I can't. You know I can't."

He exhaled slowly with a soft hum. "How'd you find out?"

The question brought some of the anger back, and Claire had to let go of his hand.

"I don't think we should talk about that now. You're still sick. I don't . . ." She sniffled. "You have no idea how scared I was when you fell out."

George smiled weakly. "It's okay. I'm already at the hospital. If I have another heart attack, they already have a room for me."

Claire chuckled and sighed. She looked into his eyes with hardly any malice. "It was my anniversary present. As soon as you gave me that necklace, I knew you bought it for someone else."

George nodded. "I, I knew I messed up." He shook his head. "After I gave it to you, the very next day I realized what I did. I thought you might get suspicious, but I hoped you wouldn't. I knew you were smart, but I hoped . . ."

Claire waited, but he didn't finish that sentence. "Why'd you let her name that boy George Jr.?" she asked. This was completely different than she expected her confrontation to go, but it was probably for the best. Yelling and screaming was only good for third-grade recess.

"I didn't want her to," George said. "I told her not to, but she . . ."

"Kim."

"Kim, she's . . ." He cleared his throat. "She's a strong-minded person. A lot like you, baby. I couldn't give her a good enough reason *not* to name him George, and once she sets her mind to something." He shook his head. "She's, she's a lot like you."

Claire would have hated that comparison had she not met Kim herself. "You moved her from New York?" she asked.

George nodded.

"Why would you do that?"

"I, I didn't have a choice, Claire. I thought about breaking it off and coming to Texas without her, but she wasn't going to forget about me just because I was gone. She would've found me and put me on child support. You would've found out anyway if I went to court."

Claire didn't believe that. "You loved her?"

George looked away and the room went quiet. Claire didn't think he would answer, but he sighed heavily and met her eyes again. "Yes, Claire. I loved her. I luh, love her. I love the twins, too."

Claire knew this was the case, but it was still like a dagger through her heart. A blade so deep it pierced her very soul. Her tear ducts twitched, but she wouldn't cry in front of this man. Not now, and not ever again.

"Why would you do this to me?" she asked. "How could you do this?"

George's eyes watered and the tears wet his cheeks instead. In sixteen years of marriage, this was the first time she ever saw him cry. "I'm sorry, Claire. I am so, so sorry. I never meant for this to happen. I, I never wanted it to go this far. When I met her, I knew it was wrong. It was wrong for me to talk to her, and it was wrong to sleep with her, but I did it.

"You were at home taking care of our children, and I was, I was so stressed out at my job, and I had this big family I created. Everything seemed so hectic at home, but it was different when I was with her. She calmed me, and she made me happy, and there were no responsibilities."

That was laughable, but Claire let him finish his story.

311

"But then she got pregnant," he said. "And just like that, everything was messed up. I still loved you, and I didn't want you to find out. But by then I, I loved her, too, and the only way to keep it a secret was to stay with her. I started living with *both* of you, and things spiraled out of control so fast. I had to move her down to Texas, and I had to be there for you and for her and our kids and the twins. Oh, my God, Claire, please forgive me."

He sobbed openly. This was the most pitiful she'd ever seen him, but George's explanation only deepened Claire's contempt. He ran from the family *he created*—only to create another one? This man disgusted her more than leeches, rats and snakes combined, and it showed in her eyes. George saw the change and tried to switch gears.

"But, but I'm glad it's out in the open now. I love you, Claire, and you're the *only* woman I care about. I want us to be a normal family again. I want to be with *our* kids—no the twins. I don't care about Kim anymore. I only want to be with you."

His words were heartfelt, and Claire believed him, and if he told her that the day after she found the first card, she might have taken him back. But Claire was a different woman now. The whole ordeal changed her, and she could never go back to the way she was. She shook her head solemnly.

"It's over between us, George. We're getting a divorce."

His eyes widened and he grabbed her wrist. His touch was cold and unfamiliar.

"Please don't say that," he begged. "It doesn't have to be over, Claire. It doesn't have to be." He tried to sit up, but the pain was too much for him. His arm trembled, and sweat quickly sprouted on his forehead.

Claire pulled her arm away and placed her hands on his shoulders. She pushed him back to a lying position and patted his chest lightly. "George, I'm going to leave. I know I'm upsetting you, and I don't want you to get any worse. Lie down and stop hurting yourself."

"No."

"Shhhh," she cooed. "It's all right. Kim's on her way, and I'll bring the kids by later for a visit."

George's mouth fell open. "Kim?"

Claire nodded. "I called her already, before you woke up. She should be here any minute."

George's confusion was priceless, so Claire didn't tell him she made the call posing as a nurse. She smiled and turned her back on him for the very first time. When she stepped out of his room, she knew she was stepping into a brand new life, and she did so with boldness and confidence. She left sixteen years of her life behind her, but that was all right. She still had a whole lot of life left in her.

When she got to the ground floor, Claire passed a grieving mother of two at the hospital's main entrance. The young mother looked up at Claire. There was a hint of recognition when they made eye contact, but Kim didn't stop to ask if they'd met somewhere before. At that moment, Kim was only concerned with her man, and whether Claire was still interested in the house across the street was totally irrelevant.

ᴄ᷾᷾᷾᷾᷾᷾᷾

When she got back to her Lexus, Claire found her cellphone lying on the passenger seat. She didn't realize she'd
left it, but considering the morning's drama, it wasn't too
surprising. She had a multitude of missed calls. Most of
them were from Becky, so she called her back first.

"Hello?"

"Hey, Becky."

"Claire! Oh, my God! What took you so long to call
back?"

"I'm at the hospital. Where are the kids?"

"We're here at your house," Becky said. "What are
you, you're where?"

"At the hospital," Claire said. "George had a heart
attack."

Becky gasped. "Oh, no!"

"It's okay," Claire said. "He's going to be all right. I'm
on my way home. What are the kids doing?"

"I took them out to breakfast," Becky said. "And then
we went to the mall because you weren't answering your
phone. I kept them out as long as I could, but we ran out
of stuff to do. I brought them back two hours ago."

"You're still with them?"

"Yeah, I'm here."

"That's good," Claire said, and then she had a horrible thought. "You didn't let them go in the garage, did
you?"

"The garage, no. I didn't let them, and I don't think
they did."

"Oh, man," Claire said with a hand to her chest. She started the Lexus and backed out of her parking spot.

"What's wrong?" Becky asked. "What happened to George?"

"I broke his bike," Claire said. "I went to town on it this morning before the constable showed up."

"George has a bike?"

"His Harley," Claire said. "When he saw what I did to it, that's what made him have the heart attack."

"Are you serious?"

"Yeah, but it wasn't all my fault. He's been having chest pains for a while now. I didn't even know he had heart problems, but yeah, when he saw the bike, that's what made him fall out. I was standing there, yelling at him, and he had a heart attack right in front of me."

"Why'd you break his bike? *How* did you break it?"

"We have to talk about it later," Claire said. "Where are you now? Where are the kids?"

"They're in their rooms, I think. I'm in the living room."

"Becky, I need you to make sure none of them goes down to the garage. If they see that bike, I don't know what I'd do. I don't know why I did that. I still can't believe it."

"Okay," Becky said. "No one will go down there. Are you gonna be here soon?"

"Fifteen minutes," Claire said. "Thanks a lot, for everything. I gotta go."

"Okay," Becky said, and they disconnected.

Claire called information next looking for a nearby wrecker service. The operator gave her the number she needed and then transferred the call to them. Claire chewed off her pinky nail while the phone rang.

"Plummer's Towing."

"Hi," Claire said. "I need to get a motorcycle picked up from my house."

"Where you taking it to?" The man on the other end had deep southern twang, and he sounded like he had a jaw full of snuff.

Claire racked her brain for the name of George's favorite motorcycle shop. "Um, Cycle, no, uh, *Custom Cycles*, on Camp Bowie."

The man on the other end grunted. "Where we picking up?"

"My, my house," Claire said. She gave him the address.

"That's a nice little trip," the tow guy noticed. "What's wrong with your bike?"

"It's smashed up," Claire said. "It got wrecked pretty bad."

The man grunted again. "Hmph. I cain't get nobody over there for at least an hour."

"That's fine," Claire said. "Thank you."

✑

When she got home, Claire didn't want to park in the garage, but she couldn't park in the driveway either because she'd have to move when the tow truck got there. She left her Lexus on the curb instead, and it looked so out of place she knew she wouldn't get away with her plan. The kids were going to find out about daddy's bike no matter how diligent she was.

Inside Claire found Becky in the living room alone.

"Hey, girl."

Becky jumped up to embrace her.

"Claire! How's it going? Are you okay?"

"I'm all right," Claire said. "Where are the kids?"

"They're still in their rooms. They're so quiet. Did you serve George the papers this morning?"

Claire put a finger to her mouth. "Shhh! We'll talk later."

"Oh. Okay. How's George?"

"He's doing well," Claire said. "Listen, I appreciate all your help today, but I have to talk to the kids. Lord knows this is going to be one of the hardest things I've ever had to tell them."

"You're going to tell them about the divorce?"

Claire put a hand to Becky's lips this time. "Shhht! No, not yet. I'm talking about him being in the hospital. They're going to be so worried."

"Oh," Becky said. "It'll be okay. You sure you don't need anything else from me?"

"No," Claire said. "You've already been such a big help. I appreciate everything, really. I love you, girl."

"When are you going to tell me what happened?"

"How about later on tonight," Claire offered. "I'll call Melanie, and maybe we can get some more bumpy face."

"That's a great idea!" Becky exclaimed. "I love that bumpy face!"

ᕐ

Claire thought she'd have a hard time explaining George's heart attack to the kids, but they were surprisingly brave throughout the whole ordeal. Once they were assured their father was definitely not going to die, every question they asked was to feed their curiosity.

"Did he die for a minute, and then they brought him back to life?" Stacy asked. She sat on the couch on her mother's right side. Nikki sat quietly on Claire's left, and George Jr. sat Indian-style on the floor between her legs.

"No," Claire said. "At no point did your father die for a minute."

"That would've been cool," George Jr. said. "If he saw a light, and then he had to run *away* from the light so he could come back alive."

"That's not *cool*," Nikki said. "Don't you know Daddy's hurt right now?"

"Mama said he was all right."

"He is going to be all right," Claire confirmed. "But right now he is still sick. He's in the hospital, and I don't know how long he's going to be there."

"Does he have a zipper on his chest?" Stacy asked.

Claire frowned. "A zipper?"

"When Bridgette's dad had a heart attack, he came back home with a zipper on his chest," Stacy informed.

"That's because he had *surgery*," Nikki said. She was more solemn and irritable than the younger two.

"Could they unzip it and see his heart?" George Jr. asked.

"I should hope not," Claire said with a frown. "What she's talking about is probably staples they put in to keep his chest closed. Once it heals, they'll take the staples out, and it will just be a long scar."

"They really use *staples*?" George Jr. was astounded.

"They do if you have surgery," Claire said. "But we don't need to talk about that, because your father didn't have surgery. He had a small heart attack, and if he takes care of himself when he gets out, everything will be fine."

"When is he going to get out?" George Jr. wanted to know.

"I don't know," Claire said.

"Can we go see him?" Stacy asked.

Claire nodded. "We're going in a couple of hours. Did y'all eat lunch yet?"

"I ate a corny dog," Stacy said.

"I had some chips," George Jr. reported.

Claire shook her head in dismay. "Why don't y'all go find something to wear to the hospital, and I'll make something to eat before we go."

George and Stacy scurried off, but Nikki lingered on the couch. Claire put an arm around her shoulder.

"You all right?"

Nikki nodded. "Is Dad really going to be okay?"

"Of course," Claire said with a furrowed brow. "Why would you ask that?"

Nikki shrugged. "I didn't know if you trying to make it sound good so the children didn't get scared."

Claire chuckled. "No, I wasn't. And I take it you're not a child anymore?"

Nikki shook her head. "I'm not a child. I'm a young adult."

"Oh, well excuse me, madame," Claire said.

"I forgive you," Nikki said and got up with the gracefulness of a princess.

⁓

With the kids busy in their rooms, Claire got started on a tuna salad. She still didn't think she could get George's bike picked up without anyone knowing about it, and she was right.

The wrecker showed up at three o'clock, and his arrival was nowhere near secretive. Not only did he pull his noisy truck into the driveway, but he got out and knocked hard on the front door. Claire rushed to answer it, but by then Stacy and George Jr. were on their way as well.

Claire cut them off in the hallway. "Y'all go back to your room!" she ordered.

"Why?" Stacy asked. "Who's that?"

"It's a tow truck," Claire admitted. "He's going to take your daddy's motorcycle to the shop again."

Luckily George shipped his bike off fairly often, so they swallowed the story easily enough.

"Can I watch?" George Jr. asked.

"No," Claire said. "Go back to your room."

"Why can't I watch?"

Nikki emerged from her room then, and Claire was at her wit's end.

"None of you can watch! Now go back to your rooms. All of you! Your dad's in the hospital, and I'm stressed enough as it is."

That didn't make a lot of sense, but the kids didn't argue. They went back to whatever they were doing, and Claire went outside to direct the truck driver. They got George's busted bike loaded up and shipped off in just fifteen minutes, but Claire was sure she hadn't heard the last of it.

And she was right.

After lunch Nikki crept into her mom's room looking more forlorn than a gazelle at a hyena convention. Claire was ironing a blouse, but she stopped to see what the girl's problem was.

"What's wrong, honey?"

Nikki made her way to her mother's bed and took a seat slowly. Claire went and sat next to her. Nikki wore blue jeans with a long-sleeved black button-down. Her long hair was down, and she had a large bang hanging over her right eye.

Claire thought she wanted to finally give her feelings on George's heart attack, but it turned out her daughter was a lot smarter than she gave her credit for. Nikki had her mom's intuition as well.

"What happened to Dad?" she asked as soon as Claire sat down.

Claire's heart shot up in her throat, but she tried not to show it. Her thoughts immediately returned to the night before, when she held a gun to George's head and thought she heard a sound behind her. If that was Nikki, then this child had to be on the verge of a mental breakdown.

Claire got up and closed her door. She came back and sat with her hands in her lap. "What do you mean, honey? I told you, your father had a heart attack."

"Why did the tow truck take his bike?" Nikki asked.

Claire couldn't believe the bad vibes she was getting. "Nikki, why are you asking me about your father's bike?"

"You asked George how he would feel if Daddy didn't come home," Nikki reminded her.

Claire knew right then she was in a heap of trouble. She regretted ad-libbing such a delicate conversation even more now.

"What are you saying?" she asked her daughter.

Nikki sniffled and a thick tear rolled down her cheek. Somehow she still had the strength to look her mom in the eyes. "I just want to know what happened."

Claire wished there was a big hole she could jump into. "Nikki, you're just a—"

"*I'm not a baby*," the adolescent spat. "I'll be fifteen in *four months*."

Claire was startled at first, and then she reached for her daughter's hand. She cradled it and squeezed softly. "Yes. You will be. You are a big girl." Claire still didn't want to tell her about the bike, but Nikki would think horrible things about her mother until it was out in the open. That was even more unbearable.

"I can tell you what happened," Claire said, "but you're not going to like what you hear. This is *real* big girl stuff I'm talking about. I didn't do anything wrong. I think you should just accept that. But if you want the truth, I won't keep it from you. It's going to hurt, though. . . ."

With the whole weight of the issue fully in her hands, Nikki hesitated. She decided she didn't like being in the dark any more than her mom did. "I want to know."

Claire took a deep breath and sighed. "All right." She regarded her daughter intensely. "You're a lot braver than I was at your age."

Nikki smiled hesitantly.

"The reason I asked George about your dad not coming home," Claire said, "is because I found out he's been cheating on me."

Nikki's mouth fell open.

"Yeah," Claire said. "That's pretty much how I felt. But it's worse than that, Nicole. Not only is your father cheating on me, but he's been with the other woman for *eight years*. They have children together. Twins."

Nikki stared at her mom like she was watching a magic trick. "Nuh-uhn."

Claire nodded. "Trust me, I wouldn't lie on your daddy, especially about something like that."

Nikki shook her head in bewilderment. "Daddy has some more kids?"

"Yes, he does," Claire said. "They were at the hospital earlier today. That's why we had to wait a while before I took you guys. His girlfriend was there, too."

"Oh, my God, Mama . . ."

"I'm going to divorce him," Claire said. "I didn't know how you kids would feel about it, so that's why I asked George Jr. that question. I regret it now. It didn't do anything but stir up a hornet's nest."

Nikki was speechless.

"I didn't want you to see them take the bike," Claire went on, "because I got so mad I beat your dad's motorcycle with a sledge hammer. I called the wrecker to pick it up because I'm ashamed of what I did. I didn't want you guys to know about it—at least not until I told you about the divorce."

Nikki looked like she was having second thoughts about the big girl drawers she put on. "You broke Daddy's Harley?"

"I flattened it like a pancake," Claire admitted.

"So Dad really *did* have a heart attack?"

"What did you think?" Claire asked. "You don't think *I* did something to put him in the hospital, do you?"

Nikki didn't nod, but she was on the verge of it.

"I was mad at your father," Claire said, "but I could never hurt him—not even if I wanted to. Trust me."

Nikki smiled and a whole world of weight lifted from her small shoulders.

Claire threw her arms around the child, and Nikki laid her head on her mother's shoulder.

"How do you like being a big girl?" Claire asked.

"It sucks," Nikki admitted. "But I feel better."

They held onto each other for a while, and then Nikki looked up and frowned.

"Do I have another little brother, or do I have a big brother?"

Claire chuckled. "Another *little* brother."

Nikki rolled her eyes and moaned. "That sucks, too."

"I'm glad we're finally on the same page," Claire said.

CHAPTER TWENTY-FOUR
A STRATEGIC MEETING

Claire called at five to make sure her husband had no other visitors before she took the kids to Jackson Memorial. The whole time they were there Claire expected Kim to round every corner, but Ms. Pate was no longer at the hospital, and she didn't show up again during the kid's visit.

Claire wanted to ask George if he told his mistress the truth yet, but they were never left alone and she didn't get a chance. But it didn't matter anyway. Soon everyone would know all about his sordid deeds.

Nikki already knew her father's secrets, but, as instructed, she didn't let the cat out of the bag. She hugged her daddy and smiled at him and doted on him, and Claire thought she should get an Oscar for her performance.

George watched his wife's eyes a lot during the visit, and each time he saw the same message behind her dark pupils: *You're an asshole, I'm only here for the kids, and we're still getting a divorce.*

When it was time to go, Claire almost laughed when a nurse asked if she wanted a cot so she could spend the night.

"Uh, um, no thank you," she told her. "I definitely do not want to spend the night. Not now and not ever."

In the background George watched solemnly like an old, desperate man, but Claire had no sympathy for him. She gathered her brood around her and didn't look back.

"Come on, y'all. Let's go home, get some ice cream."

"Bye, Dad!" George Jr. called over his shoulder. "I can't wait for you to come home."

Claire and Nikki locked eyes and exchanged a knowing look.

"Yeah," Claire said. "I can't wait to see how that turns out, either."

⌒

Later that evening the kids started to miss their dad again when it was time for bed, but they weren't too upset about it. George wasn't around for them most of the time when he was healthy. Plus Claire knew they got a lot of their cues from her, and since she wasn't crying and moping around the house, they had no inclination to do so, either.

Her girlfriends came over at eleven, and it was a struggle to keep them quiet until the youngsters were officially asleep. Later they posted up in the den with three shot glasses, one bottle of bumpy face, and a whole lot of catty estrogen. Melanie and Becky wanted to hear all about the battered motorcycle and the look on George's face when Claire finally got her chance to shut him down, but the conversation eventually made its way to Kimberly Pate's *audacity.* The girls had different views on that subject.

"She loves him," Claire said. "I could hear it in her voice when I called her. I saw it in her eyes. She loves George's dirty drawers."

"That's the problem right there," Melanie argued. "You shouldn't be in love with somebody else's husband."

"She doesn't know he's married."

"You don't know that." Melanie leaned forward and poured everyone another shot. She spilled a fourth serving on the coffee table and plucked half dozen Kleenex to wipe it up. "Ooh, I'm sorry."

"I got it." Claire grabbed the tissues and cleaned the mess herself. She then took her glass and turned it up with her comrades. The liquor was strong, but this was her fifth shot. She was already somewhat inebriated, and the alcohol was going down with more and more ease.

"She wouldn't put up with him if she knew he was married," Claire guessed.

"You don't know what bitches will do nowadays," Melanie warned. "Some hos *like* to be the other woman."

"She went to her house," Becky said.

"Yeah, I went to her house," Claire said. "She didn't know me at all. Even when I told her my real name she didn't have any recognition."

"What about when she went to the hospital?" Melanie questioned. "She had to know he was married by then."

"I'm the one who called her," Claire countered. "I told her I was a nurse, and I didn't say anything about him being married. Plus I saw her on my way out, and she didn't say anything to me."

"She been keeping her mouth closed all these years," Melanie said. "She ain't got no reason to say nothing now."

Claire shook her head in exasperation. "Look, whether she knows now or not isn't even the point. What I need to figure out is where she wants to go from here. Does she want to be with him anyway, or does she feel the same way I do? And if she still doesn't know he's married, who should tell her?"

"Wow," Becky mused. "Can you imagine that? If it was your boyfriend of eight years, this man you've got children with, and someone calls you one day to say he's been married the whole time?"

"Don't nobody care what she feels like," Melanie said.

"I do," Claire said, and the conversation skipped a beat.

"Why?" Melanie wanted to know.

"Because I was her," Claire said. "I was in the same boat with her. I know how I felt when I found out what was going on. She's going through the same thing. Plus I'm about to divorce George and take everything he has. What do the twins get out of it?"

"Forget them twins," Melanie said with a frown. "That's *they* problem."

"No man is an island," Becky warned.

Melanie sneered at her. "What?"

"That's John Donne," Claire said.

The clarification didn't help. "So, what that mean?" Melanie asked.

"It means *they* matter just like *she* matters," Claire said. "Just like *I* matter, just like *you* matter. We're all in this together. No one's out there all by themselves."

"Bitch don't matter to me," Melanie said.

Becky didn't have a seventeenth-century poet to quote for that one. "Are you going to tell your kids about the twins?" she asked instead.

Claire shook her head and looked up to the heavens for guidance. "I don't know. What do you think?"

Becky shrugged. "Are you asking me or Jesus?"

Claire grinned and shook her head. "I'm asking *you*, dingus."

Melanie laughed. "I think you should tell them," she said.

"Me, too," Becky said.

Claire frowned. "Tell them their dad was a *freak*?"

"*No*," Becky said with a giggle. "You don't have to tell them *that*."

"How else can I put it?" Claire wondered. "I know I have to tell them something, but I'm still worried about how they'll react to the divorce, let alone those twins. You should've seen Nikki's face when I confided in her."

"Tell them a lot of great men had relations outside of their marriage," Becky suggested.

"Great men like who?" Claire wondered.

"Well, like Thomas Jefferson for one."

"You sure picked one hell of an example," Claire said. "They have Jefferson family reunions every year, and they fought like hell to keep those black people out."

"They *eventually* let them in."

Claire rolled her eyes. "Girl, we're going to have to work on your persuasion skills."

⁓

The next few days crept by like years, and time did more to heal the Hudgens' wounds than any medication could have. The kids went back to school on Monday and Claire returned to work the same day. No one at the office knew about George's heart attack or the divorce, so there were refreshingly few condolences to deal with.

The morning hours were slow that day, so Claire had time to call her lawyer and update him on the recent developments. Trevor was blown away by the news of George's heart attack, and he was equally shocked by Claire's new proposition.

"You, you want to, what?"

Claire sat up in her seat with her elbows on the desktop. She chewed on the back of her pen and looked around to make sure no one was eavesdropping. "I think it's the right thing to do," she said.

"Well, I don't know if that's even *legal*," Trevor argued. "I, I have to say I never heard of anything like it. Not to mention how much this would affect your case. If we can find a judge who will allow it, she's likely to get half of everything you would've got."

"Yes, I know that," Claire said. "And I'm okay with it. As long as I get the house, I don't mind splitting the rest."

There was a long pause and then a big sigh on the other end of the line. "Where'd you get this idea, anyway?" Trevor wanted to know.

"From TV," Claire said quickly.

"Nothing good ever came from *TV*," Trevor muttered.

"Don't be so negative," Claire kidded. "Just because most lawyers are soulless bloodsuckers doesn't mean you have to follow suit."

"Ouch, ouch and ouch," Trevor said. "You know I'm not like that. I'm just looking at things from a legal perspective."

"Well, answer me this," Claire said. "Do you think those twins are entitled to any support?"

"Well, of course I do."

"And Kim," Claire said, "you don't think she deserves anything?"

"I don't know if she does or not," Trevor said. "She's not my client, and she has nothing to do with my case."

"She has everything to do with this case."

"But only as evidence."

"Yeah, and that's what I want to change," Claire said. There was another pause and another big sigh from Trevor Smiley. "What were you watching on TV, anyhow?" he asked.

Claire giggled. "It was an infomercial for Jerry Ampler."

"Aw, jeez."

Jerry Ampler was one of the most notorious trial lawyers in Texas. The majority of his cases were frivolous fender benders, and it was rumored he had nearly half of the state's trauma doctors and chiropractors in his pocket. But not everything he did was bad.

"It was about the Netavan trials," Claire reported. "He was asking women to call if—"

"If they had a miscarriage in the last three years," Trevor interrupted. "And if they were prescribed Netavan during that time period. Yeah, I saw the commercials."

"That's what gave me the idea," Claire said.

"For a class-action divorce?"

"Yes. I was already thinking we should do something for Kim and her kids, and I believe that's the best way. We should both go after him, at the same time."

"Well, first off I don't believe that's possible," Trevor said. "And secondly, have you had any contact with Ms. Pate? Does she know about the affair yet, and more importantly, does she want to stay with George afterwards? 'Cause if she still wants to be with him, chances are she's not going to get on board with this."

"Let me deal with that on my end," Claire said. "What I need you to do is see if you can get this started in the courts."

"Exactly how do you plan on dealing with it on your end?" Trevor wondered. "I can't write up a thing until I know Kim is down with it."

"I'm having lunch with Kim today," Claire said.

Trevor was almost to the point that nothing she said surprised him. Almost.

"Come again."

"I called her this morning," Claire said. "I told her I wanted to meet with her so we could talk about George, and she said okay."

"She didn't ask what it was about—and who you were for that matter?"

"I told her who I was," Claire said. "She remembers me from when I went to look at the house across the street from her."

"You did what?"

"It's a long story," Claire said. "All I know is she remembers me, and she didn't seem too surprised I wanted to talk about George. She didn't ask a lot of questions. She just said okay, she would meet me."

"You . . ." Trevor sighed again. "You know what, I don't even want to understand all of this. If you and Kim want to sue George at the same time, then have her call me tomorrow and I'll get to work on it. How you do it is not my business. I work for you."

"That's right," Claire said with a grin. "You do work for me, don't you?"

"Yes, ma'am. So if you ever need me to file a brief or lose my briefs or anything like that . . ."

Claire cracked up. "Lose your briefs?"

"Actually I wear boxers, but—"

"Good day, Mr. Smiley."

"Good day to you, Claire. And good luck with Kim."

Claire left the office at noon and made it to the Don Pablo's on Hulen Street in just five minutes. She didn't see Kim's car in the parking lot, but when she entered the restaurant the hostess asked if her name was Claire.

"Um, yes, it is."

"This way, please. There is a woman waiting for you."

Claire's stomach twisted in knots as she followed the young lady through the colorful restaurant. She didn't feel this nervous when she met Kim the first time, but they met under a pretense then. This time Claire was about to drop a nuclear bomb, and Kim would have time to look at her and scrutinize her or maybe even attack or belittle her.

The hostess led her to a small booth near the kitchen. A waiter walked by as they approached. He carried a huge platter with four sizzling plates on it. The hostess stopped to let him pass, and Claire stopped, too. When the waiter was gone Claire saw Kim sitting alone at the booth. Kim was nervous, too. She looked around the restaurant anxiously. Her eyes froze and narrowed when they landed on Claire.

It was clear she recognized Claire not only as the woman who visited her home last week, but also as the woman she saw at the hospital on Friday afternoon. Kim didn't look angry or annoyed by Claire's presence, but her confusion was immeasurable.

"Here you go," the hostess said and placed Claire's menu on the table across from her husband's girlfriend.

Claire took her seat slowly, and the two women stared deeply into each other's eyes.

"Your waiter will be right with you," the hostess said and disappeared into the scenery. George's two women didn't speak for a full ten seconds.

Claire always thought Kim was attractive, and even in her state of distress she was still pretty today. Kim wore a white sleeveless dress that had a ballet neckline and blue floral prints. She wore her hair pulled back in a pony tail and had barely any makeup. Her face was smooth, with no worry lines, but you could see the stress in her eyes.

Claire wore tan slacks with a dark blouse she found in the back of her closet. The slacks were loose fitting, except around her hips and thighs. The blouse was form-fitting with a V-neckline that pulled attention to her generous bosoms. Claire wore lipstick and eyeliner and was just as stressed as Kim was, probably more so. She couldn't keep her fingers from trembling, so she kept her hands in her lap.

Kim's voice was shaky, but she made the first move. "You're Claire, right?"

"Yes," Claire said. "I'm the one who called you this morning."

"You called from the hospital, too," Kim said. "I remember your voice."

"Yes, that was me, too," Claire said. "I'm sorry I lied to you about being a nurse."

"You also lied when you came to my house," Kim recalled. "You said you wanted to look at the place across the street."

"I'm sorry about that, too," Claire said with a sigh. "But I wasn't trying to hurt you in any way. Please forgive me."

Ms. Pate didn't say whether she would or wouldn't. "What do you want with me?" she asked, and that surprised Claire immensely.

"You mean, he hasn't said anything?"

"Who?" Kim wanted to know.

"George," Claire said. "I thought he would have told you by now."

Kim shook her head hesitantly, and Claire could see her inner turmoil. On one hand she already knew, or had a good idea. But on the other hand, Kim didn't want to know what was going on. Claire realized this woman loved George as much as she did. That was even more reason for Kim to stay with him after the divorce.

"My name is Claire Hudgens," she said. "When I came to your house, I told you it was *Hutchens*, but it's really Hudgens. George is my husband."

Kim took the news much like Claire did when she found the first card. Kim stared with shock and then disbelief. She shook her head, put a hand to her mouth, and looked down at her menu. When she met Claire's gaze again, Kim's eyes were filled with tears. They fell thick and heavy, and Claire had never seen anything so painful. Her eyes welled, too, and their waiter didn't know what to think when he approached the booth.

"Uh, hi, I'm Kyle. Do you, um, would you like some water?"

Claire shook her head and Kim nodded and the waiter got away from them as quickly as possible.

"I'm so sorry," Claire said when he was gone. "I know exactly how you feel. And I'm not just saying that."

Kim sniffled loudly, and Claire dumped the silverware from her napkin and offered it to her. Kim took the cloth and blew nose into it. "I knew it," she breathed. "I knew there was something going on with him. He's never at home. I'm not stupid."

"Neither one of us is."

"Why you, why you didn't tell me?" Kim bawled.

Claire knew that question would come up, but she still didn't have a good answer for it. She wiped her eyes and shook her head slowly. "I'm sorry. I was being selfish."

Kim blew her nose again and squinted through her tears.

"I found out George was cheating over a month ago," Claire said. "At first I didn't know for sure, so I started following him around. He led me to you, and I saw your kids, and I knew we were going to get a divorce. But I had to meet you first. I went to your house, and I lied to you. I don't know what I wanted really, but I had to meet you.

"I lied about who I was because I didn't want George to know yet, but I didn't take time to think about how it affected you because, because I didn't care about you right then. Even though we were in the same situation, I didn't care about your feelings. And I was wrong for that. I'm sorry."

Their waiter came back with the water and didn't ask if they were ready to order yet. "I'll, uh, I'll give you some more time."

"How, how long have y'all been married?" Kim asked when he walked away. She had her tears somewhat under control, but she couldn't control the quivery quality of her voice.

"We've been married sixteen years," Claire said. and Kim's eyes flashed open like she got slapped. "He was my high-school sweetheart," Claire went on.

"*Sixteen years?*"

"We have three kids," Claire said. "Our oldest is in high school. The youngest is in the fourth grade."

Kim was too shocked to respond.

"When I found out George had twins with you," Claire said, "that was worse than knowing he was cheating in the first place, so I know how you feel."

Kim shook her head. "I can't believe this."

"It's true," Claire said. "George has been splitting his time between you and me. He tells me he's going out of town for business, but he goes straight to your house. I know this for a fact because I followed him. I don't know what he tells you when he leaves for a week at a time, but he doesn't go where he said he would. He comes straight to my house. He's been playing both of us for a long time."

"I met George eight years ago," Kim said, still in a daze.

"I know," Claire said. "When he first met you, everything was perfect. You didn't have any children or responsibilities, and he used to run to you to get away from the stress at home with me and my kids. But then you got pregnant, and he says everything changed."

"He told you that?"

"I confronted him Saturday," Claire said. "I told him I was getting a divorce, and that's when he had the heart attack."

Kim's tears dried up in a fire of bewilderment. "He told me he had high cholesterol," she recounted.

That was a surprise to Claire, and she was pissed all over again. "That's why he said he had a heart attack?"

Kim nodded, her eyes big and beautiful.

Claire put a hand to her temple and shook her head. "I can't believe he hasn't told you about me yet, but considering everything else he did, it's not that big of a surprise. He's still a snake and he's still trying to play us, girl. When I told him I knew about you, he said he didn't want to be with you anymore. He said he wanted to be with me and he didn't care about the twins."

That brought Kim the rest of the way from woeful to angry. "He said *what*?"

"Listen," Claire said. "I'm really sorry about all of this, and I definitely don't want to argue. George has been playing both of us for fools, and we have to stick together if we want to get him back."

Kim nodded vaguely. "What did he say about the twins?"

"I don't know if he meant it," Claire said, "but he did tell me that. He says he wants to be with only me and my kids. He says he doesn't care about you or the twins."

Kim's nostrils flared.

"But this is a weasel we're talking about," Claire said. "I'm sure if you tell him that you know about me, he'll tell you the exact same thing. I don't think George cares who he's with at this point, so long as he gets to keep one of us."

"Shit," Kim said with a sneer. "He ain't staying with *me*."

Those words were like music to Claire's ears, and she couldn't help but smile.

"That's what I hoped you'd say." Claire brought her purse to her lap and dug for her lawyer's card. "I'm going to divorce him," she said. "I was going to get him for everything, but I keep telling myself you should be involved.

339

George may not have married you, but he did you just as wrong as he did me. We should work together on this case."

Kim took the card and studied it briefly. "But I can't divorce him. He's just my boyfriend."

"You've been with him for eight years," Claire said. "That makes you his common-law wife."

Kim's eyes narrowed as she considered this. "You want us to divorce him at the same time?"

"My lawyer is against it," Claire said. "He said that would entitle you to some of the alimony, and I'd have to split the properties with you. But I told him this is what I want to do. I think the twins deserve just as much as my kids do. And if you don't want to be with George anymore, then we should work together to ruin him."

Kim thought about it a few seconds more. "You're not going to take him back?" she asked.

"Um, hell no," Claire said. "What about you? Do you still want to be with him?"

"Not if what you're saying is true. If they'll let me divorce his ass, then that's what I want, too."

Claire stuck a hand over the table. "Then it's a deal. If you call my lawyer tomorrow, he'll set everything up."

Kim took Claire's hand and shook it. "You say you and him have *three* kids together?"

"Yeah," Claire said. "And my boy's name is *George Jr.*"

Kim had been through a myriad of emotions already, but she still had enough in her to register disgust at this. "*That's* why he didn't want me to name my son George! Aw, hell yeah. We gon' get his ass!"

"Yeah, we are," Claire said with a chuckle. "And I want to be the one to tell him."

CHAPTER TWENTY-FIVE

THE FINAL CHAPTER
MOVING ON

Claire had a message for her when she got back to the office. It was from Jackson Memorial, and when she called back, they told her George was scheduled for release later that evening. Claire thought that was a perfect time to tell him about the class-action divorce, but there was one more thing she had to take care of first. Stacy and George Jr. still didn't know about the break up, and Claire had to give them the bad news before she left their father stranded at the hospital.

Claire was nervous about the talk when she picked the kids up from school, and they sensed something heavy was on their mother's mind.

"What happened?" Stacy asked from the backseat. "Is Daddy all right?"

"Did he have another heart attack?" George Jr. guessed, already on the verge of despair.

"No," Claire said. "Your dad is perfectly fine. But that is what I want to talk to you about. He's getting out of the hospital today."

"That's good," George Jr. noted.

"Yeah, why you not happy?" Stacy asked.

███ off

"Why *aren't* you happy?" George Jr. corrected her.

"Shut up!" Stacy hollered and then asked, "Why aren't you happy, Mom?"

"He can't walk?" George Jr. predicted.

"Why don't y'all be quiet until we get home and then she'll tell you!" Nikki snapped.

Her siblings immediately piped down, and Claire gave her oldest daughter a grateful nod in the rearview mirror.

⌒

When they got home Claire ushered her family to the living room before they could disperse and get started on their homework. She directed all of them to sit on the couch while she took a seat across from them on the loveseat. They were starting to get worried, so she opened the meeting with a smile.

"You know, you guys really have surprised me lately. I'm very proud of the way you've handled yourselves since your dad went to the hospital."

George grinned brightly, but Stacy and Nikki's smiles were guarded.

"You've been acting like grown-ups," Claire went on, "and I'm glad because I have a real grown-up thing to talk about."

"Uh-oh," Nikki said.

"Uh-oh, what?" Stacy asked.

"There's no *uh-oh*," Claire said. "We're a family, and no matter what happens, we're going to handle it as a *family*. We're all we've got, so we're going to stick together, right?"

They all nodded.

"Right?"

"Yes," they said in unison.

"Okay." Claire leaned forward in her seat and sighed. "All right, now what I want to tell you, I don't want you to think of your father any differently. He's a good man. He loves you and he takes care of you as best he can. You guys all love your dad, right?"

They nodded again.

"You love him, and you know he loves you, too, right?"

They looked around at each other before nodding this time.

"Well, I have to tell you something that might make you angry at your father. But I don't want you to be. Just keep thinking about how much you love him, okay?"

No one responded.

"Your father is not coming home with us when he gets out of the hospital," Claire said. Stacy gasped, and Claire kept talking before she could interrupt. "Your father had, he had an *accident* a little while ago," Claire said. "He did something with another lady that he shouldn't have done. But we still love him, right?"

They were confused as hell, but they nodded.

"What your father did with this other lady," Claire went on, "accidentally made a *baby*. You remember we talked about where babies come from?" she asked George Jr.

"From your stomach," he said.

"That's right," Claire said. "So what I'm trying to tell you is your dad likes this other lady a whole bunch, and they had a baby together—actually, they had *twins* together; that's *two* babies. Do you guys understand what I'm saying?"

"Daddy cheated on Mama," Nikki clarified.

Claire wouldn't have used those choice words, but they did the trick. Stacy's mouth fell open, and George Jr.'s eyes bugged.

"That's, that's right," Claire said, "But we're not going to talk about what he did or why he did it. He was wrong, and we'll just leave it at that. The reason I'm telling you about it is because there's two things you need to understand: The first is your father and I are going to get a divorce. So he won't be living with us anymore. The second thing is about the twins. They are your brother and sister. Even though I'm not their mother, your father is their father, too. And that makes you all *related*."

"You're getting a divorce?" Stacy asked.

"Yes," Claire said. "But that doesn't mean you won't see your father anymore. You can still see him whenever you want."

"I got another brother?" Stacy asked next.

"You have another brother *and* another sister," Claire said. "They're twins. They're in the second grade, so they're eight years old."

"I'm nine!" George Jr. observed. "Does that mean I'm not the youngest anymore?"

"That's right," Claire said. "You have a little brother and a little sister now."

"Daddy cheated on you?" Stacy asked again.

"Yes, but it's okay," Claire said. "I'm over that now. I just want you guys to understand there will be changes in our lives."

"Where are the twins?" George Jr. asked.

This was going a lot better than Claire hoped. "They live in Irving," she said. "The twins' mother is named Kim, and I had lunch with her today."

Now Nikki was taken aback. "You did?"

"Yes, honey. I told Kim about the divorce, and she wants to help out. She says she doesn't want to be with your father anymore, so he can't go live with her, either. She's very upset with him."

"So where is Daddy going to live?" Stacy pondered.

"I don't know," Claire said. "But he gets out of the hospital today. I'm going to see him and tell him what's going on."

"Can I go?" George Jr. asked.

Claire got up and went to put an arm around him. "Not this time, sport. Today we need to have a private talk, just Mommy and Daddy."

Stacy and Nikki threw their arms around her for a big, group hug.

"Man, I can't believe Daddy cheated on you," Stacy said.

"I forgive him," Claire said, even though that was not yet the case.

Claire left for the hospital at six p.m. She thought Kim might be there, or that maybe Kim had confronted

George already, but neither of these was the case. When Claire walked into his room, George still had the smug look of a man with a backup plan.

"I thought you wasn't coming to see me no more," he said without looking away from the television mounted on a far wall. George sounded like his old self again, and he looked better, too. His bald dome was recently shaved, and all of the color had returned to his face. He didn't look sick at all anymore. The oxygen line was gone, as well as his catheter.

He watched an old re-run of *Family Matters*, and he clearly wasn't worried about a thing in the world. That made Claire's news even that much more rewarding. She went and sat on the corner of his bed. George looked over at her and rolled his eyes.

"What do you want, Claire? I read your little papers again, and you're out of your goddamned mind. I already got me a lawyer, and he's gonna tear that case to pieces. The lake house? The timeshares? All of my savings? Shit, your lawyer must be as dumb as you."

His venom was potent, but Claire smiled. "Aw, George. Don't be like that."

He crossed his arms over his chest and sneered at her. "Be like what, Claire? Did you read that shit your lawyer filed, or are you stupid enough to think you're going to take me to the cleaners? You might get some alimony and a little child support, but that's it! You're not getting my cars, and you're not getting my house. You're not getting shit else you got on that paper. Do I look like Boo Boo the Fool to you?"

Claire almost answered in the affirmative, but the more he talked, the dumber he sounded, so she let him keep going.

"What's gon' happen," George said, "is I'm gonna give my lawyer more money than you gave yours, and he's gonna tear your lawyer to pieces. And after it's all said and done, you'll be lucky to get *anything* from me. I'm the one who went to the service, Claire. I'm the one who went to college. I'm the one who has a good job. You ain't got shit, and you know it, and you're not going to come up off of me. Uh-uhn. If you want a lake house, you need to get off your ass and work for it."

"Wow." Claire put a hand to her mouth and chuckled. "Three days ago you wanted to be with only me, and now you talk to me like this?"

"That's 'cause I ain't got time to play with you, Claire. If you want to back off of this stupid-ass divorce, then things will be different. But I ain't got nothing good to say to you while you got this clamp on my nuts. I'm gon' be all right, Claire. I don't need you."

Claire couldn't help but laugh then. She tried to maintain composure. "Oh, excuse me."

"What the hell's so funny?" George wanted to know. "You think I'm shitting you? You think you really stand a chance in court?"

"No," Claire said, shaking her head. "It's not that, George. I'm laughing at how you said you'd be all right. I wanna know something: Are you going to be all right at Kim's house, or do you plan to be all right somewhere else?"

George sensed a trap. "What's it to you?"

"Well," Claire said, "I had lunch with Kim this afternoon, and I don't think you're going to be able to weasel your way out of it this time. You didn't even tell her about the divorce, George. How stupid is that? How long did you think you were going to keep her in the dark? I hate to tell you, but Kim's on our side now. She not taking your sorry ass back, and we're *both* taking you to court."

A divorce lawyer's retainer: $3,000.00

Lunch at Don Pablo's: $32.54

The look on George's face when he realized he was screwed from both ends: Priceless.

"What, what are you talking about?"

Claire sighed airily, still chuckling. "Don't worry about it, sweetie. You just get you some rest. You're gonna need it." She stood and headed for the door. "And while you're at it, you might want to find yourself another ride home from the hospital—and somewhere to stay."

She made it all the way to the hallway before he called out to her.

"Claire, wait."

But of course she didn't stop.

There was a lot that could've gone wrong with Claire's plans. George could've hired a high-profile attorney like he threatened. He could have fought for delay after delay and drug the divorce on for years, or Kim might have gone back on her word and picked George up from the hospital when he was released, but fortunately none of that happened. When George got out of the hospital he had to go and stay with one of his old Air Force buddies, and that was just the beginning of his downward spiral towards obscurity.

For the divorce, George hired a competent attorney named Miles Schaefer. Mr. Schaefer had a pretty good success rate, but he was ill-prepared for the mountain of evidence Claire and Kim piled against him.

They all met in court two months after George checked out of Jackson Memorial. It was only a pre-trial hearing, but it was then that Mr. Schaefer fought against what was to be the most crucial aspect of their case: Should Ms. Pate be allowed to divorce George as a "common law wife," and should she and Claire be allowed to divorce George at the same time?

To Mr. Schaefer this was a no-brainer. He approached the judge's bench with poise and confidence. Claire and Kim watched fretfully from the plaintiff's table.

"Your Honor," Mr. Schaefer said, "what these people are trying to do is *ludicrous*. My client was never married to Kimberly Pate, neither legally nor common law, and Mr. Smiley has no merit to include her in these proceedings. I ask the court for her immediate dismissal."

That sounded like a good defense to Claire, but her lawyer stood calmly and approached the bench as cool as a cucumber. Trevor wore a smoke gray suit with a black tie, and he was thoroughly prepared for such an argument.

"Your Honor, I beg counsel's pardon, but I believe Ms. Pate has as much to do with these proceedings as Mrs. Hudgens does."

That got a loud *humph!* from George, who sat alone at the defense table, but everyone else paid keen attention.

"I will prove," Trevor went on, "that the defendant, Mr. George Hudgens, did in fact have two wives at the same time, Mrs. Claire Hudgens and Ms. Kimberly Pate. He carried on functional and emotional marriages with both women for nearly a decade. He split his time with them equally, had children with both of them, and planned for the future with both of them.

"Now, while it is true Mr. Hudgens never had an official marriage ceremony with Ms. Pate, citing the Texas Family Code section 2.401: Their relationship falls well within the range for a common-law marriage due to the fact that they cohabitated for more than eight years, and also due to the fact that on December 24, 2009, at a Christmas party at Ms. Pate's place of business, Mr. Hudgens did indeed refer to Ms. Pate as his 'wife' to her employer as well as to two of Ms. Pate's coworkers."

That comment put a strange look on a few faces in the courtroom, Claire's and George's included, but his lawyer wasn't fazed.

"By counsel's own definition," Mr. Schaefer argued with a bored expression, "my client could not have had a common-law marriage with Ms. Pate. Your Honor, at no point did Mr. Hudgens cohabitate with Ms. Pate. My client lived at home with his *only* wife, Mrs. Claire Hudgens.

"We will admit that my client had *some sort* of relationship with Ms. Pate, but he had a wife and children at home, and that's where he lived the majority of the time."

Trevor already warned Claire about this tactic, and he also briefed her on what they should do if this issue was raised. *Perjury* is an ugly word, but it was the least Claire would do to make her husband suffer.

"Your Honor, if you will allow me," Trevor said and half-turned towards the plaintiff's table. "Mrs. Hudgens, will you please tell the court how often your husband spent the night with you over the past eight years?"

"He was only there half the time," Claire lied, "if that."

George looked like he was having a baby, but there was nothing he could do. He was the biggest liar in the courtroom, and no one would believe him over Claire, not even his own lawyer.

"I'm going to allow this," the judge decided. "I believe both Ms. Pate and Mrs. Hudgens are married to Mr. Hudgens, and if they choose, they can both divorce him at the same time."

George shot to his feet while Claire muffled a snicker.

"That's not true! She's lying!"

"Take your seat," the judge ordered.

"But she's lying! I was with her most of the time!"

"Take your seat, Mr. Hudgens, or you'll have more than her to worry about!"

George took his seat, and Claire leaned back and took in the whole measure of his misery. His pain was well-warranted. With the decision to allow Kim as a co-plaintiff, the judge effectively sealed George's doom.

The trial lasted another month, and Mr. Schaefer fought his hardest to get every piece of evidence dismissed, but in the end everything went as expected.

George lost the case and had to pay for his infidelities many times over. Claire got her house and Kim got the home in Irving. Claire got $500 a month in child support, and Kim got $350. That was a good chunk of George's income, and it was separate from the $600 he owed both women in alimony for the next five years.

George's lawyer argued insanely that they couldn't take 70 percent of a man's income, but the judge was unwavering. George would have $200 left to live on every week, and many people in this great nation survived on less than that.

The judge gave each vehicle to whoever drove it most at the time of the divorce, and he let George keep the lake house. Claire got $42,000 from her husband's savings, Kim got $33,500, and George kept a measly fifteen hundred for himself.

All in all, Claire was very satisfied with the results of the divorce. George didn't pick up his kids for the first three months afterwards, either out of spite or because he was busy at his part-time job installing satellite dishes, but he eventually did return to their lives. He continued to miss scheduled visitations every now and then, but who could blame him? Last Claire heard he had a third job somewhere in the mall, and he still couldn't get his motorcycle out of the shop.

It wasn't the death she envisioned when Claire first set out to kill her husband, but it was pretty close. George got shunned by both of his life-long loves, and the divorce made headlines in all of the local papers. The women of Overbrook Meadows were horrified to learn a real live bigamist lived among them, and no one would even go to the movies with George once they found out who he was.

Claire and Kim, on the other hand, emerged from the turmoil with an intimate bond neither of them expected. They were so close, Claire sent Kim an invitation to her annual Labor Day barbecue later that year.

And so it was that four months after the divorce, George's two ex-wives met at one location with no violence involved. Also along for the festivities were Becky, her daughter Courtney, Melanie, her son Trevon, and her husband Anthony. Nikki and Stacy invited a few friends from school, and by three p.m. Claire's backyard was bustling with excitement that Saturday afternoon.

Claire never threw a party of that magnitude without George's help, but there were plenty of extra hands pitching in. Melanie and Becky helped set everything up, and Anthony took control of the barbecue pit. Claire had plenty of time to get acquainted with the twins and shoot the breeze with Ms. Kimberly Pate.

Their relationship started under such rocky conditions Claire didn't think she could ever make friends with George's mistress, but Kim was polite, easygoing, and very appreciative of Claire's openness and acceptance. Kim got along amiably with Becky and Anthony as well. Melanie held out for a little while, but even she warmed up to George's other ex-wife eventually.

There wasn't much to dislike about Kim, once you got to know her. She was a hardworking single mother.

She had her own house, her own car, and her own income. She'd been duped in the past, but she was stronger and wiser for it, just like Claire.

Kim would probably never become a core friend like Melanie and Becky, but she would always be welcome at Claire's house, and her children would always be recognized as George Hudgens's seeds.

⌐⌐

By the time everyone reached their limits of food and fun, the sun had begun to set on Claire's modest two-story home. She started clearing off the tables, but Stacy distracted her with a peculiar question.

"Mama, who's *Trevor Smiley*?"

Claire almost dropped a pitcher of tea. "Huh, who?"

Stacy held up her mom's cellphone. "Some man's on the phone," she said. "You saved his number with the name *Trevor Smiley*. Who is he?"

"It's just some guy," Claire said nonchalantly. She took the phone from her daughter and ducked into the garage, where it was a lot quieter. Her heartbeats started to quicken before she put the cellular to her ear.

"Hello?"

"Hey. Long time no see." His voice was deep and smooth. It immediately took Claire back to his couch, and his tongue, and the hairs stood on her arms.

"How are you doing, Mr. Smiley."

"*Mr. Smiley*? Aw, it's not that bad, is it? I'm not your lawyer anymore."

Claire knew he was going to say that just like she knew he would call, but she still didn't know how to respond to him. "Thanks for the work you did on my case," she said.

"Aw, it was nothing. Things just sort of fell into place by themselves."

"Don't be so modest," Claire said. "You know you did a good job. Most lawyers wouldn't have fought so hard for the husband's mistress."

"Most lawyers don't have a crush on you," he said.

Claire began to feel warm, but it wasn't uncomfortable this time.

"I waited four months before I called you again," he said.

"I noticed. Is that the average grieving period after a divorce?"

"It is if you didn't like your husband."

Claire didn't have a response for that.

"You don't sound very happy to hear from me," Trevor noticed.

"It's not that," Claire said. "I've got a bunch of people here. We're having a barbecue."

"Is it a party for Nicole? Her birthday's Monday, right?"

"I can't believe you remember that."

"I remember all of your children," he said. "I still remember their dates of birth. I could probably tell you their *socials*, but I don't want to keep that in my head . . ."

Claire gave him all of that information for their lawsuit, but that was a long time ago.

"Do you like me?" he asked bluntly.

Claire blushed and was glad no one was around. "You, you know I like you."

"Then why haven't you called?"

"I don't know," Claire said. "I guess the circumstances of how we met kinda bummed me out. I didn't think it was right to get caught up in something like that. I didn't want to be made a fool of."

"I would never do that to you."

"Trevor, you say all the right things, but face it, you were my divorce lawyer, and you came on to me. Not only was it *inappropriate*, but you've got the opportunity to do that all the time. I didn't want to be a notch on your belt."

There was a pause. "You know you're hurting my feelings, right?"

"I don't mean to," Claire said. "I'm just being honest. Some people might consider what you did *sleazy*."

"Ouch."

"I'm just saying."

"Do you think I would treat you that way?"

Claire shook her head. "I'd like to think you wouldn't."

"Let me ask you something," he said. "What would you do if you worked at a funeral home, and the man of your dreams—your *soul mate*—walked in and said he wanted to bury his wife?"

"A *funeral home?*"

"Okay, maybe that's a bad example. But you see what I'm saying, don't you? I'm not talking about just some good-looking guy. I'm talking about the *only* man for you . . ."

"You don't feel that way about me."

"Claire, it's been four months since the last time we talked, and I haven't thought about any woman *but* you. I've never gone out with a client other than you.

"I'm sorry I wasn't more professional when you walked into my office. But when I see something I want, when I see something I *need*, I've got to go for it. Even if it cost me my license, you would have been worth it."

This man was the best when it came to flattery. He made Claire feel like no one else could.

"Would you like to have dinner?" she asked.

"What? You're kidding."

Claire chuckled. "No. I'm serious."

"Well of course I would!" he bellowed. "I'll take you to dinner in *Paris* if you want."

"No." Claire giggled. "Something local would be fine."

"When?" Trevor asked. She could hear his excitement building.

"I don't know," she said. "Why don't I call you to-morrow and we'll talk, and then we'll let it go from there."

"That's the best thing I've heard all month," he said. "Man, I'm shaking over here. I haven't been this excited since high school."

Claire hadn't either, but she wasn't going to tell him that. "It's just a date," she cautioned. "I'll call you tomorrow and we'll see how it goes . . ."

"All right. I can't wait to hear from you."

"Okay. Bye." Claire hung up and leaned with her back against her Lexus. She smiled and slid the cellphone into her pocket. She returned to the party a few minutes later with her spirits high and her eyes aglow.

EPILOGUE
THREE YEARS LATER

The dogwood trees were back in full bloom. Gentle breezes snagged soft, pink petals from nearby branches and set them adrift into the atmosphere. Some caught a ride on a thermal and were thrust even further towards the heavens. These flowers twisted and flipped in the air like tiny ballerinas.

A handful of this natural confetti made it all the way to Claire Hudgens' backyard. The petals glided back to earth like feathers; some landing on the large tables set up and meticulously decorated for the occasion.

And that was just fine.

There were already colorful floral arrangements adorning the arch and pillars erected for today's festivities. A beautiful cream-colored carpet ran between two sections of seats. The chairs had white covers that were almost as beautiful as the bride's gown.

Out front visitors' cars stretched for blocks on both sides of the street, but only the white limousine occupied the coveted spot in Claire's circular driveway.

Inside, the living room was full to capacity; humming with excited energy. Guests dressed to the nines filled the whole bottom floor, in fact, but only a small number of visitors were allowed upstairs.

Even still, never had so many people been in Claire's bedroom at the same time. Stacy lounged on her mother's bed looking very much like a princess in her purple chiffon dress. She had her hair down, her lip gloss glistening, and a bit of rouge on her already rosy cheeks.

Stacy was a high school freshman now, but unlike her sister, she knew how to take full advantage of the next four years, the most precious time of her young life. She had a cellphone in one hand, and a lock of hair twisted around her finger in the other. Stacy stared out into nothingness and popped her chewing gum with a wistful smile on her face.

"Mmm, hmm," she said into the phone. "Well, if you liked me you'd be over here . . . Yo grandmamma is still gonna be in the hospital *tomorrow,* that's not an excuse . . ."

Nikki shook her head and rolled her eyes at her little sister. She turned back towards the bathroom and leaned against the doorframe. Her dress was virtually identical to Stacy's, but Nikki was eighteen now. She would be leaving for college in a couple of months, and her womanly physique was no longer that of a child's.

Nikki had long dancer's legs like her mom and a thin waist. Her bosoms blossomed back in middle school, but Nikki was comfortable in her skin now. She wasn't a makeup fanatic like her sister, but she no longer wore oversized shirts and baggy pants to hide her physique.

Nikki looked over her mother's shoulder and made eye contact with Claire in the bathroom mirror. Claire smiled and winked, and Nikki grinned back. Her mom's eyes were large and beautiful, and Nikki had never been so proud.

Melanie stood on Claire's right, brushing her friend's hair one last time before they put on the veil. Melanie's gown was lavender, and Claire thought she was as lovely as an angel. Melanie replaced her tight curls with a straight weave a couple years ago. Today her hair was jet black and shoulder length. She was still round and top-heavy, but Melanie exuded confidence and poise. She smiled softly as she brushed, and Claire could feel the love in each stroke.

Becky stood on Claire's other side grinning like she had the most delectable secret. She stared at her friend's reflection in the mirror with a hand over her mouth. Becky filled out her lavender gown a lot differently than Melanie, but Claire couldn't say either of her bridesmaids looked better than the other.

Becky's eyes twinkled, and a tear actually rolled down her cheek. She brushed it away quickly and giggled to herself.

"What's your deal?" Claire asked.

Plenty of attractive women showed up for the wedding, but no one within a thirty-mile radius was as beautiful as this bride was. Claire's ivory gown was strapless, with a sweetheart neckline and beaded lace draped down the sides. She opted for a chapel train that was lightweight, shimmering satin, soft and contouring.

Her hair was longer now, and it was full and vibrant. She wore it straight today, dark-colored with hints of auburn. Her skin was smooth, her complexion flawless. Claire's eyes were bright and hopeful. Her smile was almost childlike.

"I always cry at weddings," Becky explained and sniffled pleasantly.

Claire nodded. "I'm hoping I don't start crying, too. How's everything looking down there?"

"It's all *wonderful*," Becky said dreamily. "Everything looks so nice. Everyone's so pretty."

"Did you see my brother-in-law?" Melanie asked with a handful of Claire's locks. "I hope he ain't drunk already."

Claire looked sideways at her. "You'd better be kidding."

"Uh-uhn," Melanie said. "But we just glad he don't smoke crack. We got one of them in our family, too."

Claire rolled her eyes but couldn't help but laugh.

"I'm just playing," Melanie said. "You know I wouldn't invite no alcoholic to your wedding."

"You're a fool," Claire said. "But I do thank you for not bringing your drunk brother-in-law. Did Rickey come?" she asked Nikki.

Her daughter smiled warmly. "Yes. He's here."

"*My, my, my,*" Melanie said without looking up.

"What?" Nikki asked.

"You're the *last* one I thought would get a boyfriend," Melanie said. "I thought you'd be in college before you finally noticed boys."

"I still don't notice them," Nikki said.

"Tell that lie to your mama," Melanie kidded.

Nikki looked around for an escape. "What about *Becky*," she said. "Mark is here, too."

Claire raised an eyebrow and looked over at her friend. Becky's smile was immediately wall to wall. She looked down at her toes.

"Did he bring his daughter?" Claire asked.

Becky nodded. "We all came together."

"That's great," Claire said. "I look forward to meeting her."

"Have you hit that yet?" Melanie asked.

Becky's eyes grew large.

Claire looked back at Nikki and gave her friend a short elbow to the thigh.

"*Melanie!*"

Melanie looked back, too, and laughed. "Oh, I didn't know she was still back there."

"Y'all don't have to worry about me," Nikki said. "I know *all* about that stuff."

Claire frowned but Nikki laughed.

"I'm just kidding, Mom. *Dang.* Lighten up."

Claire gave her a long look before returning her gaze to Becky.

Melanie watched her, too.

Becky looked around nervously. "What?"

"How *are* things going with you and Mark?" Claire asked. "You do a lot of smiling—"

"And giggling," Melanie added.

"And giggling when we bring him up," Claire went on. "But you don't talk about him much."

"We're taking it slow," Becky said. She held her hands together and rocked like an adolescent. "I don't want to get too carried away. You know how it is when you put everything you've got into something, and it turns out to be something totally different than what you expected?"

Claire knew *exactly* how that felt.

"So far so good, though," Becky said. "He's hard-working. He has a good relationship with his family. He makes good money. He's no *Trevor*, but he does okay."

Claire nodded.

"Not too many out there are like Trevor," Melanie agreed.

That made Claire smile. "Yeah, he is something," she mused.

Everyone knew Claire's soon-to-be-husband was attractive, but it was Mr. Smiley's earning potential the girls were referring to. Since winning Claire's divorce some three years ago, Trevor had enjoyed a boatload of success, most notably the highly publicized divorce of Sam and Pamela Brookshire.

When one of the city's most influential couples divorced last year, the trial made headlines for weeks. Much to everyone's surprise, Mrs. Brookshire relied on a barely known attorney named Trevor Smiley to take her millionaire hubby to the cleaners. Claire's man racked up an eight-digit settlement for her, and no lawyer in Overbrook Meadows was more in demand now.

"Is Kim coming?" Becky asked.

Claire shook her head. "No. I didn't send her an invitation."

Claire spent a lot of time getting to know Ms Pate after the divorce. It no longer made her uncomfortable to see her ex-husband in the twin's eyes, but Claire still didn't want George's mistress at her wedding.

"I don't see why you didn't invite her," Melanie spat. "You already gave her half of George's money. You might as well let her get drunk at your reception, too."

Claire didn't acknowledge that. Melanie knew the money was for the twins, but she never fully came to terms with Claire's forgiving nature in that regard. If it was up to Melanie, Kim would be destitute, dragging her babies to different women's shelters every night.

Claire looked up at the sound of someone ascending the stairs. George Jr. rushed into the bedroom and squeezed by Nikki at the bathroom door. He stepped in front of Becky and held a cellphone up to the gorgeous bride.

"Say cheese, Mama," he instructed.

George Jr. looked smart in his little tuxedo. His hair was short and edged perfectly. His legs and arms were longer now, and his resemblance to his father was uncanny. He was still an unabashed nerd, but he grew into a handsome young man. Claire couldn't have been more proud of him.

"We're going to take pictures downstairs," she said, but he snapped a shot while she was talking and quickly turned tail.

"Thanks."

Nikki grabbed his arm before he made it too far. "Come back here, sneaky."

"Let go!"

She pulled him back into the bathroom, and George Jr. stood uneasily, smirking suspiciously.

"What's that picture for?" Claire asked.

"For Trevor," he admitted.

"Uh-uhn." Claire shook her head.

"He's using you," Melanie informed. She put the brush down and stroked Claire's hair one last time with her hands. "Don't you know it's bad luck for him to see her before the wedding?"

"He says a picture doesn't count," George Jr. responded. "He says we have a lot of technology today, and we should take advantage of it to get around old *dinosaur* rules like that."

"I see you've been coached well," Claire said. She stuck out her hand. "Give it here."

George Jr. gave up the phone, and Claire deleted his photo. She turned and pointed it at Melanie. "Give me a pose."

Melanie put her hands on her hips and flashed a big, cheesy smile. Claire laughed as she took the picture. She gave the phone back to her son.

"Okay, go give it back to him."

"But I didn't get a picture of you."

"It's okay," Claire said. "I'm playing a trick."

George Jr. grinned and took off again. Nikki went with him.

"He's going to tell him before he shows him the picture," Melanie predicted. "You know how they are."

While it was true her two men had a surprisingly close relationship, Claire didn't think her son would spoil the joke at all.

"He'll get him," she said. "Trevor may be his best bud, but George is a mama's boy through and through."

Becky stepped forward and put a hand on her friend's shoulder. "I'm so happy for you," she said. Her eyes started to leak again, and her smile was as tender as they had ever seen it.

Claire reached up and held her hand. She put her other arm around Melanie's waist and squeezed both girls very tightly.

"Thank you guys," she said. "I never would have made it to this point without you. I'm giving my first toast to the best two friends a girl could have."

"No, the first toast is definitely for you and Trevor," Becky insisted.

"Just try not to leave this one in financial ruin," Melanie said.

"George is doing better now," Claire said.

Melanie frowned. "Girl, you know he's not."

Claire chuckled softly. "Okay. I promise."

THE END

ABOUT THE AUTHOR

Keith Walker is a graduate of Texas Wesleyan University where he earned a bachelor's degree in English with specification in education. Keith started writing in the fifth grade and he has won many awards and contests since then. Keith is an avid poet who performs at various venues throughout his hometown and neighboring cities. He lives in Fort Worth, Texas with his wife and two children. Visit him at *www.keithwalkerbooks.com*.

2010 Mass Market Titles

January

Show Me The Sun
Miriam Shumba
ISBN: 978-158571-405-6
$6.99

Promises of Forever
Celya Bowers
ISBN: 978-1-58571-380-6
$6.99

February

Love Out Of Order
Nicole Green
ISBN: 978-1-58571-381-3
$6.99

Unclear and Present Danger
Michele Cameron
ISBN: 978-158571-408-7
$6.99

March

Stolen Jewels
Michele Sudler
ISBN: 978-158571-409-4
$6.99

Not Quite Right
Tammy Williams
ISBN: 978-158571-410-0
$6.99

April

Oak Bluffs
Joan Early
ISBN: 978-1-58571-379-0
$6.99

Crossing The Line
Bernice Layton
ISBN: 978-158571-412-4
$6.99

How To Kill Your Husband
Keith Walker
ISBN: 978-158571-421-6
$6.99

May

The Business of Love
Cheris F. Hodges
ISBN: 978-158571-373-8
$6.99

Wayward Dreams
Gail McFarland
ISBN: 978-158571-422-3
$6.99

June

The Doctor's Wife
Mildred Riley
ISBN: 978-158571-424-7
$6.99

Mixed Reality
Chamein Canton
ISBN: 978-158571-423-0
$6.99

2010 Mass Market Titles (continued)
July

Blue Interlude
Keisha Mennefee
ISBN: 978-158571-378-3
$6.99

Always You
Crystal Hubbard
ISBN: 978-158571-371-4
$6.99

Unbeweavable
Katrina Spencer
ISBN: 978-158571-426-1
$6.99

August

Small Sensations
Crystal V. Rhodes
ISBN: 978-158571-376-9
$6.99

Let's Get It On
Dyanne Davis
ISBN: 978-158571-416-2
$6.99

September

Unconditional
A.C. Arthur
ISBN: 978-158571-413-1
$6.99

Swan
Africa Fine
ISBN: 978-158571-377-6
$6.99$6.99

October

Friends in Need
Joan Early
ISBN:978-1-58571-428-5
$6.99

Against the Wind
Gwynne Forster
ISBN:978-158571-429-2
$6.99

That Which Has Horns
Miriam Shumba
ISBN:978-1-58571-430-8
$6.99

November

A Good Dude
Keith Walker
ISBN:978-1-58571-431-5
$6.99

Reye's Gold
Ruthie Robinson
ISBN:978-1-58571-432-2
$6.99

December

Still Waters...
Crystal V. Rhodes
ISBN:978-1-58571-433-9
$6.99

Burn
Crystal Hubbard
ISBN: 978-1-58571-406-3
$6.99

Other Genesis Press, Inc. Titles

Other Genesis Press, Inc. Titles (continued)

Blood Seduction	J.M. Jeffries	$9.95
Bodyguard	Andrea Jackson	$9.95
Boss of Me	Diana Nyad	$8.95
Bound by Love	Beverly Clark	$8.95
Breeze	Robin Hampton Allen	$10.95
Broken	Dar Tomlinson	$24.95
By Design	Barbara Keaton	$8.95
Cajun Heat	Charlene Berry	$8.95
Careless Whispers	Rochelle Alers	$8.95
Cats & Other Tales	Marilyn Wagner	$8.95
Caught in a Trap	Andre Michelle	$8.95
Caught Up in the Rapture	Lisa G. Riley	$9.95
Cautious Heart	Cheris F. Hodges	$8.95
Chances	Pamela Leigh Starr	$8.95
Checks and Balances	Elaine Sims	$6.99
Cherish the Flame	Beverly Clark	$8.95
Choices	Tammy Williams	$6.99
Class Reunion	Irma Jenkins/ John Brown	$12.95
Code Name: Diva	J.M. Jeffries	$9.95
Conquering Dr. Wexler's Heart	Kimberley White	$9.95
Corporate Seduction	A.C. Arthur	$9.95
Crossing Paths, Tempting Memories	Dorothy Elizabeth Love	$9.95
Crush	Crystal Hubbard	$9.95
Cypress Whisperings	Phyllis Hamilton	$8.95
Dark Embrace	Crystal Wilson Harris	$8.95
Dark Storm Rising	Chinelu Moore	$10.95
Daughter of the Wind	Joan Xian	$8.95
Dawn's Harbor	Kymberly Hunt	$6.99
Deadly Sacrifice	Jack Kean	$22.95
Designer Passion	Dar Tomlinson Diana Richeaux	$8.95
Do Over	Celya Bowers	$9.95
Dream Keeper	Gail McFarland	$6.99
Dream Runner	Gail McFarland	$6.99
Dreamtective	Liz Swados	$5.95
Ebony Angel	Deatri King-Bey	$9.95
Ebony Butterfly II	Delilah Dawson	$14.95
Echoes of Yesterday	Beverly Clark	$9.95
Eden's Garden	Elizabeth Rose	$8.95

Other Genesis Press, Inc. Titles (continued)

Eve's Prescription	Edwina Martin Arnold	$8.95
Everlastin' Love	Gay G. Gunn	$8.95
Everlasting Moments	Dorothy Elizabeth Love	$8.95
Everything and More	Sinclair Lebeau	$8.95
Everything But Love	Natalie Dunbar	$8.95
Falling	Natalie Dunbar	$9.95
Fate	Pamela Leigh Starr	$8.95
Finding Isabella	A.J. Garrotto	$8.95
Fireflies	Joan Early	$6.99
Fixin' Tyrone	Keith Walker	$6.99
Forbidden Quest	Dar Tomlinson	$10.95
Forever Love	Wanda Y. Thomas	$8.95
From the Ashes	Kathleen Suzanne	$8.95
	Jeanne Sumerix	
Frost On My Window	Angela Weaver	$6.99
Gentle Yearning	Rochelle Alers	$10.95
Glory of Love	Sinclair LeBeau	$10.95
Go Gentle Into That	Malcom Boyd	$12.95
Good Night		
Goldengroove	Mary Beth Craft	$16.95
Groove, Bang, and Jive	Steve Cannon	$8.99
Hand in Glove	Andrea Jackson	$9.95
Hard to Love	Kimberley White	$9.95
Hart & Soul	Angie Daniels	$8.95
Heart of the Phoenix	A.C. Arthur	$9.95
Heartbeat	Stephanie Bedwell-Grime	$8.95
Hearts Remember	M. Loui Quezada	$8.95
Hidden Memories	Robin Allen	$10.95
Higher Ground	Leah Latimer	$19.95
Hitler, the War, and the Pope	Ronald Rychiak	$26.95
How to Write a Romance	Kathryn Falk	$18.95
I Married a Reclining Chair	Lisa M. Fuhs	$8.95
I'll Be Your Shelter	Giselle Carmichael	$8.95
I'll Paint a Sun	A.J. Garrotto	$9.95
Icie	Pamela Leigh Starr	$8.95
If I Were Your Woman	LaConnie Taylor-Jones	$6.99
Illusions	Pamela Leigh Starr	$8.95
Indigo After Dark Vol. I	Nia Dixon/Angelique	$10.95
Indigo After Dark Vol. II	Dolores Bundy/	$10.95
	Cole Riley	
Indigo After Dark Vol. III	Montana Blue/	$10.95
	Coco Morena	

Other Genesis Press, Inc. Titles (continued)

Indigo After Dark Vol. IV	Cassandra Colt/	$14.95
Indigo After Dark Vol. V	Delilah Dawson	$14.95
Indiscretions	Donna Hill	$8.95
Intentional Mistakes	Michele Sudler	$9.95
Interlude	Donna Hill	$8.95
Intimate Intentions	Angie Daniels	$8.95
It's in the Rhythm	Sammie Ward	$6.99
It's Not Over Yet	J.J. Michael	$9.95
Jolie's Surrender	Edwina Martin-Arnold	$8.95
Kiss or Keep	Debra Phillips	$8.95
Lace	Giselle Carmichael	$9.95
Lady Preacher	K.T. Richey	$6.99
Last Train to Memphis	Elsa Cook	$12.95
Lasting Valor	Ken Olsen	$24.95
Let Us Prey	Hunter Lundy	$25.95
Lies Too Long	Pamela Ridley	$13.95
Life Is Never As It Seems	J.J. Michael	$12.95
Lighter Shade of Brown	Vicki Andrews	$8.95
Look Both Ways	Joan Early	$6.99
Looking for Lily	Africa Fine	$6.99
Love Always	Mildred E. Riley	$10.95
Love Doesn't Come Easy	Charlyne Dickerson	$8.95
Love Unveiled	Gloria Greene	$10.95
Love's Deception	Charlene Berry	$10.95
Love's Destiny	M. Loui Quezada	$8.95
Love's Secrets	Yolanda McVey	$6.99
Mae's Promise	Melody Walcott	$8.95
Magnolia Sunset	Giselle Carmichael	$8.95
Many Shades of Gray	Dyanne Davis	$6.99
Matters of Life and Death	Lesego Malepe, Ph.D.	$15.95
Meant to Be	Jeanne Sumerix	$8.95
Midnight Clear	Leslie Esdaile	$10.95
(Anthology)	Gwynne Forster	
	Carmen Green	
	Monica Jackson	
Midnight Magic	Gwynne Forster	$8.95
Midnight Peril	Vicki Andrews	$10.95
Misconceptions	Pamela Leigh Starr	$9.95
Moments of Clarity	Michele Cameron	$6.99
Montgomery's Children	Richard Perry	$14.95
Mr. Fix-It	Crystal Hubbard	$6.99
My Buffalo Soldier	Barbara B.K. Reeves	$8.95

Other Genesis Press, Inc. Titles (continued)

Naked Soul	Gwynne Forster	$8.95
Never Say Never	Michele Cameron	$6.99
Next to Last Chance	Louisa Dixon	$24.95
No Apologies	Seressia Glass	$8.95
No Commitment Required	Seressia Glass	$8.95
No Regrets	Mildred E. Riley	$8.95
Not His Type	Chamein Canton	$6.99
Nowhere to Run	Gay G. Gunn	$10.95
O Bed! O Breakfast!	Rob Kuehnle	$14.95
Object of His Desire	A.C. Arthur	$8.95
Office Policy	A.C. Arthur	$9.95
Once in a Blue Moon	Dorianne Cole	$9.95
One Day at a Time	Bella McFarland	$8.95
One of These Days	Michele Sudler	$9.95
Outside Chance	Louisa Dixon	$24.95
Passion	T.T. Henderson	$10.95
Passion's Blood	Cherif Fortin	$22.95
Passion's Furies	AlTonya Washington	$6.99
Passion's Journey	Wanda Y. Thomas	$8.95
Past Promises	Jahmel West	$8.95
Path of Fire	T.T. Henderson	$8.95
Path of Thorns	Annetta P. Lee	$9.95
Peace Be Still	Colette Haywood	$12.95
Picture Perfect	Reon Carter	$8.95
Playing for Keeps	Stephanie Salinas	$8.95
Pride & Joi	Gay G. Gunn	$8.95
Promises Made	Bernice Layton	$6.99
Promises to Keep	Alicia Wiggins	$8.95
Quiet Storm	Donna Hill	$10.95
Reckless Surrender	Rochelle Alers	$6.95
Red Polka Dot in a World Full of Plaid	Varian Johnson	$12.95
Red Sky	Renee Alexis	$6.99
Reluctant Captive	Joyce Jackson	$8.95
Rendezvous With Fate	Jeanne Sumerix	$8.95
Revelations	Cheris F. Hodges	$8.95
Rivers of the Soul	Leslie Esdaile	$8.95
Rocky Mountain Romance	Kathleen Suzanne	$8.95
Rooms of the Heart	Donna Hill	$8.95
Rough on Rats and Tough on Cats	Chris Parker	$12.95
Save Me	Africa Fine	$6.99

Other Genesis Press, Inc. Titles (continued)

Other Genesis Press, Inc. Titles (continued)

Order Form

Mail to: Genesis Press, Inc.
P.O. Box 101
Columbus, MS 39703

Name _____
Address _____
City/State _____ Zip _____
Telephone _____

Ship to (if different from above)
Name _____
Address _____
City/State _____ Zip _____
Telephone _____

Credit Card Information
Credit Card # _____ ☐ Visa ☐ Mastercard
Expiration Date (mm/yy) _____ ☐ AmEx ☐ Discover

Qty.	Author	Title	Price	Total

Use this order
form, or call
1-888-INDIGO-1

Total for books _____
Shipping and handling:
  $5 first two books,
  $1 each additional book _____
Total S & H _____
Total amount enclosed _____

Mississippi residents add 7% sales tax